FLESH AND IRON

THE FLARE HUNG suspended in the sky, trailing droplets of glowing white incendiary. The light it cast was a monochrome of white and stark shadow. But it was enough to reveal to Baeder what lay in wait amongst the tree line. No more than a hundred metres away, separated by just one grid of cassam paddy, Baeder saw hundreds, if not thousands, of faces staring at him. Insurgents lying in wait, their eyes white with intent, looking at him.

Then with a roar that built up into a thick wall of sound, the Carnibalès charged.

A WARHAMMER 40,000 NOVEL

FLESH AND IRON

Henry Zou

To my grandfolks. For all the stories they told me when I was young.
Especially the ones with ghosts, dragons and fighting apes.

A BLACK LIBRARY PUBLICATION

First published in Great Britain in 2010 by
The Black Library,
Games Workshop Ltd.,
Willow Road, Nottingham,
NG7 2WS, UK.

10 9 8 7 6 5 4 3 2 1

Cover illustration by Raymond Swanland.

A CIP record for this book is available from the British Library.

A CIP record for this book is available from the British Library.

UK ISBN: 978 1 84416 814 9
US ISBN: 978 1 84416 815 6

See the Black Library on the Internet at
www.blacklibrary.com

Find out more about Games Workshop
and the world of Warhammer 40,000 at
www.games-workshop.com

Printed and bound in the UK.

IT IS THE 41st millennium. For more than a hundred centuries the Emperor has sat immobile on the Golden Throne of Earth. He is the master of mankind by the will of the gods, and master of a million worlds by the might of his inexhaustible armies. He is a rotting carcass writhing invisibly with power from the Dark Age of Technology. He is the Carrion Lord of the Imperium for whom a thousand souls are sacrificed every day, so that he may never truly die.

YET EVEN IN his deathless state, the Emperor continues his eternal vigilance. Mighty battlefleets cross the daemon-infested miasma of the warp, the only route between distant stars, their way lit by the Astronomican, the psychic manifestation of the Emperor's will. Vast armies give battle in His name on uncounted worlds. Greatest amongst his soldiers are the Adeptus Astartes, the Space Marines, bio-engineered super-warriors. Their comrades in arms are legion: the Imperial Guard and countless planetary defence forces, the ever-vigilant Inquisition and the tech-priests of the Adeptus Mechanicus to name only a few. But for all their multitudes, they are barely enough to hold off the ever-present threat from aliens, heretics, mutants – and worse.

TO BE A man in such times is to be one amongst untold billions. It is to live in the cruellest and most bloody regime imaginable. These are the tales of those times. Forget the power of technology and science, for so much has been forgotten, never to be re-learned. Forget the promise of progress and understanding, for in the grim dark future there is only war. There is no peace amongst the stars, only an eternity of carnage and slaughter, and the laughter of thirsting gods.

PROLOGUE

'TELL ME, LIEUTENANT,' the old woman said, 'did my son fight well?'

'Mamsel,' said the lieutenant, taking off his khaki cap and mopping his brow. 'I've never seen a man fight like he did.'

'I know this,' the lieutenant continued slowly. 'From the time that your son was assigned to my platoon, even though he was native, he was one of us. If it were not for his bravery and his knowledge of this land, my men and I might not be here now.'

The tall lieutenant sat down, folding his long limbs on the steps of the stilt-hut next to the old woman. He looked awkward in that village, clad in his sweaty fatigues of tan, khaki and pale creamy green. They sat together for a while, on those rickety wooden steps, watching the river ebb beneath their feet through the gaps in the planks.

'We were the same in many ways, he and I. I would tell him of my native Ouisivia, of the bayous and the steaming swamps. How the men of the 31st Riverine and I would ride through those waters on motored boats fighting swamp orks. He would tell me about Solo-Bastón, and how he would spear-hunt with his father along the riverbanks here. We were not so different.'

The old woman seemed to be half listening. As she stared vacantly into the river, there was something on her mind that she could not bear to think about. Finally she relented.

'Tell me how he died,' she said. She locked eyes with the lieutenant for the first time, eyes buried within a nest of weathered wrinkles and hardened from a life in the wilderness. 'I need to know.'

'Guiding my men through the rainforests of Bastón. He died in the service of the loyalist cause.'

'But how?' she persisted. 'If you do not tell me, I will never sleep again.'

And so Lieutenant Eden Barcham of the 31st Riverine Amphibious told the old woman a story of the Solo-Bastón insurgency and the part her son had played.

Lieutenant Barcham, a swift boat commander, had been one of the first officers in his regiment to be selected for deployment to Solo-Bastón. They had mobilised a force of eight thousand Guardsmen to quell an insurgency so far from their homes they had never heard the name of the place before. Although founded on the world of Ouisivia, the Guardsmen of the 31st Riverine had been especially requested by the Ecclesiarchy for their specialisation in jungle and semi-aquatic warfare. But deployment had been four months earlier and, since then, the insurgent heretics of Bastón had proven to be far more tenacious than the Imperial forces had estimated. They called themselves the *Carnibalès*, a phrase meaning 'martyrs who eat meat' in the local dialect. The enemy used the terrain well when they fought and melted into the civilian population when they chose not to.

Since Barcham first set boot in the dense rainforests of Bastón, Inawan had been assigned to Barcham's platoon as a guide. A young warrior from one of the few remaining loyalist tribes who had not joined the insurgency, Inawan had spoken to Barcham in fluent Low Gothic and, in turn, Barcham referred to Inawan as *Kalisador* Inawan – the native word for a practitioner of weaponry. The mutual respect would serve them well for the hellish months to come.

The first months had been far worse than Barcham had expected. The Ecclesiarchy, the ruling authority on Solo-Bastón, had dismissed the insurgency as a minor revolt against Imperial agricultural settlements. The reality was far more severe. Within the first week, Barcham had seen combat three times. In the worst of these engagements, he lost two of his four amphibious Chimeras to ambush in the muddy estuaries. The insurgent heretics had surged out of the rainforests and into the river, armed not with javelins and machetes, but with lasguns and bolters. The slow-moving Chimeras languished in the river, taking pot shots from the riverbanks.

The battle had drawn on for forty minutes until the enemy was chased into the wilderness by the swooping Vulture gunships. In the aftermath, two of the armoured carriers were ablaze in the water, cast along the stream like funeral pyres. Barcham lost eleven men of his forty-man platoon and swore never again to use amphibious Chimeras in a river patrol. Such ponderous machines died slowly in the water.

In the days after the attack, the local insurgents began distributing hand-drawn leaflets to the villages in the region claiming that the Imperial soldiers had been massacred. They challenged Imperial forces for control of the province and began to recruit loyalist tribes into their insurgency.

Lieutenant Barcham did not let this slight go unnoticed. He requisitioned inflatable Riverine assault landers for his platoon and, with Inawan leading the way, they propelled themselves deep into regions that had been lost to Imperial control. Again the enemy fought a game of hit and run but, this time, the 31st Riverine took the fight to them, strafing the enemy in their motored boats with guns blazing. The insurgents melted into the wilderness and issued no more leaflets.

Barcham's platoon equipped all subsequent patrols with either inflatable landers or swift boats – ten-metre-long shallow draft vessels that housed a crew of six and one precious pintle-mounted bolter. They made many forays into the heartland with their flotilla of swifts. At night, they drew their vessels into a protective circle, like the frontiersmen of Old Terra with their steed-drawn wagons. They slept in cramped bunks in the vessels' bellies, and ate their rations cold so as not to light fires and draw the attention of insurgents. When it rained, and it often did, the troops had to deal with sleeping in the downpour and tramping about the boat in ankle-deep water.

'It was miserable,' said Lieutenant Barcham to the old woman, 'but Inawan helped to pull us through it. He could brew hot tea from foraged water roots and tell vivid stories of folklore. Little things like that helped keep our minds intact.'

'When it wasn't miserable it was sometimes exciting,' the lieutenant continued with a wry smile. 'The enemy learnt to fear us. We'd come upon their secret hide-aways, rafts tethered on the water bearing caches of arms and ammunition. At first they would run inland and we would chase them with firepower, unleashing volley after volley into the undergrowth until we had flattened the area.'

In the fourth month Lieutenant Barcham was called away from clearing operations and ordered to mount an inland patrol on Chimeras. The platoon was to carve a path into the central rainforests in order to exert their influence on isolated inland tribes. They were to ride into the sloping hills along a winding dirt road, flanked on both sides by a strangling mass of gum-sap trees and clusters of epiphytes.

The lieutenant did not see the merit in such an exercise and Inawan agreed that it was unnecessarily dangerous. It had become common knowledge by then that the insurgents were using lasguns and even missile tubes from unknown sources. The sloping rainforest would be a perfect ambush point for the entire duration of the patrol.

But a Guardsman's first objective is to obey orders. So it came to pass that Barcham's platoon set forth in four separate Chimeras, each carrier housing a squad of ten Riverine Amphibious. When they arrived at each village, the Chimeras went through one at a time, training their turreted multilasers on the stilt-huts for protection.

As they came to the fifth and last village on their route, Lieutenant Barcham began to instinctively feel 'the churns'. It was something a veteran Guardsman picked up the longer he was deployed: a finely honed instinct that warned him something was amiss, a cold dreadful nausea at the bottom of their bowels. All Guardsmen knew of the churns and, in the past four months, Barcham was more than familiar with the feeling. He could not exactly express his concern but something was wrong about the village. Inawan was similarly grave and he vigilantly trained a vintage autorifle on each thatched window and door they passed. To their relief, the platoon passed the village without event and reached their designated checkpoint.

Although they had not spotted any signs of enemy activity, Barcham and Inawan agreed that their presence was certainly known to the insurgents by now. Deciding not to make camp in unfamiliar territory, the lieutenant hoped to race the dusk and return to base camp before nightfall. As they came down the mountain, the sinister fifth village was the first settlement they reached on the return path. Here the dirt road funnelled into a ravine that led a winding path through the hamlet. It was late afternoon and the monsoonal skies were swollen rain clouds, cradling the village in deep shadow.

Tribesmen lingered along the dirt road but fled at the sight of the platoon. They faded into their stilt-huts, some sprinting away to shutter their windows and bar their doors. Barcham ordered the four Chimeras to advance in single file, cautiously nursing their engines down the slope. Once again they rumbled through the village unmolested, coming around a bend in the path. The first carrier in line negotiated the steep twist.

That was the signal for the ambush.

Las-fire, rockets and heavy calibre rounds drummed down on the armoured carriers. The Chimeras rocked on their suspensions, hammered from all directions by enemy fire. Guardsmen scrambled towards the vision slits of the Chimeras, firing blindly out with their las-guns.

'Get going! Don't stop moving!' Barcham barked into the vox-unit. It would be their only chance to sur-vive the ambush.

Insurgent heretics swarmed out from hiding, rushing in to mob the Chimeras. Some of them were not even armed, pelting the carriers with rocks and debris. Oth-ers were Kalisadors, armed tribal warriors who, according to Imperial intelligence, were ferociously cruel in combat.

Lieutenant Barcham socketed his bayonet onto his lasrifle just as the top hatch of his carrier was pried open. An insurgent Kalisador slithered into the com-partment, brandishing a machete and machine pistol. The Bastón warrior was garbed in traditional battle-dress, a loose cotton tunic and breeches with calf-length sandals bound by intricate hemp cord. Around his shoulders, torso and headdress was the chitinous plate of a cauldron crab, heavy and dark grey. Fluttering paper litanies and shells woven into coloured string clattered against his armour. Around his legs and hips, beards of knotted string interwoven with coloured glass proclaimed, in its way, the great reflexes and stamina of the warrior and the great length of his sword arm. This was the ritualistic battledress of a heretic; the lieutenant recognised this, as Inawan spoke often of the superstitions of his people.

The lieutenant fired once from the hip at point-blank range. The shot flashed white in the confined compart-ment, hot and brilliant. In the sizzling haze the insurgent bounced off the metal decking and lay there unmoving. The lieutenant stepped forwards to inspect the body.

That was when the hatchway swung open again. A hand appeared, tossed in a grenade, and slammed the hatch shut. Lieutenant Barcham dropped into a crouch and turned his back to the grenade. It went off with a stiffly concussive report. Something stung his back. 'Direct hit!' he shouted at his men, turning to inspect the damage.

That was when he saw Inawan curled up on the floor. His insides were spilling out from the middle of his torso. Inawan wore no chitinous plate, or the trinkets and fetishes of heretic Kalisadors. He simply wore loose cotton garments bound at his calves and forearms by intricate rope work, eschewing the heretical magicks of the insurgents. Inawan had professed a strong faith in the Emperor and that was all he had needed to protect him from the guns and bullets of his enemies. Barcham had never met a man more stoic in his belief.

But there was no time to mourn. 'Don't stop to fight back! Just keep moving,' the lieutenant shouted at his driver. The remaining Chimeras fell into line, following their lead.

'We were shooting as much as we could, in any direction,' Barcham recalled to the old woman. 'The men were hosing guns out from their vision slits, lobbing grenades out from the hatches. The enemy chased us, hugging the tree line and firing as they came.'

Of the four carriers, two remained, but in weary condition. Black smoke plumed from their engines, small fires fluttering from the treads. Snipers popped shots off their battered hulls and mortars burst before them, sending shrapnel hissing through the jungle canopy.

But the platoon moved on, down another narrow gulley and up a sharp cleft in the terrain.

'Once we crest this gorge, we'll be in open ground and they won't follow,' Barcham urged his men over the vox systems.

Gunning the last dying splutters from their engines, they cleared the final crest. The enemy fire waned as the Chimeras surged on and left them behind. But the platoon did not stop for another five kilometres, until one of the carriers finally rolled to a halt, its engine dead and its armoured compartment filled with oily black smoke. By now, Vulture gunships were making low attack runs on the village and its surrounding region. The Imperial retribution was furious and coils of orange tracer lit up the sky long into the evening.

Back at the base camp, Lieutenant Barcham waited to gather his dead. Throughout the night Vultures touched down to refuel, bringing back with them the plastek body bags of his broken platoon. They would unload the remains of his men before whooping away on their turbine engines, back into the night. The dead – fifteen men in all – were laid out on the parade ground. The injured – twenty-two including Barcham himself – were taken to the infirmary. Three Guardsmen remained unaccounted for. The insurgents had cut out the livers of those who had been left in the field for several hours, but Barcham did not tell the old woman this. The practice of ritual mutilation was *bating bating*, a grave insult to the dead and strictly forbidden.

'My platoon was no more,' the lieutenant concluded. 'Not one man emerged unharmed.'

Within a week, those of his platoon with minor injuries were dispersed into other fighting units. Lieutenant Barcham, limping with shrapnel in his left leg and lower back, was placed on temporary administrative duties until recovery. He was a grade three – wounded with grievous bodily harm – and given two weeks' recuperation.

But before they were disassembled, the men who survived held a service for the fallen. Kalisador Inawan was included in the platoon's registry and buried with full honours, as befitted a Guardsman of the 31st Riverine. Back home on Ouisivia, fallen soldiers were set adrift in the bayous. Here their bodies were cast on rafts down the waters of the Serrado Delta.

'That is how your son died. If there were more loyalist men on Solo-Bastón like him, this war would already be over.'

CHAPTER ONE

OUT ACROSS THE oceans of Solo-Bastón, far beyond where the muddy inlets gave way to thrumming tides, the water became a foamy jade. From those frothing waves rose the towering might of an Imperial Argo-Nautical, a warship of distant Persepia. From its forward-jutting ram prow to its stern, the Nautical was a vast floating gun battery. The solid, blue-grey sheets of its hull towered over the water like a fortress, sloping up on an incline towards the deck. The Argo-Nautical dominated the ocean, eclipsing the horizon as it drew astern with an offshore platform. Its sheer bulk made the support girders of the platform appear frail and dwarfed even the Vulture gunships roosting on the landing pad.

Upon the platform, the high officers of the Bastón campaign were assembled with their accompanying ceremonial guard. They had been summoned by

Cardinal Lior Avanti, head of the diocese on Solo-Bastón, acting governor-general and, without a doubt, the most powerful Imperial authority on the planet. Rarely was such a meeting requested of them; the staff officers shifted uncomfortably as they stood to attention.

Also present was Major General Gaspar Montalvo of the Caliguan Motor Rifles. He sweated in the sun underneath a furred mantle and a full suit of burnished copper. Accompanying him were two of the tallest, most imposing men in his regiment. The soldiers were men of the 105th Motor Rifles, a mechanised formation from the oil-rich world of Caligua in the Bastion Stars. They wore loose-fitting jumpsuits of dusty brown with pads of ballistic mesh sewn into the thighs, chest and shoulders of their utility uniforms.

Standing opposite was Fleet Admiral Victor de Ruger of the Persepia Nautical Fleet. He stood smartly in his sky-blue dress coat, with silks arranged in layers across his left shoulder and a feather-crested helm curled under one arm. A coterie of attendants and officers flanked him, bearing his personal shield, standard and refreshment towels on platters. Persepian Nautical Infantry were arrayed in ordered ranks behind him in their chalk-blue frock coats and polished chrome rebreathers. Lasguns fixed with boarding pikes were held vertically in salute, a bristling forest of steel that glinted with oceanic reflection.

Almost unnoticed, Brigadier Kaplain stood off to the side. He hated ceremony, like all men of the Riverine Amphibious. Regardless, Kaplain had shaved and even pressed his uniform that very morning. A tall, thin man of late middle years, the brigadier looked more like an administrative clerk than the commanding officer of the wild Ouisivians. He wore fatigues of muted swamp camouflage, standard issue amongst all Guardsmen of the 31st Riverine. Even as the docking ramp of the Nautical was lowered towards the rig platform, Kaplain continued to smoke his tabac. There was no way that he was going to salute a man who had never earned his right to be saluted.

Overhead the Nautical sounded its boarding horns, braying with tremulous urgency. Air sirens whooped as the boarding ramp locked into position. Below, the assembled soldiery snapped their heels and stood to attention in unison. Kaplain sighed wearily and stubbed out his tabac with the heel of his boot.

Slowly, with measured strides, Cardinal Lior Avanti descended the ramp. Avanti was overwhelmingly tall and upright for a man of so many centuries. Although the skin of his face was like veined parchment, his features were heavily boned and well proportioned. A web of metal tubes sutured to his nostrils trailed into his voluminous robes, connecting him to a life-support system deep within his attire.

His every movement was deliberate and sure, exuding a great conviction that he could do no wrong. His holy vestments of embroidered tapestry, rich with midnight blue and purple, cascaded in perfectly measured lines, strangely unmoving despite the whipping ocean wind. Over this he was draped in a cope of needled gold and a lace train of tremendous length. Behind him, walking two abreast, sisters of the Adepta Sororitas in white power armour carried his lace train for a length of eight bearers.

The cardinal finally reached the ramp's landing and levelled his gaze on the Imperial officers. He drew an imperious breath.

'Gentlemen. Every morning I pray for victory. Do you?' Avanti asked.

Major General Montalvo risked a sidelong glance at Admiral de Ruger, syllables stuttering behind their teeth but not forming any words. Kaplain, however, kept to the old regimental adage – 'Keep your chin down, your eyes high and your mouth shut.' He did exactly that, keeping himself towards the rear of the assembly. For Kaplain, this entire meeting was a farce. He would have much preferred to be back on base camp where he was needed. In the past few days they had experienced a spike in insurgent activity and there were even rumours that they had lost favour with the local loyalists in the surrounding provinces. In his opinion, he had much better things to do than curry favour with the Ecclesiarchy, but orders were orders.

The cardinal approached Major General Montalvo and placed a hand on the officer's shoulder. The squat, pugnacious general shuffled uncomfortably from foot to foot for a brief second. Kaplain almost pitied the man. He was already sweating profusely underneath his fur mantle and copper plate and doubtless the cardinal's attention did little to abate his condition.

'It hurts my heart,' the cardinal proclaimed. He turned to address the entire assembly before continuing. 'It hurts my heart to think that men of the Imperium are not fighting hard enough or faithfully enough to have ended this war already.'

Montalvo looked to Admiral de Ruger for support. De Ruger simply stared straight ahead to attention, evidently glad that he was not the object of the cardinal's ire. When no help was forthcoming, Montalvo gritted his teeth. 'We are operating at maximum capacity considering the situation. Strategically, the enemy hold the mainland and its super-heavy siege-batteries,' he conceded.

'Yes, I've already heard enough about the curtain guns that it hurts my head at their mentioning. I've known about these siege-batteries since you landed. I can't figure out why, with so many troops at your disposal, you cannot wrest control of these defence silos from the enemy?' At this, Avanti directed his gaze on Admiral de Ruger, expecting an answer.

Kaplain was now more amused than before. Admiral de Ruger, a thin man with avian features, long of face and long of neck, began to fumble for an explanation. For a moment, the wide-eyed look on the admiral's face threatened to dislodge the monocle he wore over his left eye. It amazed Kaplain that two of the most dominant military officers in the subsector were being terrorised by an old man with barely functioning joints.

'We've performed numerous bombing runs but the canopy is dense and the super batteries are well fortified due to terrain. But we will send more, increase bombing runs twofold, supplies allowing.'

Avanti leaned in close, a smile curling the corners of his mouth, but there was no mirth in his slitted grey eyes. 'Then why can we not dissuade these indigenous savages from undoing the good work of the God-Emperor here? What is it about these savages that His armies cannot overcome?'

Now it was Admiral de Ruger who looked to Montalvo for support. Neither officer spoke a word.

'Because they're holding the super-heavy battery on the mainland and blasting the snot out of our transport craft every time we attempt to deploy anything,' Kaplain called from the rear.

The brigadier could not help himself. He would bring an end to this farce. He had little regard for the Ecclesiarchy. As far as he was concerned, the military and theology were distinctly separate entities and he did not answer to the cardinal. Pushing his way through the ceremonial troops, jostling aside platter bearers and junior attendants, Kaplain emerged at the front of the assembly.

'What my comrades here are trying to say, in the simplest terms, is that the insurgents have captured the island's big gun. This big gun blows up big boats. But we need big boats to deploy troops onto the mainland, and we need big boats to run supply lanes in order to sustain any mass mobilisation. But as long as this big gun remains in enemy hands, we have to skulk beyond their range.'

Although Kaplain's fellow officers were glowering at him with unrestrained anger, the brigadier continued. 'So, for the past four months, we've been sending piecemeal patrols into the wilderness and getting thoroughly licked. I would send in an expedition, but my esteemed comrades here,' Kaplain gestured at his fellow high officers, 'outrank me, and refuse to do anything but send high-altitude bombing to disable the guns. They don't seem to understand that the heavy canopy cover and terrain protect the battery and renders it almost impervious to bombardment, and I can't send my boys out there without support. And that, my surly friend, is why these savages are tying your hosieries into a knot.'

There came a collective gasp from the audience. Several members of the Adepta Sororitas took a step towards the brigadier, their plated boots thudding with intention. For a moment, Kaplain wondered whether his Ouisivian manners had pushed the cardinal too far. But the cardinal began to chortle. His laughter wheezed through bundles of tubing that connected his nostrils to pressure filters hidden beneath his voluminous robes, sounding like a discordant metal organ.

'Well said, brigadier. I appreciate your candour,' commented Avanti with his eyes twinkling. He turned back to Montalvo and de Ruger. 'You could learn much from this man. You propose a different method, brigadier?'

The generals began to trip verbally and wring out excuses. They listed a lack of sufficient logistics, supplies and even blamed the monsoonal weather. But the cardinal had ceased to pay them attention.

'It's hot and I don't like this weather. I need to retire to my chambers,' the cardinal decided. 'Brigadier, if I give you authority to commit to an inland operation, can you break this stalemate?'

Kaplain nodded. 'Yes. But my men will need low altitude overhead support. I won't send my soldiers out there into enemy territory without any lifelines. I expect Vulture gunships and Persepian aviators to ghost them.'

'Pure folly,' the admiral interjected. 'The enemy have access to anti-air weaponry. I will not expose my fliers on low altitude runs.'

'Stop saying words,' the cardinal ordered. 'You will give the 31st Riverine all the support they need to conduct this operation. I want those guns silenced with all possible haste.'

The officers knew that all discussion was over. The admiral saluted crisply, and Montalvo slapped the breast of his armour with the flat of his palm in respect.

The cardinal turned his back on them. 'Excellent! Dismissed.'

The assembly dispersed swiftly as the generals stalked away towards their waiting Valkyries. Already the engines were whirling to life and ready to airlift them back to their mainland provinces.

Kaplain watched his fellow officers leave, growling angrily and snapping at their attendants. Chortling, the brigadier reached into his breast pocket and slid out a tabac stick.

'Are you an intelligent man, brigadier?'

Kaplain looked up, the tabac hanging unlit between his fingers. Cardinal Avanti stood before him, smiling with only his mouth. Despite Kaplain's considerable height, the cardinal was far taller and thinner, towering over the brigadier with his spectral shadow.

'That can be subjective,' Kaplain said, staring up at the cardinal. He was not intimidated by Avanti, if that was what the cardinal was trying to achieve. The old man moved in closer, far closer than would be considered a polite distance.

'I'd like to think you are. So I'll tell you this, brigadier.' The cardinal leaned in towards Kaplain, smelling strongly of ointment and rose powder. 'If you ever patronise me like that again, I will have you executed for contempt of the Emperor's servants. That's just how it works, my boy. Dismissed.'

Kaplain said nothing as Cardinal Avanti and his lace bearers slid up the docking ramp. Cardinal or not, the next time Avanti threatened him like that, Kaplain swore he would shoot the man himself. That was the way the 31st Riverine worked on Ouisivia.

CHAPTER TWO

AT THE CENTRE of the Bastón mainland, at equal distance from the western seaboard and eastern peninsula, the Earthwrecker was a conduit of maritime dominance. A rail-mounted artillery piece based on the Earthshaker design, the super-heavy Earthwrecker was an immense artefact of war. It lay dormant in a subterranean rail network built specifically for its containment, a military installation situated in the Kalinga Curtain and stationed with six thousand PDF servicemen. Unstoppable, undefeatable, its machine pulse could be felt across the archipelagos. Girdled by hills and powered by iron-hulled engines, it was manoeuvred ponderously by way of rail-track to any number of firing vents carved into the hillside.

The Kalinga Curtain covered an area of thirty-five square kilometres and contained an entire underground rail system and hundreds of anti-air raid structures. The subterranean complex was said to have been mostly hand-dug by eighty thousand local residents during the first stages of Imperial rule.

Inevitably, it was the first target of the Carnibalès and fell into insurgent hands in the early stages of the war. With its eight-tonne rocket-propelled warheads, the Carnibalès had managed to thwart every Imperial attempt to land troops or supplies onto the mainland. Insurgent forward observers, usually no more than rebel peasants with hand-held vox-units, kept a vigilant watch for Imperial movement. When such movement was spied, the inevitable warheads would roar. The Imperial Guard lost thousands to the Earthwrecker in those early stages of conflict.

The Persepian Nautical Fleet wasted thousands of tonnes of munitions in relentless bombing sorties in an effort to neutralise the threat but to no result. The gun's very presence emboldened the insurgency. It allowed a dissident force of ill-equipped agriculturalists to stalemate many times their number of disciplined, well-trained Imperial Guard.

EVERY FEW DAYS, the shores of mainland Bastón would light up with the rolling thunder of detonations. For several hundred metres along the eastern coastline, amphibious transport vessels would disgorge waves of Guardsmen who waded through the sand, lancing the air with las-fire. The Guardsmen of the 31st Riverine Amphibious practised their live fire drills here. In between the monotony and terror of river patrols, the men of the 31st worked on their land assault tactics in the hope that soon, maybe in the coming weeks, the Serrado siege-batteries would be silenced. When that day came, the Imperial armies would deploy en masse and come to grips with the enemy. Until then, they trained.

Against the backdrop of ocean and jungle, these Guardsmen were quite a sight. Bronzed and tall, they wore fatigues of swampland camouflage: a splinter pattern of pale, milky green and dusty tan that had been produced for the jade swamps and sandy riverbanks from whence they came. Sweating in the subtropical heat, many of the troopers cut the sleeves and legs off their standard-issue fatigues. It was entirely against regulation, but Riverine officers understood the men under their command and, by their nature, draconian discipline would likely have an adverse affect.

They committed many other offences that were against regulation too. Bandoleers of ammunitions were slung across their chests exposed to dust. Autoguns were shortened, the webbing around their hips was loosened, magazines were taped and blades hidden. Above all, the threat of infection in sweltering climates prevented shaving and every man was thickly bearded. Each a minor infraction within itself, their accumulated discrepancies earned them quite a reputation amongst the other Imperial regiments they served with.

On this day it was the men of the 88th Battalion of the 31st Riverine Regiment that came ashore for their assault drills. They were five hundred and fifty men in all, transported by a flotilla that lined up for the race to shore. The forty swift boats got a head start, for they had to arrive first. Their lean-bladed profiles painted in the cream green and tan of the Riverine colours bounced atop the tidal waves as their gunners swept the beach with their mounted bolters. Next came the inflatable assault landers, black rubber and U-shaped. Each

carried a twelve-man squad of Riverine troops. Behind
them came a support squadron of fifteen gunboats, flat
hulled and fifteen metres in length. These were robust
vessels resembling squat river barges, each housing a
single autocannon or heavy flamer. Oversized flags of
the 31st Riverine, displaying the sword and dragonfly,
flew proudly from most boats; a glorious touch.

The waters of Solo-Bastón were clear, far too clear
when compared to the silty bog that the Riverine were
accustomed to on Ouisivia. The vessels beached themselves too far out from the shore and the men in the
rubber landers splashed into the water, dragging their
inflatables behind them. The sand was loose too – not
like the sucking mud of home, which was firm and slippery. Here and there a Guardsman tripped and fell into
the waist-high water, resurfacing with laboured gasps.

'Secure positions at the sandbanks. I don't want any
piecemeal formation like last time,' barked Colonel
Fyodor Baeder of the 88th Battalion.

The colonel ran at the front of his men, taking care to
lead the pack. At thirty-three years standard, he exerted
himself more than any of the younger men. He took
care to lead by exemplary performance, as respect
between the soldiers of the 31st and their officers was
difficult to earn and easy to lose. These were resilient
men, and Baeder knew that they did not respect him.
He was a new officer amongst their ranks, transferred to
the 88th Battalion after their last commanding officer
'disappeared' during a cleanse operation.

It did not help that theirs was a lawless world. On
Ouisivia, the steaming semi-habitable swamplands created rugged men who eked out a living netting for
shrimp or hunting for gator or swamp rat. It was either
that, or join the Guard. Colonel Baeder himself had

been born and educated within the sheltered administrative parishes and, like many of his fellow officers,
had attended military academy in the urban heartland
of Norlens. He was not welcome amongst these
swampmen and he knew it.

'Hold this line steady,' Baeder yelled as he crashed
belly-first into the sand dune. He dragged the last
ounces of strength from his lactic-burnt limbs and
made sure to edge himself ahead of his men. They
leopard-crawled through the sand, heaving and grunt-
ing. Something popped in the colonel's lower rib, but
he could not stop or his men would make their disdain
well known to him. 'You move like old people dance!
On! On!' Baeder urged, with a confidence his body did
not feel. Over their heads, the gunboats and swift boats
shredded the rainforest ahead with heavy support fire.
The noise and exertion was physically deadening.

Finally, they reached a long sandbar before the tree
line. The Riverine lay prone behind their lasrifles and
snapped sheeting volleys into the vegetation, chopping
down trees and brush. Under the combined firepower
of the battalion, even the thick-limbed gum-saps
leaned and fell over.

'Cease fire! Cease fire!' Colonel Baeder yelled
hoarsely into the battalion vox-unit. The firing with-
ered and died away. Exhausted, his men rolled over
onto their backs, staring at the sky. Others tugged their
canteens from their hip webbing, taking long, throat-
bobbing gulps. Baeder had no doubt that it was not
purely water his men were drinking.

'Well done, ramrods. Seven minutes and eighteen
seconds. Best time this week.' Despite his weariness,
Baeder did not wish to show fatigue or thirst in front of
his new battalion. Instead he hauled himself up and

began to move down the line on shaking legs, making ammunition and weapon checks.

After the battalion was settled, Colonel Baeder stood before his line of soldiers. They lounged on the sand before him, canteen bottles uncapped, looking up at him while shielding their eyes from the early morning sun. Baeder liked to think he was what an Imperial officer should look like but he knew that was likely not to be the case. He was not tall compared to most of his men, and certainly not as thickly shouldered. Rather, he was slight of build, with a young boyish face and, unlike the other men of the 31st, Baeder could not summon more than patchy stubble on his chin and neck. He knew it would be a long while, if ever, before the battalion would be used to him. But despite his appearance, Baeder had a fine martial record, and his neck bore the scar of a swamp ork's teeth. The bite formed a ridged scar two fingers from his jugular as testament to his experience. Baeder knew how to run a battalion and he would make these men understand.

'Today was an acceptable time. It has been our best all week. Incidentally, this week has been far the worst since I joined this battalion. I don't know if it is boredom, or the lack of a tangible fight, but we are getting lax. We cannot allow the 88th to become the worst battalion in the 31st Riverine.'

The men began to murmur. They knew what was coming and some even cursed openly and loudly.

Baeder nodded. 'Reorg. We're running the drill again until we can hit under six flat. Be up and ready to move in five minutes.'

By mid-afternoon, the battalion had run the drill another five times over. Their clothes were crusted with a fine evaporation of sweat and seawater. At the end of the sixth landing drill, most of the men lay face down in the sand with their eyes closed. Some, less fortunate, were dry retching into the sand. Colonel Baeder moved briskly down the line, hiding his weariness well. He worked relentlessly, first moving to each and every man, praising him for his efforts and offering him water. Next, he gathered his captains and sergeants together for an analysis of their performance. Not once did he sit or slake his thirst. Finally, after his duties were fulfilled, Colonel Baeder left his battalion strewn across the sand at rest, and slipped into the tree line on his own.

Staggering into the humid darkness of vegetation, out of sight, the colonel braced his arms against the trunk of a gum-sap and bent over double. He vomited. He emptied his stomach until he tasted the acidic burn of bile and his lungs locked up with exertion. Completely and utterly drained, Baeder collapsed as the straining ligaments of his hamstrings went out underneath him.

'I knew I would find you here.'

Colonel Baeder craned his head and saw a tall, thin figure standing before him in crisp fatigues. The man stood with his hands on his hips, shaking his head.

'Brigadier Kaplain, sir.' Baeder struggled to push his back against the tree and rise to salute.

The brigadier waved him down. 'At ease, at ease. You've done enough for today.' Crouching down next to the sprawled out colonel, Kaplain proffered him a canteen of water.

'How are you settling in with the 88th?'

With a heave of effort, Baeder wedged his back against the tree into a slumped sitting position. 'They are a hard bunch. It takes more than some dog-pissed inspirational speech to get them moving. Constant action is what they need.'

Kaplain laughed. 'Speeches? This isn't some war hero story. Leave the talking to the Commissariat.'

'True as that may be, I'd like to instil some sense of trust between the men and me before we may have to mobilise as a battalion. So far I've had the platoon on rotational patrols, fragmented puissant business.'

Kaplain smiled. 'Let me guess – the closest you've got to combat so far has been reading patrol reports from your platoon commanders?'

'I need a cure for the itch, sir,' Baeder shrugged.

The brigadier clapped the colonel on the back knowingly. 'If your legs can still move, take a walk with me, the Persepian Nautical Fleet are bombing the hills again. It's a glorious if wasteful sight.'

The two staff officers meandered back out onto the beach as squadrons of winged craft climbed to high altitude overhead. As they scaled the slippery tusks of igneous rock that littered the coastal slopes, bombs were already spilling out over the high hills of the mainland.

Kaplain gestured at the undulating horizon, carpeted in green. Explosions were swelling up in the distance, tiny bubbles of orange that burst into rolling black smoke and flame. The hills were trembling as the chain of explosions popped and expanded. 'Those damned siege-batteries. Who would have thought that a handful of insurgents could stalemate twenty divisions of Imperial fighting men.'

'I understand that the Persepian Aviation boys have been flying sorties to the mainland night and day. We've barely had any sleep from the constant noise,' Baeder replied. Although they were too far off to be seen, Baeder could imagine the Marauder bombers of Persepia, painted chalk blue, devastating the landscape on wide banking runs.

'The Earthwrecker sunk another one this week, you know. High Command have kept the sinking classified, but word will be out sooner or later,' said Kaplain.

'Sir?'

'A Persepian Argo-Nautical. The warship *Thrice Avenged* attempted to land fourteen thousand Motor Rifles onto the mainland just two days ago. It managed to sail within visual distance of the island before the super-heavies began firing ordnance on it. One shell went clear through the hull and the whole mess went down within minutes. We lost about ten thousand Caliguans and almost the entire crew. What a disaster.'

Baeder was not sure how to accept the news. In a way he was angered by the High Command's relentless stupidity. It was not the first time the Nautical Fleet had lost one of its precious warships to the siege-batteries. If the two warships sunk in the early days of the war did not teach them to stop deploying the vessels, then the subsequent three sunk in the following months should have. Yet they persisted, sending one after another of the great warships towards the mainland loaded with supplies, fuel and men, hoping that this one would make it through unnoticed by the siege-batteries and their distant spotters.

Rudimentary logic would have concluded that, where one tactic has failed, trying it repeatedly would not increase the success rate. But that was exactly what High Command had continued to do. The war had begun with a full complement of twelve great Nautical warships, a dozen floating fortresses that should have stopped the war within days. Now, four months later, they were left with seven and were no closer to finishing the war than when they had started.

'That's a mess, sir. Are the pilots homing in on the exact coordinates of these super-heavy pieces? My men are getting testy. We're burning out from the waiting, sir.'

Faraway, the explosions began to calm. Fire, like an emergent sun, glared on the horizon, burning thousands of acres. Kaplain watched the pyrotechnics for some time before replying. 'A deeply fortified gun piece. We know it's dug-in on a range of hills known as the Kalinga Curtain with a cannon large enough to compensate for the cardinal's glaring insecurities. We have approximate locations from old PDF schematics, but the gun is embedded in an underground system and the Persepians are too scared to fly any lower. We probably haven't even scratched its paint job.'

Judging by the crease of Kaplain's brow, Baeder knew there was something the brigadier wanted to say. Finally, Baeder could wait no longer. 'What will High Command do now then, sir?'

'High Command wants me to send troops into the heart of Bastón. I'm going to send you.'

'Sir?'

Kaplain nodded. 'The siege-batteries are preventing us from launching any sustained assault on the mainland; you know this. The Motor Rifles need fuel and transport for their vehicles and it's obvious the Persepians are trapped out at high anchor. The Riverine are the only regiment who have a foothold on the mainland. We can't take this island ourselves, but we can send in a smaller probing force to find and disable this gun. I'm sending the 88th to fix this mess.'

'Sir. We're not ready. The 88th Battalion is not cohesive yet. I've been with my men for four months! We have not even operated at a company level. Any of the other battalions are more tightly knit, even the 76th, frag it, even the 123rd would do a better job.'

'Don't make this harder than it has to be, Baeder.' Kaplain suddenly looked very weary. 'It doesn't get any easier for me to send men to their deaths. This will be a dangerous operation. You will lose men, colonel. But we need this done, and I can't entrust a lesser battalion with the job.'

BEFORE THE INSURGENCY, the Serrado Delta had been the major artery of trade for mainland Bastón and its infant islands. Ramshackle fishing trawlers from upriver would ply their daily catches amongst the coastal villages. Along the banks, makeshift markets sprang up here and there, motor-canoes and rafts laden to the tipping point and tethered by the rushes. There they sold all manner of fruits and vegetables from local water gardens, pungent spices or urns of fermented fish.

For the past few months, the Serrado Delta had become hauntingly empty during the day. Insurgent attacks had concentrated on razing agricultural settlements, leaving burnt scars of earth where production had once been abundant. The only trade barges that traversed the delta during daylight hours were the coffin makers, who had more business than they could supply.

At night, refugees meandered downstream in sad, sodden convoys. They were mostly tribes fleeing the turmoil of the inland wilderness, hoping to reach Imperial-controlled territory without being spotted by insurgent heretics. Since the early days of war,

Persepian aviation had dropped leaflets on isolated settlements promising them safety under the bulwark of
Imperial military presence. For most tribes, fleeing was
a far better option than staying on their ancestral lands.
At best, tribes considered neutral were harassed constantly by insurgent propagandists, rounding up their
young men for recruitment or demanding exorbitant
taxes. At worst, tribes who were heavily vested in agriculture or revealed to be Imperial loyalists were
considered lost to the old ways, often becoming the target for raid or massacre by insurgent warbands.

One such tribe were the people of the Taboon. Like
all tribes of Bastón, they were a loosely-related kin
group of extended family forming a network of elaborate social hierarchies. Together they had travelled for
eight days down the delta, sailing only under the cover
of night. There were eighty in all, crammed onto all
manner of propeller canoes, junks and tow barges.

Like most tribes, they revered the strength of their
warriors. The people of Taboon had two such men, also
known as Kalisadors. The indigenous people of Bastón
had never been a warlike culture and it was not uncom-
mon for tribes of two or three hundred people to be
represented by a single Kalisador warrior. As such, the
entire pride, history and prestige of the tribe was vested
in a single man. These Kalisadors were of special status.
In times of inter-tribal conflict, Kalisadors would
engage in one-on-one combat in a ritual mired in ceremony and etiquette under the audience of both tribes.
There was an air of festivity during these bouts, with
much dancing and drinking. Fights were often only to
first blood, and upon the completion of the duel the
inter-tribal conflict would be resolved, forever and
indisputably so. The Bastón tribes had a great fondness

for festivity and any excuse was made to duel their tribal champions, anything from territorial disputes, to the loss of rural produce. This method of conflict, of course, had been before the insurgency.

Times were much harder now and the Taboon looked to their two Kalisadors for guidance. Luis Taboon was a Kalisador of old, a man of greying years. He had settled many illustrious victories for the Taboon and, although he was old, his wiry frame was known for his fast knife disarm, a specialty of his, as well as his elaborate pre-duel dance ritual which none could match. There was also Mautista Taboon, a very young man, third cousin of Luis, with narrow shoulders but long limbs and a fierce mane of hair. Although Mautista was young, he showed much promise, having already mastered the Kalisador art of stick and dagger.

During their exodus, the two Kalisadors had led the way. Although they knew their unarmed expertise and tribal weapons were no match for the insurgent firearms, the pair had kept a sleepless watch over the convoy. Remaining vigilant, they navigated ahead of their tribe in a single-motored sampan, singing loudly to frighten away bad luck and evil spirits that lurked in the treetops. When the tribe broke camp during the day, the pair gathered volunteers to spear for cauldron crab in the shallow mud. Although they had not slept or rested, the Kalisadors always gathered more food than the others of their tribe.

Now, eight days into their trek, the pair were haggard. The past days had chipped away steadily at their constitution, grinding down their resolve and their stamina until they were sore and short of breath. But they were close to safety now. The pair knew this and probed their sampan far ahead of the column. It was dark and the trees extended their branches far over the river in an arch overhead. Vines fell around them at head level, while the nocturnal animals watched them from the murky darkness with glazed, glowing eyes. Mautista clapped a machete against a straight stick in timpani that warned away ghosts while Luis sang, for his voice carried well whereas Mautista's did not. Night was a frightening place in the rainforest but they pressed on. Ahead, they could see the lights of an Imperial camp. It meant safety and they would not stop now.

'Praise the Lord-Emperor. We're finally close,' said Luis in his trembling baritone. Although age had shrunken his frame it had not robbed him of his voice and Mautista was comforted by that same calmness which warded away evil. Beyond them, the winking lights and search probes of the Imperial blockade played across the water.

'These Imperial soldiers, are they good men?' asked Mautista. Although he had seen some of the Planetary Defence soldiers at trade markets, Mautista had never spoken to off-world Guardsmen before. He took out his straight dagger and laid it anxiously across his lap. The sight of the naked steel helped to calm his trembling hands. He was nervous, but he could not work out why.

Luis nodded enthusiastically. 'They are good men. I met a sergeant from a distant land once in my younger days. They have strong faith in the Emperor.'

Suddenly the older Kalisador began to smooth out his balding pate. 'How do I look? We must show our ceremonial best, warrior to warrior as we meet these men.'

'You look fine,' Mautista replied.

In reality, the older Kalisador looked more than weathered. He wore a tunic and loose shorts of grey hemp, plastered to his gaunt limbs with days of accumulated mud. The ceremonial rope bindings on his forearms and calves were dry and fraying.

Mautista imagined his presentation to be remarkably similar. The breastplate of cauldron crab shell had chafed his underarms raw, bleeding into his shirt and drying in trickles down his arms. The many pennants and bead strings that adorned his attire had been lost in their trek. In particular, Mautista had lost a hoop of beaten copper he had worn against his right hip. The copper crescent had been a gift for tracking down a gang of cattle rustlers deep in the Byan Valley and beating all five of the men with a binding club until they were dark with bruises. In gratitude his village had gathered their harvest money and commissioned a local artisan to shape a tiny sliver of precious copper into a crescent symbolising the return of cattle horns for their brave Kalisador. Mautista would have very much liked to show these off-world warriors his medal, and perhaps compare their deeds.

'Look at their lights and guns,' marvelled Luis in awe.

They were very close to the blockade now. At the narrowest point of the channel ahead, the Imperial Guard had erected a series of pontoons and sandbags into a floating blockade. A flashing siren light marked the military checkpoint, spinning in fast, pulsating circles. Behind the wall of sandbags, Guardsmen played drum-like searchlights across the black water. Despite the evening darkness, Mautista could see the silhouettes of men with guns prowling along the blockade wall.

Luis leapt to his feet, waving his arms frantically. 'Friends! Friends!' he cried, rocking the boat with his jumping. Immediately, a searchlight swung to bear on them, its harsh white beam cupping their entire vessel. Mautista threw up his hands to shield his eyes.

A deep voice, crackling from vox speakers, barked out of the white void. 'Halt. You are entering the Imperial safe zone. State your business.'

Giddy with excitement, Luis reached into leather pouches sewn into his tunic and began to pull out the leaflets that Imperial craft had dropped for them. Many were crumpled, others were melted into furry wads by river water, but they were all the same. Luis tore them out of his pouches and thrust handfuls of them before him like an offering. 'We are loyalists seeking safety within the military zones!' he replied.

There was a long pause before the vox speakers clicked again. 'Come closer but stay a distance of five metres from the checkpoint, then switch off your engines and keep your hands above your heads.'

Hands shaking, Mautista nursed their keel motor towards the blockade. Up close he could see almost half a dozen soldiers in thickly-padded jumpsuits, each training a lasrifle at their vessel. Directly to their front, another soldier took the cap off his head and waved them in like a flag.

'Switch off the engine,' Luis hissed to him. Careful not to make any mistakes or sudden movements, Mautista shut off the propellers and let the sampan glide in to close the gap. Then with slow, exaggerated movements, Mautista and Luis laced their fingers behind their heads.

Leaping over the sandbags, the soldier with the cap waved at them. 'Welcome to Checkpoint Watchdog. I'm Sergeant Descont of the Caliguan Motor Rifles. Sweet merciful frag, do you boys look like you need a drink.'

Mautista almost sagged with relief. After spending eight days constantly looking over their backs and fearing discovery, the notion that they had found safety was enough to drain all the adrenaline that was left from his body.

'Where are you from?' the sergeant asked.

Luis began to speak, exposing his wrists to the soldiers as a gesture of peace. 'We are the Taboon people, from the inland Byan Valley. There are more of us, eighty more, further back upriver. We are fleeing–'

The sergeant cut him off with a lazy wave of his hand. 'Sure. Sure. Eighty, got it. I'm going to let you boys come through the checkpoint while I vox my superiors. Then we can see about bringing up the rest of you.' With that, Sergeant Descont flashed the thumbs up to his men and turned to go. Another soldier, still aiming his firearm on them, motioned with his head towards a chained docking picket behind the barricade.

By the time Luis and Mautista had tethered their boat to the floating checkpoint, a group of soldiers were waiting for them. Luis and Mautista hopped off the vessel onto the gently shifting surface and immediately reached out to thank the Guardsmen with grateful handclasps.

The soldiers shrank back, chuckling and shaking their heads. 'You're not touching me with those filthy paws, indig,' laughed the closest soldier.

Mautista exchanged an uncertain look with Luis. The young Kalisador had expected men of good Imperial faith to be kinder, but these soldiers simply stared at him from a curious distance. He noticed these were tall, powerfully-built men. Well-nourished and well-trained, more powerfully built perhaps than even the Northern Island Kalisadors who lifted heavy stones and hand-wrestled. They all wore glare-shades and chewed constantly.

'You're one of those fragging indig warriors, uh?' drawled one of the soldiers as he spat his dip. 'I hear you boys do all sorts of slap-happy unarmed fighting, uh?'

Mautista saw Luis bristle with indignation. The soldier swaggered forwards with a pugnacious smirk until he was face-on with the old Kalisador. The old man levelled his gaze on the soldier, the wiry muscles of his jaw twitching slightly. 'We know how to duel with bare hands. But we also duel with twin sticks, war clubs, daggers and machetes.'

'Is that so, indig?' cawed the soldier, as he turned to his friends. Turning around, he thrust his lasrifle before Luis. 'How does that compare with one of these?'

The soldiers burst out laughing, but Luis said nothing. Mautista had to admit that the lasrifle was impressive indeed. Sleek and matt black, with a long silver snout and a leather strap that the soldier wound loosely around his forearm, the lasgun was quite frightening. It had a lean, uncomplicated design that did not hide its purpose to harm. Mautista was startled to think that all their years of devotion to the Kalisador arts could be undone by any man with basic knowledge of these firearms.

'Trooper Nesben, stow it for later,' barked Sergeant Descont as he emerged from the command tent. Strangely enough, the sergeant wore glare-shades now too, and spoke to the Kalisadors with a detached anonymity. 'You've got clearance. Bring up the convoy,' he said, pointing at Mautista.

Unwilling to compromise safe passage for their tribe, the Kalisadors avoided eye contact with Trooper

Nesben and his jeering cohort as they turned to retrieve
their sampan.

'Not you. You stay here,' Sergeant Descont said, aiming his index finger on Luis.

Mautista felt a surge of sudden uncertainty, but Luis
simply nodded. 'Go and get the others. I'll be here
when you get back. I'm sure they just need me to
answer some questions.'

The young Kalisador was not so certain, but he
clasped hands with the old man and slipped away.
Later, as he loosened the moorings of his sampan,
Mautista realised his earlier elation had long since
washed away and he only yearned to be away from this
checkpoint. These soldiers, he knew, were not good
men and he only hoped the Imperial authorities in the
safety zones were kinder. Suppressing his instinctive
fear, Mautista was only glad that he had slipped Luis a
butterfly blade in his palm before they parted.

THE PEOPLE OF the Taboon were huddled in their vessels
just beyond a natural bend in the river. As Mautista
rounded the turn in his sampan, pinched and mal-
nourished faces looked at him anxiously. His family,
for they were all related in some way, peered at him
from their overcrowded boats. He saw Fernan and her
four girls; she had not eaten for a week so her children
would not go hungry. There was Cardosa the village
carpenter, Mautista's second cousin, and Lavio the net-
mender, both strong men who were now weak with
fever. Even Bustaman the village elder was jaundiced
from starvation. In all, eighty desperate faces looked to
Mautista for hope.

'We are here. The Imperial armies are up ahead and
we are free to go through. We will be safe then,'

Mautista called out to them as he steered his sampan close.

Word spread quickly along the cluster of vessels. An excited babble of voices filled the humid evening air. For the first time in eight days, the hushed and fearful silence was lifted and the Taboon spoke loudly and freely amongst themselves. Motors were gunned loudly and vessels throbbed ahead, eager to meet the check-point.

'We have done it, Bustaman,' said Mautista as he drew his sampan alongside the elder's trawling vessel. 'We've led everyone to safety.'

The village chief, leaning over his trawler, sighed. The folded creases and wrinkles that webbed his face appeared deeper than they ever had before and Mautista immediately knew something was wrong.

'We did not guide all of them. One of our youngest members, Tadeu, died tonight. Hunger and fever took him. We must bury him together, chief and Kalisador,' the old man wheezed weakly. He spoke softly, so as not to alarm the other people on the trawler, and it was evident that not all of the tribe knew yet.

'Tadeu? Tagiao's newborn son?' Mautista hissed with a mixture of frustration and disbelief.

Bustaman nodded. 'Yes, we must bury him now, so as to not bring the dark spirits with us when we journey into our new home.' Weakly, with arms not thicker than bone, the village elder held a small bundle to his chest and prepared to climb over the trawler and into Mautista's sampan.

'Wait, Bustaman,' Mautista said. 'You are sick. I can bury Tadeu myself, I can perform that rite as Kalisador. You go on ahead with the others and receive water and food.'

The old man hesitated, halfway over the trawler. 'I am the elder, it should be me.'

'You cannot help anyone in your state, elder. I am Kalisador and I have a duty to protect my tribe, including you. Please go,' Mautista said as he reached out to take the bundle from the old man's arms.

Bustaman had no strength to argue. He sagged back onto the deck of the trawler, his shorts and tunic flapping loosely around his skeletal frame. As the trawler steered away on the steady chopping of its engines, Bustaman and the others waved at Mautista. The Kalisador waved them away, and found himself drifting alone on the delta as the throb of their engines faded.

'The Emperor protects,' Mautista murmured to himself as he drew the points of the aquila swiftly across his chest. Peering into the depths of the riverbank, the spaces between the trees created yawning pits. Even though Mautista had grown up in the rainforests, the night had always been a time of ghosts and daemons in Bastón folklore. Gripping his striking stick in one hand and a machete in the other, Mautista prepared to find a place in that forest to rest little Tadeu.

THE SOLDIERS SAID nothing to Luis Taboon as they waited for his tribe. The only sounds were the chirping of insects and the occasional ring of the spittoon as a soldier spat his dip, so it was a welcome relief to Luis when he spotted the flotilla of river craft approaching the checkpoint.

'My people!' said Luis, beaming proudly at the men around him. Sergeant Descont nodded, almost in blank-faced affirmation.

Searchlights raked across the flotilla as it meandered closer on the steady *chut chut chut* of ageing motors.

This time, however, Luis was glad the soldiers did not point their rifles as it would have frightened the children, many of whom had never seen an off-world soldier before.

Sergeant Descont raised a loudspeaker to his lips and issued a static-laden command. 'Welcome to Checkpoint Watchdog. Please moor your vessels to the right side of the bank and disembark. We have fresh water and rations waiting.'

By now Luis noticed torch beams criss-crossing the riverbank to his left, just before the checkpoint. Soldiers waded out into the water to pull the smaller boats in to the shore and help his people onto the land. Luis was surprised at the swift efficiency and preparation of these Imperial soldiers.

Sergeant Descont escorted Luis onto the riverbank where the Taboon were sitting around on the loamy soil, hungrily digging into ration parcels. Soldiers moved amongst them with jerry cans of water, issuing tin cups. The soft, muddy earth had never felt so secure beneath Luis's toes. The Kalisador sat down in weary gratitude and was content to just fall asleep.

'Have some grub,' Sergeant Descont said, handing Luis a parcel in brown plastek foil. 'Standard-issue ration. It's good eating,' he promised.

Luis tore open the package with his bare hands, spilling the contents onto the ground. Tubes of sugared fruits, tins and packets fell out like a new harvest and Luis ate with the enthusiasm of a man who had not eaten properly for eight days. There were tinned curds, cereal crackers and tubs of meaty paste. The tribe marvelled at the foreign food and packaging, trading and taste-testing everything with childish awe. A village fisherman held up a tube of fruit-paste triumphantly, declaring, 'This must be what the wealthiest lords and cardinals eat every day!'

Luis plucked up a tin labelled *lactose syrup, sugared* and placed it into a pouch for safekeeping. The bits of torn packaging and foil he lovingly folded into squares and placed into pouches too, as souvenirs he could one day show the younger generations of the tribe. He would tell them of the time that Imperial soldiers saved the Taboon people.

'All right, people, enough time for eating. Up! Up!' shouted a newcomer. He moved amongst the tribe, ushering them to stand; a rake-thin man, with glare shades perched on a hatchet nose. Like the other soldiers, he wore a jumpsuit of light brown, layered with mesh in some parts but, unlike the others, he wore a series of stars and badges on his sleeves. It was obvious, even to the tribe, that this was a higher-ranking soldier simply by the way he walked and spoke if not by his uniform.

'All right, indigs! I am Captain Feldis of the Caliguan Motor Rifles, 10th Logistics Brigade. I'll be taking you to your new settlement where you can get sorted for registration and camp details. Get up, put away what you are doing and get moving. Go!' he shouted, kicking the dirt for emphasis.

The atmosphere changed very quickly. Soldiers began to haul people up by their arms, trampling or knocking over their food and water. The Taboon looked confused and suddenly hurt, and Luis shared those feelings. The Kalisador turned to find Sergeant Descont and ask what was happening but instead he found Trooper Nesben leering in his face.

'Come on, indig. It's time to get settled,' he smirked, jabbing Luis in the ribs with the butt of his lasrifle. The soldier tugged the knives and warclub from Luis's harness, throwing them into the dirt. The Kalisador had never felt so helpless. One by one, the Taboon were herded by soldiers into a marching line. Widow Renao tried to leave the marching column and head back to her canoe, but soldiers gently yet persistently escorted her back into the line. She pleaded that she had to retrieve her possessions from her boat first but the soldiers were not listening.

'Get these dirty indigs out of here for processing,' the captain whispered to Sergeant Descont. Luis overheard their exchange and wished Mautista was with him, but of the young Kalisador there was no sign.

MAUTISTA COVERED THE makeshift grave with handfuls of peat. Wiping his damp hands on his trousers, the young man slid a volume of Imperial scriptures from his hip pouch – *The Scriptures of Concordance*. Unwrapping the muslin cloth, he opened the book on his lap, careful not to smear the pages with his soiled hands. Dirtying the sacred text would be blasphemous. When he was a child of ten, Mautista had accidentally dropped his scripture book into the swine pen. The village preacher found out and lashed him a dozen times with a switch stick. It had left a lasting impression on him.

Kneeling before the tiny cairn of heaped soil, Mautista began to read aloud the 'Resting of Saint Carlamine'. Despite Imperial teaching, superstition was bound to the Bastón psyche. By reading the prayer, Mautista would quell the angry, tragic soul of the child. He hoped the words would placate Tadeu, so the child's ghost would not follow him, clinging to his back and bringing him misfortune.

As he read, a chill spread through his limbs. The words tripped in his mouth and Mautista rose suddenly to his feet. He looked around him, peering into the gloom. Something had spooked him. A feeling of foreboding had yoked down on his shoulders. Looking at the grave, Mautista shook his head at how unnerved he had become. He reasoned that the past few days of starvation had diminished his rationality.

Regardless, the rainforest lingered in the strange hours between dawn and night. The nocturnal animals had receded to their dens and the birds of morning were still asleep. It was dark and silent and Mautista did not wish to stay for any longer than he had to. He finished the last prayer and scurried back to his canoe, as fast as his legs could slosh through the water. The feeling of foreboding did not leave him.

BY THE TIME the Taboon marched to their destination, the sky was indigo with predawn morning. The tribe had threaded their way along a dirt path carved out of the cloying undergrowth until they reached a wide clearing. Here the ground was ugly and barren, stripped bare of any vegetation. An abrasive chemical stink hung in the air, no doubt the solvent used to disintegrate this swathe of nature.

An Ecclesiarchal preacher waited for them in the clearing. Dressed in sombre robes of black, edged with gold, the preacher cut a stoic, solitary figure. As the tribe was led into the clearing, Luis tried to wave towards the preacher. To the tribes of Bastón, the Ecclesiarchy had always occupied a role of guidance and faith and their preachers were considered family by many. Luis tried to flag his attention, but the preacher avoided eye contact.

'Stop waving and get into line with the others,' Captain Feldis snapped at him. The Taboon were forced into a rough line, flanked on all sides by upwards of thirty soldiers. The tribe were uneasy; Luis could feel it. After their ordeal, most did not have the mental faculties to process what was happening. Luis himself was confused. He could not grasp how or why they were being treated in such a way. Surely, once the soldiers handed them over to the care of the preacher, they would be allowed to go free?

The captain approached the preacher and saluted stiffly. 'Where do you want the children?'

'Set them aside first, I don't want them causing a fuss like last time. We need them in a good state for the plantations,' the preacher said flatly. He paused and laughed, 'Assimilation is what's needed for these filthy indigs. Inter-breed them with pure Imperial blood when they are of good breeding age.' These were the first words to come out of his mouth and in an instant Luis knew their ordeals were not yet over.

Soldiers waded into the crowd of refugees with their rifle butts, dragging the youngest children away. The tribe erupted hysterically, pleading and plaintive. Fernan drew her four girls into her arms like a protective mother bird. Strong hands wrenched her children away and Fernan collapsed to her knees, pulling at her hair, but silent. She simply had nothing left, not even to make a sound.

'Do not fear. Your children will be well treated and given Imperial education in our institutions. We are simply protecting them from ignorance, so they may have a better life,' the preacher announced.

The tribe was not calmed by his words: many continued to struggle and the soldiers began to use their rifle butts with rigorous force. Strangely enough, some of the soldiers seemed uncomfortable, even ashamed at what was occurring and many, including Sergeant Descont, stood to the side and looked away. Briefly, Luis considered the butterfly blade that Mautista had slipped him, tucked away beneath his wrist braces. His hands tingled at the thought of driving the leaf-shaped shard up into Trooper Nesben's chin, but he did not. To do so would not bode well for his people.

After a brief struggle, the children were loaded onto a waiting military truck, parked at the edge of the clearing. It had all been prepared, Luis realised. The soldiers had obviously done this before. Some of the Guardsmen wandered about casually, chatting amongst themselves and lighting tabac. For Luis, it was like a surreal dream. He kept waiting for something to happen to make his semi-lucid reality normal again. He wanted the preacher to tell them that it was simply a test of their faith in the God-Emperor, that they had passed and that another truck would be arriving shortly to take them all to their new settlement grounds.

'Line them up!' Captain Feldis barked.

'I can't watch this,' Luis heard a soldier say to Sergeant Descont. The sergeant shook his head. 'I can't do this either. That's why I wear these,' he said, tapping his glare shades. 'I don't have to look them in the eyes this way.' With that the sergeant padded away.

They spoke as if Luis were not even there. Several other soldiers, shaking their heads sadly, filed out of the clearing. Not one soldier acknowledged them or looked at them. Only a dozen Guardsmen remained in the clearing, Trooper Nesben and Captain Feldis amongst them.

'Have they been given their last meals?' the preacher inquired of the Captain. Feldis smiled tight-lipped and nodded, before leading the preacher away from them.

Luis's head was reeling. For the first time, in the dawn light, he noticed the barren earth was rugged with trenches. Shallow pits that were eight or ten metres long and two metres wide, lining the earth like tilled soil. He looked at his people, and his people all looked at him. Everyone Luis had known in his lifetime looked to him, their Kalisador, for an answer and he had none to give them. In the background the officer and preacher continued to chat as if nothing out of the ordinary were occurring. It was not real, Luis told himself.

'–but it turns out I could buy it cheaper if I purchased three at once,' the preacher said to the captain as they passed by. The Kalisador caught the tail end of their very ordinary conversation and he snapped back into reality.

'Kneel! Get those rural knees onto the rural soil now!' shouted a soldier. 'Don't turn around,' barked another as they moved behind the tribe. 'Eyes straight ahead,' they shouted from behind.

Luis felt his throat turn dry. His shoulders began to tremble. Off to the side, lounging against the side of the truck, the captain and the preacher continued their conversation about local poultry prices.

'Find marks. Set to rapid. Ready!' The Guardsmen shouted in unison from behind. The old Kalisador suddenly felt no reason to turn around and see what they were doing. There was no point or hope in doing so. With regret, he slid the butterfly blade from its concealment and wished that he had died fighting. But the time for that had long passed. Without further warning, the Guardsmen began to fire their rifles.

CHAPTER THREE

CHAPTER THREE

THE SOUND OF gunfire travels wide in the wilderness. Its distinct report reverberates amongst the trees, sending animals scarpering up the trunks and startling flocks of birds into flight. The echo lingers for long after, interrupting the flow of nature with its rude, artificial presence.

Although Mautista knew little of firearms, he knew enough to recognise its sound in the still air of dawn. Especially the sound of multiple shots, crackling with a constant rhythm. The Kalisador knew instantly that something had happened to his people. If he closed his eyes and steadied his breathing, he could almost hear the screams, distorted behind the threshing blasts of weaponry.

Warily, Mautista guided his sampan close to the checkpoint once again. He steered the outboard motor by the tiller, the engine throbbing gently while his

other hand gripped a machete. Before him, the checkpoint was strangely empty. The searchlights tilted down
limply in their mounting brackets and no soldiers were
in sight.

It was only then that Mautista saw the empty boats.
All along the right side of his approach, the ramshackle
assortment of his tribe's transport bobbed and bumped
against each other in the morning swell. They were
tethered like despondent beasts, the tribe's possessions
bundled and roped, lying unclaimed upon their backs.

'You there! Come closer!'

Looking back to the checkpoint, now less than fifty
metres away, Mautista saw the outline of a Guardsman
appear on the pontoon. The soldier stood there, staring
at him. Mautista froze, staring back. There was a long,
awkward period of indecision as both men simply
stared at one another. Then another figure appeared on
the pontoon, shouting something at his fellow soldier.
The lasrifle in the second soldier's hands forced
Mautista into action. Groping for a cloth bundle containing foodstuff and medicine, Mautista propelled
himself off the sampan and into the water with one
fluid motion.

A las-shot sparked into the side of the sampan. It was
the first time Mautista had been shot at and the proximity of death ignited his body with twitching
movement. Another las-shot sizzled into the water
sending up a geyser of steam, forcing him to plunge
underneath the surface. Brown water gurgled around
him as river debris darkened his vision in thick, blackened clots. The Kalisador swam, his limbs carving the
water with desperate, life-saving strokes. By the time he
resurfaced, Mautista emerged just in time to see the
sampan he had left behind erupt into a shower of

splinters. The boat was blown upwards and out of the water, spinning in mid-air as pieces of wood and tin peeled away. Up on the pontoon, a soldier was raking the water with a mounted weapon, something Mautista recognised from Ecclesiarchal teachings as a heavy bolter, a weapon used by the Emperor's crusaders in the early wars of scripture. A rapid succession of what resembled burning hot embers erupted across the water as the heavy bolter swung back and forth. Not waiting another moment, he cleared the short distance to shore with practised strokes and surged out of the water headfirst. The shallow riverbank pulled at his ankles as he sprinted towards the tree line, acutely aware that the bolter would no doubt be tracking his back.

For a brief, absurd moment Mautista considered allowing himself to be shot. His tribe were probably gone, and he had failed them as a custodian of his people. There was nothing left for him in this world. But it was a passing moment and his warrior's instincts pushed him onwards. All around him, thick gum-saps fell, throwing up a solid wall of splinters and mulched vegetation. Mautista hurdled a log as bolt-shots stitched the ground to his front. He continued to run, deeper and deeper into the rainforest even as the bolter stopped firing. He ran and ran and did not stop until his lungs were seized from exertion and he could no longer tell where he was.

COLONEL FYODOR BAEDER, stripped to the waist in the afternoon sun, made his way around Riverine Base Camp Echo with a purpose to his stride. The men of his battalion were 'bombing up' on the parade ground, prepping their kit for their first true taste of conflict on Bastón. There was a general air of excitement on camp and even detachments not assigned to the 88th were lending a hand with the preparations. Soldiers laid out all their equipment neatly on plastek groundsheets, cleaning and repairing. He darted around them, and stopped to allow a forked lifter delivering pallets of rations from the storage sheds to pass.

Riverine Guardsmen from other battalions passed by, carrying stamped boxes of ammunition and strongboxes of rifles. They were sweating under the relentless heat but everyone on base worked tirelessly to get the 88th Battalion ready for their operation. It may have been his battalion preparing for operation, but it would be the entire 31st Riverine that was preparing for war.

'Fyodor, you lucky bastard. Enjoying the attention?' Colonel Tate called out to him from the open entrance of a vehicle hangar.

'Enjoying doing something for once,' Baeder replied, grateful for an excuse to wander underneath the shaded hangar roof.

Colonel Tate and a handful of his men were smeared in machine grease. The hangar was sour with the smell of polish, promethium and burnt rubber. Behind them, a line of swift boats secured in tow racks was being worked on by the Guardsmen – hammering, tinkering and mending. Sirens sounded as an engine block was winched up towards the ceiling by a clanking pulley system.

'Leave some of them for us. I don't want you doing too thorough a job and leaving us squatting in ditches,' Tate joked.

'I think there will be plenty of insurgents left by the look of things,' Baeder responded. 'But if it'll make you sleep better, I can try to go easy on the ones we do find.'

Tate laughed and his men laughed with him. Baeder had known Ando Tate since they were both junior officers serving in Snake Company back in their early days. Ando Tate, with his broad grin, had been a natural amongst his men, rough and hardy despite his privileged upbringing. Baeder had always admired his ability to lead so effortlessly; it was something he never believed he could do.

'So what's the word, Fyodor? When are you lot moving out?'

'06.00 tomorrow. I'll be making last inspections at 04.00. It's really happening this time.'

Colonel Tate whistled appreciatively. 'Wish I could be there with you, brother.'

'I do too. But I'll see you out there soon,' Baeder said, clasping forearms with his old friend. As he turned to go, Baeder called over his shoulder mockingly, 'Don't mess up my boats either, Ando!'

Hurrying against the flow of traffic, Baeder passed beneath the girders of a guard tower. Despite being situated in a designated safe zone, soldiers manned the defence turrets constantly against insurgent mortars far out in the wilderness. Rows of green canvas tents were erected underneath its protective shadow. It was there that Baeder found the H-block administrative quarters, a rectangular green tent with spray-stencilled writing on the entrance flap. A corporal saluted and escorted him inside to meet the bored-looking admin clerk at the front desk.

The clerk, a red-faced captain sweltering in the heat, flicked the colonel a lazy salute as he entered. Judging by the spreading patches of sweat darkening his uniform, and the red rash on his neckline, it was evident to Baeder that the captain did not want to be stuck in administrative duties.

'Captain Brevet, sir. What brings you here?'

Baeder saluted sharply. 'A request came in that Brigadier Kaplain required me for a matter of great urgency. Any idea what that's about?'

Displaying no sense of urgency, Captain Brevet began to rifle through a sheaf of papers. He mumbled to himself as he worked until finally he triumphantly produced a slip of paper. 'Ah!' he announced, 'it says here, that an insurgent has been captured while on patrol. Brigadier Kaplain requests that you be present during interrogation, before you leave for the operation.'

'Very well. I will find him at the command post, I gather?'

The captain nodded. 'Yes, but do you need transport? It's a ten-minute walk,' he said, smearing his brow with his cap.

'No. I'll be fine, thank you, captain,' said Baeder turning to go.

'Wait, sir. Is it true? Your battalion is moving out to clear the siege-batteries so we can break this stalemate and finish this war?' the captain asked.

'We'll try,' Baeder responded.

Before he could say anything else, Captain Brevet swivelled on his seat and shouted at the only other man in the tent, a lieutenant standing only an arm's length away. 'See to it that the colonel gets a ride to the command post! Immediately!'

The lieutenant led Baeder out the back of the admin tent and down a narrow lane of storage sheds, until he found a sergeant smoking tabac underneath the shade of a signpost. 'Take the colonel to the motor pool, immediately,' he ordered the sergeant.

After threading through the base for some time, Baeder found himself outside a docking hangar marked *Motor pool – H Block*. Here, the sergeant deposited the colonel with a corporal who was unfortunate enough to be caught lounging on the bonnet of an all-terrain four wheeler. 'The colonel here needs to get to command post. I have important things to attend to so you'll have to take him.'

The corporal looked around desperately but there was no one else in the hangar. Reluctantly tugging his flak vest on, he saluted Baeder. 'All right, sir. Command post it is.'

As the pair strolled out towards a parked four-wheeler, a young trooper carrying two buckets hurried past. 'Timmons!' shouted the corporal. 'Come here for a second. Where are those damn buckets going?'

The trooper wandered over. 'The boys over at boat shed F have oil leaks on one of the swifties. They need buckets.'

'Give me those. I'll take them, it's just a short walk. You drive Colonel Baeder over to the command post right now!' snapped the corporal as he snatched the buckets from Trooper Timmons.

Trooper Timmons scrambled into the vehicle. He gunned the ignition then stared blankly at the fuel gauge. 'Sir,' he began, 'there's not enough fuel in the tank. If you don't mind waiting I can send one of the other troopers to go requisition some from the fuel depot.'

Baeder could not help but laugh. The Guardsmen of Ouisivia were terrifying soldiers in a firefight, but the majority were swamp dwellers at heart. If they did not have their lasguns in hand, they preferred to be boozing, sleeping or smoking in any combination. 'Emperor bless the Ouisivian way,' Baeder chortled, 'but I think I'll walk instead.'

* * *

INSIDE THE COMMAND post, it was dark and unlit. A single lume-globe hung, suspended from the canvas tent by a black cable.

Around the lonely pool of light stood three men of the 31st Riverine, all of whom Baeder knew well. Present was Brigadier Kaplain, as well as the two most senior men in Baeder's battalion. Evidently, Kaplain had summoned the key commanders of the 88th to be present at the interrogation.

'Baeder, sir,' nodded the closest officer, a man with an ork skull tattoo scarring his face from forehead to chin tip. Like Baeder, the officer was clean-shaven. The finely-inked bones of a greenskin hid his entire face beneath a mask of black and ivory.

'Major Mortlock,' Baeder responded. As Baeder's second, Cal Mortlock was one of the most feared men in the battalion. His brutal look commanded a hushed reverence among the rank and file and the men simply referred to him as a monster, but never to his face. Despite outward appearances, like Baeder, the officer was born and raised in the relatively sheltered provincial parishes of Ouisivia and was thus remarkably soft-spoken for a man with ork teeth etched into his lips.

Standing off to the side in silence, Baeder noticed Sergeant Major Giles Pulver staring at him while picking his teeth with a huntsman knife. The sergeant was the most senior non-officer in the battalion, a rough-shed of pure Ouisivian frontier stock and a swamp rat through and through. He wore non-issue snakeskin boots and a flak vest over his bare torso in total disregard for regulation. His beard was longer than any other soldier's, his uniform more faded and his hands more calloused. In short, he was everything that Baeder was not. The contempt that Sergeant Pulver held for the slim, unassuming colonel was palpable.

'Sergeant Pulver, how do you do?' said Baeder.

The sergeant took his time to answer, working the blade between his front teeth with a surgeon's precision. 'Fine,' he replied finally in his thick, Ouisivian drawl.

If Brigadier Kaplain noticed the terse exchange between officer and soldier, he chose to ignore it. 'Fyodor Baeder, we've been waiting for you. How are the preparations?'

'Excellent, sir. Prowler and Serpent Company are both prepping to schedule. Seeker Company is a little late as usual. They have engine problems with several boats but Captain Fuller will have them sharp in time, I'm sure. As for Ghost Company, well they've been ready since morning and are chomping at the bit to deploy.'

Kaplain mulled over the news like fine wine. 'Good to hear. I have something to show you, colonel, it's quite different from what we've encountered previously.' The brigadier beckoned into the unlit depths of the command tent and two Riverine troopers stepped forwards and hurled the bound captive unceremoniously beneath the pool of light.

'Lord of Terra…' Baeder gasped.

Lying there, at his feet, was an insurgent. He was a native Bastón man and, like most of his people, slender and light of frame from poor nutrition. At first glance he looked just like any other insurgent, a rural villager in mud-stained sandals, his joints bulging with sinew from a lifetime of farming. But there was one startling difference – the man had no eyes, just a smooth sheath of skin where eyes should be.

'Can he see?' Baeder asked.

'Oh yes, quite well by all accounts,' Kaplain replied. 'He was caught taking potshots at passing river patrols with an autogun just six hours ago. Apparently led our platoon on a merry chase through the wetlands too so yes, I would say he has no problem with eyesight.'

Baeder knelt down to inspect the captive, taking care to keep a hand over the autopistol at his hip. The captive turned his eyeless face towards him in a parody of a stare. Baeder backed away, thoroughly unnerved. 'What do you know about him, sir?'

'He first claimed to be a local fisherman. Don't they all? After initial questioning he admits he is an insurgent, a *Carnibalès* by night and local river bargeman by day. He says his name is Orono of the Musan people. That's all we've gathered from him so far,' said Kaplain.

Baeder noticed the brigadier used the term Carnibalès, a native word for the insurgent fighters. As far as he was aware, *Carni* was indigenous for meat-eater, virile symbolism of the warrior, while *Balès* meant cabal. In essence the insurgency referred to themselves as the carnivorous cabal, a theatrical name if any.

'Let me at this meatball. I'll knock the corn out of him,' growled Sergeant Pulver.

'Not now, sergeant. Civility for our guest, please,' Major Mortlock interjected. He grinned monstrously at the captive, the tattooed incisors on his lips pulling back to reveal his natural teeth. If the captive was frightened, he hid it well beneath a show of jaw-clenched defiance.

'Are those mutations?' Baeder asked Kaplain.

The brigadier shrugged. 'He claims he was born with them. But I'm not convinced – you can see fresh scar tissue around his eyes and some scabbing on his upper brow. He's the first captive to show signs of mutation but you should see the weapons we've been taking from his friends.' The brigadier led them towards a folding table at the edge of the tent and flicked on the desk lamp. Upon the steel surface autoguns, a lasgun and several sidearms were arranged in neat rows.

'Look at this,' Kaplain said, picking up an autogun. 'It's not Imperial issue, it looks home-brewed, but the working mechanisms are too precise for them to be producing indigenously. Imperial Intelligence suspects that advanced working mechanisms are smuggled onto the planet before being batch-assembled with native components.'

Baeder inspected it carefully, testing the weight in his hands and cocking the weapon. The brigadier was right, the autogun was roughly manufactured with a stock and body carved from soft gum-sap wood. While the wood was shaped roughly, showing uneven chisel marks in most places, the metal firing mechanisms were of advanced Imperial design. It was likely that the finer working mechanisms were sourced externally and then mass-produced on Bastón. The same could be seen of the lasgun, its body and stock constructed of cheaply-stamped metal.

Passing the autogun to Major Mortlock for inspection, Baeder blew a breath of disbelief. 'External sources then? The Carnibalès are getting off-world aid?'

Kaplain nodded. 'Every patrol into insurgent country turns up at least one crude weapons factory.'

'The ramrods from Sergeant Traiver's company turned in a seventy-year-old grandmother last week. She had her grandchildren mass-producing gun stocks in the smoking shed,' Pulver added with a dry laugh.

'Underground workshops, house-factories, canoe-borne bomb makers. Fragging everywhere nowadays. We intercepted a poultry truck this month. Every bird carcass had a plastek wrapped lasgun firing-mech sewn into its arse. Four hundred and eighteen poultry birds. Four hundred and eighteen lasgun mechs which were undoubtedly off-world and smuggled,' Mortlock reported. 'Creative little bastards, aren't they?'

A frown creased Kaplain's face. 'The guns have always had us scratching our heads for months, but now the mutation sends alarm bells ringing. Although this is the first sign of mutation we have encountered, I'm beginning to suspect that something is influencing the course of events here.'

'What?' Baeder asked.

'The Dos Pares,' Kaplain said. 'It means "Two Pairs" in the native tongue.'

'Dos Pares!' echoed the captive from the centre of the tent. 'Dos Pares!' He was swiftly silenced by the kicking boots of the troopers standing over him.

'What the frag does that mean?' said Sergeant Pulver.

'Intel is unsure at present. But we believe it's the name of whatever cause, faction or leadership the insurgents are rallying under. Most captured insurgents mention the title in some way,' Kaplain replied.

'Or arms suppliers,' Baeder mused. He had indeed heard of the 'Two Pairs' before. He had filed enough patrol reports from the past few weeks alone to notice that the Dos Pares were a recurrent theme in the insurgency.

'Either way, they are keeping them well-armed and organised,' Kaplain said. He selected another autorifle from the desk, this one even cruder than the last, with a chipped wooden stock and a blunt-nosed barrel of

sheet metal all held together in places by rubber band-
ing. Despite its poor craftsmanship, there was no
mistaking the 6.65mm hollow point ammunition in its
drum magazine.

'Men, we have suspected for some time that this is no
indigenous revolt. There are outside influences at work
here. I wanted you all to see today that this insurgency
has escalated beyond disenchanted natives causing
mischief. Neutralise those siege-batteries quickly, so we
can put an end to this mess.'

AT 06.00, THE five hundred and fifty men, four companies
in all, slipped out onto the waters of the Serrado Delta
before the moon had peeled away from the sky. Although
the delta was not the longest river of Bastón it was certainly the largest, connecting a series of major river
systems, some of which fragmented the landmass into a
series of jig-sawed islands. In parts, the delta became so
narrow that the trees above met in an arch, forming a net
of dappled greenery above. Its variable width, combined
with seasonal variations in flow and the presence of
rapids and waterfalls, made navigation extremely difficult.
Although pre-operational maps and navigational data
sheets had been meticulously researched by Imperial
intelligence, pre-planned routes would require a large
measure of luck and guess work. The wilderness had
always been the insurgency's one greatest ally.

Once on the narrow delta channel, they were forced
to navigate as a trailing convoy, the swift boats leading
the tip of advance. Behind them came the tubby gun-
barges, flanked on all sides by inflatable landers ready
to engage any threats along the riverbank. Each man
carried one month's worth of provisions, a full combat
load of ammunition and spare canisters of fuel.

Overhead, a single jet engine Imperial Lightning flew overwatch. Admiral de Ruger had, with great reluctance, spared the Riverine a single piloted aircraft to provide scout and reconnaissance. Baeder suspected de Ruger had not wanted the Riverine swamp rats to steal his glory and the admiral had made it clear, under no uncertain terms, that his pilot would only provide cover for eight hours of the day, and even then, no further than eight hundred kilometres from the green zone. Beyond that range the convoy would be left without nautical support of any kind. Despite this, the combat aviator was an enormous boost to battalion morale. Although unseen in the deep-water wash of dawn, the Lightning's tail-lights were clearly visible, winking like a guardian star that ghosted the battalion. It was a benevolent presence that reminded the Riverine Guardsmen below that they were not quite alone. His call sign, appropriately, was Angel One.

It was a common saying amongst the troops that, although the Imperium still ruled Solo-Bastón, the wilderness belonged to the insurgency. Unfortunately, the wilderness was also four-fifths of the Solo-Bastón landmass, with the Imperium holding the remaining rural provinces and seats of government. As a result, the 88th Battalion would venture deeper into the Bastón rainforest than any cleanse operation or patrol, well beyond the range of timely Vulture gunship support and certainly beyond the range of standard artillery.

As the battalion flotilla left the docking piers of Base Camp Echo that morning, the officers and men lined the shores, standing in stoic silence. The 'Ferryman's Post' was played on a bugle, accompanied by the steady crump of artillery in salute. It was an honour usually reserved for fallen Riverine Guard as their funeral barges carried them away on the bayou.

LIEUTENANT TOMAS DUPONTI was a real Persepian officer. When he did something he did it right and he did it with flair. He was a combat aviator of the 245th Nautical Squadron, and he fought the Imperium's wars from a cockpit at supersonic speeds and prided himself on four dogfight victories.

For the past four months he had been flying his Lightning interceptor over Bastón. The enemy here could not summon any aerial threat to challenge him and Duponti had suffered the tedium of high altitude reconnaissance mapping with nary a skirmish in sight. When he heard that he had been the only pilot selected for a low-altitude escort mission in cooperation with advancing ground troops, Duponti had never been happier. Finally, with the wind at his back and the canopy at his wing tips, he felt like a combat pilot again.

Lieutenant Duponti was one of many Nautical aviators who scrambled Lightning interceptors from the flight decks of a Persepian fleet. The planes, painted a powdery blue, were a workhorse of the Persepian Nauticals. They were light and clean to handle, unlike larger, more cumbersome craft, and their fuel efficiency meant they could probe further inland than any other Imperial flier on Bastón. In that time, Duponti had become quite adept at high-altitude surveillance, boring though the task might be, and had been recommended for this combat mission by Admiral de Ruger himself.

Of course, reconnaissance flights were by no means risk-free. Only two weeks ago, Duponti had been

forced to fly at a significantly lower altitude due to
monsoonal storm clouds. The gale had buffeted his
little craft with sledgehammer force and, during the
entire flight, his Lightning had rattled with the force of
wind and rain. Descending low for his homeward
flight, an unseen insurgent gunman put a heavy bolter
round through his engine. Bleeding smoke and fire,
Duponti put his plane down on an emergency strip in
the rainforest, forty kilometres out from the closest
Riverine outpost. The lieutenant abandoned his burning craft on the strip, escaping into the underbrush
with his hand vox and service laspistol. There he hid,
neck deep in mud, watching insurgents converge on his
position. He was paralysed with fear for almost an hour
as heretics swarmed over his wreck, tearing off pieces of
fuselage as trophies. It took that long before a platoon
of Riverine Chimeras reached his position and scattered the insurgents back into the sodden jungle.
Duponti had struggled out of his hiding place, his grey
flight suit slathered in mud while waving his white
undershirt above his head. He had come so close to
dying that day.

   Still, it was nothing compared to a combat flight. By
06.00, when the 88th were scheduled to deploy,
Duponti had already been in his cockpit for a good two
hours, wired in anticipation. He soared north over the
Calista Hinterlands, going as low as he dared to,
slightly beyond the range of ground fire but close
enough to watch the canopy streak beneath his wings.
The exhilaration, combined with the G-force on his cir-
culatory system, made his entire body throb with
intoxicating energy.

   De Ruger had outlined his task as overwatch – a simple support role. For an eight hour shift, Duponti

would be on standby aboard the warship *Iron Ishmael* waiting for an emergency call from the 88th while occasionally flying out as reconnaissance for the battalion. Importantly, it was a low altitude mission and Duponti would be in range of enemy ground forces, and they within range of his autocannon. In a way, the lieutenant saw it as a duel.

'Angel One, this is Colonel Baeder from Eight Eight. We are on the move, over,' a voice crackled over Duponti's headset. The message was like a jolt after hours of static wash and Duponti swallowed his stimms.

Clicking his vox piece, Duponti took a deep breath. 'Eight Eight this is Angel One. Lieutenant Tomas Duponti reading you loud and clear. I'm fuelled and ready to scramble, over.'

'Good to hear, lieutenant. How many squadrons do we have as support? Over.'

'Just me, sir. Over,' Duponti admitted.

There was a hesitant pause at the other end. 'Lieutenant, say again. Just your squadron? Over.'

Duponti chewed his lip beneath his flight mask. 'No sir, no squadron. Just me and my bird. Over.'

The aviator thought he heard some cursing in the background before the colonel spoke again. 'One flier? Admiral de Ruger must have been feeling generous.'

Duponti understood the colonel's concern but there was little he could do about it. Orders were orders. 'Sir, I'm just one man,' Duponti began. 'But I fly damn hard and I'll do what I can. We can both forget about the admiral's eight hours per day. I'll be on call twenty-four hours and fly recon as much as I can take. I'll sleep in my flier if I have to, it's the best I can do sir. Over.'

'Thank you, lieutenant. I appreciate that,' crackled the headset. 'Look, we won't need you right now so get some sleep while you can. I have a feeling that over the coming weeks you'll become my favourite person, Duponti. Expect to hear from me plenty, over.'

'I'll catch a nap when I can, sir. Nothing further? Over.'

'Nothing further. Out.' The vox-channel went dead.

With that Duponti tilted his Lightning into a tight ascent. His pupils were dilated and his breath was coming sharp and fast from the stimms. There was no way he could get to sleep now. The dawn sun bathed his cockpit in a hard orange glow and Duponti continued to chase it, engines burning as he climbed the sky.

CHAPTER FOUR

MAUTISTA WANDERED INTO the village in a daze.

He had no idea how long he had been walking, or how far he had walked. He only knew that his bleeding feet had carried him into a rural hamlet, deep inland.

It was a village that Mautista did not recognise. Rows of huts with roofs of rusting corrugated metal lined a dirt road. Poultry pecked aimlessly on the ground, fish dried on racks in the sun and old men squatted on the stoops of their huts. Behind both rows of homes, a grid of paddy fields provided much of the village's sustenance and trade during the dry season. It was a familiar sight, like most Bastón villages, but Mautista had never been here before.

'Where are the Dos Pares?' Mautista began to howl. 'Where? If they defend Bastón, where are they when it matters?'

The villagers shrank away from the newcomer who had wandered into their town. Most walked briskly in the opposite direction, darting frightened glances in his direction, and even the wandering poultry were startled by his outburst.

'Where are you? Show yourselves!' Mautista screamed. Mad with grief, he stumbled towards the closest hut. A middle-aged woman shushed her curious children into the house and slammed the tin sheet door, just as Mautista reached it. Delirious, he began clawing at the door. He knew that every village in Bastón had a contact with the insurgency in some way, whether it be child-spy or fisherman but, either way, the Dos Pares had eyes and ears in all places.

A handful of stout village men encircled him warily – the mad man in Kalisador garb, dishevelled though he was, was no less a frightening sight. They surrounded him but kept a hesitant berth. 'Fetch help,' one of them decided, and with that they left Mautista well alone to howl at the sky. Soon, most of the village had shuttered their windows and barred their ramshackle doors, leaving Mautista to vent his anger alone.

Mautista collapsed on the ground and fell asleep. When he awoke, he was roused by the rumble of engines. He felt as if he had slept for hours, but it could not have been for long as the villagers had yet to re-emerge. Bleary eyed, Mautista pulled himself up and looked down the single dirt-track that led out of the village. Shielding his eyes from the sun, he saw approaching vehicles in the distance. As they rumbled down the winding dirt road from the hills, he could make out an agri-truck and a rural autobus. By the time the vehicles applied their squealing brakes, Mautista was waiting for them alone in the middle of the dirt-track. He already knew who these people were – they were insurgents of the Dos Pares, they were Carnibalès. The truck and autobus ground to a halt just metres before him, wheels throwing up a fan of dust.

Almost twenty Carnibalès fighters piled off the vehicles – an entire insurgent warband. At first glance they looked like any other villagers, clad in rural canvas garb and salvaged scraps of PDF leather armour. But there was a ferocity to their demeanour. Mautista had seen livestock bandits before and these men had the same ruthless look about them. Some were shaven-headed while others styled their hair into oiled topknots. Many others hid their faces beneath wound strips of leather so only their eyes could be seen. One brute even had traditional protective scripts tattooed into his shaven scalp: text and diagrammatic shapes criss-crossing his entire head and neck.

'I want to join the Dos Pares cause,' Mautista began. 'I want to kill Imperial men–'

The brute with the tattooed scalp punched him in the jaw before he could finish speaking. Before he realised what had happened, Mautista was on his back looking up at the sky.

'Balls of a great ape,' spat the insurgent. 'Who do you think you are? Coming into our region and causing enough trouble for these folk to send for us.' The insurgent stamped down on his ribs with the flat of his hemp sandal. 'Well we are here now. Is this what you wanted?'

Mautista did not have a chance to reply. The other Carnibalès swarmed over him, beating his prone form. The Kalisador fought back even as the warband laid into him, groping out and catching someone's hand in the kicking, stamping mess. Immediately, Mautista began to apply a wristlock, one of the basic principles of Kalisador duelling known as 'defanging the snake'. He applied pressure by bending the victim's hand even as someone stepped hard on his ankle. A kick broke his nose with a wet snap. Someone else began to pull at his mane of hair but Mautista would not relinquish the wristlock. The Kalisador swore to himself, even as fists pounded the back of his head, that he would break that hand if it cost him his life. Finally, as his vision hazed from concussion, he wrestled the hand into an unnatural angle and snapped it. There was a popping crunch, but Mautista had no time to savour his victory. The beating continued as the village crowd gathered around, watching.

EVENTUALLY, THE BLOWS wilted and slowed. With one last kick, the Carnibalès warband parted away and towered over the Kalisador. Mautista did not know what he looked like, but judging by the blood rolling in oily sheets down his forehead, he must have been a mess. He breathed heavily and bubbles of blood frothed at the corners of his mouth. He staggered onto his feet, wincing as bruised joints clicked into place.

One of the insurgents in the mob began wailing. 'He broke my hand!' he shouted, nursing his shattered wrist. 'Frag! He broke it!'

The insurgents glared at Mautista as one. Twenty wild, ferocious men staring at him with murderous rage.

'He fragging deserved it,' Mautista managed to say. When he smiled, blood drooled out of his numb lips.

The insurgents immediately surged forwards, a swarm of flailing fists. The Kalisador turtled up, shielding his head from the worst of the blows. Rough hands seized his clothing, pulling and tearing at him. For each hand that lingered too long, Mautista reached out and snapped fingers. Disarming an opponent's weapons or neutralising his ability to fight was one of the primary methods of Kalisador unarmed fighting and, although Mautista had never excelled in that area, he was more than capable against untrained combatants. Mautista continued to break fingers and he counted seven digits. It was the only thing that kept his mind off the pain.

When the insurgents had finished with him, Mautista was wedged against the wooden fence palings of a poultry coop. His left eye had swollen shut and his right eye was almost the same. Hazily he could see villagers forming a curious ring around the Carnibalès who encircled him. In a way, Mautista was glad he could not see them properly, if he had perhaps he would not have been so brave.

'I broke seven of your fingers, something to remember me by,' the Kalisador croaked. He tried to laugh, but it hurt to breathe and he trembled instead. He was sure they were going to kill him. He wanted them to kill him. He wanted to die so he could see his tribe again. The insurgents edged in closer, several of them nursing mangled hands. Then tattoo-neck slid a knife from his rope belt with slow deliberation. Mautista tried to get up.

'Tacion, enough. That one is a tough and very stupid boy,' called a man as he stepped from the autobus's accordion doors. The Carnibalès parted to let him through and Mautista almost thought he was not a man at all. He was one of the tallest men Mautista could ever remember seeing, taller even than the offworlders. The man's entire bone structure seemed elongated, with shank-boned forearms and tall blades for shins. This unusual appearance was enhanced by white chalk daubed all over his skin and black paint smeared on his mouth and around his eyes. With slow, unfolding strides, the man approached Mautista, his ex-PDF leather armour creaking.

'I want to become a Carnibalès,' Mautista wheezed.

'Yes, you do,' agreed the ghost face. 'I can see that you do.' He crouched down next to the Kalisador and cupped Mautista's head in his hands. His fingers were cold and strong, pinning Mautista's head against the fence. With thumb and forefinger, he stretched the skin around Mautista's eyes, while peering into them.

'Are you looking to see if I lie?' said Mautista without flinching.

Ghost-face smiled in reply. 'No. I'm checking for concussion.' Finally satisfied, ghost-face gripped the backplate of Mautista's crab shell, levering him upright with surprising ease. As he patted dust and blood off the Kalisador's breastplate, Mautista realised that he was a full head and shoulders taller.

'Are you of the Dos Pares?' Mautista dared to ask.

'I am a Disciple. One of many direct students of the Dos Pares. I will tell you my name once you tell me yours.'

'Mautista of the Taboon people,' Mautista began, and then haltingly corrected himself. 'I was of the Taboon people.'

'I am Tabinsay. I have the authority to recruit you to become a Carnibalès. Is that really what you want?'

'I'm bleeding all over the dirt, am I not?'

Tabinsay clapped his hands in soft amusement. 'Very true.' Standing up, the Disciple beckoned towards his men. 'Blindfold our guest. We'll take him with us.'

Mautista did not even have time to say his thanks before the mob was on him again, binding his hands with cord and lashing a cloth around his eyes with a brusqueness that was all too familiar. Soon they were frog-marching him up onto the agri-truck, ready to take him to the inland hills.

MAUTISTA BEGAN TO count in his head, slowly, one by one, focusing his mind on the rhythm of one number following another. The road up the hills was rough and nauseous. Blindfolded as he was, Mautista felt every bounce along the dirt-track as the truck's wheels sought purchase along the steep climb. So it was of great relief when the truck finally lurched to a halt. Mautista had lost count by then and he had no idea how long it had been.

As the blindfold was wrenched off his head, Mautista squinted out of the truck's flatbed and took in his surroundings. They were in an isolated village, so deep inland that the air seemed thick with leaves. Everywhere he looked, vines and creepers criss-crossed his vision, while drooping beards of curtain figs touched his head from an eighty-metre high canopy. Amongst the deeply ridged trunks of moss pillars, rings of lean-tos crouched beneath their girth. Mautista had expected some kind of military base like the PDF installations from before the war, or perhaps a fortress of some kind. This settlement, with its scattering of lean-tos, was not where the proud resistance was based. Or, at least, that was what Mautista had envisaged.

'Is this the Dos Pares camp?' Mautista asked the insurgent seated next to him. The insurgent shot him a knowing smile.

'You'll see.'

And see he did. The insurgents concealed their vehicles with tarpaulins before stooping into a nearby lean-to. The sheet of tin, propped against sprawling taproots, concealed a trapdoor below it. Mautista slid down feet first, followed by the insurgents one after another. The opening was barely wide enough for his shoulders and once inside it was little better. They moved along at a semi-crouch, scraping their heads against the low wooden rafters above. Luminite strips glowed dull blue along the tunnel, sometimes branching off in forks, leading them deeper and deeper into the subterranean depths. At certain intervals, Mautista had to avoid knocking over caches of arms: strongboxes of ammunition and lasguns propped upright against the walls.

'Who built these?' Mautista asked.

'We did,' replied Tabinsay from behind him. 'The Dos Pares planned this, and our people dig. Sometimes I don't see the sun for weeks,' he said, his white pallor almost luminescent in the dim lighting. 'We come out only in the night.'

In some parts the tunnels dipped into wider, larger bunkers, their walls supported by interlocking logs and hard-packed clay. Some of these bunkers were lined with rows of sleeping cots, while others were storage sheds. One in particular was some sort of crude weapons factory, scattered with workbenches and tools of a metal smith. The insurgent labourers looked up from their work to glare warily as Mautista crept past them.

'Through here,' Tabinsay instructed, pointing at a small, square opening in the wall no more than fifty centimetres in height and width. It would no doubt require Mautista to crawl on his hands and knees, an agonising task considering the injuries he had sustained. But on he crawled through the serpentine stretch, as his bruised ribs rubbed against the ground the entire way.

Mautista shimmied out into a bunker, Canceo following close behind. He found himself in another underground chamber girded by logs and lit by vapour lanterns. The sodium glare illuminated overlapping maps and charts on the walls. More paper spillage lined the floors, printed leaflets of propaganda showing crude pictures of happy, smiling villagers standing over a trampled Imperial aquila.

'Simple, but fine illustrations, aren't they?'

Mautista was surprised to see a trio of tall, white-painted men squatting around the bunker where he didn't see them before. Like Tabinsay they too were raw-boned and lean – somehow stretched – yet there were subtle differences. One of them, the closest to Mautista, had long tendrils of hair, like white tentacles that seemed to merge seamlessly with the flesh of his scalp. Another Disciple seemed even more distorted, the bones of his shoulders and knuckles distended to thick, rock-like proportions. The abnormal changes fascinated Mautista and the Kalisador instantly knew that these men were somehow different from the regular Carnibalès.

'Yes. Quite beautiful,' Mautista replied, picking up a leaflet. While looking at the sketched renderings of the joyous villagers and the Imperial defeat, the Kalisador thought about the Taboon people and felt a strong yearning. There was something to the strokes of ink on that paper which stoked a surge of pride in him. For the first time since the massacre of his people, Mautista's anguish was replaced by a hot spike of purpose.

'You no doubt wish to join our cause? Otherwise you wouldn't be here alive,' said the Disciple with the flesh-ridged scalp. He spoke to Mautista while barely acknowledging him, working a guillotine rack with deft, practised fingers, chopping wide sheaves of papers into smaller blank leaflets.

'More than anything,' Mautista proclaimed.

'I'm curious, Kalisador,' said the one with distorted shoulders. When he spoke, his voice was low and garbled, as if his jawbones were too wide for his skull. 'You look a frightful, bleeding mess. Why?'

'I can explain that,' said Tabinsay. 'We beat him. Hard. But he wouldn't stay down, kept fighting back and even broke the hands of several of my best shooters.'

Suddenly, all three Disciples in the bunker looked up and regarded him with raised eyebrows of respect. 'A true Kalisador,' said one.

'We can find a place for you in the insurgency, if you are willing to learn amongst normal Bastón-born men – farmers, boatsmen and beggars alike.'

Mautista nodded. 'Of course.'

'Good,' grunted blunt-jaw. 'Blood-brother Tabinsay will take you to the barracks. You should clean up, rest. Tend to your injuries. We'll call for you before dawn tomorrow and assign you to a training mob.'

'When do I get a gun?' Mautista asked.

'Soon. Now go,' said the Disciple, waving him away.

For the first several days, the 88th Battalion slid along the Serrado Delta. They travelled slowly, particularly along the narrow winding inlets. There amongst the needle rushes and overhanging bowers, insurgents liked to take potshots at passing river patrols and, in such confined areas, the snipers often picked off two or three soldiers before melting into the wilderness. As a consequence, the convoy crept with their engines humming quietly, guns facing all directions, all eyes scrutinising the dense undergrowth for any signs of irregularity, perhaps the curve of a hat, or a patch of cloth amongst the green.

However, the battalion received no fire in those few days of the operation. They were still close to the green zone and it was well known that the insurgents were terrified of straying too far along the coastal regions. They were too frightened to come within range of Imperial support weapons to engage troops so close to Imperial-controlled provinces.

They were far too frightened of the Vulture gunships.

This close to the seaboard base camps, a Vulture gunship could be voxed and en route within minutes. With an operative distance of five hundred kilometres, the gunships threatened a wide radius of wilderness that the Carnibalès insurgents had taken to calling the 'death circle'. Only the hardiest or bravest insurgents dared to operate within the death circle. At any moment, a Vulture could rise above the canopy, its presence heralded by the ominous *whup whup whup* of turbine engines. The sound itself was enough to send insurgents scrambling into hiding. There the Vultures would hover above the canopy, pivoting on the spot while hunting for movement. Once sighted, the Vulture would sound its guns, thunderous and clapping like a locomotive chattering through a tunnel.

Vultures were heavily favoured by the 31st Riverine. Back home on Ouisivia, the swamp orks were so wary of these war machines that they considered them an incarnation of Gork's wrath. And indeed, there was a crude resemblance; painted in the jade green and tan of the Riverine with its sloping, pugnacious profile, the Vulture was a predator in the field of war. A chin-mounted heavy bolter was housed below the cockpit, while two autocannons were cradled in hard points beneath its wings. These weapons discharged in rotation so that while one fired, the others would load, generating enough firepower to flatten a hectare of mangrove into quagmire within a minute.

But the Riverine pilots preferred to hit and run, strafing the enemy with conservative bursts of fire. In one swooping charge, the tracer trials from its combined arms seemed to merge into one puff of orange flame. With such air dominance at their disposal it was little wonder that the insurgency resisted attacking the 88th Battalion during the early stages.

But a flotilla of such size is hard to miss and Colonel Baeder made no attempt to hide their presence. Either way, the insurgency had operatives in most villages. Most settlements clustered along the waterways, and the flotilla passed them often. The grey-brown water from the sea served as highway, laundry, sewer and bathtub, and curious villagers watched them with trepidation. Soon, when they travelled out of range of Vulture support, the enemy would be waiting for them. Colonel Baeder knew this. His men knew this also and it was only a waiting game.

CHAPTER FIVE

THE 88TH BATTALION headed south, threading along the
river towards the deep subtropical depths of Bastón.
According to Baeder's maps, the super-heavy battery
would be a hard three weeks of sailing, weather per-
mitting. But out in the wilderness, the maps and
calculations amounted to nothing. The swell of monsoon season varied the channels, flooding new inlets
into the delta's arterial spread and creating dangerous
rapids where the water had been calm. The foliage
spread in the wet season with roots snaking out into
the water, clogging propellers and beaching vessels
atop nests of mangrove. Slowed, frustrated and snagged
by terrain, the flotilla became spread thinly, losing formation as vessels lagged behind.

Although the Riverine Amphibious were expert
boatsmen, their home world of Ouisivia had not prepared them for the conditions of jungle fighting. There,

their chosen terrain had been flat, low lying wetlands; saline fens where the climate was humid but tolerable. On Bastón, the rainforest seemed to exist as a single, seething entity that attempted to thwart the off-worlders in any way organic. The air was steaming, a shimmering pall of fetid heat that sat heavily on the lungs. Sweat glued their fatigues to them in wet, peeling swathes, so much so that most of the men went bare-chested.

Worst of all were the insects, constantly biting and darting like dog-fighters. The buzzing sand-biters had a sting that could penetrate even the flak vests, leaving an itching welt that swelled to the size of a thumb. Drenched in constant sweat, the bites became puffy and raw. The Guardsmen scratched themselves constantly. It amazed Colonel Baeder how a simple insect could deteriorate morale so dramatically.

Baeder tried to instil confidence in his men by not allowing the climate to defeat him. He steamed under his full-length fatigues and boots, sweating so badly that his spare uniforms became stiff and board-like. He refused to scratch his bites although they burned like throbbing embers beneath his sticky uniform. Above all, he displayed a calm he certainly did not feel inside, navigating as best he could by the maps he had been given. One wrong turn and his men would forever see him as the weak, pallid high-born officer who would become the target for all their collective torment. It was a fine line he walked between focus and boredom.

Baeder was still lost in thought when his vox headset crackled. 'Sir, this is forward scouts, reporting,' came the soft, metallic voice on the other end. Roughly half a kilometre upriver, three swift boats maintained a constant lead on the flotilla as forward scouts and it was

their job to stay in constant vox contact, updating the
battalion on terrain changes ahead.

'Go ahead. Report,' the colonel said, dismissing vox
protocol altogether. Judging by the urgent whisper,
Baeder knew something was wrong; he could not
account for it, but he could hear it in their voices.

'Sir, there are bodies floating in the river and some
piled up on the riverbank. I think I see more tangled up
inland, but I can't be sure.'

Baeder's entire back tingled when he heard this.
'Understood. Hold position where you are and stay
edged. We will be up to meet you shortly.'

The colonel was riding in an up-armoured swift boat
at the front of the column. Acting fast, he ordered his
crew of five to vox for a reinforcement section. He
required three assault landers, and one extra swift boat
to join him. A gunboat equipped with a heavy flamer
was also requested to lend onsite supporting fire. The
rest of the battalion was to maintain a defensive formation and power down their motors until further
command.

Major 'Ork Skull' Mortlock, standing at the prow of
his swift boat, answered him. Mortlock had been with
the battalion for two foreign campaigns and by all
rights should have been promoted to colonel when
their previous battalion commander had perished. But
elements of brigade leadership had deemed the major
too much like the wild men under his command and
assigned Baeder, a staff officer from Operations Command, to the 88th instead. Watching him standing on
his swift boat with the sleeves torn off his fatigues and
a helmet sitting askew atop his death's head, chin
straps hanging loose, Baeder realised why the command feared Mortlock. They feared him because he was

everything that most Riverine officers tried to be, but could not be.

'Ready to go?' Baeder called out as his swift boat drew astern.

'That depends, sir,' Mortlock began. 'What's in store?'

'The scouts have reported some suspicious activity ahead. We're going inland to investigate.'

'A fight, sir?' Mortlock asked eagerly.

It was an act, Baeder knew, and a good one. Mortlock was not the pugnacious thug that he portrayed himself to be, but it was good for morale. A timid leader did not lend his soldiers much confidence.

'I can't say,' Baeder replied, then paused. 'But they've found something we should look at.'

Mortlock raised his lasrifle, addressing the three squads of Guardsmen in assault landers that had drifted alongside. 'Did you hear that? Let's see if we can get ourselves a good fight!'

The men in the landers roared, clattering their rifle butts in approval. Baeder smiled. The major certainly had a way with the rank and file.

THE VILLAGE OF Basilan had recently been rebuilt. A long-range patrol from the 31st Riverine, Snake Company of 506th Battalion, had reached the village at the limits of their patrol route. Upon witnessing the state of disrepair that the village had suffered during the war, the company had offered to rebuild the local chapel and schoolhouse. A mortar fired into the village had blown the roofs off both buildings and inflicted considerable damage to its structure.

Snake Company had stayed for three days, foraging corrugated metal and forest wood for the repairs. On the third morning, Vultures chute-dropped medical supplies onto an old PDF landing strip and Snake Company Chimeras had ferried the supplies back to the village. The villagers had sorely required antibacterial soap as the jungle heat bred infection and soap was a precious commodity in Bastón, even long before the war. For the first time in months the people of Basilan tried to re-establish their fishing trade along their little strip of the Serrado Delta.

By the time Colonel Baeder came across their little strip of the delta, all the Imperial aid had become undone.

A dozen bodies bloated with gas remained buoyant in the water. Bodies of more villagers were scattered on the wooden pier overlooking the river. Some had even managed to reach their boats but had died there before they could cast off. There was even what appeared to be the remains of a woman tangled high up in the branches of a riverside gum-sap. Baeder had seen killing before, but there was something about the still, secretive nature of the rainforest that disquieted him.

Quietly, the inflatable slid into the reeds of the riverbank. Baeder and Mortlock had joined the assault landers and they splashed into the knee-deep water with the platoon. Baeder noticed half a human hand nodding softly amongst the tall needle grass. He signalled for his men to thumb lasguns off safety as he unholstered his autopistol. Behind them, the remaining crews of the swift boats and scouts waited under the protective gaze of a heavy flamer barge.

Sergeant Luster sloshed next to Baeder with a worried look. Like all swamp-born Ouisivians, he was a big man with a thick neck and shoulders broadened by a childhood of swimming and dragging trawl nets. It was disconcerting to see a man like Luster so spooked. 'Sir, should we call another platoon?'

Baeder weighed up his chances. Once inland, he would have only his platoon to rely on. The battalion was another half a kilometre downriver. Then again, if he called up a company-strength formation to sweep the area only to find nothing, he would cause undue tension on already combat-stressed soldiers. He decided against it. He would do the job with the men he had at hand.

'No, sergeant. We'll go in as is.'

Sergeant Luster did not look pleased and neither did the troopers as they waded up the riverbed and secured the perimeter of the bank. All along the tree line, there was no movement nor sound. Birds did not like the stench of rotting death and the area was eerily quiet except for the soft lapping of water. A dirt path carved into the dense net of greenery wound its way deep towards the village.

'Mortlock, split the squads into two. I'll take the main path with squads one and two. You take squad three and ghost alongside the path well hidden. If we get hit, hook around and flank them. Got it?'

Mortlock gave him the thumbs up and promptly melted into the undergrowth with his section in tow. Splitting their advance would not only leave them less vulnerable to ambush, it also split the command elements of his battalion, so that both commanders would not become casualties if misfortune befell them. But it also divided their already meagre firepower and some of the Riverine growled and muttered visibly. Baeder did not blame them: the unfortunate female victim, dangling stiffly from the high branches above, cast an ominous pall on the entire task.

They set off up the path cautiously, taking care to walk on the edge of their boots and roll onto the balls of their feet to minimise noise. As they moved out of the dappled sunlight into the shadows of mossy trunks, Baeder felt a chill that overwhelmed even the maddening heat.

The devastation was all encompassing. Human remains were scattered in deliberate hiding places, stuffed between branches, noosed up in vines or loosely buried in soil. The act of killing was outstripped by the morbid cruelty and unspeakable acts performed on the victims afterwards. With one curt hand signal, Baeder brought Trooper Castigan and his squad flamer to the front. Tactically, it was a sound decision, but mentally, Baeder liked to have the tongue of ignition flame by his side.

'If we were back home, I'd say this the craft of swamp orks,' Mortlock said over the vox headset.

'I don't think the ferals were ever this brutal. Cover us and stay put, I'm moving my squad into the village proper,' Baeder instructed.

Mortlock and his section lurked at the tree line just beyond the paddy fields as Baeder and his men fanned out into the village. The hamlet had been built at the centre of a large square field of cleared rainforest and buffered by agrarian fields. The people here had grown cassam tubers and the paddies were chest high in water during the monsoon season with broad hand-shaped leaves skimming the water surface. The huts were built on stilts overlooking the agrarian plots, their sagging roofs giving them the look of tall, tired old men.

Holding their lasguns at neck level, above the water-line, Baeder and his squad waded into the paddies. The soil was unexpectedly mushy and Baeder's first step plunged his chin below water, his mouth gulping mud. With the ground yielding to the ankles with every step, their progress was slow and vulnerable. Behind every leaf frond Baeder expected something to be lurking and waiting but nothing moved. Here and there, the body of a villager could be seen floating face down, shot from behind as they fled across the paddies. The team cleared each hut in turn, Trooper Castigan moving in first with his flamer and Baeder following with pistol in hand as the rest of the squad surrounded the structure. Inside, the remains of half-eaten meals could be found on the rush mats, evidence that the attackers had come quickly. Baeder envied the simple life that these people had lived before the war. The villagers must have formed family circles on the hut floors, sharing roasted cassam tubers, fermented fish and the boiled leaves.

A wail from outside brought Baeder around sharply. The colonel darted out of the hut, forgoing the short ladder and jumping straight into the paddy water with an ungainly splash. His soldiers were already plough-ing through the water towards the source of the scream. One hundred metres away, a woman stood in the mid-dle of a distant paddy, her head and shoulders visible but shaded by cassam fronds. She was Bastón-born, judging by her loose linen shift and large shell earrings, traditional garb amongst indigenous women. She wailed again and once she saw the soldiers she would not stop wailing. Troopers surrounded her, aiming their lasguns as Baeder waded closer.

'Hush, hush,' Baeder hissed pleadingly, unsure of what to say. He held up his hands and lifted his finger off the trigger of his pistol to show he meant her no harm.

She was young, her face unmarked by the traditional dotted tattoos around her eyes that would show she was a married woman. Her hair was wild from where she had pulled at it and her eyes were rheumy from weeping. As Baeder moved closer, she continued to garble and wail unintelligibly.

'Slow down, speak to me,' Baeder called to her. 'Speak to me,' he said again, holding his hands out in front of him.

'I'm standing on a mine!' she wailed.

Baeder's gut lurched at her words, but he fought down the panic. 'Get back,' he said to his men. Whether it was their pride or the culpability of placing their commander in danger, the Riverine hesitated. 'Stop horsing around! Get back!' Baeder shouted. As his troops retreated to a safer distance, Baeder edged closer towards the woman. 'How did you come to be standing on a mine?'

'They forced me to...' she managed to say before trailing off into sobbing murmurs.

'I need you to tell me everything that happened, or we can't help you.'

The woman took a breath but was well beyond composure. 'Two nights ago, monsters came during dusk. They killed and killed; they killed everyone. They made me do this so I could warn everyone who found us about what happens when we support Imperial bastards.'

'Monsters? Do you mean insurgents?' Baeder asked.

'No! Monsters!' she insisted. 'Our Kalisador killed one and left it in the trees, over there,' she said, pointing to the eastern paddy. Baeder motioned for four of his troopers to investigate without looking away from the girl.

'Can you promise me you won't let the monsters eat my liver when I die?' she asked suddenly. Baeder understood vaguely what she meant. The Bastón-born had a superstitious fear of mutilation after death, as they believed they would suffer the pain in the afterlife. Despite the best efforts of the Ecclesiarchy to neuter the old beliefs, elements of them persisted and had experienced a resurgence since the war. By all reports, the Carnibalès had a habit of eating the livers of their victims. Many of the Guardsmen bodies that Baeder had seen at the base camp morgues had been mutilated.

'Yes. We can protect you and take you to the next village we pass.'

'No. I can die here, at home. I can die now, now that you'll protect me. Stand back,' she said softly.

Baeder's eyes widened in shock. He opened his mouth but before he could say anything, the girl took a step. He was only five metres away when it happened. The mine expanded in a blistering bubble of white water. With a fractional second to act, the colonel hurled himself backwards and was submerged. Underwater he heard a loud, wet burp and then his ears were ringing. He hoped the water would be enough to slow the ballistic properties of shrapnel as the force of the detonation spun him around. He felt as if he were caught in a whirlpool. His vision became clouded by a frothing mass of churned mud.

As he surfaced, the first thing Baeder did was to scream for his men to report injuries, but he could no longer hear the sound of his own voice. He'd been deafened. His men rushed towards him, asking for orders or checking his condition, but he could only hear the gurgle of his own ears. Baeder struggled in a daze, feeling as if he had taken a sledgehammer blow to the skull. Troopers stood around him. He saw flickers of a man screaming into the vox, presumably to Mortlock, but he could not hear a word of it. Further away, he caught a glimpse of the four troopers he had sent away, dragging something between them. Blinking rapidly, Baeder lost his footing and slid back into the murk, his lungs filling rapidly with water as the world spun in directionless circles.

Mortlock knew the sound of explosions on water. He had become accustomed to the dull, resonant clap and the gusty roar of liquid. In the distant agri-ponds, he saw a spear of water shoot into the air, white and vertical.

'Move and engage!' Mortlock shouted into his headset.

The Riverine dispersed into an open file advance, sweeping out of the tree line with lasguns levelled. Mortlock hacked at the cassam fronds with a machete. As he slogged his legs through the mire, he could hear the muffled shouts of men in the distance.

'Burn these huts as we go!' Mortlock instructed his squad flamer. The major had not liked the eerie quiet of the village from the start and he wanted to take no chances with enemy hiding places. The trooper juiced his flamer with a short, liquid burst and began belching a curved line of flame at the walls of each structure. He triggered on the move, raking the flames back and forth along the buildings. Each hut, cobbled together with irregular wooden planks and scrap metal, caught easily, the flames whirling some twelve metres into the air.

As the fire-team pressed on, the squad vox-unit began to receive from Baeder's squad. Connected to a bulkier vox array on Trooper Colham's back, the vox receiver piece transmitted the confusion directly from Baeder's position for Mortlock to hear.

'Mortlock, this is One. The colonel is down but uninjured, no casualties to report. We had a fraggin' native set off a booby trap. Dumb indig scared the hell out of us. Request cover, over.'

'This is Mortlock's escort. We're on our way. Stay calm and hold position. Out,' relayed Colham on the run.

By the time Mortlock reached them the colonel was waiting for him, his silver hair matted across his forehead, his chest swelling in great heaves. 'Major–' he began imperiously.

'Are you good, sir?' Mortlock asked.

'I'm fine. A little headache and some bruised eardrums. That's not so important right now.'

'Sir–' Mortlock began.

'Not now, major. Look at this,' Baeder said. Mortlock followed the direction of Baeder's pointing index finger and saw there, held afloat by four troopers, the body of a subhuman monster.

'This does not bode well,' Mortlock said, scratching his chin as he was wont to do when in contemplation.

The 'monster' was spread-eagled on the ground at their feet. It appeared human but beyond the continuation of two legs, two arms and something resembling a head, the similarities ended. Sergeant Luster cut away the insurgent's leather face bindings with his bayonet, peeling them away like loose skin. Beneath its flat, almost inverted face was more mouth than anything else, with a wide, slack maw so deep that its gaping throat was lost to shadow. The skin that covered its body was thickly wrinkled, forming a hard rind that resembled the peel of dried fruit. When Baeder touched it, it felt rubbery and slightly yielding, causing him to rub his hands on his trousers gingerly.

Most tellingly, it wore calf length trousers of white canvas and a leather jacket with one shoulder plate. The leather was a shade lighter where the PDF insignia had been stitched off. There was no mistaking the scavenged apparel of an insurgent. Parts of uniforms foraged from dead PDF troops, mismatched with traditional garb, had in a way become a uniform of sorts for the insurgency.

Baeder sucked his teeth. 'The taint. Guns. These insurgent warbands aren't fraggin' around with us are they? This is serious.'

'You reckon this is a mutant? Not just some awry genetic accident in the womb?' Mortlock asked.

'Let's be pragmatic, major,' Baeder said. 'This is extensive mutation. The thing barely looks human. It's just too much to be natural.'

Mortlock nodded, his brows knitted in deep concern. 'What do you want to do with it?'

'Burn it,' Baeder said. 'I'll log the report to the Ecclesiarchy. They should be intrigued to learn about ruinous mutations among the insurgency.'

CARDINAL AVANTI STROLLED out onto the flight deck of the *Emperor's Anvil* and into the hard sun glare of the open sea. His bodyguard of battle-sisters in their alabaster armour trailed behind him, keeping even the Persepian armsmen at a respectful distance.

Avanti had a fondness for morning strolls along the flight deck. He walked the full length of the great Argo-Nautical, inspecting the string of parked fighters and bombers. Often, he ran a white-gloved finger along the painted metal and if it came away with dust the flight crew would be flogged. Sometimes, depending on Avanti's mood, he would be merciful or he would not. It was, he believed, good for discipline and the upkeep of faith. It reminded these soldiers that, despite their guns and training, the ultimate power lay within the Emperor and his highest servants – the Ecclesiarchy.

As Avanti circled the fuselage of a Marauder bomber, peering at the waiting aircraft with cold scrutiny, a young Ecclesiarchal page clattered down the steps of the bridge tower. He appeared to be in a rush, his face red from exertion.

The boy halted just short of Avanti's bodyguard and bowed, gasping hard to restrain his breathing in the presence of the cardinal. 'My lordship, there is an urgent vox transmission that requires your attention. It is a Captain Brevet from Riverine Base Camp Alpha.'

At this, the flight crew who had been standing next to their bomber in an apprehensive huddle, relaxed visibly. Some still bore the flog-marks of Avanti's discipline from several days past.

'You have been excused today,' said Avanti, addressing the crew chief directly. 'But consider this, anything shy of the perfection of duty is negligence towards the Emperor. To neglect the will of the Emperor is to invite slothfulness into your soul. It is the first step towards damnation,' Avanti said, wagging his finger with a mirthful gleam in his eye.

The crew chief stiffened visibly. Although he was a lifer with combat honours and thirty years of service to the Guard, he could do naught but nod. 'Yes, your lordship.'

It gave Avanti little pleasure to cut short his morning stroll, but he considered himself a pragmatic man. He soon found himself in the command tower of the Argo-Nautical. The vessel was at high anchor and the command bridge, usually thrumming with activity, was largely empty but for a handful of junior officers on standby. Avanti dismissed them. He preferred to handle intelligence personally and decide what it was that the military seniors could and could not know. It simply made things so much easier.

'My lordship, may I speak?'

It was Palatine Morgan Fure, a sister-soldier from the Order of the Steepled Keep. She was a short, well-muscled woman with a stern, broad jaw and heavy cheeks set like chapel stones. She wore power armour of form-fitting ivory plates, a bolter mag-clamped to her cuirass.

'Yes, child, you may,' said Avanti.

'I can take this vox message in your stead. Your lordship should not have to negotiate the petty foibles of a field officer.'

Avanti nodded. Palatine Fure was, in his opinion, one of the most loyal individuals he had ever encountered. She was intense, not only in her physical demeanour but in all manner of focus and piety. She and her company of sisters had been assigned to him for the better part of a decade since his ascension to cardinal and Fure had taken upon herself the task of his safety with a vigilance that bordered on the obsessive. She slept four hours a day, devoting the rest of her time to her training as a monastic militant. In her supervision of Avanti's guard detail, the cardinal had never feared for his safety, no matter where he travelled. Avanti enjoyed the rightful obedience he wielded over her and allowed her to display her devotion whenever it pleased him.

Fure snatched the vox receiver from a towering command bay and keyed the frequency.

'Speak,' she commanded, with total disdain for Imperial Guard protocol.

'Halo,' crackled the other end, using the call sign for high-ranking Ecclesiarchal members. 'Halo, this is Riverine Base Camp Alpha. I am Staff Liaison Captain Brevet. Who am I speaking to?'

'You are speaking to Palatine Morgan Fure. What message do you have?'

'I must speak with either Cardinal Avanti, or any staff officer of high command.'

'I am his aide. You may speak to me.'

'As you wish,' said Brevet with an electronic sigh. 'This morning our base camp received intelligence from the 88th Battalion gathered during the course of Operation Curtain.'

'Yes. And?' Fure snapped.

'Well, they retrieved the corpse of a slain insurgent. The corpse bears extensive signs of mutation.'

Palatine Fure looked to Cardinal Avanti. The cardinal waved his knurled hand once, in dismissal. 'Is that all?' she said in a flat tone that revealed no emotion. Before Captain Brevet could summon a reply she released her finger over the transmit button and hung the handset back in its bracket.

Avanti tutted to himself, drumming his fingers as he thought. 'This is a good thing,' he decided finally.

'A good thing, my worship? I thought we were to allow the Imperial Guard to know only what we needed them to know,' Fure asked.

'It was only a matter of time before they realised this is no simple peasant uprising. At least now we can use the influence of Chaos as legitimacy for waging this war,' Avanti cawed.

'But, my worship,' Fure said with a dull look. 'These mutations only began to occur many months after we began repossessing the land from the natives.'

Avanti sighed. Palatine Fure was a stoic servant, but she was frustratingly simple at times. Some people were just not set up to think politically. It was indeed true that the Imperial authorities had begun to uncover the beginnings of otherworldly influence many months after the Ecclesiarchy had begun to claim indigenous land for agricultural use, but that was no longer relevant.

For the past two years Avanti had implemented a policy to reclaim the land for Imperial use from the indigenous tribes. The local PDF had been given Ecclesiarchal clearance to forcefully evict the indigenes from their lands. The parameters for 'force' were open to interpretation. It had been a glorious time of productivity for the Ecclesiarchal coffers. Convoys of PDF trucks rumbled into the heartlands to claim regional provinces for direct use of the Ecclesiarchy. Those very same trucks would return, their cargo holds swollen with Bastón tribals ready for placement into work camps.

To Avanti's concern, the natives had begun to fight back, in small resisting mobs at first. Trucks began to disappear. Then isolated outposts both civilian and military were burned and razed. The Imperial authorities had not suspected those primitives capable of such a thing. Then the resistance became organised. Roving mobs became warbands; random acts of violence became planned raids. Rumours began to surface of a faction known as the Two Pairs. That was when the Imperial Guard from distant worlds began to deploy. For a moment, things hung in the balance for Avanti.

The involvement of Guard forces meant the cardinal did not have the autonomy to pursue Ecclesiarchal interests at a whim. It frustrated him that officers would be so daring as to question why he was ordering both the killing of insurgents and civilians. Now things were falling into place quite nicely. If Chaos were indeed exerting influence on the insurgency then it was a good sign as far as Avanti was concerned. Now he had legitimacy to cleanse the mainland of its inhabitants and he would be right in doing so.

'Palatine, if the inland is corrupted, then we will scour it clean,' Avanti declared, using the impassioned tone that he reserved usually for sermons. 'We will have to sanctify the land of Bastón so that further generations of good Imperial citizens may make use of its soil.'

CHAPTER SIX

AT EXACTLY 16.00 on the one hundred and twenty-second day since deployment, the Persepian fleet steamed one of its grand Argo-Nauticals – the *Manifest Destiny* – to within sighting distance of the mainland. Their intent was to sail the vessel, by cover of darkness, into the placid Torre Gulf. From there, fourteen thousand Guardsmen would be deployed with supplies and motor fuel to establish an Imperial foothold on the island and reinforce the Riverine Amphibious already on the mainland.

It was a brave effort. Eight kilometres out from the coastline, Carnibalès spies planted in the coastal villages alerted the enemy of the Imperial movement. Three minutes later, the first Earthwrecker shell landed in the water just shy of the *Manifest Destiny*. Despite its gargantuan bulk, the Argo-Nautical was rocked by tsunami-level tidals created by the warhead. The second warhead, howling on contrails across the sky, did not miss. The hyper-velocity round – more missile than ordnance shell – split the Nautical's deck and released its charge inside the ship's hold. The resulting explosion whitened the night sky. Within the Imperial administrative cities occupying the coast, thousands of loyalists were awakened from their sleep by light streaming through their windows. Upon waking, their first sight was of a mushrooming cloud out on the horizon. They knew, one and all, that the Earthwrecker had spoken and Imperial salvation had been denied again.

MAUTISTA'S EARLY DAYS of training were hazy and fragmented. It did not seem so long ago that he had lived an enviably simple life as the warrior custodian of his people. Now he shared an underground bunker with fifty other recruits, their living spaces confined to narrow cots three shelves high. His days became a blurred routine of training, eating and negligible amounts of sleep. He was no longer subject to the troubles or joys of common life. Mautista no longer worried about the dry season harvest. There were no village festivals to look forward to, nor the courting of village girls. He knew exactly what his training day consisted of, from the moment the instructor roused them from sleep to the time he collapsed exhausted in the early morning. Mautista felt like his life had already ended.

The absence of any distraction allowed his mind to focus only on the task at hand. Upon receiving his standard-issue kit – a press-stamped lasgun and canvas bandoleer – Mautista began his indoctrination. He learnt the basic use of a firearm and its maintenance. He learnt how to shoot and, at night, their instructors would take them above ground to practise their shooting at nocturnal game. Mautista came to enjoy the firing, especially the reassuring recoil against his shoulder. He remembered the mix of awe and frustration he had felt when he had seen those soldiers brandishing their brutal las weapons at Luis. That same fear drove him on to master the rudiments of insurgent warfare.

The days were long and they trained hard for eighteen hours of the day, with short breaks in between. Recruits were expected to volunteer for an insurgent warband within two weeks of training, but they were also expected to be ardent supporters of the Dos Pares philosophy, known as the *Primal State*. When they did rest, the insurgent recruits would be lectured on the insurgent cause, philosophy and their many grievances towards the Imperial cult. In essence, the Primal State was a renaissance of the old religion and culture of pre-Imperial Bastón, yet at the same time there were distinct elements of anarchy, of revolution and of a strange, foreign theology known as *Kaos* in the native tongue. Here too, the Kalisador's keenly-focused mind excelled, and he engaged his instructors in lively theological debate. The destruction of the Taboon had deteriorated his faith in the guidance of his Emperor and the philosophy of Mautista's instructors suddenly made so much sense to him.

So great was his advancement, that Mautista was soon singled out amongst the recruits. There were hushed whispers that the insurgent leaders were watching him, that he would be a candidate for becoming one of the Dos Pares Disciples. So it came as no great surprise that, on the fifteenth day of Mautista's indoctrination, an instructor came to visit him.

'They're here for you,' said his instructor just as he had returned exhausted from a night training march. Mautista had just collapsed into his cot when he realised his instructor was standing over his bunk. 'Get up and pack your belongings.'

'Who is here for me?' Mautista groaned wearily.

'I am,' said a tall man, standing outside the underground barracks. His face was daubed in chalk and ink, his forehead deeply knotted with bony growth. Dressed in leather armour, with a lasrifle slung across his back, it was obvious that he was a Disciple of the Dos Pares.

Mautista immediately sprang to his feet. 'Why?'

The Disciple said, 'The Dos Pares have granted an audience with you.' It was the phrase every recruit wished to hear. It meant that he was selected to become a Disciple, a leader of the insurgency. Or at least have the chance to be deemed worthy. Whether successful or not, no recruits ever returned to their warband again.

'Pack your belongings,' the instructor said. Mautista was not sure, but he thought he saw a taint of envy sour his instructor's expression.

Mautista reached beneath his bunk and pulled out a roped bundle. Since his recruitment he had eschewed his Kalisador garb. His possessions were meagre – a lasgun, a canvas bandoleer, a canteen and a scavenged PDF leather jacket with one metal pauldron on the left shoulder. This was all he owned beside the canvas rural garb upon his back.

'I'm ready,' he told the Disciple. With that Mautista left with the tall man to meet the Two Pairs.

THE DOS PARES, to most, was a standard bearer of rebellion. In the old language it translated to 'Two Pairs'. It became a synonym of unity steeped in an even older culture. To most, even to the common insurgent who was farmer by day and guerrilla by night, the Dos Pares was nothing more than a spiritual motif. The words were inked in the propaganda posters distributed by the guerrilla network, or whispered amongst old men in drinking dens.

Most Bastón-born did not truly know who or what the Two Pairs or the Dos Pares were. There were many who believed it was simply a term that encompassed the insurgency as a whole. Others still, believed the Dos Pares to be nothing more tangible than a philosophy, a rebel ideal that had spread from the jungle interior to the outer provinces.

The Disciples, however, knew the truth. These select few saw the Dos Pares as flesh and blood. To them, the Dos Pares was the physical, driving force of the entire insurgency. They were the masterminds of strategy, the leaders who trained natives in modern forms of combat and the entire reason that the Bastón-born insurgency had not already collapsed under the Imperial war effort.

Since the early days of Imperial aggression, the natives were rallied by the Two Pairs. These mighty beings taught all they knew to their Disciples, nurturing both their minds through instruction and their bodies through chemical treatment. This cadre of Disciples in turn marshalled a crude yet determined force of heretic rebels against the Imperium. Although many thought of the Dos Pares as a product of vivid propaganda, very few knew them to be real.

Mautista however, would be one of those privileged few.

* * *

A DISCIPLE BY the name of Phelix took him through the tunnel complex, through the tracts of freshly excavated tunnels. Mautista was led down passages he had never known existed. Only while lost in those claustrophobic depths did Mautista realise the enormous scale of the underground earthworks. The tunnels resembled bowels of freshly uprooted soil, coiling and uneven. Finally, Phelix and Mautista emerged in one of the many gun production facilities hidden underground. There amongst the workbenches, milling machines, lathes and grinders, Mautista met the Two Pairs.

The Dos Pares were four men. Four identical men.

That is, Mautista could not think of any other way to describe them. They looked like men in all aspects of physical semblance, that much he was sure of. But there was a solid presence to their power, an aura of overwhelming control that was beyond their physical appearance. They were men who seemed to make no mistake. There was a perfection to them that seemed to defy mortality of men. In that sense, they seemed inhuman.

The Two Pairs were tall. Taller than even the lithe Disciples, so tall that Mautista's head barely reached the middle of their torso. And how big those torsos were! An expansive ribcage and solid abdominal wall that rose like the wall of a fortress, matched in proportion by the rest of their body. Next to these giants, the Disciples looked like children suffering malnutrition. The Two Pairs wore simple loincloths of hemp, their bare muscles daubed with white from their shaven heads to the bulges of their calves. Like their Disciples, black kohl was smeared into their eye sockets and around their mouths so that they appeared as white, ghostly spectres. That's what they looked like, Mautista decided – like ghosts from another world.

'Come here and let me look at you,' commanded one of the four. There was a certainty to his voice, as sure as the sun would rise.

Mautista stepped before the quartet of white titans. The back of his neck knotted with anxiety. The simple act of the Two Pairs looking at him caused his nerves to seize up in awe. With men such as these leading the insurgency, there was no way they would fail. Mautista was sure the insurgency would succeed simply because these men said so.

'Tell me, Mautista Taboon,' began one of the Two Pairs, 'what is the role of a Disciple?'

'A Disciple leads warbands into battle against Imperial forces. He uses his men as a force multiplier against numerically superior forces by disrupting supply lines, raids, ambushes and harassing their area of operation,' Mautista answered automatically, as if from rote.

'A Disciple is a teacher. He takes that which he learns from us and he disseminates it amongst all people,' said the first giant. 'The Disciple is an embodiment of the primal state of Kaos, and he empowers others with this same conviction.'

'A Disciple is our mouthpiece. He goes where we cannot, spreading the insurgent cause while imparting his militant methods upon everyone, from child to grandmother,' rumbled the second.

Mautista nodded once, timidly.

'He is not just a soldier, but an operative. The operation being the expulsion of Imperial influence from his birth land. You must learn from us, and what you learn you teach to others,' said another.

By now Mautista could no longer discern where the voices were coming from. The Four seemed to speak as one.

'I understand.'

'Good. Come closer.'

One of the giants took a syringe from the steel work-table. Mautista had seen such things before. A local PDF medic had often visited his village before the war, once every two months to inoculate the children against tropical infections. The needle looked much the same, but this one was much larger and filled with a dark red liquid. Mautista did not dare ask what it was for. Instead he simply proffered his arm towards the waiting giant.

'This will change you,' the giant said. 'But it is the only way you can learn from us within such a short amount of time. Time is not on our side and every day the Imperial forces grow stronger. We must accelerate the process: expand your mind and your body.'

Mautista did not understand, but the giant was so soothing in his tone that Mautista was no longer listening. He felt the needle slide into his bicep vein, intensely cold and intrusive. For a moment he was overcome by a surge of euphoria. And then the pain came.

It travelled up his arm, into his shoulder and then speared into his heart. It was a deep pain. He felt it in his marrow. It felt as if his entire body was being crushed together from all directions. Once, as a child, Mautista had a molar extracted by the village iron-smith. The pain was comparable, except this time it penetrated every bone and organ in his body. Mautista opened his mouth but could not scream, the pressure on his lungs was too great. Locked up and seizing, the pain intensified. Dark spots feathered his vision.

The Two Pairs made soothing sounds at him. 'An inevitable side-effect,' said one.

'It will pass,' said another.

'But if you die, then the warp wills it. What will be, will be.'

The Two Pairs continued to stand there, watching Mautista, doing nothing as he spasmed unceremoniously on the ground.

One of the giants knelt down next to Mautista. 'This will continue for several hours. Perhaps most of the night and tomorrow. You will live if you choose to live but it is easier to let go,' he whispered.

HIGH ABOVE THE tunnel complex, above the topsoil and undergrowth, it was raining again. Misting the air silvery grey, the monsoon washed down in sheets, shivering the canopy.

The 88th Battalion flotilla travelled at its slow, constant pace unperturbed. Hoping to avoid the worst of the torrential flooding along the main channel, the convoy snaked north-east along an inlet parallel to the major delta. They had made good progress in the past few days and, according to their charts, the first of the super-heavy batteries was no more than four days' travel to the east, five if the weather was poor.

Baeder's intention was to reach the large rural settlement of the Lauzon people by the end of the day. It would be a steady forty-kilometre stretch if the flood tides did not hamper their progress. By all accounts, Imperial intelligence had marked the Lauzon community as loyalists and there they could resupply their provisions and prepare themselves for the assault on battery one. From that point on, they would be less than one hundred and fifty kilometres from the super-heavy and enemy presence would undoubtedly become dense. The siege-batteries were the lifeline of the insurgency and the region would be fiercely defended.

Sergeant Major Pulver rode at the rear of the column, his swift boat bringing up the rear guard. Pulver considered himself an infantryman at heart, always preferring short stints on an inflatable assault lander that could get him close to the enemy, quickly. He had been born and bred on the feral marshes of Ouisivia and the cramped, claustrophobic confines of the swift boat's hab quarters did not suit his temperament. It made him irritable.

'Frag this, sergeant, I can't even get a decent meal in,' Trooper Sceri shouted from under the cover of the pilothouse awning. The torrential downpour sleeted sideways and, although the trooper huddled beneath the pilothouse eating his rations, rainwater was filling his mess tin.

'Suck it up, Sceri,' Sergeant Pulver called from the rear deck. He made no effort to even look at the young trooper.

'Did you hear?' said Sceri, trying to change the topic. 'The colonel apparently saved some boys the other day when they made that landing. Word is he walked face-first into a landmine so the others wouldn't have to. That's some heroic business. He's a true ramrod.'

That got Sergeant Pulver's attention.

'The colonel is a fragging meatball is what he is,' Sergeant Pulver said, stamping sodden serpent skin boots through the puddles towards the pilothouse. 'Who is he trying to impress with that idiotic gesture?'

Trooper Sceri shrugged sheepishly. He looked down, trying unsuccessfully to tip rainwater from his mess tin without losing any of his dehyd gruel.

'He could have gotten himself killed. That would have landed us in a cluster-frag, I guaran-fragging-tee it. I don't have faith in this colonel more than I can throw him, but this early into the mission, losing our commanding officer would be death for morale,' Pulver concluded.

Sceri said nothing. He continued to pick gingerly at his steadily diluting food.

'High-born overachievers always have something to prove.'

'Suppose we frag him later.'

The door to the pilothouse slid open and Corporal Schilt sauntered out onto the deck.

Pulver was not surprised. 'Plotting again, Sendo. Your mother was a snake,' he said dryly.

Corporal Sendo Schilt was a wiry little man, with a face like a snub-nosed swamp bat. His irises were a slit-eyed blue and, when he smiled, he showed pointy canines. Schilt was a man the sergeant would not turn his back on. As a sergeant major, Pulver had seen Guardsmen come and go, but Schilt was one of those rare few who were survivors. It did not surprise Pulver at all that Schilt would kill any officer who put him in unnecessary danger. In a way, a man like Schilt was a liability.

'Of course. I'd wager that our colonel volunteered us for this suicide mission to pad his career record,' Schilt hissed.

'It's too early to be talking about fragging him, corporal,' Pulver said. 'But if he pulls any more chivalrous rubbish that endangers both the mission and our boys, I'm going to put him out.'

'Yeh, well this mission is suicide. A lot of us have come to that conclusion. We're not happy either. If it comes down to our skin, well then we're acting. I know boys within the battalion who'd be willing to get the job done, sergeant, if you get my drift.'

'Keep your sights on the objective, corporal. Until then, I'll decide how best to keep this battalion intact, with or without the colonel,' Pulver said darkly.

JUST SEVENTEEN KILOMETRES out from Lauzon province, the scouting lance of three patrol craft stopped. Their motors idled as their guns panned the area around them. It was still raining and visibility was reduced to a grey curtain no more than ten metres in each direction. The downpour threw up a mist as it pounded the river surface, swirling like a landlocked cloud.

The way ahead was blocked by a dam. Crudely constructed of logs piled one over another, it stretched the entire fifteen-metre width from riverbank to riverbank. Despite the rising water levels, it rose just high enough to prevent the shallow-draft vessels from crossing.

Lieutenant Riddle, commander of the scout lance, voxed immediately to the main line of advance. 'Sir, we have solid obstruction here. The locals have decided to dam up for the wet season and it's a bloody no go.'

'How big is this dam, lieutenant?' Baeder voxed back.

'Nothing my men and I can't handle, sir. Do you want me to remove it? It might take a while.'

'Only remove as much as we need to get past. I don't want us to be held accountable for fragging up the livelihood of local farmers, understood?'

'Yes, sir.'

With an unspoken efficiency, two of the swift boats went to shore while one remained in the channel to provide overwatch. Riverine Guardsmen fanned out to secure the clusters of tendril beards overlooking the water as a work team waded out to clear the obstruction.

In the flash tides, the footing was treacherous. Riddle and his volunteers clung on to clumps of needle rushes as the water pushed up against their thighs. Each man held an entrenching tool, a small fold-out shovel issued for digging gun pits and shell scrapes. They were the only tools at hand for dislodging the logs from their foundations. The Riverine worked quickly, unearthing clumps of soil holding the dam in place. The rain drummed off Lieutenant Riddle's head and, clad in shorts, his joints were soon numb from the cold.

'Sir! There's no foundation to this dam!' shouted Trooper Wiman.

Curious, Riddle picked up a mossy branch that had shed from a nearby tendril beard and plunged it underwater, jabbing for the part of the dam that was obscured by water. The strong current tore the branch from his grasp. Riddle watched as the branch resurfaced on the other side of the dam and was carried away on the tide. Wiman was right, the dam had no middle nor bottom. It was simply a skirting of logs that obstructed the surface of the river and roughly half a metre below it. Dams were meant to stop water, not allow it to pass underneath.

This was not a dam. This was a boat trap.

Panic began to set in. 'Clear it!' Riddle shouted, kicking at the logs. 'Clear this quickly!'

As his men began to set to at a frantic pace, Riddle sprinted back towards his swift boat. He scrambled aboard, ploughed into the pilothouse and tuned his vox.

'Calling all formations! Obstruction is not a dam, prepare for insurgent activity. Calling all–'

Riddle let the vox speaker fall away from his mouth. In the distance he could hear the distinct popping and cracking of small-arms fire. As he peered out from the rain-streaked windows of his pilothouse, he caught glimpses of movement amongst the deep trees.

They lost all sense of order. The vox-channel was suddenly alive with the shouts and screams. But Riddle did not pay attention to the vox. He had more pressing matters at hand. Outside, he could already see muzzle flashes and hear the reports of loud, point-blank gunfire. Streaks of pale las-light lit up the rain curtain. Grabbing a lasrifle from the gun rack, the lieutenant threw open the cabin door, firing as he went.

FLASHES OF LIGHT, rotating, sparking, lancing, rippled along the left side of the riverbank. Insurgent skirmishers scurried in between the trees, their shapes barely visible in the sleeting rain.

Standing on the bow, Baeder saw a skirmisher make a dash between two gum-saps. Tracking his movement with the scope of his lasrifle, Baeder put him down with a clean shot. The man dropped hard, disappearing from view.

'Ambush on portside! Enemy infantry sighted!'

The swift boats and gun-barges opened fire. Autocannons, heavy bolters and belt-fed heavy stubbers poured fire into the wilderness. Above the gunshots, Baeder heard the crackle of wood as trees were felled and shorn branches crashed.

Enemy shots stitched the portside of Baeder's vessel. Sergeant Volcom threw back a tarpaulin that had diverted rain off their bow-mounted heavy bolter,

stood up and began to fire. But a Carnibalès sniper was
already in waiting. The insurgent, unseen, fired two
shots. The first spanked off the bolter's mantlet but the
second entered the sergeant's sternum, throwing him
back with an upward spray of blood. He fell, dead,
onto the deck. Then someone ran a row of las-shots
along the swift boat's deck railing, forcing Baeder into
cover.

'Frag!' Baeder bellowed. He sprinted into the swift
boat's pilothouse as another las-round hissed over his
head. Inside, Corporal Bellinger had knocked out one
of the windows with the butt of his lasrifle and was
picking shots with his gun against the windowsill.
Rainwater was spraying onto the vox array and delicate
navigational banks inside the boat but now was not the
time to be fussy. Baeder popped out the plexi-pane of
another window panel and squeezed his trigger on full
auto. White las-shots beamed out from the Imperial
positions, criss-crossing with the pink of insurgent las.
A trio of insurgents began to set up a mortar plate
beneath a stand of tendril beards and Baeder juiced his
entire clip in their direction. The rain made it hard to
see what he was doing, but by the time his muzzle
stopped flashing, all that could be seen was a toppled
mortar and no more insurgents.

An inflatable lander exploded nearby, struck by a
missile. Baeder saw the smaller craft cartwheel in the
air, its black rubber flaming and shredded. It landed,
belly up, the entire squad of Riverine lost to the explosion. The insurgents were targeting the troop-laden
landers now with support weapons; portable missile
launchers and even mortars aimed point-blank at a
horizontal axis. The landers ripped across the river on
outboard thrusters, disgorging Riverine Guardsmen

into the shallows, ready to assault up the steep embankment.

Baeder knew the Guardsmen rushing up towards the tree line would be scythed down by hidden gunmen unless the battalion provided accurate covering fire. The gun-barges which had, up until that point, not fired their main weapons for fear of fratricide would have to be brought into play. Risk be damned, thought Baeder.

'Bellinger!'

'Sir!'

'Vox air-support then ground support. Tell him there are friendlies, danger-close, assaulting the tree line. Pick his shots and be clean about it!'

'Sir!' said Corporal Bellinger, picking up the water-logged vox receiver.

Baeder turned his attention back to the men scaling the slope towards the gunmen amongst the trees. Their bayonets were fixed and they fired as they ran. Guns barked from the foliage, dropping Guardsmen back into the frothing delta. Baeder continued to shoot into the silver haze, picking out targets when he could see them, firing blind when he could not.

THE MAIN THRUST of the ambush came up behind the 88th Battalion, jamming them from retreat. From out of the rain, motored sampans, cutters and keel-hulled trawlers carved a direct path towards the rearguard. These were a motley collection of vessels, up-armoured with sheets of hammered metal, but there were lots of them. Collectively dubbed 'spikers', these boats had been prevalent since before the war as the chosen trans-port of estuarine bandits. Now they were the mainstay of insurgent raiders, crude yet simple to produce in great numbers.

Sergeant Pulver found himself firing the stern-mounted heavy stubber as Trooper Sceri fed the belt ammunition. Both enemy and Imperial vessels manoeuvred tightly in the river confines. The constant swerving and jinking of the motored vessels caused las-fire and gunshots to lacerate the air wildly.

'Keep this thing moving! They're all over us!' Pulver bellowed at his coxswain.

A motored sampan laden with insurgents firing auto-guns streaked past them, stitching the hull of the swift boat as they passed. Pulver tried to track them with the mounted stubber but the sampan was much lower, and the swift boat was moving at great speed. As they passed each other, the stream of tracer went wide, streaking over the insurgents.

'Damnit,' Pulver swore as he corrected his aim.

The insurgents were using the speed of their smaller vessels well. They never stopped moving, churning the water white as they twisted and turned around the swift boats, hitting and running. Pulver's coxswain pivoted their boat as another sampan ripped past, spraying ammunition. As the boat settled, they found themselves face on with another spiker.

'Ram the fragger!' Pulver shouted.

Their target was a fat-hulled trawler, its prow augmented with a beak of cold-rolled iron so that it resembled a broad, frilled fish. Pulver's swift boat cut a sharp angle and sped straight forwards. The bladed profile of a swift boat was streamlined for ramming and all fifteen metres of hull cut into and over the spiker. The trawler was shaken apart under the impact of the larger vessel and forced underwater. Insurgents, many of them broken by the collision, were swept up by the rushing waters.

Pulver slid on the slick deck and fell as the swift boat jammed hard in another evasive manoeuvre. A missile missed them, skimming across the foredeck to explode far out in the trees beyond. The river fighting had become so dense that it was hard to tell whether the missile had been friendly or insurgent.

Nearby, close enough for Pulver to reach out and touch, a swift boat met an incoming spiker head on. They missed each other by a matter of centimetres, both vessels moving at full throttle. They passed each other firing, but the Imperial bow-gunner was better. He laced a cord of fire perpendicular to his boat so that the insurgents sped face first into it. At eight hundred and fifty rounds a minute, the heavy bolter emptied the canoe of all enemy life in seconds.

Twenty metres out, Pulver saw an assault lander collide with a keel-hull. Riverine Guardsmen immediately boarded the enemy vessel, piling on with bayonets fixed. The insurgents could not match the aggression of soldiers who had trained for years if not decades. They were Guard, damn it! Pulver couldn't help but laugh at the absolute chaos of the engagement. Regaining his footing, he dragged himself up behind the heavy stubber and rattled off a short burst. It was only then that he realised his ammo-feeder, Trooper Sceri, was no longer in sight. The trooper must have been thrown overboard at some point, inbetween the weaving and ramming. Cursing as only a sergeant knew how, Pulver continued to blast tracer into the fray. He would avenge Sceri by punishing the insurgents. He would make them regret their decision to ambush the 88th Battalion. He wanted to know that, when the survivors returned to their camps, they would have lost more than they gained – that was the Ouisivian way.

UP ON THE embankment, amongst the shuddering rushes, Major Mortlock fell off the bow of his swift boat and onto the soil. His was the only swift boat that had joined the assault landers in charging inland, but there was no way he would miss this.

Immediately, las-shots drilled into the ground around him. The hard rain blurred his vision and he could see shapes flitting amongst the trees, snapping shots at them. The enemy were well dug-in, hidden amongst shallow ditches and even up in the trees. Coordinated gun nests were chopping down his advancing men, tumbling them back down the sloping riverbank as they appeared over the top. They were killing his boys and that made Mortlock irrationally mad.

'Come on, Riverine,' Mortlock roared. 'Are we soldiers? These are dirt farmers! Show them how it's done!'

A grenade went off in the trees nearby. For a moment his world blurred and spun. Clods of dirt filled his vision. Mortlock tumbled, fell, staggered back up and lifted his weapon of choice – a fen-hammer. In reality it was a small four-kilogram carburettor, stripped from a boat motor and hot-welded onto a metre of solid steel piping. The weapon was crude, weighty, and common on Ouisivia for crushing ork skulls. Swamp orks were known to survive multiple bayonet stabs, but a blow from a fen-hammer could lay down even the toughest greenskin.

Mortlock crashed into the undergrowth, half-blinded by rain and bomb shock. He lashed his hammer in wide arcs, the valves and ridges of the hammerhead tearing chunks of wood from a gum-sap. Insurgent gunmen, surprised by the Guardsmen in their midst, began to flee. Mortlock brought his hammer down on the back of a sprinting insurgent, bringing him down heavily. He swung again, mangling the barrel of a lasgun that had swung up to aim at him. Wielding the weapon two-handed, Mortlock chopped like a lumberjack, his shoulders and forearms rippling with hard muscle. Insurgents scurried in his wake, screaming of a skull-faced ghost that could not be killed. Mortlock chased them, splintering, breaking and pounding.

Riverine Guardsmen followed Mortlock through the break he had carved in the insurgent position. They fell amongst the slit-trenches of their enemies, engaging in close-quarter fighting. The rain reduced visibility and churned the ground slippery with mud. It was a savage tussle, the conditions and terrain negating all skill. Grenades exploded, point-blank. Bayonets and knives glinted in the grey.

Something bumped Mortlock from behind and he reeled, instinctively lashing out with a backfist. The punch narrowly missed Colonel Baeder.

'Sir?' Mortlock yelled above the clashing.

Baeder was already bleeding from a cut above his brow and his lower body was grey with mud. 'I came as quick as I could. Didn't think I'd let you do all the work, did you?' Baeder said, flexing the fingers of his power fist. It was a standard design issued to staff-officers, with an external power pack that limited its battery life. Baeder kept one in the vessel's stow trunk and only unpacked it when the situation was bad. It was now very bad.

There was no time for further talk. An insurgent splashed out from a nearby slit trench with an outthrust bayonet. Baeder swatted at the weapon with the palm of his power fist, tearing the weapon away from the insurgent and breaking his wrists with the kinetic force. With his free hand, Baeder fired two shots into the insurgent's chest, dropping him down onto his rear. The battalion had already lost too many men that day and Baeder was determined to inflict heavy casualties on the insurgent force, deterring them for the weeks to come.

Together, Baeder fought back-to-back with Mortlock as insurgents melted out from the smoke and downpour. Although he could not match Mortlock's strength or ferocity, Baeder considered himself an infantryman first, and an officer second. He fought until his limbs felt loose and hollow. He slid in the mud, fell to his knees and even took a stinging war club in the thigh, but he kept a constant pace of attack with fist and pistol.

'Is this what you wanted when you woke up this morning?' Baeder bellowed at the enemy. His troopers joined their voices in an enormous roar. Baeder fired his autopistol into the trees, banging out six or seven shots for emphasis. Mortlock continued to press on with his rhythmic striking. Slowly, step by grinding step, the Imperial Guardsmen dislodged the enemy from their positions.

'EIGHT EIGHT, THIS is Angel One. Report status, over.'

'Angel One. Holy frag! We are taking some heavy fire. Insurgents all over us along the east bank and up our arses.'

Lieutenant Duponti's fighter was hovering some eight hundred metres over the canopy below. He had ghosted the region flying back and forth in the rain, watching his fuel gauge with anxious attention. The weather conditions were bad and high winds hammered his craft, rattling the cockpit. After what had seemed like hours of inaction, it was finally happening. Below him, amongst the sprawling greenery, he could see strobes of light dancing along the Serrado Delta. Ambush.

Yet there was little he could do. With nervous frustration, Duponti tuned his vox frequency to the battalion channel and listened to the wash of screams and gunfire down below. The insurgents were too close to the flotilla for him to use his arsenal, so he paced across the sky, describing impatient circles amongst the storm clouds.

Finally, unable to handle the wait, Duponti nursed his Lightning through the slamming gale and horizontal rain to a lower altitude. There, he could make out distinct explosions, the firepoints of gun barrels and even the flaming wreckages on the delta. Just being so close to the fighting made his fingers itch over the firing stud of his flight-stick. His practised eyes could spot the Imperial battalion making a counter-assault along the riverbank. White las-beams like flickering spider webs criss-crossed the enemy positions. Pink beams of enemy fire stung back. The fighting went on like that for some time until the pink las-fire began to wither and die away. On the Imperial vox-channels, he could hear that the insurgents were breaking away.

'Angel One. This is eight eight.'

Duponti started in his seat. This was it. 'I read you, eight eight. What can I do?'

'We've got them reeling. They're peeling off. Can you chase them down and clear them out? We can't afford to have any stragglers coming back later for more when they feel brave again.'

'Sir, I'll scare them so much they'll turn themselves in.'

'Loud and clear. Make them hurt.'

With that, Duponti threw his Lightning down towards the rainforest. It came down fast with his machmetre needle hovering at close to four hundred metres a second and the view outside the cockpit a blur of melted greys and greens. He clipped up and banked at the last fraction of a second, skimming up across the canopy before slowing and announcing his presence with a volley of hellstrike missiles. Explosions rolled away underneath him. He was going too fast to make out targets, but he knew where to hit so he dived back and forth over the trees. He heard enemy fire snap past. Ground gunners blazed up at him. In reply, Duponti spread lascannon fire through the canopy.

'Angel One is dry,' Duponti voxed. He spat out the last of his hellstrike missiles and began to gain altitude. The ground forces voxed something in reply but Duponti could only hear the howl of blood in his ears as the speed of his attack runs crazed his circulation. Looking down, a swathe of rainforest was burning bright and hot. As a veteran pilot, Duponti never ceased to be awed by the destruction he was capable of inflicting. He banked his strike fighter around and checked his fuel gauge again.

'Eight eight, this is Angel One. I'm all out of shots and low on fuel. Anything further?'

'No, Angel One, we've got them running. Thank you. Out.'

With that, the vox-link clicked dead. Although it was unspoken, Duponti knew the gratitude of infantry when he heard it. Still running on the residual adrenaline, Duponti crested his plane high, tore off his flight mask and whooped loud. He promised himself one hot brew when he returned to the Argo-Nautical. He deserved that at least before he refuelled and flew out once again.

THE INSURGENTS FLED, chased by fire into the hills.

Dead men were scattered alongside broken trees. An entire section of the rainforest, mostly along the water-line, had been deforested by intense gunfire. On the delta, three swift boats and five assault landers were now flaming rubber carcasses reflecting orange onto the river surface. Of the men, nineteen had been killed in action with a further five injured. Slighter injuries were common amongst almost all the Guardsmen who had assaulted the riverbank.

Colonel Baeder moved along the shore, crouching by each dead Riverine laid out in neat rows. He made sure to find out which of the men in his battalion were killed. He had gone to great lengths to remember each and every man in his battalion by name, even though most did not know that, and he would at least make the same effort to know who had died.

Through the billowing smoke, medics rushed back and forth bearing drip bags and field dressings. Most of the flotilla was moored by the riverbank as injured men were ferried off their vessels. Many Riverine sat in a daze along the sloping embankment as the adrenaline of combat was replaced by exhaustion.

Baeder found himself standing before the body of a trooper called Beldia. Baeder remembered him as a support gunner of Three Platoon, Serpent Company. He had even listened to Beldia's story about blowing up an ork swamp hovercraft with a heavy stubber just weeks ago in the company mess hall. Although Baeder had never known Beldia personally, he knew the man had been a boastful soldier but an accurate shot. The body before him had a laswound in his throat and a filmy glaze in his eyes.

'Beldia. He was a stout one,' said Sergeant Pulver, picking his way through the broken undergrowth.

'Yes, I knew of him.'

'You didn't know him,' Pulver said flatly. In his fist, the sergeant gripped a clutch of ident-tags, red and gory. He held the metal tags in front of Baeder and threw them on the ground at his feet. 'These are all the men who died today because you did not stick to the main route.'

The sergeant's lacerating words stung Baeder into shock. 'Sergeant. This was an ambush. The enemy were well dug-in and waiting.'

'And you fed us straight to them. What the frag were you thinking? Were you thinking at all?' Pulver spat.

Baeder curled his power fist in anger. Baeder knew Pulver was a veteran soldier – a lifer – there was no way he could honestly believe Baeder was responsible for the ambush. He knew it and Pulver knew it. There was something else that had ignited the sergeant.

A handful of Riverine squatting in ditches turned their heads curiously. It would not be long before the entire battalion knew of this exchange. 'Sergeant Pulver,' Baeder began, choosing his words carefully. 'If you have something to say to me, then say it directly. But no soldier in his right mind would believe I was the cause of this engagement.'

'You are a glory hound, sir. This entire engagement, this entire mission is a result of your hunt for rank,' Pulver said accusingly.

Baeder gritted his teeth. 'Sergeant, this mission was not of my choosing. It was simply a task assigned to me and one that I intend to complete. Your job is to liaise between myself and the soldiers under my command. You are a senior soldier, act like it.'

Pulver spat his dip into the river, a wild hateful look in his eyes. 'You have not earned your right to be my commanding officer.'

In any other regiment, Baeder would have had his sergeant major executed by a commissar. Hell, Baeder had every military right to shoot Pulver himself then and there. But this was not any other regiment. It was, time and time again, not the way things were done on Ouisivia. Besides, his men adored the sergeant major and such an act would damage morale if not incite outright mutiny.

'This is not finished, sergeant,' Baeder said, 'but you should know this is not the time. We are deep in enemy territory, cut off from support of substance and responsible for the most crucial undertaking of this entire campaign to date. You will not turn the battalion with infighting. Is this clear, sergeant?'

'It's clear enough. I won't, but I can't guarantee that some of the boys won't air their grievances in some way.' And with that dark threat Pulver stalked away.

Baeder shook his head. No matter how hard he fought, or how hard he tried, the sergeant major would always view him as the 'other'. Their backgrounds were too different and their leadership styles were mutually antagonistic. Yet the ultimate responsibility of command fell on him as a colonel and, in the end, he was indeed accountable for every death in his battalion. The only thing he could do in a time of war was to mitigate the casualties while getting the job done. He just wished that Kaplain had not thrust this monumental task upon his shoulders so early in his command of the 88th.

'Bury the dead,' Baeder said to a passing junior officer. 'We need to press onto Lauzon province to treat our wounded. Have our men bombed up and ready to go in thirty.'

The subaltern nodded, saluted and sprinted away. Left alone again, Baeder took his bush cap off his head and rubbed his face. There would be a long way to go yet before they could silence the siege-batteries, and most likely many more casualties to tally. He only hoped he could hold the battalion together for long enough to get there.

CHAPTER SEVEN

IN THE DAYS following the chem-injection, Mautista noticed changes. Changes in his body, but changes deep in his thought processes too. It occurred to him that he no longer missed his Kalisador armour. Since the day that he had lost his people, Mautista had clung to his armour as the last reminder of his old life. But his cognitive process was sharper now: logical and uninhibited by sentiment. He discarded the old breastplate of hardened shell because there was no need for it any more; it was a rational conclusion. He felt, for lack of a better word, enlightened. As if his mind had been placed in a higher place, a place where petty things like ego did not trouble him. It made him sure of himself, surer than he had ever been.

His body changed painfully. Every day his joints ached and at night it was worse, especially his shins, his shoulders and deep in his liver. He grew rapidly from a height

of one seventy centimetres to almost one ninety in a matter of days. The chemical injections continued,
administered daily by the Dos Pares. Although they hurt
less with each successive treatment, the pain never went
away. Mautista became spider-thin, almost distended. The
Two Pairs assured him it was a necessary side-effect of his
treatments. In turn, Mautista asked no further questions.

The Four became Mautista's teachers, alongside
twenty-two other prospective Disciples. Mautista even
dared to call them by their names, although he knew
he could never consider them friends. These were not
men or comrades; they were, in a way, guardians of a
cause greater than any single individual.

During this time, Mautista came to know the Four
personally. There was Jormeshu, there was Atachron
and there was Gabre and Sau. They came from a distant
star, although where, they would not tell. They knew
things that no Bastón-born could know and their phys-
iology seemed superhuman. During a particular
training exercise in ambush methods, a fledgling Disciple was crushed by his own poorly-rigged log trap. One
of the four – Gabre – simply levered the half-tonne log
off the dead man and Mautista saw with his own eyes
the way Gabre barely strained to lift it.

To his great astonishment, Mautista learned that it
was not the first time beings like the Four had set foot
on Solo-Bastón. They told them that for thousands of
years, others like the Four had come down on Bastón
and selected the healthiest young boys from various
tribes and taken them away into the stars. It coincided
with the folklore that Mautista had known since childhood, of eerie white titans descending from the rain
clouds to steal children away forever. These four were
like those very same star visitors.

The Two Pairs even revealed that their kind had a name. Although Mautista did not know what the name meant, each of the Four carried an emblem on their loincloths, a female face fanged and serpentine, painted in bruised red. They called themselves Legionnaires of the Undivided; they called themselves the Blood Gorgons.

THE LAUZON COMMUNITY appeared in the dusk of post-storm, as the waning orange of day glowed on the edge of an otherwise grey horizon.

As the 88th Battalion flotilla rounded a bend in the river, they saw tall houses of beaten sheet metal made taller by the stilts that held them. Between the trees and houses on either side of the channel, strings of multi-coloured glow-globes laced the open air with a gaudy yet welcoming fluorescence.

Baeder voxed ahead, reaching the village chief on an open channel, and brought the convoy to a halt just shy of the village watchtower. There the battalion disembarked and waited in the soft glow of twilight. They waited with their weapons stowed, for entering a village while armed was against Bastón custom. But although the Lauzon were marked as loyalist on the map, Baeder had learnt not to trust his maps and would not let down his guard. A skeleton crew working on rotating shifts would man the vessels at all times. The flotilla drew up a defensive rectangle on the water, their guns covering all arcs of fire.

As Baeder waited for the welcoming party to arrive he began to make a mental map of the area. Like many riverside villages, the Lauzon community was built up in tiers along the Serrado Delta overlooking the river as its main source of trade, commerce and thoroughfare.

The town was one of the largest Baeder had encountered outside of the Imperial-controlled provinces, with
houses three or four ranks deep on the sloped banks.
Defensively, the town spaced watchtowers at both ends
of the river and a low fence that separated the cassam
paddies from the township further inland. Baeder estimated, by the sheer amount of homes and the large
extended families usually housed in each, that the Lauzon had a population of at least a thousand if not
more. It was a bustling town by rural standards and the
war did not seem to have diminished that.

When the welcoming party trailed its way along the
waterline, it did so with customary flair and festivity. The
Lauzon chief, a portly man in his late middle years, led
the procession looking slightly ridiculous in his oversized
headdress of tightly-wound cloth, layered with painted
fish scales. Behind him wound a ribbon of local girls carrying urns of water. The village Kalisadors, all five of them,
a sizeable amount for any one tribe, walked behind the
procession looking very serious. Baeder was interested in
these men the most, as they each wore a suit of shell
armour handed down through the generations and heavily customised according to tradition, deeds and history.
They walked like trained fighters, their hips steady as they
strode with each step.

As they neared, Baeder offered his hand for the chief
to shake, but the man smiled broadly and shook his
head. 'None of that, good colonel!' he laughed, latch-
ing onto Baeder with a wide embrace. Adapting
quickly, Baeder hugged the chieftain before accepting
the water jug from a Lauzon girl. The chieftain moved
on to hug Sergeant Pulver and Baeder chortled softly as
the sergeant major stiffened involuntarily, before patting the chief on the back.

'I am Tusano Lauzon. Come, come, you are welcome to make camp under our protection,' Tusano said, beckoning them all to follow him. 'We will get very drunk tonight!' He laughed as he led the weary string of Guardsmen towards his town.

THE MEN MADE camp around the cassam paddies, pitching two-man bivouac tents on the higher dry ground that girt the watery pastures. It was the first time in almost nine days that the battalion had a chance to stretch out cramped limbs on dry land and Baeder used it as a chance to refresh his men.

Soldiers dispersed out onto the river to swim or cooked a hot meal over a proper gas flame. Some of the more dedicated boatsmen took the opportunity to tighten up the creaks and stutters of their boats. Baeder himself relished the chance to wade out into the delta and scrub the grime from his body and beat his uniform against flat river stones. It was night by then, the delta lit by the pink, blue and yellow glow-globes strung up overhead. After he was thoroughly refreshed, Baeder took it upon himself to make a camp inspection before turning in for the evening.

Many of the soldiers huddled around portable gas burners boiling ration packs. Light wounds were attended to with the deliberate care afforded by a break in operations; ammunition and supplies were redistributed. Baeder crouched with each group he came across, doling out small quips and thanks for their efforts. There was no mention of Pulver's insubordination and overall the men were excited and still riding on the high of a successful combat engagement. Stories of gun fighting, some embellished, most much funnier in retrospect than at the time, drifted merrily from

camp to camp. It was a way to deal with the otherwise
stifling trauma of post-combat and Major Mortlock was
the worst of them all, bellowing uproariously as he
strode about camp, inciting laughter wherever he went.

Around the perimeter of the paddies facing the dark
edges of the rainforest, a small picket had been set up
on two-hour shifts throughout the night. The fire-team
on first shift had no chance to clean or recuperate and
knelt amongst the mud with their guns aimed vigilantly into the depths of the wilderness. Baeder
brought them hot tea and cereal biscuits from the officer's stores. It was a small token, but the Guardsmen
were appreciative of the gesture.

As he returned wearily to his own tent, Tusano Lauzon strolled down from the township. 'Colonel, you
must join me for a meal,' he cried out. 'You must share
your stories with me.'

Baeder was in no mood to humour the chieftain. He
was exhausted, he was sore and his eyes were stinging
from lack of sleep. But custom was custom and it
would do the Imperial cause no favours to offend the
few remaining loyalist tribes. He hung his head and
sighed bitterly into his chest. By the time he looked up,
Baeder had forced up a weary smile.

'Tusano, hospitality in such trying times can't be
refused,' Baeder said, following the chief.

He was led up some wooden beams embedded into
the dirt hill as crude steps, winding his way through the
cramped jumble of houses. They came to a long shed-
like structure with a warm orange glow shining from
the windows. A chalkboard outside the entrance with
last month's fishing quotas and lost property marked
the shed as the community hall. As Baeder stepped
inside the rush-mat interior, he was immediately taken

by the earthy smell of rural cooking. Two village fishermen were laying out steaming clay platters on the rush
mats around which sat thirty-odd family members of
the chief: aunts and uncles, nephews, nieces and many
grandchildren. On Bastón, the fishermen were custom-
arily appointed the village cooks, as their knowledge of
their product and how to best cook it became a source
of pride for every trawler, netter or angler. Baeder was
suddenly very hungry indeed.

They began to eat with no great ritual, as was the way
on Bastón. The indigenous people had a fondness for
good honest eating and no fanfare was made of the matter. For a time, nothing was heard in the hall but
appreciative murmurs in between chewing and clinking
of spoons. Baeder dipped roasted cassam tubers into a
salty paste of fermented shrimp and ate heaping spoon-
fuls of cassam leaves sautéed in lard. The villagers piled
salads of minty leaves and crunchy water sprouts onto his
bowl accompanied by fish steamed in its leathery skin.
Strangely enough, Baeder even developed a liking for a
clear sour broth made from the bones of an aquatic rep-
tile and bitter greens. The meal was light, savoury and
extremely sharp on the tongue and soon Baeder found he
had eaten far more than he was comfortable with. At the
conclusion of the meal, urns of indigenous alcohol were
brought to the fore, a salted elixir that signified the end
of the eating and the start of conversation.

'How is trade?' Baeder asked, as one of Tusano's
young nieces poured him a thimble of drink. Since the
war, many thriving communities had succumbed to
poverty and starvation. Those who were self-sufficient,
like the Lauzon, often became the target of insurgent
tax collectors, gathering a substantial portion of a village harvest.

'Very bad,' Tusano cried, throwing his hands up in exasperation. 'No one trades along the delta any more, and any food we keep in our stores is taken away by Dos Pares men.'

At the mention of the Dos Pares, a senior Kalisador who was sitting at the back of the room shot the village chief a cold, silencing glare. Tusano bit his lip and began to drift on about a lack of trade routes and inflated prices of engine oil for their river vessels. Baeder noticed the awkward exchange but said nothing about it.

'Do the Dos Pares men come often?' Baeder dared to press. Again he noticed Tusano shifting a sidelong look to the Kalisador at the other end of the hall before answering.

'Sometimes,' he shrugged. 'But it's better now that we have come to a forced agreement. We supply them with cassam plants every fortnight. What choice do we have? We are not a fighting people and they ride into town with so many guns.'

'Do they control this entire region?' Baeder asked.

Tusano poured him another drink from the urn and offered the thimble up to Baeder's lips. Baeder took the offering, knocking it back with one stinging gulp. Only then did Tusano continue speaking.

'They are more active upriver. Here, we receive the odd Imperial patrol and that keeps them quiet for a while. But there is really not much we can do. They take what they want and force us to comply. We just try to survive day to day,' Lauzon said sadly before slurping his liquor.

'I take it they don't know you are loyalist?'

Tusano shook his head. 'Oh, no. No, no, no. The Busanti people, three days' walk inland, were massacred for harbouring an Imperial preacher just two months ago. It is too dangerous.'

Baeder was not a religious man. But the idea that these people were forced to hide their allegiance for fear of death made him feel helpless.

'What choice do we have?' said Tusano as he noticed the dark look on Baeder's face. He poured Baeder a third drink and changed the topic. 'Here, drink and tell me what it is like in the Imperial Guard.'

'Master Lauzon,' Baeder said. 'I get the feeling you are trying to get me very drunk.'

CORPORAL SENDO SCHILT had just finished scrubbing and oiling his lasrifle, uttering the last few words of the Litany of Cleansing as he did so. The rain had been hell on its working parts, clogging the delicate mechanisms with an oxidised green carbon build-up. Schilt loved his lasgun. He had even named her, and so it came as no great surprise to his squad-mates when he chose to attend to his weapon before he attended to himself. With a surgeon's precision he scrubbed and scraped his disassembled lasrifle. Only when he had performed the weapon's final function test upon reassembly, squeezing the trigger with empty clicks, did he attend to his own needs.

Like all the Riverine, Schilt had suffered under the subtropical conditions. His feet were white and swollen from waterlog and it was a great relief to peel off his wet socks and splay his toes in the cool, loamy soil. He applied a soothing balm to the sweat rash and insect stings that formed angry red continents across the surface of his skin, cursing Colonel Baeder for every bug-bite he had suffered.

His mood did not improve until he ate his boiled ration pack, a tin of ground meat and nuts in a starchy gravy. He even emptied the calorie-dense concoction into a mess tin for the purpose of dipping crackers and accompanied this with a tin cup of hot infusion. It was a far cry from eating the rations cold out of the packet on the run, and improved its otherwise questionable palatability. Overall, it was the best meal Corporal Schilt could ever remember eating.

Finally satisfied, Schilt lay back on his groundsheet, clad only in his shorts to air his aching body in the cool night air. Around him, a group of Riverine crouched around a burner, passing a hip flask back and forth. Although Colonel Baeder had expressly ordered a ban on all consumption of alcohol during the operation, the Riverine soldiers understood it differently. To them, it simply meant 'do not get so drunk that you get caught fighting and end up being court-martialled'.

'Did you hear? The colonel is a lunatic. He ran up with the assaulting platoons during the ambush today to snag a piece of the fighting,' snarled a gristly heavy stub gunner named Colder as he passed the flask over to Schilt.

'The man is a glory-hound. We wouldn't even be in this mess if he didn't drag our battalion on this suicide mission,' Schilt said as he took a long swig.

'Glory or not. As long as I die with lasgun in hand, I'll be happy,' muttered another trooper, his words already slurred by alcohol.

'Die if you want to, but I plan on living for a while longer. This colonel has no sense of self-preservation. He's going to get us all killed.'

'We already lost Neydo, Chael and Kleis today,' said Colder.

Schilt took another sip of the flask and smacked his lips. 'I wonder what would happen if I slit the colonel's throat. Mortlock too. Finish them both right quick.'

Schilt was not afraid to air his opinions in the company of these men. Although the twenty-odd Riverine sitting with him were from various platoons and companies, they formed a closely-knit fraternity within the battalion. Together, Schilt's boys shared a strong opinion on how the battalion should be run and took the ruffian pride of the Riverine Amphibious to extremes. For the most part they kept to themselves and the other Riverine steered clear of them. Each of these men had a subtle cold streak about them that was disturbing. Others within the batallion even nicknamed them the 'creepers'. In any other context, they would be called a gang and that was what made them so dangerous.

'Mortlock ain't so bad,' burped another trooper.

'Yeh, but he's with Baeder. If we smoke them both, then Pulver will take charge. It'll be smooth sailing if that happens I guaran-fragging-tee.'

'How about the company commanders? Captain Gregan, Captain Steencamp, Fuller and even that young one – Buren?'

Schilt snorted dismissively. 'They have nothing over Pulver. True command authority will fall to the sergeant major.'

The group went on like that for some time, treading a fine line between complaint and outright mutiny. As the night wore on and the drink flowed more freely, the men became louder and more daring in their protestation. Finally, a sergeant from Five Platoon stalked over and ordered them all to retire to their tents before an officer found them. Slurred and stumbling, Schilt's boys crawled into their bivouacs.

Schilt, however, could not sleep. Stirred by his fiery words and numbed with toxicity, he wandered out towards the edge of the paddy fields near the tree line to relieve himself. He tried to appear sober but he walked far too upright to remain convincing. The village chief had placed volunteer villagers as sentries on the edge of the camp, rural men armed with machetes and long, two-pronged forks used to uproot cassam tubers from their watery pits. The men greeted Schilt, who waved them away, murmuring something under his breath. The village sentries smiled knowingly and chuckled amongst themselves.

His mind fogged by drink, Schilt wandered far too long and much further away than he would have liked. Soon the sentries and the gas burners of the tents dis appeared from view. Clad only in his shorts, Schilt wandered deeper into the rainforest, the undergrowth cutting open the soles of his feet. It was not until he realised that his feet were bleeding that he also realised he was lost. Abruptly, the corporal decided he was tired and he sat down beneath a large tree in the darkness.

Night was a frightening place in the jungle. Drunk and lost in its shadowy folds was not a good time to come to that revelation. Tendril vines reached out of the depths like deep-sea tentacles, and the branches suffocated his surroundings with an oceanic darkness. Schilt reached into his hip webbing and drew his bayonet. Although the corporal had forgotten his boots, his flak vest and his beloved lasgun, he had, for some reason, had the foresight to shrug on his webbing before he left. The bayonet was a wide blade, serrated along one edge with a slightly hooked tip that the Riverine dubbed a 'gretchin skinner'. Although it was no lasgun, the wirebound handle felt solid and good in his palm. He sat there with knife in hand, his desire to relieve himself overcome by the desperate need to find his way back to camp.

Suddenly, Schilt spotted a flickering light in the distance, like a mirror reflecting the moon. Schilt began to lurch towards it, groping his way through the trees. In his stupor, Schilt saw it as a light from a standard-issue gas burner. It never occurred to him that it could be something else entirely.

As he continued to stumble forwards, he saw the light again. A beam of light, white and glaring, which prescribed a slight arc before disappearing again. He wanted to call out but opening his mouth made him feel sick so he walked faster. Several hundred metres away, branches snapped and cracked, echoing loudly in the night. It sounded like a herd of beasts ambling through the undergrowth.

Then he saw it again. A beam of light. And then another. And another. Dozens of lumite beams moving in the distance.

It was not the Riverine camp.

Schilt stopped in his tracks and listened. He could hear voices now, coming closer. They were hushed voices talking in the dark, thrashing through the undergrowth towards him, but so many voices that they merged into a seething hiss. It could not be the base camp. Schilt was certain of that. Whatever it was could only be moving towards the Riverine camp. Turning, sprinting, Schilt ran in the opposite direction, hoping to reach the camp before they did. He did not even notice the weeping cuts in the bottom of his feet as he ran and ran.

* * *

SERGEANT PULVER STROLLED along the boardwalk pier, shacks rising in tiers along his left, the muddy waters flowing by at his right. It was already late in the evening and the rickety pier was empty. Pulver was rather fond of the quiet, as it gave him a rare opportunity to gather his thoughts in between the duties of a senior NCO.

Nursing a poorly-rolled stub of tabac, Pulver walked down the pier which stretched the entire length of the river-town. The soles of his snakeskin boots thudded a wholesome, mellow beat on the warped wooden slats. It was a pleasing beat and it helped him to think about the task ahead. They were close to the siege-batteries now, close enough to warrant a large-scale ambush on their flotilla, not a minor task considering the ramshackle disposition of the enemy. In a matter of days the 88th would be at their primary objective. The fight that waited for them there would be the worst yet, Pulver was sure of it. What he was not sure about was his faith in Colonel Fyodor Baeder.

The man was a career officer, pure and simple. His mind was technically brilliant and, as a strategist, Baeder was more than sound. But in Pulver's opinion, Baeder had a fault inherited by most Imperial commanders – he tried too often to be a hero. The annals of Imperial history were richly embroidered with courageous last stands, glorious victories against the odds and dazzling displays of swordsmanship. From fleet officers to mighty Astartes, these were all grand men, Pulver did not doubt that. But he hated it. When it came down to the running of an army, Pulver wanted a stern, no-nonsense planner. The idea of following a romantic leader forging ahead towards suicidal martyrdom did not appeal to the pragmatic sergeant in the slightest.

Yet to him, Baeder was exactly that. The colonel's need to earn the respect of his men drove him to prove his worth as a true ramrod Riverine constantly. Pulver did not need that. What he needed was a commander who could get the job done, quickly and quietly with minimum loss of his soldiers. There was hope yet, however – Baeder was not all bad. Admittedly, Baeder had proven faultless so far, contrary to his chivalrous ways, and even the ambush had not been his fault, despite Pulver's heated misgivings. So far, with a mixture of luck and balls, Baeder had pulled them through intact. But it worried Pulver that sooner or later, their luck would run out and Baeder would run them all headfirst into a slaughter.

Pulver sucked his tabac and flicked the glowing end into the water. Wars were not won by officers delivering thunderous one-liners, while waving their sword against a faceless horde of enemies, Pulver mused bitterly. Wars were won by clearly written memo notes in the chain of command, efficient logistics and precisely coordinated pieces on a planning map. Men like Baeder appalled him, and it appalled him more that Imperial narratives were rife with men of his ilk.

He was lost in dark thoughts such as those for quite some time, pacing the entire length of the boardwalk over and over. Finally, Pulver resolved that if he did not occupy himself in other ways, he would likely shake out some alcohol from his men and drink himself to sleep to alleviate the tension. It was something he hoped to avoid.

After some deliberation and four tabac sticks later, he decided to explore the Lauzon township, particularly the docking sheds that he had passed on several occasions. As a soldier, he had a natural curiosity for the war-making

of various cultures and to study the littoral vessels of the
Bastón would allow him to analyse the insurgent spikers
in their unconverted forms. It could perhaps be
considered trespassing, but Pulver convinced himself
that it would be an intelligence-gathering exercise.
Besides, the Ouisivians had a loose concept of property.

The docking shed was a semi-cylindrical structure of
corrugated metal that reached out into the eastern
riverbank. Although the shed door was secured by padlock and chain, Pulver had been raised in the fen
swamps by his trapper father who supplemented their
meagre income by less than legitimate means. The
sergeant considered it the one good thing his father
had left him, and with nimble fingers he made short
work of the padlock with the tip of his bayonet and the
end of a webbing clip. Creaking the iron door open,
Pulver slid inside and eased the door shut behind him.

Inside, a sodium lantern illuminated a clutter of
mooring ropes, buckets, empty canisters and the detritus of forgotten, rusted tools. A rectangular docking
space large enough to park three Chimeras side-by-side
dominated the centre of the shed, and a cluster of dark
vessels crouched on the water.

He moved from boat to boat inspecting each by
hand, with the appraising eye of a man who had spent
much of his life bobbing about on buoyant materials.
They were old, these boats, perhaps close to some one
or two centuries.

Pulver lowered himself into the small two-man sampans, testing their fluted hulls by rocking them with his
weight. Next he moved on to the larger trawler vessels
with their double outboard motors. These were the flat-
nosed metal hulls that combed the Bastón estuaries,
the single most important commercial workhorse for

the Bastón people. But most impressive of all were the keel-hulls, capable of coastal travel and powered on a rear motor so large that it took up fully one third of the vessel's ten-metre-long frame. Pulver had come to know these as the most dangerous of all the insurgent spikers. Its heavy propeller thrust engines gave them a stability to mount support weapons that would capsize smaller sampans and canoes, but their speed was so much greater than that of the ponderous trawlers. Pulver had seen keel-hulls up-armoured with scrap metal, a scythe blade affixed to the prow and mounted by flak thrower or autocannon. In such a configuration, the keel-hulls could threaten even the mighty swift boats.

There were other boats mixed in the dock too: shuttle ferries, skiffs, scows and even a few water-bikes. Pulver climbed from one to the other, rocking them with his weight, checking their motors. Finally at the end of the docking shed, covered by a tarpaulin, Pulver came to a vessel he did not recognise as a native boat. It was low and flat in its canvas sheet, with a distinctive shape that the sergeant found strangely familiar. Pulver jumped off the end of a trawler onto a motor canoe and then onto the docking ramp to inspect the strange bundle. Gripping the tarpaulin, he hauled it off in one heavy pull.

Underneath was a rigid-hulled inflatable. The very same assault landers used by the 31st Riverine Amphibious. The regimental symbol of a long sword with the gossamer wings of a serpent-fly sprouting from the hilt was painted across the front gunwale.

'Frag and feathers. What is going on here?' Pulver muttered to himself. Even from where he stood, he could see the unmistakable smears of dried blood where someone had tried to wipe it away with a wet cloth. The inflatable was covered in it. Strings of shrapnel punctures scarred one side of the boat and the outboard motor had been stripped away. It left little doubt as to the fate of this vessel's previous occupants.

As Pulver stood, still grappling with the notion of how the bloodied remains of an Imperial vessel could end up in the storage shed of a loyalist town, he heard a rapid series of footsteps patter behind him. Pulver instantly reached for the lasrifle slung across his back. The weapon was never more than a hand's reach away. Turning, he saw that the door to the storage shed was now wide open.

A cool draft billowed from the entrance. It chilled the perspiration on Pulver's skin. Immediately, the sergeant experienced 'the churns' in his belly, a nauseous warning that coiled up in his bowels. He heard the patter of soft steps to his right.

He brought his lasgun up to his shoulder just quick enough to see a Kalisador hurtling towards him.

Pulver aimed but the Kalisador disarmed him, twisting the weapon against the hinges of his wrists. The disarm happened efficiently, with a neurological smoothness that came only with practised muscle memory. One moment Sergeant Pulver was holding the weapon up and the next it was flying into the open water, sling and all. It was then that Pulver knew better than to draw his bayonet. He knew the Kalisadors were experts at disarming their opponents, a pattern of techniques known as defanging he had already heard too much about. A refugee Kalisador had performed it as a parlour trick for the Guardsmen back on base in return for tabac.

'Defang this,' Pulver growled, grabbing the back of the Kalisador's skull and delivering a headbutt to the bridge of his nose. The Kalisador stumbled backwards, momentarily stunned. Under the sodium lights, Pulver could see his assailant was not a big man, rather he was wiry and corded like most Bastón-born. Pulver was considered a 'spark-plug' by his men but the Kalisador was even smaller than him. Pressing his advantage, Pulver clinched the back of his neck with one hand and began to hammer his face with the other.

Although he had never received any formal hand-to-hand training, no Riverine sergeant could rise through the ranks without a measure of scrappy brawling that was well received within the regiment. The power of the bigger man surprised the Kalisador and, for a moment, the smaller fighter staggered. But muscle memory once again took over and the Kalisador squirmed out of Pulver's grip, created distance with a swift back-pedal and drew a straight-edged dagger from his waistband.

'You little bastard,' spat Pulver, backing away. His hands groped behind him for a weapon but he found none.

The Kalisador glided forwards in a low stance, tracing an elaborate pattern in the air with the glinting tip of his dagger. Then, like a coiled serpent, he struck. Pulver gritted his teeth and rushed forwards at the same instant, throwing off his attacker's timing. The stab, aimed at his liver, was jarred and Pulver took the blow on his forearm instead. Knowing that the Kalisador would not make the same mistake again, Pulver seized the knife arm in both hands and hurled himself over the edge. Both men went into the docking space and hit the water with a shuddering splash.

The water was shockingly cold. Pulver couldn't see a thing, but he maintained his grip on the knife hand. In a way, it was his lifeline and there was no way he would let it go. Twice, Pulver tried to come up for air but bumped his head against the bottom of a vessel. With one hand he clung to the assailant's knife hand, with the other, he pushed the Kalisador's head down below, keeping him beneath the water. His lungs were straining, his chest seizing up painfully.

As his vision blurred, Pulver finally emerged through the gap between two trawlers. He gasped and struggled to take in great heaving lungfuls of air. In the water below, the struggling Kalisador began to slacken. Pulver stayed there, gripping with the last of his strength until the Kalisador stopped moving. He stayed there for many minutes after. Sure that his assailant posed no further threat, he let the weight sink. With his combat fatigues heavy with water, Pulver crawled up onto the pontoon, his lungs still labouring painfully. There he sprawled out on the wooden planks, swearing and trying to catch his breath.

EVEN FROM SUCH great heights, Duponti could see the mass of movement below. A throbbing mass of twinkling lights was converging on the 88th Battalion coordinates, sweeping in from all three sides of the inland jungle. There were so many of them converging on the position that they dispensed with stealth altogether. Down there, Duponti estimated perhaps close to five or six thousand torchlights.

'Eight eight, this is Angel One. Come in, eight eight.'

His urgent vox message was once again met by silence.

'Eight eight. This is Angel One. Multiple enemy movements converging on your position. Come in, eight eight.'

Again the dry hiss of static.

'Frag it!' Duponti swore, smashing his fist into the flight panel in frustration. The enemy were no more than three hundred metres away from the camp now. The one saving grace was that the rainforest was incredibly dense and notoriously difficult to move through, especially in the night. Duponti knew the movement would be slowed to a crawl as they chopped through the tangled undergrowth.

Retuning his frequency, Duponti began to cycle through the alternate vox-channels for the battalion. His warnings, growing in desperation, went unheard. The battalion was, after all, on temporary stand down and the only manned vox would be on the primary channel.

Duponti was almost screaming now. 'Eight eight! Enemy movements now one hundred and fifty metres from your position!'

In final exasperation, Duponti threw his voxsponder aside. He would have to go in himself. Nudging his strike fighter down, he began to level out slowly in an attempt to hide his presence from the enemy until the last possible moment.

As he closed in, Duponti fired a flare. The phosphorus flare ignited in the air, hovering in the sky like a newborn star. Amongst the showering trails of chemical illumination and the harsh artificial light, Duponti saw them clearly. Thousands of Carnibalès heretics brandishing firearms and polearms were massing together at the edge of the jungle. Thousands of them like a surging, chittering mass of soldier mites. In a creeping, pincer formation they surrounded the battalion camp. Duponti toggled his weapons to armed and primed them for an attack run.

CHAPTER EIGHT

IT WAS ALREADY late into the night before Colonel Baeder managed to extract himself from the village chief and his hospitality. The 88th Battalion camp was silent, his men either asleep in their tents or passed out on the soil.

Baeder picked his way through the camp, careful not to wake any of his men from their much-needed rest. He could not help but notice that some of the prone figures clutched flasks or had even managed to barter urns of fermented alcohol from the local Lauzon. Baeder had ordered there to be no consumption of alcohol but he had not expected the order to be heeded. It was more an attempt to dissuade the Ouisivians from their otherwise probable excess. He himself had humoured the village chief with a sip or two of the vile local brew.

There would only be four or five hours before dawn and, although Baeder wanted nothing more than to rest his aching body before reveille, he knew it would be prudent to check on the sentry pickets. Although Tusano had volunteered nine village men and a Kalisador as sentries, battalion NCOs had also appointed a roster of five Riverine to patrol the forest edge. The unfortunate Guardsmen assigned to patrol the camp perimeter had forgone their one night of rest and visiting them would be the least an officer could do. He carried a wicker basket in each hand, laden with leftovers from the chieftain's feast, a much-needed morale booster for the on-duty Guardsmen.

Yet Baeder felt something was wrong as he neared the edge of camp.

He could not hear the distinct chatter of vox reports on the primary vox array that the team of five should have been manning. In fact, as he neared the gun pit where the five should have been, he saw the vox array had been tipped over in the dirt.

Baeder dropped his food baskets and went for his autopistol instead. He could see the five Riverine sentries lying face down. Each had a glistening wound on the back of their skulls, blunt trauma inflicted by blows from behind. Of the volunteer villagers, there was no sign, but Baeder could make out mud tracks leading away from the gunpit towards the camp. He considered sounding an alarm, but opted for a more subtle approach. He cocked his Kupiter .45 automat pistol and slid after the footprints in the mud.

The horrors unveiled themselves to Baeder slowly. At the first two-man tent Baeder tracked the prints to, he found the occupant Riverine inside were dead, their throats slit and the ground damp with enormous blood loss. The next tent was the same. Baeder counted nine good men, lost in one night without so much as a shot being fired. Ten metres away he counted ten; Corporal Huder unceremoniously dumped into a clump of bracken with multiple stab wounds, still holding a hip flask in his hands. The corporal had likely been drinking alone at the edge of camp when he met his fate.

At the third tent in a row, Baeder stuck to the shadows. He saw four murky figures standing around the canvas tent, obviously keeping watch. Even in the darkness Baeder could see the glint of weapons. Three of the men carried machetes and a fourth leaned against his two-pronged cassam spear. They were unmistakably the village volunteers and judging by their hunched, tentative postures, they were in the act of murdering Baeder's men.

Baeder emerged from the shadows confidently, his pistol held behind his back. 'Good evening, gentlemen!' he said clearly.

The Lauzon tribesmen started. As he walked towards them, they looked at him with stunned expressions, grasping for words. Baeder knew it was the split second moment where they were deciding whether they could construct a passable excuse for what they were doing inside the battalion camp, or whether they should rush the officer and overwhelm him. Baeder did not give them that luxury. He swung his pistol out from behind his back and popped off two shots in fluid succession. Two of the murderers collapsed wordlessly. Baeder caught the third as he leapt at him with a raised machete, shooting him twice point-blank in the chest. He put down the fourth man as he turned to run. Baeder showed the murderers the same absence of mercy they had undoubtedly shown his men.

Alerted by the popping gunshots, another Lauzon murderer emerged from the tent flap, his business of killing interrupted. The machete he brandished was already wet with threads of blood. As he sprinted the several metres towards Baeder, he received a pistol shot in the abdomen. But small calibre rounds never guaranteed putting an opponent down, especially when he was running on desperation. Baeder back-pedalled and fired two more shots, both finding their mark in the murderer's torso. Yet he kept on coming. With an eight-round clip, the autopistol had one shot left. Baeder fired his last round into the attacker's neck, almost pushing the pistol barrel against him. There was a great burst of blood, but still the murderer rushed at him. A firearm's lack of stopping power was every Guardsman's worst nightmare. He remembered his power fist, locked up in the stow trunk on his swift boat, but it was too late to lament.

Baeder threw his spent autopistol aside and grappled with the man's machete. They stumbled, pushing and straining in the clinch until they toppled over into the tent. Both went down in a tangle of canvas, rope and whipping limbs. Baeder found the man rolling on top, his many gunshot wounds pouring all over him. The murderer struggled, groaning and breathing hard in Baeder's ear. It was the worst experience of combat Baeder had ever suffered. With a final heave, Baeder swept his attacker and gained top position. By then, the pistol shots were draining away the attacker's strength and the villager, with his wide crazed eyes, was beginning to go limp. His movements slowed and finally, with a shudder, he was still. Baeder released his hold on the man's machete handle and kicked him away.

The sounds of their struggle brought out the lurking silhouettes of the other Lauzon murderers from a nearby tent. But by now Riverine were emerging in various states of undress, half-asleep but gripping lasrifles.

'Insurgents,' Baeder bellowed, pointing at the Lauzon. Immediately, a las-shot snapped out and dropped one of the Lauzon silhouettes. There was pandemonium as Riverine bolted out from their tents, simultaneously tugging on boots and fatigues and loading lasrifles. A great clamour roused the battalion from their sleep.

But before the quiet was truly broken, up in the sky, a phos-flare was released.

'Angel One,' Baeder muttered to himself.

The flare hung suspended in the sky, trailing droplets of glowing white incendiary. The light it cast was a monochrome of white and stark shadow. But it was enough to reveal to Baeder what lay in wait amongst the tree line. No more than a hundred metres away, separated by just one grid of cassam paddy, Baeder saw hundreds, if not thousands, of faces staring at him. Insurgents lying in wait, their eyes white with intent, looking at him.

Then with a roar that built up into a thick wall of sound, the Carnibalès charged.

DUPONTI DROPPED HIS Lightning like a stone, blazing away with hellstrike missiles. He strafed the length of the enemy advance, jamming his finger hard on the trigger button. Within seconds he had made his run, gaining altitude again.

He craned his head about to inspect his damage. A wall of fire, two hundred metres in length, danced along where the farm met the forest. It consumed an entire strip of cassam paddies along with a shard of the first of the enemy wave. But from his vantage point,

Duponti could see sprinting figures detach from the trees at the left and right flanks of the battalion camp. Mobs of tiny, surging people converged towards the Imperial position down below, seemingly unafraid of the Riverine las-volleys blistering them. Duponti was already out of hellstrike missiles, but he banked around anyway, determined to add his lascannons to the engagement.

'Angel One, this is Baeder,' crackled Duponti's headset. 'It's heavy down here. How many can you see from where you are?'

'They are moving in from all three sides inland, the delta is clear. I count thousands. I don't know if there are more under the canopy. Can you reach your boats?'

'My men barely have their britches on. Frag! This was a trap, the Lauzon sold us out.'

'I'm coming down to give them hell,' Duponti promised.

'Give them what you can. We need all the time we can get. Out.'

Major Mortlock threw himself down behind a low irrigation ditch and blasted a fan of las-fire to his front. Riverine Guardsmen spread out in a thin line around the camp, digging in behind the drainage canals or even the chest-deep water paddies to repel the enemy offensive. In the first few minutes of shock, the Riverine fired wildly, unleashing every firearm in their arsenal. Smoke and grit choked the air in a gagging, swelling cloud.

Yet still the insurgents came. Mortlock was uncertain whether it was the light, but some of those rushing faces were terrifyingly inhuman. There were mutants amongst them. Under his scope, Mortlock was sure that

some were not even true insurgents. Some were not
armed. Mobs of shrieking Bastón-born sprinted out
from the rainforest, some clutching rocks, war clubs,
machetes, even tools of agriculture. The insurgents
amongst them, the ones who had guns and knew how
to use them, blasted the Riverine lines from a distance
of no more than thirty or forty metres. The short space
between opposing forces soon became clogged by the
dead and wounded as small-arms fire whipped back
and forth.

Mortlock knew to pick his shots. Here and there, he
could spot the leaders of the pack offensive. They were
unmistakably tall and glowed almost white in their
warpaint. These gaunt warriors directed the attacks,
urging mobs of attackers towards weak points in the
Imperial line. Mortlock lined up a particularly rake-
thin insurgent whose face was as white as a corpse. He
breathed out and fired, dropping the insurgent as he
was brandishing an autogun over his hand and yelling
encouragement to his men. The pallid man rose to his
knees, still screaming. Mortlock put two more shots
into his chest, this time pinning him down for good.

Smoke and intense heat from the burning cassam
paddies washed over them. Mortlock's eyes stung. The
air became searing. Dim shapes hurtled out of the
smoking haze. Mortlock tried to shoot them down
before they reached the battalion lines. There were so
many. Troopers Carlwin and Vere on either side of him
fired on automatic. Carlwin fell, a thrown hatchet in
his chest. Above the roar of gunfire, the vox-unit on
Trooper Vere's back blared with competing voices. Platoon commanders were screaming orders above each
other.

'Enemy are mutants,' crackled the vox.

'Enemy are not mutants. Enemy are native insurgents.'

'Enemy are mutant insurgents. Archenemy forces flanking left and right.'

Mortlock ripped the vox receiver from Vere's back. 'Shut the frag up!' Mortlock screamed into the airwaves.

No clear order could be gleaned. Communication between the various units broke down. The voices continued to step over each other. 'Clear nets! All units! Clear nets for vox silence!'

'Mortlock!' Baeder screamed as he dropped belly down next to him. 'I need Serpent Company to go and pack their belongings fast, grab ammunition and rations, ditch the rest. Then Prowler, Ghost and Seeker in that order. After we're set to go, we'll make a fighting withdrawal. Got it?' he shouted. Unable to use the vox, Baeder had taken to doing things the old-fashioned way – he was sprinting from officer to officer, heedless of the firestorm that sliced around him.

Mortlock nodded in between reloading his clip. 'Serpent, then Prowler, Ghost and Seeker, in that order. Got it!'

With that Baeder got up, without regard for the volume of enemy fire, and ran to relay his order to the other junior officers. Rounds punched the dirt around him as the colonel sprinted in a crouch. He bellowed a curse at the enemy and Mortlock soon lost sight of him.

'All right! You heard the Colonel. Serpent Company, move out!' Mortlock shouted. He pounded out sixteen shots in rapid succession to keep the enemy down as Serpent Company disengaged from the firing line to retrieve their belongings.

An insurgent with a threshing flail leapt over the irrigation ditch and into the Riverine lines. Mortlock's suspicions were confirmed – the insurgent's lower jaw and mouth merged into a tiny, spiked orifice; a certain sign of mutation. It brought its threshing flail down hard on the back of Trooper Roscher and then once across his neck, killing the man as he rolled over. Mortlock blasted up with his lasrifle, catching the insurgent underneath the chin. Without turning to look, Mortlock tore a grenade from his webbing and hurled it into the night, deterring any follow-up attack on their position. Frustrated, the enemy shredded the lip of the ditch with a flurry of las-fire as Mortlock and the men around him kept their heads down.

The fighting was the heaviest Mortlock had encountered on Bastón. It might have even been the heaviest he had ever encountered. A rocket exploded thirty metres away, showering him in mud and blood. He began to get flashbacks of the swamp ferals on Ouisivia. But those greenskins were wild, like an elemental force. The insurgents running face first into their gunfire now had a logic and belief to their sacrifice. It made Mortlock's blood run cold.

It came as a great relief to Mortlock when Serpent Company returned to the lines, now dressed and prepped. He hid his fear well as he ordered Prowler to disengage and break camp. A heavy stub gunner exposed his upper body above the ditch to give them better covering fire. He fired a long ten-second spurt before a single shot blew out his eye and sent him tumbling back into the ditch. Mortlock slung his lasrifle over his shoulder and crawled over the dead gunner. The man had been Trooper Hennel of Seeker Company, a veteran of multiple engagements; he had

earned his infantryman's combat badge at the age of
sixteen. He had also been one of the best snook dice-
players in the battalion. Mortlock checked his pulse,
making sure that Hennel was dead. He then unlatched
the heavy stub gun from dead fingers and pulled out
the remaining belt of rounds from the ammo-pack
Hennel wore on his back. Holding the stubber one-
handed while he laid the belt of ammunition across
the open palm of his left, he knelt down behind the
ditch and pelted out tracer in wide sweeps. In the night,
muzzles flashed back at him; one shot in particular ricocheted off a rock to his front and showered him in
molten pinpricks of shrapnel.

'Don't be a hero,' Mortlock said to himself as he emptied the stubber and scrambled back behind cover.

AT 03.45, EXACTLY thirteen minutes after the Lauzon
Offensive had begun, the Riverine began to claw their
way backwards in a fighting withdrawal.

They trampled over the remains of their tents and
non-essentials as the fighting receded into the camp-
site. Riverine dragged their wounded with them,
determined not to leave them behind as they were
forced to do with their dead. It was a sad, weary retreat
with none of the glory implied in a 'fighting withdrawal'. Their shots were desperate as insurgents
hounded them, attacking in mobs before concentrated
firepower scattered them away to regroup.

Baeder led a rearguard, two solid fighting platoons of
Prowler Company with Captain Buren attempting to
delay the thousands of rabid insurgents at the banks of
the delta as the battalion loaded up onto their
transports. Sergeant Pulver joined them from the
direction of the Lauzon settlement. A crowd of

emboldened villagers had followed him, hurling stones. Not at all fazed by the aggression, Pulver mustered four or five troopers, turned and directed a steady volley of fire at the Lauzon mob. The villagers broke at the sign of the first shot.

It was a messy affair and although Baeder collected eighteen frag grenades, he had used them all before they even reached the bank. By the time Baeder was rushed onto a departing swift boat, he had depleted three lasrifle mags and two clips from his autopistol.

And still the enemy followed them, surging into the water like a stampede. They hurled rocks and flaming alcohol jugs and those with crude firearms sang out parting shots. The gun-barges with their heavy flamers washed sheets of fire behind the flotilla, forcing the enemy up the banks. As they passed through the channel of the Lauzon township, some of the boat gunners began to fire on the houses in anger. Baeder voxed for them to cease fire and conserve ammunition.

They remained alert as insurgents followed them up river, hounding them for five kilometres with potshots from the trees. Each attempt was met with a thunderous volley from the heavy weapons on board the Riverine vessels until, finally, the enemy gave up.

Under the husky light of dawn, the Guardsmen finally dropped down on their decks, completely burnt out. Their faces were black with greasy ash and their throats stung from smoke. The fighting had taken a heavy toll on the battalion. Forty-five dead and a further nine wounded. The 88th Battalion lost more men in that one night of fighting than they had for the entire duration of the war.

In the following morning, aerial reconnaissance from Angel One reported an estimated six hundred insurgent casualties. Bodies littered the entire Lauzon rural fields and down into the delta itself. The grim assessment did not embolden Baeder at all. The fighting had been ferocious, the enemy had been determined, and the battalion had not even reached their objective yet.

THE TRIBES OF Solo-Bastón had lived on the mainland and surrounding islands long before the arrival of the Imperium. Indeed, they continued to occupy their traditional land in the decades after the Ecclesiarchy formally annexed the islands. Although portions of the land along the coastal regions were dedicated to administrative cities and certain land had been given agricultural leases, fundamentally the use and enjoyment of the inland by the natives continued with little disturbance from the governing authorities after annexation. As long as the natives prayed to the God-Emperor and paid their rural tithes, there would be peace.

The uprising, however, changed that. The inland and surrounding islands became red zones. It was said that the Imperium controlled the cities and the Carnibalès controlled the rainforest. It was also true that ninety-five per cent of the landmass on Bastón was rainforest. As a result, the Imperium clung to their coastal provinces while the insurgency raged like a stormy sea around them. On their small, mobile craft, the Riverine Amphibious were the first to deploy to the mainland and reinforce the remaining PDF elements. The coastal regions became the last bastion of Imperial control on Bastón. Yet slowly, even that was beginning to change.

On the one hundred and thirty-fifth day of uprising, a riot erupted in the administrative province of Union City, sixteen kilometres north-east of the Torre Gulf.

Carnibalès propagandists, disguised as inland traders, whipped up a frenzy of hate in the back alleys of Union. Excited, frenzied and intoxicated, for an entire day heretics rampaged through the city, killing Imperial officials and their families. Non-natives were beaten, stripped and mutilated, their bodies tipped into the Union Quay harbour. It took three thousand Riverine Guardsmen two days to restore order to the city and by then the damage had been done. Entire blocks of Union had been consumed by fire and bodies littered the streets and hung from street poles.

CHAPTER NINE

'LOOK AT THIS glorious land,' said Cardinal Avanti, sweeping his arms in a gesture that took in the expanse of broken, deforested earth before him. 'Waiting for the seed and harvest of honest Imperial folk.'

Brigadier Kaplain watched as his fellow officers Montalvo and de Ruger nodded in clockwork agreement. Inwardly, Kaplain sighed. The land before him had been freshly chain-felled by Caliguan transport tractors and the spillage of broken trees all lay in one direction like the unburied dead, the smell of sap still strong in the air. Guardsmen of the Caliguan Motor Rifles were still in the process of registering and loading native tribesmen onto waiting troop-trucks. These men and women had, until the morning of that day, been ancestral owners of this land for thousands of years. But by mid-afternoon, the Ecclesiarchy had already moved in on one of

Bastón's many rimward islands and declared it annexed for the glory of the Imperium.

'Where will these people go?' Kaplain asked, pointing at the miserable line of homeless tribesmen at the edge of the clearing.

'Oh, don't worry, brigadier,' Avanti said off-handedly. 'We have settlement camps set up waiting to train them in the methods of agriculture and mining. They will soon be under the employ of the Administratum as labourers so they need not go hungry.'

Kaplain rubbed the bridge of his nose wearily. He had been a soldier for long enough to recognise a conquest when he saw one. But the people of Bastón had been loyal to the Imperium before the insurgency and now the remaining loyalists were being punished for the actions of a rebellious minority.

From their observation deck atop a Caliguan tractor, Avanti and his three high officers watched the clearing process under the shade of servitors bearing lace parasols. Eight Adepta Sororitas bodyguards, including Morgan Fure, stood to attention with them, aiming their boltguns at the tribesmen in the far distance, although in Kaplain's opinion there was clearly no need.

'Do you think that perhaps by taking the land away from the remaining loyalists, we are aiding the insurgency with new recruits?' Kaplain asked gently.

'Are these not loyal citizens of the Imperium? What use are they to the Imperial cause if they languish in their primitive ways? Are they not better put to use on worthwhile tasks?' Avanti questioned, raising his stark white eyebrows.

Kaplain didn't answer. He could feel Palatine Morgan Fure penetrate him with her silent stare.

'Besides, this insurgency is only a by-product of our administrative efforts here in Bastón,' Avanti continued. 'It is unfortunate, but inevitable, that rebellion should arise when we are only doing it for their own good. Some people will never learn.'

At this, even Montalvo and de Ruger started in confusion. 'Your grace? The rebellion began as a consequence of your efforts?' de Ruger spluttered.

Avanti waved his hand dismissively. 'Oh, yes. I thought I might as well inform you all now, that this rebellion began as a result of the indigenous population's protest at our plans to transform their primitive island nations. The rebellion became larger than we expected, that's all.'

The revelation suddenly made Kaplain quite nauseous. The Imperial military had been led to believe for the entirety of the campaign that the insurgency had been an independent act of rebellion against Imperial authority. Now the cardinal was admitting the natives were acting in retaliation to their heavy-handed policies. Kaplain was shocked and, judging by the reaction of the Caliguan and Persepian officers, it was a revelation to them too.

'Your grace,' Kaplain began, choosing his words slowly. 'You mean to tell us, that… you started this war and made us come down to clean it up?' he said, suddenly angry. He looked at his fellow military officers but knew instantly he would garner no support from them. Both men, although surprised at the sudden turn of events, did not seem bothered. They wandered away to retrieve refreshments from waiting choral-boys, leaving Kaplain to deal with Avanti alone.

'Don't look so offended, brigadier,' Avanti chortled. 'It's not like we started cleaning them out knowing they would fight back. This war was an unexpected consequence. Who knew that a bunch of dirty indigs with clubs could cause such a fuss?'

Kaplain shook his head, trying to digest the cardinal's statement. 'You started this? This insurgency was not a revolt, but a reaction?'

'I did. I'm proud of it too. This planet was a waste of the Emperor's natural bounty. We are turning it into something productive for the Imperial settlement so that man can enjoy the fruits of his own labour.'

By the scowl on Kaplain's face, it was evident that he was not convinced.

'Brigadier, when you pick a fruit from a wild tree, does that fruit not become yours by virtue of your labours?'

'Not if my labour included genocide,' Kaplain said quietly.

There was a flutter of anger across the cardinal's face, brief and quickly repressed. 'The Emperor decreed that land unused is land wasted. What man creates by the efforts of his own labour becomes his by the laws of nature. This planet was empty when we came here, devoid of sovereign authority. Do you understand, brigadier? Or are you stupid?'

De Ruger and Montalvo, returning with drinks in hand, chuckled amongst themselves.

Then Morgan Fure began to speak. 'Regardless, brigadier, theology is beyond your right to question. You only need to know two things. One, the insurgency has escalated beyond our initial estimates and now they have betrayed us by turning into common heretics. Two, your duty is to quell these new-found cultists. Nothing else is relevant.' It was the first thing Kaplain had heard her say.

The cardinal clapped his hands in slow, mock applause. 'You can see why I like her,' he said to the three generals.

There was nothing more Kaplain could say and he knew it. One wrong word and he would end up on charges of heresy and he did not much feel like giving the cardinal and his hard-faced bitch that satisfaction.

'Besides, it seems that military intelligence has gathered enough evidence of Ruinous influence amongst the insurgency. All the better reason to deal with this heretic scum as quickly and as efficiently as possible. Would you agree, brigadier?'

Kaplain could not shake the feeling that even if the Ruinous Powers did have a hand in this conflict, it was only the result of the Ecclesiarchy's callous course of actions that invoked them somehow. The universe worked in strange ways; even as a simple soldier he knew that. But he did not voice his opinion.

'May I be excused, cardinal? If there is nothing further you wanted to show me, the weather is hot and I don't want to keep my driver waiting in this heat,' asked Kaplain.

Avanti nodded without looking at him.

Kaplain snapped the heels of his boots together with a terse thud and saluted his fellow officers. He made a conscious effort not to address the cardinal during his salute before he stamped down the ramp of the tractor towards a waiting four-wheeler.

Once Kaplain was well out of earshot, Avanti leaned in to Fure. 'Watch that man,' he whispered. 'I have a feeling he may cause some mischief before our work is done.'

The palatine, like the cardinal, had learnt to smile without her eyes. She twisted her lips and nodded obediently.

MANY OF THE prospects were dying. They were dying through their bodies rejecting the chemical treatments or they were dying through the intensity of training. Mautista was determined not to become one of those who fell by the wayside.

The first Mautista saw die had been Abales who had, in another lifetime, been an artisan of the Ogalog peoples. They had only been three days into their Disciple induction when the artisan's blood rejected the chemicals. His joints had swelled to acute proportions as his bones had lengthened, until finally his muscles and ligaments collapsed under the strain. They found Abales dead on the fourth morning, curled up in a ball of agony. His kneecaps had split out of his legs and his shoulder blades had torn out of his upper back.

Five more had perished in the two weeks after that. The chemicals poisoned their blood, causing the veins to puff up beneath their skin in cases of angry black thrombosis. The protruding arteries were soft to the touch and minor vessels mottled their bodies. Even the prospects that survived were afflicted by the malady to some degree. It was for this reason that Mautista believed they daubed themselves in white chalk and kohl in a morning ritual. No fully ordained Disciple ever appeared before the Carnibalès soldiery without the corpse-white warpaint of their caste.

For those who survived the system shock of physical transformation, more would fall victim to the intense training methods of the Dos Pares. Early in their induction, Gabre of the Blood Gorgons led the recruits to

Yawning Hill, in actuality a tiered mountain cliff in the upper hinterlands of Bastón. The sheer slabs of cliff that rose three thousand metres above the ground were all but impossible to climb. Only the hardiest foragers, searching for eggs of the rare cliff-dwelling bantam, dared to brave the ascent. The foragers worked in four- or five-man groups with the aid of securing rope and relay teams, and even then, only during the warmest seasons with well-stocked supplies for a three- or five-day climb.

The prospects were made to scale the vertical heights during the monsoon season, with no rations and only a small pickaxe. They set off alone, edging their way up the cliffsides as rain and high wind pelted them. For Mautista, the intense mental focus of the climb far out-stripped the exceedingly difficult physical aspect. For minutes, even hours at a time, he would pause, splayed across the rock face as he studied his next move. The rain slicked the rocks, or loosened others, and he would reach out with trembling fingers to test the next handhold. It was like a game of rook that required unrelenting focus, a game that lasted for three whole days and in which a mistake at any point would result in death. Several times Mautista lost his grip on the slippery stones, clamping on by the tips of his fingers, clenching his cramped forearms through the sheer determination to not die. He caught snatches of sleep whenever he could find a ledge stable enough to sup-port him, but even then never for more than one or two hours at a time.

On the third night, as he neared the peak, the wind became unbearably strong. At times it pounded him with a tangible force, pulling at his hair and wedging gaps of air between his body and the cliff. During these times Mautista would press himself against the rock and close his eyes, feeling the gale rippling across his back and howling mockery into his ears. It was only during these moments of bleakness that Mautista truly realised the purpose of this trial. He was frightened to the point of trembling. Physically and mentally he was depleted. This was what the Two Pairs wanted to know. At the final hour of the final war, would Mautista lie down and die? Or would he press on to achieve the Primal State?

Suddenly, Mautista experienced a rush of endorphins. He felt a focus that he had not felt even before the climb. He could fall backwards and let the wind carry him away, or he could climb to the top. The logic was so pure and his fate was entirely within his own grasp. He had achieved clarity of mind free of affliction. Slowly, hand over hand, Mautista clawed his way upwards. It no longer mattered to him whether there were ten metres or ten hundred metres to reach the peak. He would climb to the top, and then he would kill a platoon of Imperial Guard and climb it all over again if he had to.

When his hand finally dragged him over the edge, Mautista found Gabre and Sau had set up a base camp. Several of the other prospects had already made it up before him. They were changed men, walking with a sure, steady stride. It had taken Mautista two days and three nights to complete the ascent, surviving on rainwater and moss, but he had finally made it. Despite their newly-transformed physiques, six of the remaining sixteen had not survived the climb.

Mautista knew this was a way of culling the unsuitable. The Disciples were the backbone of the Carnibalès, the visible leaders, the field commanders and more importantly the teachers of the common insurgents. The Two Pairs made it known that ill-prepared Disciples would become a taint, polluting the insurgency itself. For the ten remaining prospects, their training as Disciples could now begin.

'CHAOS IS NOT an entity. Chaos is a state of existence. It is the Primal State.'

Jormeshu was, for the first time, in his full rig of battle armour. No longer clad in a loincloth, he appeared even larger than before, his voice made sonorous by the vox speakers housed in his enormous breastplate.

'The Ecclesiarchy has taught you that Chaos is evil. That order and the rule of law should navigate the history of mankind.'

The ten Disciples nodded in agreement. They sat in cross-legged obedience on the dirt floor of an underground bunker, watching the Legionnaire prowl back and forth like a caged behemoth. Mautista had never seen armour like Jormeshu's before. The suit had a slab-like quality to it, sheathing Jormeshu in plates thick and heavy. The colour was a deep shade of red, so deep it shone like lacquered black-brown. Yet at the same time, thorns and filigree chased the edges of the suit in leaping, energetic angles so that the armour appeared organic somehow. It was as if the suit had a life and voice of its own and had chosen Jormeshu as its host. Mautista had never seen anything so wonderful.

'But man was not made for order or law,' Jormeshu rasped. 'By nature man is flawed. It is an inevitable part of mankind. Man strives to increase his power, his influence, and he does this through his imposition of order and authority. Life is a continual struggle for one man to be better than the next man. Law and order stagnates this power struggle.'

The Disciples shouted in approval, raising their fists into the air. Jormeshu's boots, shaped like cloven hooves, thudded against the packed earth as he strode up and down, adding to the crescendo with tremendous force.

'But Chaos is change. It is a constant flux, like the delta which continues to flow, it is evolution. It is the way forward for mankind. The Imperium fears us because it fears change, it holds onto antiquated notions of sentiment. Even you, at one stage, feared change.'

He was right, Mautista knew. To become Disciples they had forgone their previous lives. At first he had held onto the memories of his life as a Kalisador and as a Taboon villager, but those sentiments had stopped him from progressing. They stopped him changing. The Dos Pares had often spoken of finding inner tranquillity through the path of Chaos and it was Mautista's ascent up Yawning Hill that allowed him to understand in part what they meant.

'Remember this. It is change through liberation; we will free you from the chains of the Imperium and allow you to exist as you want. Exist as you are in a Primal State. Morals are simply a construct of man. Yet man is but stardust, we are the same material as the earth, the sky and even bacteria. All matter does not abide by law, as nature does not abide by law. We should accept this. If you kill a man because the sight of him offends you, is it not the way of nature? Is it not as elemental as the tree that is felled by the storm? If the man you kill cannot defend himself then that is the way it is. There should be no moral attachment to it, because therein lies the stagnation of law and order.'

Mautista understood this too. Since he had become a Disciple he had already killed a man. The man had been a villager who had ridden his motored bicycle in front of an insurgent convoy. Fearing discovery by Imperial forces, as using the dirt roads was always a measured risk, Mautista and his training team had been pressed for time. They had blared their horns to force the cyclist off the road. As they passed, the man had looked at them. It was the look of disdain that had triggered the killing. In that second Mautista had decided the man should not exist any more. He was stupid; stupid enough to incur Mautista's attention and not strong enough to defend himself after a petty display of anger. Mautista ordered the trucks to a halt, alighted and calmly shot the man with his lasrifle. It had been a liberating experience.

'But if we are to lose our grasp of all else, then why do I still harbour a hatred of the Imperium for killing the Taboon?' Mautista asked.

'Hate is just a means. Emotions are the driving force of mankind. I ask you this, when you feel hatred, or when you feel love, or excitement. How do you decipher one feeling from another? Is it tangible?'

Mautista thought for a while and realised it was not. Emotions were an engine that drove physical action. The Dos Pares helped him channel his emotions into seeking the path of Chaos and liberation. It made him soar with joy and want to impart his revelations to all the people of Bastón. For those who did not understand the Primal, Mautista pitied them.

* * *

As MORNING CAME, so did the rain.

The raindrops bouncing hard on Baeder's face and neck woke him. He opened his eyes, still dreaming of combat, and momentarily forgot where he was. He rubbed his face to wake himself and realised his hands were streaked with dry blood. The Lauzon Offensive had not been a dream at all.

Having fallen asleep at the bow of his swift boat, hunched behind the mounted bolter, Baeder had sunk into the deep sleep of the chronically unrested. Around him, the flotilla was moving at an ambling speed, their crews spent from the previous night's fighting. There was a palpable weariness in the air.

He cracked his neck, stretched his limbs and walked around to the pilothouse. He stepped into the cabin and found Corporal Velder, his assigned coxswain, at the helm, eyelids hooded and half asleep.

'Morning, corporal.'

Velder started and snapped to attention. 'Sir,' he said, saluting.

'At ease, corporal. How much progress have we made?'

'We're about sixteen kilometres from the Lauzon township, sir. North-east bearing at coordinates B15200.'

'Very good, corporal. Stand down and catch some sleep below deck. I'll take over for now,' said Baeder as he began to peel off his uniform shirt. Blood, none of it his, had congealed the shirt to his skin. He discarded the ruined article onto the deck and, for the first time, went about as most of his men did, bare-chested beneath a flak vest.

As Corporal Velder stumbled past in a daze, Baeder knew he had pushed the men beyond their limits. They had needed rest at Lauzon, they really had. They had needed the time at Lauzon to stabilise the wounded and renew the spirits of the entire battalion. But they had left with more wounded than before. Many would not make it through the day without proper treatment. Already three entire assault landers were devoted to the supine forms of those with critical injuries, the tillers manned by on-hand combat medics drawn from other squads. Aside from human casualties, several of the swift boats were so damaged they were towed along by supply barges. One of the gun-barges had sprung a leak and many other swifties, workhorses that were close to one hundred and forty years old, were beginning to show signs of wear. Baeder feared they would not hold up for the entire mission.

He agonised about their ramshackle defences and preparations at Lauzon. They were in enemy country, and the Lauzon had been coerced into betrayal. Evidence from the massacred villages along the banksides should have warned him. But Baeder had wanted so badly to believe he could rest and water his men that he had taken the gamble. He blamed himself entirely. They were deep in the lands of the Archenemy now. He could not afford any more mistakes.

FAR BACK IN the lines, Corporal Schilt was fuming. He had almost been killed in the Lauzon Offensive. He had come precariously close to dying in some backwater hamlet on some feral planet he could barely pronounce the name of.

He had only escaped death by running back into camp and hiding in a drainage culvert while the battle had raged around him. Drunk beyond all senses, Schilt had shuddered to think what would have happened had he been forced to fight. He had simply followed the main line of retreat, making sure to keep as many Riverine between himself and the insurgent waves as possible. In his hurry to flee, Schilt had climbed aboard an assault lander rather than his assigned swift boat and was now stuck aboard its cramped crowded conditions.

It was all a rather unfortunate series of events. He was sure to never let that happen again.

'I'm going to shoot him,' Schilt declared to nobody in particular.

The men huddled around, tired though they were, began to chuckle.

'Schilt. You're drunk. Settle down,' said Sergeant Emel gently.

'I'm not drunk. Just wait and see, I'll fragging shoot him.'

In reality, Schilt's temples were still viced by the after-effects of intoxication and his breath was sour with ethanol. But in his mind, the colonel would be as good as dead.

'The colonel's all right. He's got some balls considering his staff background. At least with him, we'll never spoil for a fight,' said Emel.

Schilt shook his head sluggishly. 'If you want to die then go ahead. Me, I'm not dying here, not on this planet. Baeder is nothing but trouble.'

Emel shrugged wordlessly. The others looked away in undecided silence. But although Schilt had not gathered support here he knew his boys would share his view. It was better that his comrades did not regard his threats as anything more than the aggravated rants of a drunken soldier. It would make it easier to do away with Baeder, once he and his creepers had the timing right.

CHAPTER TEN

DUPONTI WALKED OUT of the hangar bay with the stiff, blood-tingling limbs of extended flight. The ship was quiet. Most of the personnel were sleeping soundly except for the maintenance crew working on Duponti's strike fighter.

He crossed the long grey strip of the flight deck, small and insignificant under the shadow of towering vox-mast antennas. On board the Argo-Nautical, two thousand Persepians were at rest, oblivious to the turbulent fighting many kilometres away on the mainland. The *Iron Ishmael* carried two battalions of Nautical Infantry, a squadron of Marauder bombers reinforced by four Lightning strike-fighters, as well as a crew of seven hundred sailors, crewmen and logistics units. But for now, the only man who could make a difference to the distant fighting was Lieutenant Duponti.

As Duponti made his way towards the 'iron-box' – a four-storey superstructure on the deck that housed the ship's officers – it occurred to his flight-addled mind that the operation was at a crucial point now. It was a climax. They were at war for real.

At the sentry point, two Nautical infantrymen in their neat, sky-blue waistcoats opened the enormous clam-shell entrance into the superstructure. The soldiers in their pressed uniforms, still chalky with starch, saluted Duponti as he passed. Compared to them, Duponti must have looked a dishevelled mess. He had not changed out of his flight suit for three days and thick stubble scraped his neck. For a moment, he wanted to clutch the nearest man by the shoulders and shake him, yelling as to whether he realised there was a war on. It was a momentary urge and Duponti put it down to the high spike of nerve stimms he had ingested to keep himself awake.

Duponti made his way towards the wardroom: a large officers' mess that doubled as a cafeteria. He had approximately twenty minutes to down some caffeine and load up on carbohydrates before his warplane would be ready for take-off again.

In the rectangular, steel container of the wardroom Duponti finally slumped down. He could not remember the last time he had straightened out his back against a real backrest. A handful of ship officers nursed cups of steaming caff at the big, otherwise empty metal tables. They shot him short, curious glances. Duponti was too weary to acknowledge them. He kept his head down between drooping shoulders and dug away at a bowl of gritty grain cereal.

He had not been eating long when he heard the loud scrape of chairs. The officers in the wardroom had all risen to their feet, sword-straight and in salute. Duponti turned around in his chair and saw Admiral de Ruger stride into the hall. The admiral levelled his gaze on Duponti and headed towards him.

Duponti groaned inwardly. He had never liked de Ruger. He found the man insufferably smug, far too smug for a soldier who had never gained his rank by earning his combat pins. Like most rear-echelon Persepians, de Ruger had put far too much thought into his outward appearance as a way of distracting out-siders from the fact that he had no real front-line experience. Even now in the middle hours of the night, the admiral was upholstered in a doublet of silky cyan and a cape of translucent fur.

'Sir,' said Duponti, rising to his feet. He sat back down before de Ruger returned his salute.

'How is the fighting, lieutenant? Thrilling, I'd wager,' declared the admiral in his tone that suggested he already knew the answer.

'It's getting thicker the further out I fly. These last few days have been one continuous combat zone, so thick that it's hard to call this an insurgency any more.'

'Oh, I know. How I miss the stink of fyceline,' de Ruger said, mimicking an exaggerated shiver of delight.

He didn't, of course. Duponti knew for a fact that the admiral kept himself as far away from combat as he could and had done so ever since he had been a pam-pered junior officer. Being the nephew of a Persepian consul had afforded him special status amongst the peers of his day.

Duponti slopped a spoonful of grits into his mouth. 'Sir, is there anything I can do for you?'

'I've come to let you know that your services to the Riverine operation are no longer required. You may stand down and get some rest. Clean yourself up,' smiled de Ruger. He said it as if he believed it was a good thing.

'Why?' said Duponti glumly. 'It's a full-scale engagement out there. If anything, sir, I was going to request four other pilots to help fly rotations. I can't do this alone.'

De Ruger seemed slightly taken aback by Duponti's response. 'No. No, I'm not risking any more pilots for this operation. I'm letting you know that you may stand down now.'

'Sir, the battalion are going to take much heavier casualties, especially in that kind of terrain. If I'm not flying overwatch, it could get worse.'

De Ruger shook his head. 'The 88th Battalion are expecting at least sixty per cent attrition. You don't need to work yourself to death, lieutenant. Have some dignity.'

Duponti was slouched over his bowl of cold grits, his head hanging from exhaustion. But the admiral's attitude riled him. Duponti put down his metal spoon with a clink. 'Sir, they are so close to the objective now. I've seen what it's like out there in the heartland. The inland is crawling with rallying insurgents, it's like a nest of mites out there. The insurgency grows in strength everyday, sir, I've seen it with my own eyes. For the sake of my own conscience, I need to help the Riverine neutralise that siege-battery before this war becomes unwinnable.'

The admiral was unmoved. 'When they fail,' he said imperiously, 'then Cardinal Avanti will simply return to our original strategy of carpet-bombing the inland until the heavy guns are silenced. Won't that be something? The full might of the Persepian fleet taking the mainland.'

The fact that the admiral said 'when' not 'if' was not lost on Duponti. The aviator hid his face behind a cup of tea, scowling. The admiral was a true political strategist, constantly seeking to manoeuvre himself into the cardinal's favour. Maybe he truly wanted a seat by the Emperor's golden throne when he died. Whatever the case, it did not seem likely that de Ruger had the success of the Riverine objective at heart.

'Yes, sir.'

De Ruger patted his back. It was awkward, as if the admiral were not used to contact with lower ranking men. 'Good, good, lieutenant. Now you can clean up and start looking like a real man again. I hear they are serving smoked sausages and fresh local eggs for breakfast in a few hours. Make sure you're here for those. The sausages are the smoke-cured variety from the Fragment Isles, brought all the way here from home.'

Duponti stopped paying attention. The less he acknowledged the admiral, the less likely he would be to linger around. De Ruger continued to bombast, debating with himself about the merits of fine breakfast wines and whether ham in the officers' mess was better grilled or raw cured. Finally, after several agonising minutes, he left Duponti alone.

The aviator waited until he was sure de Ruger was well and truly gone. Opening a zip pocket in his jumpsuit, Duponti took out a handful of stimms. He swallowed the pills dry. Immediately, he felt his heart begin to thump hard in his chest.

He cried out involuntarily, slapping his palms hard on the table.

The other officers sitting around quietly put down their cups to stare at him. One of them shook his head.

Duponti laughed at them, tossed his chair aside, and stumbled out to find his Lightning interceptor. Admiral de Ruger be damned, the war was just beginning.

FROM LAUZON PROVINCE, the delta widened into a basin of saline water half a kilometre broad at its widest point. But unlike the low-lying marshlands of Ouisivia, where sheets of mangroves clung to the muddy bottoms, here the rainforest continued to grow even in the water itself. According to Baeder's map, the terrain should have made for easy travel, indicating a wide expanse of water. But that was not to be.

Aquatic trees resembling stands of green coral rose out of the water and knitted a mesh of canopy thirty metres overhead. Hardy lentireeds and stringy rhizophora floated in clumps on the surface, their broad leaves speckled with salt crystals. Gas from the decomposing mud pits secreted the sinus-heavy stench of wet, rotting fruit. The foliage here had a colossal, alien quality to it, as if growth in the rough, saline waters had nurtured a strain of enormous plants that survived the conditions through sheer size alone.

The flotilla ground slowly through the aquatic forest, covering less than eight kilometres in three hours of travel. The canopy formed a greenhouse of humid air, so heavy that it could be reached out and touched like steam. Visibility was low. Sunlight that filtered through the canopy was a shade of foggy green and entire sections of boats often lost sight of each other. Fog sirens brayed constantly. After repeated slowdowns as boats sought to find each other, Baeder ordered them to maintain positional awareness through vox contact alone.

At times, Baeder felt that the entire rainforest was just an extension of the marine habitat below. Silvery shoals of fish skipped along the surface of the water, dancing on gossamer wings. Serpents slipped in and out of the water without eliciting so much as a splash. Crustaceans clung to tree bark, flies hovered in clouds and bug-eyed primates watched them from the tallest branches. The wildlife sought to claim them too; schools of tiny insects suddenly appeared on the surface of their boats, dotting the surface in hundreds, if not thousands. On closer inspection, Baeder was astounded to see that these were actually miniature frogs no bigger than his pinky nail, flitting and clustering together like condensation. Baeder brushed them away, scooping up dozens in his palm, but after a while he gave up. They simply materialised as if out of thin air.

DURING THE HEIGHT of the afternoon, at the hottest part of the day, Baeder called his men to rest. As temperatures increased, dehydration became a very real threat. Although it had not rained all day, the troopers were plastered with moisture. It was as if they had been travelling through the water itself.

Baeder himself did not rest. He ordered Corporal Velder to nurse their swift boat ahead of the battalion to meet with the scouts. The terrain was far worse than the maps had led them to believe and Baeder thought it prudent to scout ahead of the main force. Clustered and hemmed in as they were, ambush was a constant possibility.

The three scouting swifts, along with Baeder's vessel, continued sailing for a rough half hour. The going was extremely difficult and in some parts spurs of underwater roots worried their passing hulls. The boats had to navigate around miniature atolls of aquatic plants, bumping and scraping the tight confines. The water-borne jungle was like a sieve, thought Baeder, forcing the boats out of formation in order to weave around its tangled growth. The insurgents could hide thousands of men here. With this weighing on their minds, the four swifts never strayed far from each other, maintaining constant line of sight. Baeder and his coxswain stayed within the pilothouse while the boat's three other crew stayed on deck, one manning the stern stub gun and two manning the heavy bolter on the bow.

As they crept around an ox-horn bend of root systems, a village came into their view, sudden and looming. So well hidden in the jungle, the houses caught them off guard.

'Sir, was this on the map?' one of the scout boats voxed to Baeder.

'No. But this entire forest wasn't on the map either,' Baeder replied.

'Should we observe local customs and unlink ammunition from our main guns?'

'No,' Baeder decided. 'Not after last time. Keep your weapons lined up on every doorway and window.'

The village was built entirely on stilts. Support poles, some four or five metres high, kept the several dozen shack huts above the water. A system of rope bridges connected each of the various structures to each other in a web of hemp ropes and plank boards. Some of the shacks were even nestled on platforms, high in the trees, suggesting that this village was a permanent one, not just some seasonal nomadic settlement. The few villagers who squatted outside their homes fled and shut their doors as the swift boats sailed into view.

'This place looks harmless enough,' voxed the swift boat that sailed lead.

Sure enough, the town was a miserable-looking settlement in disrepair. Moss and rivers of tiny green frogs
covered the walls and sloping roofs of every building.
No one came out to greet them or at least regard the
off-worlders with curiosity. The swifts passed in single
file with Baeder at the rear, one after another until at
last Baeder's boat sailed through the centre of the settlement.

That was when the enemy fired a shot.

One lonely shot that rattled from an autogun. The
round danced off Baeder's starboard rear with an
aggressive shriek.

Immediately, the vox-channels came alive. 'Shots
heard! Location needed!'

Baeder had spotted the muzzle flash from a second
storey window of a nearby shack. It had obviously been
fired in anger, but it would be too premature to start
igniting the entire village with heavy support fire. 'Hold
your fire! My boat is going in, so cover us,' Baeder
voxed to the scouts.

They drew their boat parallel with a swinging rope
ladder that led up to the rope walkways. Snatching lasrifles from the stowage racks, Baeder and his crew
surged up onto the platforms. The five-man team
stormed up onto a lopsided house and Corporal Velder
caved the flimsy plyboard door in with a fen-hammer
from the boat's armoury.

The Riverine burst into a large room full of screaming occupants. 'Down! Down on the floor!' Velder
yelled as he brandished the fen-hammer overhead.

Baeder took a moment to assess his surroundings.
There were both men and women huddled there, along
with many children. At first glance there appeared to be
three or four families sharing one single room. The

Riverine began to search the house while Baeder covered them with his lasgun. The women started to sob hysterically and the children followed suit.

'Sir. I found it!' shouted Trooper Keidel. The Riverine was peering into a man-sized water urn. From inside, he drew out two crude autorifles and a missile tube. 'Still warm,' Keidel said, slapping the barrel of a rifle against his open palm.

Baeder looked at the four men. The Bastón men smiled at him broadly and confidently. 'No proof,' said one of them.

Another raised his hands above his head in mock surrender. 'We are not soldiers. You cannot harm us,' he said. 'Not with our children as the Emperor's witness.'

'Emperor my arse!' Baeder spat, and was surprised by his own vehemence. 'Frag it! Cuff them all!'

Corporal Velder looked at Baeder with uncertainty. 'And then what, sir? We can't take them with us.'

'We can and we will. Let these crotch-beaters know that we won't suffer their insolence any more,' said Baeder. 'Tie them up. We're going to search this whole village. Cuff these ones and leave them here for the battalion to collect on the way through.'

In Baeder's eyes, the men in the house did not seem to appreciate the severity of the situation. They were smiling smugly and claiming to be fishermen, even as the Riverine led them outside and lashed their wrists to the house stilts with plastek cuff ties. They left the four men in chest-deep water as Baeder and his four crewmen set about searching the other homes.

They had not even crossed the rope bridge to a second house when a shot rang out from across the other side of the village. Trooper Nye yelped and fell backwards. A round had entered his neck, just above the collar of his flak vest. The others crouched or dropped flat against the rope bridge.

Suddenly, Baeder was angry. He had been a career soldier for as long as he had been an adult and fighting was his duty. He had been shot at considerably in his lifetime. But the civilians taking potshots at his men stirred something within him. The Lauzon Offensive had ignited a spark and now this remote village was stirring the embers. He had lost too many men to care. Morality was now a grey area.

Baeder got up and signalled for the three waiting swift boats providing overwatch. 'Frag this place! Kill them all!' he shouted, flashing the field signals for fire at will.

The boats opened up immediately. They fired in all directions. The force of their combined arms shook the village apart, splitting roofs and tearing down walls.

Baeder watched the men they had bound struggle loose from their cuffs. One of them began to swim away from the village. He covered no more than ten metres before bolter rounds sent a bearded cecropia crashing down on him.

A male villager from another house ran out with a machete to release the other three bound men. But Baeder felt possessed. From his position high on the rope bridge he fired down on the rescuer. He did not care what motive the man had for freeing the prisoners, he cared only that his las-rounds tore cleanly through the man's torso, sending him face first into the water.

Gun barrels peeked out from behind windows and barked out with sporadic shooting. The swift boat reply was loud and terrible. Tracer fire folded the shacks into two, three or four pieces like accordion paper. One of the remaining prisoners was hit by a round. Tied up and half submerged in water, the man began to scream. His cries of anguish drew the attention of his family. Three children emerged to see what had become of their father. Howling, arms outstretched, they ran towards him.

Baeder loosened a smoke grenade from his webbing and tossed it directly down below. He would have liked to convince himself that he did it purely to force the children away from the carnage. But in the back of his mind, he knew otherwise. He had done it to deny the father a chance to see his children one last time. The men he lost in Lauzon and all the good soldiers killed under his command had not been given the chance to say goodbye to their loved ones. Baeder would not allow this insurgent that one last mercy.

The last Baeder saw of the dying man was a frail Bastón-born fisherman, utterly despondent as he tried to find his children through the thickening smoke. Baeder had denied him his last chance to say goodbye. For some reason, Baeder felt a thrill of joy. It was something he had not wanted to become. They had made him this way.

THEY FLATTENED THE village within minutes. Half of the houses became sheets of corrugated metal and wood floating in the soupy water. Those that remained standing were worried with bullet holes and las-scorch.

The sudden and overwhelming fury of eight heavy support weapons had silenced the village. No more gun barrels snuck out from cracks and crevices to dare another shot. There was a strange quiet that complemented the pall of gunsmoke. But Baeder was not yet done.

He pulled the scouts back the way they came. He would not take any chances. Voxing back to the battalion, Baeder gave them precise map coordinates of the village and ordered for mortar ordnance. There was no way he would lose another Guardsman and, in his mind, there was every chance that an insurgent could flee from the village only to follow them later, sniping from the trees. He hated these people. He quelled any empathy he once harboured for them. It was less difficult to do than he thought. Baeder simply switched off.

He could soon hear the crump of mortars and the distant whistle of their flight. All his life, Baeder had been a non-consequentialist, caged by an immovable moral code. He had lived as most men did, his actions guided by decontextualised maxims. The sin of unprovoked killing. The ethics of human empathy. The unspoken code of martial honour. Anything that may have once inhibited his actions was now nothing more than social constructs, best kept away from the battlefield. He felt they were distant, unreachable ideals.

But out here, he knew all his actions had an immediate consequence and the only consequence that mattered to him was to keep his men alive. Several weeks ago, the thought of mortaring an enemy village would have lurked like a ghost on his conscience. But now, the crackling explosions of the mortars brought him a cold and curiously morbid comfort.

CHAPTER ELEVEN

THE INSURGENCY WAS growing in force. Carnibalès propagandists were poisoning the provincial hamlets of Bastón through the power of print. Insurgent warbands distributed leaflets that depicted the Primal State as a patriotic religion that combined the animist culture of Bastón with new gods and ideologies. There were even rumours that the Carnibalès broadcast prayers at midnight on a certain vox frequency. Superstition held that, upon listening to the 'unholy' vox-channel, a shadowy wraith would stand in the corner of one's peripheral vision until they changed the frequency. Although the rumours were never substantiated, it was said that dark magic was at work and many who heard these prayers wandered into the rainforests, following ghosts only they could see.

The Ecclesiarchy attempted to counter the spreading rebel influence in their own clumsy, pugnacious

manner. Ecclesiarchal preachers accompanied Riverine patrols into the wilderness and visited the
outlying towns. Yet these preachers were overwhelmingly evangelical. They attributed the insurgency to
native ignorance, and admonished the locals for their
illiteracy and sins. The Ecclesiarchal methods did not
fare well. The preachers were viewed as a liability by
the Guardsmen. An incident in the town of Bahia
became the final straw for Ecclesiarchal involvement
in military patrols. A preacher's caustic oratory
offended the locals to the point of riot, leading to the
death of eight Guardsmen and forty-one locals. In the
aftermath, Cardinal Avanti issued a decree that clerics
were to remain within Imperial-controlled regions
unless their journeys were approved by him personally.

'ATTEN-TION!' MAUTISTA BARKED.

The motley ranks of guerrillas lined up before him
attempted to snap into parade order. The attempt was,
for the most part, sincere. Several of them were out of
rhythm and one man in the rear almost dropped his
rifle. Mautista, tall and white as a standing cadaver,
nodded his approval as he imagined an Imperial officer would do for his men.

The band of guerrilla fighters before him was his
own, the Two Pairs had given them to him. Two score
men drawn from the regional villagers. The men were
parading in a small grove near an inland village allied
to the Dos Pares cause. They were an ill-fitting bunch,
mostly new guerrilla recruits dressed in the canvas and
hemp garments of rural workers. Newly-issued canvas
munition rigs were strapped to proud chests and press-
stamped lasguns were held upright across the left

shoulder. At a distance they looked unremarkable, but from where Mautista stood, they looked fearsome enough for one reason.

Change was amongst them all.

Unlike the Disciples, each man displayed mutations of varying degrees. A few of the men carried the common gift of thorned bristles along their upper brows, while some mutations were very minor, as minor as an extra digit or three.

Yet every day, those commoners who rallied under the Dos Pares were gifted with change as long as they prayed to the shrines that the Two Pairs had erected. And what beautiful shrines they were! Tall and totemic, the pillars were of carved wood so old that they had taken on an ossified sheen. Some were the size of small busts, while others stood as high as a man. They were erected in all places, to be seen at all times, whether crouched beneath the roots of a gum-sap or nestled in a bunker shrine. Since the early days of the war, the Four had erected their shrines and, with each day, the mutations became more common.

It was not known what the origins of these totems were but Mautista knew they came from the skies. Every once in a while the totems were smuggled on board the off-world carriers that would land in the deep jungles, away from Imperial scrutiny. These off-world ships, dark and frightening, brought with them ammunition and mechanisms for the weapons the insurgency could not reproduce. Only the Four were allowed to make contact with these ships but Mautista had witnessed the nimbus of light from afar. When it came time for insurgents to carry the supplies down from the mountains to their base camps, in between the crates of weaponry would always be totems, wrapped in white shrouds and carried aloft by several men like a funeral procession.

With each shrine erected by the Four, their influence grew. Those who had joined the insurgency prayed often to these new deities, these spirits of Chaos. In turn, they experienced a change to their bodies as much as it changed their spirit. It was different from the detached and aloof religion that they had followed under the Ecclesiarchy. There the preachers had admonished them ceaselessly and in return they prayed and prayed to little effect. The power of the so-called Emperor was nothing compared to the instant gratification they received under the attentive gaze of Chaos.

'My brothers. Today we are tasked with a great undertaking,' Mautista began, drawing out each vowel in a suitably dramatic fashion. 'We are to claim taxes from a village that has not joined the cause. Although it may seem a mundane mission, I assure you it is a crucial one. The insurgency of Kaos cannot survive without the support of the people.'

An insurgent named Canao took one step forwards from the ranks. Of all those present, Canao was the most heavily mutated and therefore considered the most devout of them all. Mautista heard camp stories that, only months ago, Canao had been a very tall, very broad and very handsome village blacksmith who had courted the attention of many pretty girls, even from faraway villages. Now the muscles of his upper back and neck fused into a knotted club and his lower jaw split into two hooked mandibles. He was so very monstrous and, in his lesser days, Mautista would have envied him.

'The troop is ready, brother. We will take our payment for the cause, if not in grains then in blood.' As he spoke, the pink flesh around his mandibles peeled backwards like an eyelid and began to drool.

Mautista saluted with his long, strangler's fingers. The men fell out and began to march behind him in single file down a narrow ravine. Mautista was dressed in the cracked brown leathers of a long dead PDF officer, the seams split to accommodate his height and buckled with burnished metal plates where the gaps did not meet. For the first time, Mautista felt as if he could truly punish the Imperium. He felt like a real soldier.

THE TARGET OF the raid was a hamlet near the upper spur of the Serrado Basin. Known as the provincial canton of the Mato-Barea people, it was not a large town by any means, with a population of no more than two hundred. At least that was what the insurgent spies had reported. But the Four had imparted upon Mautista the importance of primary source intelligence and he was a keen Disciple.

Mautista and Canao hid their men in the forest and crept out alone to survey the area. They moved amongst waxy esculenta bushes, breaking up their silhouettes with branches and twigs as they had been taught. The hamlet was roughly three hundred metres away from their hiding place in the undergrowth. The rainforest had been felled for three hundred metres in all directions to provide space for their paddy fields, as well as to give a clear view of any desperate carnivores that might stray from the wilderness.

Mautista felt a chill of excitement deep in his stomach when he remembered that he would be the hunter today.

A stockade surrounded the circular cluster of water-front homes. The Bastón had never been a warlike culture and the practice of fortification had only become common since the war. The barricade was an improvised effort, piled up with disused tractors, rusted engines of agriculture and hammered together with logs from the local trees. The irregular stockade was only a metre high at some points; it would not prevent any truly determined raid. It served more as deterrence than defence.

Before its walls sprawled the ubiquitous paddies and the irrigation systems that channelled feed streams from the delta. Every once in a while the workers in the paddies would look up, scanning the area around them like a herd of cautious grazers. But they didn't see the predators who waited, just beyond their view, in the greenery.

Most of the villagers appeared unarmed, or at least poorly so. The forty or fifty farmers in the fields laboured in pairs. One would loosen the cassam tuber from its watery depths with a long fork and the other would collect it with a shovel and place the harvest into a wicker basket on their back. Their tools would be no match for Mautista's twenty devoted soldiers and their rapid-fire weaponry.

'Mautista, can you see?' Canao rasped, lowering his magnoculars. 'Over there!' he pointed with excitement.

Mautista raised his own magnoculars to where Canao indicated. He saw two Kalisadors standing behind a rusted engine block in the stockade. Their dark grey armour of crab shell and coloured ribbon reminded Mautista of a life he lived not so long ago. Immediately, Mautista both pitied and hated them. The men were so ignorant in their stubborn defence of the village. They knew nothing of the enlightenment of Chaos and Mautista regretted that he would have to kill them.

'They have guns too. This will be a problem,' Canao said, clicking his mandibles with agitation. Mautista narrowed his eyes in concentration.

It would indeed be a problem. The usual method of extortion was for the insurgents to surround the village with their firearms and negotiate taxes in the form of food harvest, cloth and perhaps even recruits. Violence was to be avoided, at least in the beginning. They could not recruit for the cause if they harmed them first. Massacre would only be reserved for hard-line loyalist communities.

Yet this approach was now complicated by the two Kalisador watchmen. They were both well dug-in behind their barricade and armed with ex-PDF shotguns. When the insurgency first took hold, almost a year before the war, the local Planetary Defence Forces were the first victims of killing. The poorly-trained reservist soldiers were killed and their armouries raided by Carnibalès forces. No doubt some of these weapons had drifted into the hands of loyalist communities as well during the course of conflict.

Mautista knew these weapons well, for the Dos Pares had given him rudimentary training in most small-arms. The Kalisadors each gripped a Mosgant90 tactical shotgun. These were quality weapons produced off-world and parkerised with a frosty black phosphate to prevent corrosion in the humid Bastón climate. Pump action with a six-slug capacity, the shotguns were incredibly accurate and could worry a target out at one hundred and fifty metres.

'Kalisadors carrying weapons of death? That is taboo,' said Canao.

'No. It is only taboo during times of peace. Now, it is not taboo. It means this village has recently lost members to violence and the Kalisadors are claiming the rights of retribution,' Mautista explained. He knew that all weapons in the Kalisador arsenal were designed to injure but not kill their opponent during ritual combat. Devices that caused irreversible harm were reserved only for the killing of a much-hated enemy beyond the point of conciliation.

Prior to the war, most Kalisadors would never touch a firearm for fear it would steal away their warrior spirit. It was a taboo device, and the Bastón were a superstitious people. If a villager were to touch a firearm, they must immediately bathe themselves for fear of bad luck. The act of pointing a weapon of death, be it gun or crossbow, was an insult beyond comprehension. The sight of the Kalisadors with shotguns ready meant they were claiming they were willing to inflict righteous retribution.

This presented a unique tactical challenge. The open paddy fields would become a clear killing zone for his men to approach. Of course, their autoguns and lasrifles had greater range over the shotguns, but killing the Kalisadors would simply result in a needless massacre of the village. At over three hundred metres, there was also no guarantee that their home-forged weaponry could accurately put down both Kalisadors.

'What shall we do?' Canao said.

'Hide the warband in the trees, to provide me with covering fire while I go in to negotiate an agreement. If they are hostile, I will run and the men will keep the Kalisadors down.'

Canao nodded in agreement, his humpback swaying as he scurried through the brush then hurried back to the others.

As soon as Mautista returned to his men, he began to relay what he had seen in a logical breakdown. He scrawled a rough outline of the area with a twig in the soil. The Four had taught him well, and he had an intuitive grasp for the tactics of off-world warfare. The knowledge they imparted upon their Disciples was impressive indeed and Mautista often wondered how fearsome those Legionnaires of Chaos would be in battle.

'I want five fighters covering the left arc, and five fighters covering the right arc at one hundred metres' spread. Keep hidden and have your weapons trained on those Kalisadors. You will provide covering fire at forty-five degree angles. I want another five covering our rear, facing the forest. The rest come with me, we will strike a dialogue with the Kalisadors. If you see me raise this signal,' Mautista raised his fist sharply, 'I want the first two groups to kill them as quickly as possible. Understood?'

The men nodded.

'Good, go about it. Canao, I need you with one of the cover fire groups. Go,' Mautista said, slapping the insurgent on his knotted humpback.

The insurgents spread out and soon melted away out of sight. Mautista was left with three young recruits, boys who only several weeks ago had been simple rural types. He could tell they were scared. They had not received the vigorous enlightenment that the Disciples had experienced. They were just boys with rifles and a month of guerrilla training.

Mautista sought to say something that would dispel their anxiety. Finally, he uttered, 'The gaze of Chaos compels you.'

It seemed to work as the Carnibalès flared their nostrils while nodding with conviction. They were working themselves up, gritting their teeth and slapping their faces.

Mautista took off across the fields. His autorifle, with its chipped wooden stock, slung casually across his back. He opened his arms as a gesture of peace. Yet as the farmers spotted him run towards them they scattered like a herd of startled livestock. Mautista knew that the white Disciples had gained quite a reputation amongst the common population, a reputation that bordered on superstitious hysteria. They were regarded as ghosts amongst some, or walking corpses because of their warpaint. Others, more pragmatic, knew them as a symbol of impending death. Mautista liked to think he was both these things as the villagers scarpered over their protective walls in terror.

'Another step and we will shoot,' shouted a Kalisador as Mautista walked within one hundred metres of the township.

Mautista stopped and studied the man. The Kalisador was built like a battering ram, with a square head and no discernable neck. The decorative beads hanging from his torso plates confirmed that this Kalisador was a great ritual dancer who incorporated unarmed fighting into his forms very well. In all likelihood, he would be a poor shot with the shotgun. But the Kalisador who crouched behind cover next to him was younger, with a smooth intelligent face. Mautista judged, by the way the younger man held his weapon, that he knew how to fire a shotgun properly. He would need to watch him the most.

'I am a Disciple of Dos Pares and my men are rebel fighters.'

'I know who you are,' roared no-neck. 'What are you doing here?'

The Four had often said that command of linguistics was as important as command of weapons in psychological operations. Mautista chose his words diplomatically. 'We are here to speak to your young men about joining the cause and, if you are willing to aid us, we would like to collect supplies.'

'We are not stupid. You are raiders,' said the younger Kalisador forcefully.

Mautista tilted his head. 'Would you shoot a fellow Bastón-born in these times of war?'

'We are Imperial citizens. We know what you lot do to loyalist settlements. Get out now or we will shoot,' yelled no-neck, thrusting his shotgun with each word.

The time for talking was over. Mautista could see it in their eyes. If he did not act quickly, the spooked Kalisadors would likely cut him down where he stood. Briefly, Mautista considered retreating and returning with more warbands in support. But the Four would not be pleased. These were just two desperate Kalisadors defending an entire village. Mautista would have to settle this himself.

He raised his fist sharply. The signal to shoot.

He found himself running in the opposite direction as gunfire cut the air around him. Rashes of volley-fire bounced out from the rainforest. For a moment, as Mautista ran towards his guerrillas, he thought they had succeeded.

But his men were not well trained. In the heat of combat, they began to fire wildly. Some of the shots kicked up the ground around Mautista as he ran. They fired without any sense of discipline, shooting in all directions. If Mautista had not spaced them out to the flanks at forty-five degree angles, it was likely he would have been caught in the teeth of their volleys.

Worst of all, the group providing rear cover forgot their orders upon hearing the gunshots and joined in the shooting. It was often a difficult task for soldiers providing cover, looking in the opposite direction of the enemy to stay on task. These men were not drilled enough and the excitement of engagement brought them running out into the open. Unfortunately, this meant Mautista was caught directly in their forward line of attack.

'Stop! Stop!' Mautista cried. 'Get back in your sectors!'

It was no use. He was too far away and the burping fire of weapons drowned out his voice. Behind him, a villager on the wall was shot down. A woman was hit in the hip and spun away. His fighters had forgotten that their objective was to put rounds on the Kalisadors to keep them suppressed. The men were firing at any target that presented itself. Mautista cursed.

He sprinted across the paddy field, hoping that he would not be killed by one of his own. His legs, little more than sinew covering lengthy bone, soon carried him far in front of his men. A shotgun blast roared. One of the guerrillas running alongside was hit in the back, his entire right torso and arm smacking into the water. Mautista's plan was falling to pieces and all because his guerrillas were not putting down enough fire on the two armed Kalisadors.

It was a disaster, but it was not lost yet. Mautista sprinted into the safety of the trees and hurled himself into the undergrowth. Once there, he signalled for his men to regroup. They did so, but only after a further few minutes of ecstatic firing. When he finally gathered his guerrillas around him, their faces were flushed with excitement.

'That was a slaughter!' Canao rasped. The men raised their weapons overhead in triumph.

'That was disaster!' Mautista spat. He lost control and slapped Canao across the face. 'Why did none of you follow my orders?'

The men, suddenly chastised, fell silent.

'You five!' snarled Mautista, pointing at the rear cover group. 'Why did you not stay in your sectors? If you disobey me again, may Chaos reject your souls!' He was frothing with anger. Spittle flew from his mouth.

'We lost one of our own today,' Mautista raged, pointing at the body out in the paddies beyond, 'because you men could not follow simple orders. When I say keep those Kalisadors suppressed, you do it! Not do it when you feel like doing it!'

The sight of the ranting Disciple terrified the guerrillas. Wispy thin and white, he became a tower of rage. He scared them. He was a wraith in their eyes.

But Mautista was not done yet. He squinted at each and every insurgent, cursing, berating and screaming at each of them individually, then as a group, then individually again. He grabbed them by the scruffs of their necks and manhandled them. His wiry limbs had become surprisingly strong and he tossed them around like children.

'What do we do now?' said Suloe, a guerrilla who had developed hard, finger-like nails across his face and upper neck.

Mautista calmed himself down to breathe raggedly. He was still clouded with red rage but he was lucid enough to at least speak normally. 'We regroup and

attack. What other choice do we have? At the very least,
I will not return empty-handed.'

As the guerrillas refreshed their magazines, Mautista
took a moment to remind them of what was at stake.
'The first fighter who fires before he is told, or breaks
orders... the Dos Pares will dispose of you accordingly.'

LIKE SHAMBLING, GRIZZLY primates, the Riverine emerged
after two days of hard travel through the aqueous
jungle. They were filthier and sicker than they had ever
been before.

Their uniforms were sodden rags, hidden beneath a
crust of gore, mud, salt and blood. The beard of every
Guardsman had hardened into a slab of dirty, dreadlocked hair. No doubt, if Baeder could smell himself or
the men around him, they would have reeked of putrid
human waste. But they had become accustomed to the
smell now and, for most, they were too tired to care if
they could.

A third of the men were sick with fever. The conditions had brutalised their immune systems and even
the tiniest grazes were prone to rapid infection. Baeder
himself had swollen glands and a head that was
clogged with mucus. This was compounded by a
chronic shortage of fresh water. Their supply barges
were down to one-fifth capacity. They did not have
enough to drink, let alone wash their infected cuts. The
river water was a cesspit of bacteria and the men who
had dared to drink from it had only become sicker,
wracked by diarrhoea.

The steaming subtropical climate turned their dis-
comfort into sweltering torture. The toils of the past
weeks were accumulating now, wearing down their
combat effectiveness. The men were not pleased and

Baeder could read it on their grimaces. Even the most ordinary tasks of manning sentry guns or refuelling the motors elicited pained groans and grumbles. Many of them had doubted the legitimacy of their mission prior to deployment and now their afflictions affirmed their dissent. Once the initial anticipation of deployment had faded, Baeder could almost hear the discontented murmurs of his men as he lay awake in his bunk at night. Yet they were too deep in the enemy interior for him to be distracted by such things now. They could only go forwards.

According to his maps, which Baeder had learnt not to rely on, the siege-batteries were entrenched no more than eighty kilometres away as they exited the basin. The river system opened out into slow-moving, almost stagnant current as they left the coastal regions behind them.

Prior to the insurgency, the Planetary Defence Force of Solo-Bastón had patrolled these inland regions. The flotilla passed the remains of PDF outposts by the water. There were guard stations erected every several kilometres, solitary blockhouses that looked over docking piers on the water. Over the months these outposts had fallen into disrepair. Veiny creepers claimed the walls and rust had corroded the mesh compound fences. The patrol boats had long since been stolen from the now empty piers. Windows were smashed in and graffiti was scrawled spitefully on the stone walls. Looking into those dark, empty windows, Baeder wondered what lay inside. The place smelt of sadness and loss; it was like looking at a portrait of someone who was already long dead.

Baeder remembered seeing pict slides of the former PDF forces during intelligence briefs, when he had been en route to planetary deployment. They were all young men clad in fresh brown leather armour. A polished metal pauldron on their left shoulder bore a cauldron crab emblem: an honorary symbol of the Kalisadors who were the custodians of the traditional tribes. They reminded Baeder of his own soldiers. It was haunting to think that most of them were now dead.

Intelligence had reported that the local PDF had numbered only six thousand strong. They played no more than a peacekeeping role and were not trained for major theatres of conflict. In reality, their one true purpose had been to operate the colossal siege-battery at the centre of the mainland against phantom enemies. When the insurgency reached its greatest momentum, the PDF had been overrun and it was reported that many of them had turned and sided with the insurgency.

Baeder saluted the guard stations out of respect as they drifted by. PDF or Guard, they were the Imperium's fighting men and they had deserved a proper burial.

'I heard some of those PDF boys could not even bring themselves to fire their weapons. That's a sad tale,' said Sergeant Pulver, stepping up on deck.

It was highly unusual and risky for any battalion senior sergeant to sail on the same vessel as his battalion commander. But for Baeder, it had been even more unusual that Sergeant Pulver had requested to do so. Baeder knew the veteran Guardsman would not otherwise do it, unless something was at stake, and so he had bent regulation, just this once.

'They could not bring themselves to fire on their own people?' asked Baeder.

Pulver shook his head sadly. 'No. Poor leadership. On my first patrol here, I found a squad of dead PDF boys in the bush. They were all still holding fully-loaded weapons. Their squad leader was shot in the back twenty or thirty metres away. He had tried to run.'

'It's not easy doing what they do.'

Pulver chewed his tabac in silence for several long minutes. Then he squinted at Baeder, eyeballing him with steady appraisal.

'I heard about what you did back in the basin village.'

Baeder stiffened. He clasped his hands behind his back, unsure of what the sergeant major would make of it.

'It takes a lot to do that for your men,' said Pulver, pausing to spit his dip. 'Takes a lot,' he repeated.

Baeder regarded the sergeant major curiously. The sergeant major had always seemed a broad, imposing man. But now, as Baeder spoke to him, he realised Pulver was a short bundle of wire and sinew.

Baeder was by no means a big man. Back at the schola tactica he had participated as a wrestler in the sixty-five kilogram division. Yet Pulver was even shorter and leaner, despite being twenty years his senior. The sergeant major had only seemed twice as large as he was through his presence. He had the brick wall disdain of a giant.

'What scares me is that it was easier than I thought it would be,' Baeder admitted. 'Razing that entire village to the ground. I... don't feel any guilt.'

'You squashed down that part of you. That's all. You might never get that back. Those people who weren't born to be combat officers, they won't ever understand that. Some do.'

It suddenly dawned on Baeder that Sergeant Major Pulver was making peace. He was bridging the rift that had been between them ever since Baeder had been assigned to the 88th. The days ahead would be hard. The battalion was already battered and they would likely lose many more. Pulver was cementing their leadership for battle. The resolve in Pulver's sun-creased face told him everything.

Baeder wasn't sure what to say. Only now did he finally understand the hostility that Pulver had shown him. The sergeant major had seen Baeder as just another officer who regarded the 88th as tactical fodder. The battalion was a single entity and Pulver was protecting it like a herd mother against anyone who would harm them, be it Archenemy or Imperial. In doing so, Pulver had made himself into a cold, logical automaton, he had given up the luxuries of compassion and choice. Baeder felt a surge of respect for the old veteran.

Pulver spat into the water. 'If we don't keep our men safe, no one will. High Command doesn't care about sending us to the meat grinder. It's us against them. That's all it is.'

'Fight and win,' Baeder said.

'Fight and win,' Pulver repeated.

THE BATTALION MOVED into what was considered the red zone by late afternoon. On their tactical maps, it encompassed a sixty-kilometre radius from where the siege-batteries were expected to be hidden. This was the heart of Dos Pares territory and, incidentally, it had been the target of a relentless bombing campaign since the early stages of war.

The signs of destruction became more evident the deeper the battalion travelled. At first there was a general thinning of the dense foliage. Further on, entire patches of jungle were flattened, visible even from a distance.

Imperial bombs had been thorough. It appeared as if pieces of rainforest had been entirely uprooted, and then wood splinters had been spread where acres of trees had once been. The shockwave of explosives flattened the areas surrounding bomb craters. Gum-saps, buttress roots, flowering cynometra, were all laid down in uniform direction. There was a strange order to the systematic destruction.

Although there was a tense, fragile silence in the air, the day passed without incident. It was not until twilight, when the sun was melting to a diffuse orange, that their overwatch flier voxed Baeder with an urgent message.

'Eight eight, this is Angel One.'

Baeder had become accustomed to that voice now. Although he had never met the pilot who had helped him time and time again, Baeder had often wondered what their saviour looked like. There was an omnipotence to Lieutenant Duponti's role. A distant, gravelly voice that had, on multiple occasions, saved the lives of his men. A voice without a face who hovered in the sky.

'Come in, Angel One. I'm reading you loud and clear,' Baeder voxed from the helm.

'I thought you should know, I may have found a loyalist village just two kilometres north-west of your current position. I picked up their distress frequency through a pre-war channel. They are requesting assistance.'

'What kind of assistance?' asked Baeder, suddenly wary. He immediately thought of a trap. This close to their objective, the insurgency would be trying everything to stop them.

'They are besieged and surrounded by a warband-strength insurgent element. There has been sporadic

Henry Zou

gunfighting for the past four hours. The village has managed to keep them at bay but it seems they are running out of ammunition. That's all I know from listening in on their broadcasts.'

'Do you think it's a trap?'

'The red zone is too hot for me to go low altitude. I'd be shot out of the sky so hard it'd knock the dirt off my boots. But they sound desperate enough over the vox. Plenty of screaming and crying. I can't speak to them directly, but I've been tuning in to their frequency for a good twenty minutes.'

'Could be a trap,' said Baeder, still unsure.

'Could be. Look, I'm not advising you whether or not to send assistance. But I thought I'd brief you on what I just picked up on my frequency.'

'Understood,' said Baeder.

'Whatever you decide, be careful, eight eight. This is deep hell we're in now.'

'Understood, Angel One. Stay on vox.'

Baeder heard Duponti whistle into his vox receiver. 'I can tell by your voice that you've already made up your mind to go in. I'll be on call. If things go wrong, I'll come down and hit hard. Over.'

'Right on, ramrod. Out.'

Duponti was right, of course, Baeder had already decided to gather a relief force. If these were loyalists, then he had a duty to protect them. Perhaps several months ago, that would have been Baeder's sole reason to gather a scouting party. But not any more. Now, all that mattered to Baeder was that his men needed water and, whether loyalist or not, the village would no doubt have a fresh supply. The monsoon season had faded for the past several days and they were parched. Clean water would go a long way to mitigating some of their ailments.

Try as he might, Baeder could not convince himself that he actually cared about whether the village truly needed help. It was simply a way to resupply their rations.

BAEDER AND SERPENT Company's Third Platoon beached their rubberised landers beneath the branches of a bomb-felled cynometra. The thirty men and their colonel spread out into an open file and swept inland under the cover of darkness. They hugged the riverbank north-west, keeping low by the rushes and moving quickly.

Baeder had chosen Third Platoon not because they were the best or most experienced, but simply because they were one of the few platoons at full fighting strength. The platoon commander was a Lieutenant Hulsen, a young officer on his first off-world campaign. Although he was a combat virgin, Hulsen was keen and possessed by the wide-eyed vigour of a newly-minted platoon commander. He wore a belt of grenades across his chest, chewed tabac without pause and swore too often. He had even managed to trade a meltagun from the base quartermaster. Baeder would have to keep an eye on the lieutenant's enthusiasm lest it ran rampant during the heat of engagement.

Pulver and Mortlock had both initially protested Baeder leading the relief force. Although it was agreed that the village was a potential water source, the threat of their battalion commander going into a trap did not sit well with the others. This far into their mission, the death of Baeder would plummet morale. Yet Baeder had insisted. Neither Pulver nor Mortlock were noted for their diplomacy and the siege would likely require more than brute force.

The platoon realised they were nearing the site of the distress beacon when the crump of a shotgun shattered the night. The shot was followed by a flurry of small-arms fire. Although it was too dark to make out anything, the direction of the shooting was clear enough to practised ears.

'Hulsen. Take a knee,' hissed Baeder as he settled down behind a waxy shrub.

'They're still fighting, then,' whispered Hulsen as he crouched down next to Baeder.

'Must be. If this siege is not some elaborate set-up, then we will need to reach the village without being caught in a crossfire. It's going to be dark and I don't want to be shot at by the very same indigs that we're here to help.'

Hulsen chewed vigorously, his jaw clenching and relaxing, his eyes wide in the gloom. 'What do you want me to do, sir?'

'We need to contact the village on their distress frequency, let them know we are going in. We need them to cover us as we make a run across the open ground. Then we'll curve up along the riverbank and enter the village from the river edge to avoid the crossfire. Understood?'

Hulsen punched the side of his helmet twice in acknowledgement. He hobbled away at a low sprint to find his vox-officer. Meanwhile, Baeder turned back to survey the land with his magnoculars. He filtered the lens into night vision and took a moment to adjust his vision.

The land was a two-dimensional monochrome green. He could see the village at two or three hundred metres to his front, the lights of the town appearing as white stars. In between the sporadic bursts of fire,

Baeder could make out defenders firing along the long village wall, and enemy gunmen hidden amongst the cassam paddies to the left of his platoon. It was obvious that the insurgents were amateurs. The very fact that the village had managed to keep them at bay told Baeder that the warband was too frightened to make any determined assault on the village. Instead, they skulked out in the rural fields, firing at the fortified town. They were probably hoping the villagers would run out of ammunition before they did. Any Imperial Guard platoon with good fire and movement could have taken that village in minutes.

After several tense minutes, Hulsen returned. 'Contact made, sir. We should get moving,' he hissed as he dropped down heavily beside Baeder.

Baeder immediately signalled for his men to rise. He slapped the helmets of his men as they ran past him. The platoon broke out into a sprint towards the walled town, rifles up and webbing swinging on their hips.

KALISADOR MANO MATO-BAREA racked his shotgun pump and fired over the barricade ledge. He crouched down quickly as the inevitable blast of counter fire kicked up sparks along the upper wall.

On the other side, he could hear the whoops and taunts of the insurgent raiders. They were creeping closer. Mano could feel them swelling with boldness as the hours dragged by, their insults getting louder and their laughter more cruel. Once he ran out of shotgun shells, the raiders would come and it would be a massacre. Mano loaded six into the breech, counting another twenty-four laid out on the ground in front of him. At the beginning of the day, the village had had five hundred shells saved up in storage, foraged and

bartered over the past months. They had been a precious insurance. He never imagined they would use up
everything in the span of a single day. Their situation
was so desperate now it did not even seem real.

The villagers were hiding in their homes, locked and
barred. If Mano strained to listen, he swore he could
hear sobs, faint and muffled, coming from the houses.
They knew that it was only a matter of time before the
raiders came. They all knew what fate awaited loyalist
villagers who refused to serve the Dos Pares.

A tracer whined overhead, followed by another ripple
of laughter.

Mano breathed heavily. He was too old to be doing
this. They had been fighting for four or five hours and
the adrenaline had long since passed, leaving him
drained. Kalisador Babaal squatted on his haunches
next to him. Leaner and younger, Babaal had spent
much of the day sprinting up and down the wall, firing
from different positions in order to keep the raiders
away. Mano had a difficult time keeping up with his
younger counterpart.

'If you give up now, we will allow your women and
children to live,' shouted a voice in the darkness.

'A curse on your ancestors!' Mano swore. He counted
to three and shoved the barrel of his shotgun over the
barricade. He fired three errant shots in rapid succession.

The exchange was followed by an awkward stillness.

Then the tiny phonetic vox placed next to Mano
began to whir and beep. It was an ageing device left in
the village by Ecclesiarchal preachers from when Mano
was just a young man. The wooden veneer was peeling
away and one of the mesh speakers was punctured.
Mano was not even certain they had been able to

broadcast distress pulses on old Imperial channels. Yet as the vox began fizzing with incoming signal, Mano's heart began to skip.

'Imperial channel bravo beacon. Do you read? Over.'

The voice coming through the speakers was barely a whisper, washed over by static, but Mano was sure he had heard correctly. He snatched up the metal transceiver from its stand and raised his voice without realising.

'Yes, receiving! We are the Mato-Barea people. We are in need of Imperial aid!' Mano screamed.

'We are a platoon-strength element of the 31st Riverine Amphibious. My men are on your map grid and will enter your village from the northern river-edge. Keep the enemy down with suppressing fire to your front. Out.'

Platoon-strength element. Those were the three sweetest words Mano could hope for. He decided, there and then, that the Emperor truly did watch over his people. He leaned over the barricade and fought with renewed hope, blasting shot after shot into the darkness. Babaal did the same and together they emptied out the remaining two dozen shells in an effort to aid their incoming rescuers.

The platoon arrived shortly after, vaulting over the left side of the village wall, where a disused plough reinforced multiple layers of rusted sheet. In the gloom he saw several dark figures drop over the wall. At first Mano thought they had been tricked. The men inside the barricade appeared to be no more than roughshod river bandits. They were the most ragged-looking Guardsmen Mano had ever seen. They looked nothing like the portraits of square-jawed soldiers depicted in those guidance pamphlets that their preachers used to hand out. These men wore ragged shorts and shredded boots, the remains of their uniforms faded to dirty white. Dreadlocked hair hung like manes from their shoulders, shaggy, brutal and wild.

But the way they moved showed they were unmistakably Guard. The troopers fanned out wordlessly to secure the perimeter of the wall. They moved quickly, setting up sectors of fire and creating intersecting arcs with heavy stub-gunners. Within seconds, the village was secured by Imperial Guardsmen who had not even spoken a word to either of the shocked Kalisadors in their midst.

Only then did a short, slim and unbearded officer approach them. Mano was not sure if it was just the waning moonlight or the angle of the shadows, but the small man seemed the most frightening out of all those hairy giants. He carried his lasrifle with bayonet fixed as if he were waiting to use it. His face was handsome, dark and slightly bat-like with an upturned nose and glinting eyes. His size was augmented by his brooding presence. In the Bastón tongue the officer had plenty of *Kamidero*, the closest translation in Low Gothic being – 'bad intentions'.

'Evening, friendo,' said the officer in a slow, drawling accent. 'Colonel Fyodor Baeder has come to save your soul.'

BAEDER HAZARDED A peek over the barricade with his magnoculars. In the grainy night vision he could see the humps of men hiding in the irrigation ditches of paddy fields. He counted sixteen men in his field of vision, loosely scattered in an arc roughly fifty metres away. He could not see if there were others, but Baeder expected there to be more men, hidden further away to provide covering fire.

Lieutenant Hulsen and Corporal Eckert crouch-ran over to Baeder's side. Eckert was young and his eyes were wide in the moonlight. He was clearly frightened.

'What's the plan, sir?' Hulsen whispered breathily.

'Let's flak them,' Eckert said. The corporal made ready to unpin a grenade from his web harness.

'No,' Baeder said, placing a hand over the corporal's chosen grenade for restraint. 'We're too close. They'll throw the grenade back. It's too much risk.'

Eckert licked his lips and peered over the barricade. 'I can hit them from here, sir. I can. It's no problem.'

Baeder shook his head again. 'No, corporal.'

But Eckert did not seem convinced. Baeder felt like a patient father chastising his over-excited son. He understood how Eckert felt. The atmosphere was charged with a quiet, deadly tension and the corporal wanted to dispel it with firepower. It was a natural instinct.

'Sir, let's finish this with flak,' Eckert pressed.

Hulsen did not have Baeder's patience. 'Damnit, Eckert! Shut the frag up! The colonel said no.'

Eckert fell silent with a thoroughly dejected look on his face.

Suddenly, a las-shot exploded against the barricade. The kinetic energy sent reverberations along the jigsawed metal. Baeder sank deeper down onto his haunches and put a hand over his helmet. A flurry of shots followed the first.

'Come out! Come out!' shouted one of the insurgents in a high-pitched stringy voice. There was a crackle of laughter.

Baeder pushed his lasrifle over the edge of the barricade and fired a string of blind shots. The laughter abated.

Lieutenant Hulsen cupped his hands over his mouth and shouted. 'Put down your arms and submit to Imperial authority!'

The insurgents mocked him in heavily accented Low Gothic. *'Purt down your arms and submeet to Eemperil'*. There was more laughter from the other side.

This made Baeder angry. 'Let's give them something to laugh about,' he grumbled. He realised that both sides were deadlocked, their weapons aimed to cut down any flicker of movement. Part of him began to panic, realising that perhaps he had exposed his men and himself to danger again. Risking a platoon for a water resupply was a reckless idea. He forced himself to suppress the thought and concentrated on the task at hand.

'Eckert, Hulsen,' said Baeder. 'Sieber, Noke, Hilversum, Bosch. I'm going to call flak! Ous?'

'Ous!' affirmed the men.

Eckert's edginess was replaced by a wide, tabac-smeared grin.

'Is this a good idea, sir?' Lieutenant Hulsen asked hesitantly.

Baeder shrugged. 'What other choice do we have to break this stalemate?' He waved his hand and clenched his fist three times for the others in the platoon. 'The rest of you, fix bayonets. You move when I move! Ous!'

'Ous!'

Baeder took a deep breath. The sting of fyceline cleared his head. Gun smoke and scorched metal. The smells helped to settle him. 'Flaks out!' he shouted.

Dark orbs were tossed through the air. They landed in the dry grass beyond the ditches with dry thuds.

Baeder put his hands to his ears and scrunched himself down. There was a concussive eruption of sound. The ground trembled. A drizzle of debris clattered off the back of his flak vest.

'Go, go! Move on me!' Baeder screamed above the ring of post-explosion. He rose and vaulted over the barricade. Smoke, white and solid, rose in coils. Baeder charged forwards and almost turned his ankle on the uneven ground. He slipped, but regained his balance. He couldn't see if his men were following him; he simply had to trust that they were.

The Carnibalès were surprised by his sudden appearance. Baeder found one of them crouched in a drainage ditch with his head down, fiddling with a grenade of his own. Baeder stabbed him with his bayonet between the shoulder blades and drove him into the mud. Las flashed in the smoke pall, pinks and incandescent whites. The screams were loud.

A Carnibalès rose out of the darkness. He appeared above the ditch, standing over Baeder. In the moonlight, his teeth were sharp and white, lined up neatly in a mouth that stretched from earlobe to earlobe. Baeder pulled up his lasrifle at the same time the insurgent brought his autogun to bear. But before either could react, the Carnibalès toppled sideways, his grin and half of his face crushed by a fen-hammer. A Riverine brought the hammer down again on the insurgent's prone form before rushing into the next ditch.

'They're running!' a Riverine shouted. 'We've got them running!'

Gripping his lasgun in blood-slicked hands, Baeder gave chase across the moonlit fields.

CHAPTER TWELVE

IT HAD BEEN a bad day for Mautista.

The sudden barrage of fire from the Mato-Barea walls had driven his warband away from their positions. Under the swift and unexpected assault, his guerrillas lost their nerve and ran. Mautista had no choice but to run with them. As they fled back into the rainforest, Mautista could not help but lament at his ill fortune. What had been the odds that he would engage Imperial military forces on his very first raid?

Certainly, Mautista had heard rumours that a large Imperial formation had been spearing inland. But the rumours had been fragmentary, drifting from village to village. The insurgency's spy networks were disparate and news often did not travel to the leaders until it was too late to be of use.

Mautista had not expected the enemy to be in his region. The last he had heard of it, the insurgency had gathered a force of some six thousand men – both Carnibalès and commoner – and ousted the Imperial force. At Lauzon it was believed they had beaten the Imperial troops into retreat. The Dos Pares had even distributed victory leaflets showing vivid illustrations of mutilated Imperial soldiers to the surrounding villages. Mautista had seen the leaflets himself; the Dos Pares claimed to have vanquished the enemy at Lauzon and released the survivors back to the coast with dire warnings for any other expeditions that might dare to probe inland. Evidently that had not been the case.

As the enemy gave chase, Mautista's warband dispersed into well-prepared escape holes. It was quite dark, but the enemy sent out searchers. Imperial soldiers with searchlights as well as village militia were thrashing the branches and shrubs in search of his guerrillas. Mautista lay in the hatchway of a tunnel, his upper body bare and covered by a fallen branch, watching the hunt. Not all of his guerrillas had managed to reach the tunnels that led back into the Dos Pares underground bunkers. Some, in their desperation, had crawled into prepared hiding places to wait out the search. As he lay in hiding with the torch beams of his pursuers sweeping over his hide, Mautista had a creeping doubt that perhaps Dos Pares propaganda had been inaccurate in their assessment of the enemy disposition. The armed Guardsmen that were hunting for him did not seem to fear him like the victory leaflets had claimed.

They found Balu first. Underneath some frond leaves the soldiers spotted the rim of a man-sized water pot buried in the soil. When the leaves were sifted aside, Balu was curled within. To his credit, Balu did not die without a fight. He hurled up a frag grenade from the pot. But the soldiers kicked the frag back over the rim and jumped away before it exploded. Just to be sure, the soldiers fired their lasguns several times into the pot, point-blank.

After some more digging, they found Phillero huddled within the buttress roots of a giant gum-sap. Mautista could not see what happened from where he lay, but he heard the las-shots and Phillero's dying yelp clear enough.

Then they found Caledo. Lifting a thatched lid, they discovered him wedged inside an escape tunnel that led deep into the Dos Pares bunker systems. Fortunately, Caledo knew what was at stake. He collapsed the entry by unpinning a grenade and holding it to his chest. The village militia who found him shouted in surprise and lunged away in all directions as the grenade went off.

To the relief of Mautista's rapidly accelerating heart rate, the pursuers then gave up. They milled about, laughing and talking and sharing tabac, but the hunting was done. They left soon after, their voices still echoing in the rainforest as Mautista extracted himself from the manhole. The remains of the warband reluctantly came out of hiding. There were only eleven men left.

'Everything fell apart today,' Canao said as they gathered by a camouflaged entry tunnel.

'Get in the tunnel,' Mautista snapped, his nerves fraying. The guerrillas, their faces gleaming with a day's sweat, looked at him with a mixture of fear and despair.

Canao ushered the insurgents into the bolt hole. 'Don't worry, we'll get some rest and begin tomorrow anew,' the veteran assured the others.

'No,' Mautista said flatly. 'No rest today. When we get back to camp no one will sleep until I say so. We are going to run fire and movement drills. We would not have been so shamed today if you lot had a shred of discipline,' he snarled.

There was a low murmur of complaint but no one dared to argue. They were beginning to fear their leader. Mautista was not sure whether Imperial officers ruled with fear, or whether they controlled their men through some other means. But as long as his guerrillas were terrified of him, there was hope for them yet.

As FAR AS calculated risks went, Baeder's gambit had paid off. The 88th Battalion unloaded over a thousand empty jerry cans from their supply barges and vessels. Seeker and Serpent Company formed a work chain from the boats all the way up to the catchment silos at the edge of the village. They passed empty containers from the vessels up the line. Sloshing, laden containers were relayed back down the line. They toiled under the gaze of sentry gunners. Both infantry on land and mounted guns on the river kept a vigilant watch of their surroundings.

Baeder joined in the labour at the front of the line. His arms burned as he plunged the canisters into the water silos, bubbling and gurgling as they filled to capacity. He hauled them, one in each hand, back down the ladder and towards the waiting work teams before receiving yet more empty ones. It was tiring work and, even in the breeze of midnight, he was lathered with sweat.

It was a great relief to Baeder's cramping forearms when the villagers arrived with midnight supper. Crustaceans, simmered in brine and bay salt, were placed in fish kettles on the ground, along with boiled cassam and vinegar. Guardsmen and villagers alike settled on the packed earth to share the shellfish: rural Bastón food in its simplest form. The battalion ate on shift rotations and Baeder kept watch. An officer never ate before his men, but when it came time for him to eat, Baeder did so with vigour. The cassam tubers were floury and still steaming, filling the stomach easily when dipped in salt and vinegars. Best of all were the various crustaceans of all sizes collected along the mud banks: spiny, clawed, segmented, yet all forms yielding a sweet white meat.

So it was with great reluctance that Baeder put down his cracked tail of crustacean as Kalisador Mano appeared amongst the supping and beckoned for him. The older Kalisador, with the thick heavy shoulders and hands, was skipping with joy.

'Colonel, I have something to show you. This you must see!' he said, his words tripping with liquor.

Wiping his mouth against a frayed sleeve, Baeder followed the Kalisador through the village. It was dark in the night, except for the ebbing blush of Persepian bombers in the far horizon. Baeder groped his way to a chapel that dominated the centre of the village. He understood that Mano was likely riding on the high of surviving to see morning, but whatever was making him so joyous made Baeder more than curious.

The chapel was an upright oblong with a pointed sloping roof. It was evident from its design that the locals had attempted to emulate the sharp angles and towering scale of Copto-Gothic architecture. But the effect largely fell flat by way of poor construction. Sections of the wall peeled away stiffly, an inevitable result of the rusting metal and wood frame that was common for most indigenous buildings. The chapel sagged several degrees to the side, and its long curtained windows gave it the bearing of a frowning old face.

Stepping inside, the chapel's interior matched its outer facade. Absent were the pews that Baeder expected. Instead an assortment of chairs, some plastek, some wood and some which resembled upturned crates, lined both sides of the chapel. A patchwork of reed rugs led up the centre aisle towards an Imperial shrine at the far end. There, above the candles, was displayed a large aquila, forged from old machine parts. It spread its corrugated wings above the shrine, heavy and dignified in a rough way. The worship shrine was a mix of Imperial votive offerings and local fetishism. It was a gaudy riot of bric-a-brac, piled together in contrasting lots. Ecclesiarchal volumes shared prominence with straw dolls, dried flowers were spread over priestly robes and multi-coloured candles burned slowly above the entire display.

Mano sat down on a rocking chair and produced a flask. He rocked on his chair and took a swig, looking out of the windows as if he had forgotten what he was doing. Another rocking chair beside him was empty. Baeder sat down next to him, waiting for him to speak. There they sat, rocking on chairs in silence, staring out into the horizon as bombs flashed.

'The Dos Pares, they have been on this world for much longer than the Emperor's servants,' said Mano finally. His voice was lowered to a reverential whisper.

Baeder pretended to nod knowingly. In truth, it was something he had not known. As far as the Imperial war effort was concerned, the Dos Pares was a populist sentiment of the insurgency, a rebellious movement that had arisen to challenge three centuries of Imperial rule. The notion that the Dos Pares had influenced the indigenous population since before Imperial settlement was something Baeder had never considered.

Two hundred and seventy years before, Imperial settlement fleets had touched down on the tropically abundant planet of Solo-Bastón. The indigenous tribes had welcomed the settlers and their Imperial missionaries as long lost human ancestry. The settlers brought with them new methods of agriculture, new customs and the teachings of the God-Emperor. All these things the indigenous tribes had embraced, blending into the folds of their tradition.

A peace had formed over the centuries. The Imperial government secured settlement on the coastal mainland and on outpost islands, building thriving metropoles of commerce and authority. In turn, the indigenous tribes maintained semi-rural cantons along the river systems, providing the central provinces with trade and taxation. Except for the jungle raiders from the heartlands, peace had been a stable commodity on Solo-Bastón.

'The Dos Pares were here before the days of settlement?' Baeder asked.

'Far longer. Back to the time of creation,' said Mano. 'But not like they are now. They were visitors from the sun and moon. I'll show you.'

Rising to his feet, Mano waded amongst the shrine ornaments, groping in the candlelight until he found what he was looking for. Slowly, he extracted a heavy object from the mess. He blew the dust from it, polished it with a flat of his palm, then brought it under the candlelight for Baeder to see.

Baeder felt his mouth slacken with involuntary shock.

Before him was a helmet. It was old. So very old that a rocky growth of mould grew like barnacles across its black-red surface. The full helm itself was very much like the ones worn by heroes of the Astartes Chapters, but there the similarities ended. Its grilled snout and slitted eyes were sculpted into a yawning, simian visage. Horns of polished ebony curled from its brow and a coif of chainmail trailed down the nape.

'What is that?' Baeder asked. Although he already knew the answer, and already dreaded the reply, he needed to hear it voiced by another man. Just so he could know he was not dreaming.

'It is a piece left behind by the visitors from the sky. We have revered this in our village for nine hundred years,' Mano declared, patting the helmet.

'May I see it?' asked Baeder hesitantly, both repelled and yearning to touch the helmet. He reached out with trembling hands and cupped it in his palms.

It was cold and heavy. Very heavy. Baeder had to clench his upper body just to hold up the twenty kilograms of solid ceramite. Upon closer inspection, the mould growth seemed organic to the helmet itself, bubbling up from the oily black surface. Despite its great age, there was no visible corrosion and the contorted cheekbones and crooked mouth looked freshly forged.

It was common knowledge that, in Bastón superstition, all inanimate objects contained a certain spirit. Plants could be sung to, and broken machinery coerced gently into operation. Holding the helmet in his hands, Baeder understood how such a myth could have been brought about. The helmet stared at him, not as a well-painted portrait would gaze upon a viewer, but stared *at him* with expression. Baeder gave it back to Mano and brushed his hands.

'This helmet changes expression. Sometimes it laughs, sometimes it cries and sometimes it is angry,' Mano said, confirming Baeder's tingling chill.

'These visitors, what did they do here?'

'Very rarely, sometimes not at all for many years, a village may have a sighting. When they do, these ghosts from the clouds choose the sturdiest village boys and spirit them away. This helmet is said to have belonged to a guro's son from a millennium ago, who was taken away to become one of the cloud ghosts. His helmet was returned to his kin as a mark of favour.'

Baeder slumped into his seat, blinking repeatedly. It did not bother him that these loyalist indigenes did not even know they were pawns of the Archenemy. Nor that they were unwilling heretics. It did not matter to Baeder. What put the fear into his core was the prospect that the Traitor Astartes were architects of this insurgency. The implication of this revelation was too much for him. He did not know what hand the Legions of Chaos were playing in this conflict. But the thought that his battalion could be the target of a scheme laid down by Traitor Astartes invoked a bowel-churning panic that he fought to quell.

'Mano. If I were you I would burn that thing.'

At this, the Kalisador's pudgy face was drawn into a frown. He hugged the relic close to his chest and angled it away from Baeder, as if to protect it. 'Why?'

Baeder shrugged. 'I do not hold any presumptions against you. But if men of an Ecclesiarchal leaning were to catch you with it, I expect even ten platoons of my battalion would not save your village.'

Mano sighed. He put down the helmet and resumed sitting next to Baeder. Again he grew quiet. 'It doesn't matter,' he concluded. 'You will leave and the Carnibalès will return. There is nothing left for us to do.' Mano rocked on his chair, drinking, lost in his own thoughts as the faraway bombing continued.

CHAPTER THIRTEEN

THE BRIDGE OF the *Emperor's Anvil* was frantic with activity. A single long-range vox from the 88th Battalion declaring that the battalion had reached the red zone had spurred the entire war effort into high alert. It was the clarion call they had been waiting for.

Above the throb of engines, the hiss of boilers and creaking of steel, boots pounded the decking. In the bridge room, movement and noise were predominant. There were too many officers wedged into a narrow space trying to do too many things at once. The relay of information between vox and staff became a slurred babble.

At high anchor on the Pan-Spheric Ocean, aboard every Argo-Nautical in the combat fleet, klaxons began to wail. It was a call to arms. All Imperial elements were to prepare for deployment.

In the officers' mess aboard the *Iron Ishmael*, onboard speakers commanded all officers to return immediately to their units. Guardsmen mobbed the corridors, all streaming towards their designated stations. As of 19.00, stand down for the Caliguan forces in reserve ended. They were to be at full readiness by midnight at the hour of zero.

Guardsmen crowded the flight deck. A restrained sense of excitement rippled amongst the assembled soldiers. The *Emperor's Anvil* was making steam, getting ready to sail.

Major General Montalvo stood on a platform raised below the antennae masts to address the assembled men. His speech was short and direct. 'Gentlemen. After so much waiting, we announce our presence. Make them fear us. Make their children's children remember the day they chose to fight the Imperial Guard.'

The Nautical fleet bellowed with sonorous engines, preparing to sail unmolested towards the Bastón coast. The energy was building as Guardsmen spread word that a Riverine battalion was on the verge of reclaiming the mainland's super-heavy defences. After months waiting at sea, the Guardsmen were eager to put their boots on dry land.

Within the troop holds of the Argo-Nauticals, Caliguan Motor Rifles were rousing from months of stand-down. In the cavernous docking bellies, tens of thousands of Caliguans were preparing their transports and organising their gear. Chimeras, armoured trucks, Trojan support vehicles parked in rows, were getting fuelled.

The atmosphere was one of loose, steady calm. Caliguan Guardsmen joked and talked as they went about their business. Although the call for action would likely be hours if not days away, every soldier was required to be on standby.

Guardsmen rattled through their labours, already laden with heavy webbing rigs and weapons. Over their padded brown jumpsuits were chest rigs with bulging pockets. With lasguns strapped to their chests, the Guardsmen rested their hands over their combat gear and waddled like pregnant women.

Despite their personal load, the Caliguan Guardsmen were stocking equipment up the rear ramps of their Chimeras. The cramped confines were stacked with boxes of ammunition, rations, grenade satchels, missile tubes, mortars and tanks of water. Considering the bulky personal combat load of each Guardsman, fitting into the vehicles would be an art in itself.

As the men worked, officers went from track to track, distributing stimms and dip for what would be an extended combat operation. The stimms would keep them alert and chewing dip promoted aggression. Alertness and aggression were the cornerstones of a Guard assault. Grimly, preachers followed in their wake, distributing last rites. The ship's bay sirens whooped every quarter-hour, marking down the time to deployment. There was a sense of bravado compelled by urgency that electrified the air.

Five hours after the call to deploy, General Montalvo toured the staging areas in person, travelling from ship to ship. Everywhere he went, Guardsmen scrambled to their feet. Tabac was stamped out by thick-soled boots. The men roared, a ferocious sound that was not quite a cheer nor a gesture of any civilised sort. It was just an expulsion of pent-up energy.

'It's time. It's time,' was all the general said.

For the final hours until they received word to mount up, the troops slept in their gear, rifles by their sides, on the metal decking of the staging areas. Officers tried to maintain their energy by parading them in platoon, then in company order, then platoon again. Restless, anxious and ready, the men thirsted for the call.

Sixty thousand Caliguan soldiers were at bay like hunting dogs, ready to be uncaged. Alongside the Persepian infantry, over one hundred thousand men pre-empting a single vox-signal. They would wait for the siege-batteries to fall quiet. When that time came, they would let the Carnibalès know – *'The Imperial Guard are coming for them'.*

THE TORRENTIAL RAIN doused the burnt jungle sodden. Precipitation churned the ash into a wasteland of silvery grey mud flats. The swathes of rainforest that remained were yellowed by defoliant, wilting like overcooked vegetables. Baeder found it hard to believe that the Archenemy insurgents still managed to resist from the interior despite the destruction.

But resist they did.

Strung up, crucified on X-beams of wood, were heat-swollen corpses. Initially, Baeder had spotted them along the riverbank, black and bulbous. From a distance they had looked like knapsacks and Baeder had not recognised what they were. It was only when the wind changed direction, carrying with it the saline stench of rot, that he realised they were the remains of the PDF troops. Evidently, they served as warning.

Ignoring the enemy theatrics, Baeder trained his magnoculars out into the distance, setting the aperture to maximum zoom. He could see the rising swell of the Kalinga Curtain, a ridge of limestone hills approximately eight kilometres to the north. Those limestone hills were layered long ago by the calcium deposits of corals and brachiopods within prehistoric reefs. Over the millions of years, monsoons had sculptured a one-kilometre chain of naturally defensible ground that the Bastón tribes had fought to control ever since the beginning.

According to intelligence, those hills would be their target. They appeared as a spine of bumpy hillocks, ravines and intrusions draped in floristic growth. Although bombing had gouged balding chunks of flora from the hillsides, the forests on the steep scree slopes were hardy. Growing in tight, irregular clumps, they clung to rock shelves and crevices, almost in defiance of the Imperial bombs.

It was little wonder that the PDF had chosen the Kalinga Curtain as the housing station for the mainland's defence batteries. Somewhere among the rugged limestone blocks, the colossal super-heavy guns were bunkered down. External military compounds studded the hilltops and hollows. Kalinga would be crawling with insurgent forces. The siege-batteries were their lifeline, with which the insurgency controlled the mainland and its surrounding waters.

This close to their objective, the battalion could no longer afford to traverse the Serrado Delta. They deviated into a minor river system. According to their maps, a minor river spur to the west ended in a blunt-headed pool three kilometres upriver. The enclosed body of water would be a defensive position for the battalion to set up camp in preparation for their final push.

For once, the maps proved accurate. At the waning of the day, the 88th Battalion made camp at a river basin with the Curtain just nine kilometres to their northwest.

Baeder estimated they would reach their target in less than half a day's sail, but first they would need to

prepare to survey thoroughly. The vessels were moored
and the men pitched camp on land, allowing them to
stretch out their sea legs.

This was a dangerous time, Baeder knew. His Guardsmen were at the limits of physical exertion. But more
than physical depletion, there existed the danger of
complacency. They were accustomed to the constant
terror of ambush now. After so long out in the wilderness, Baeder knew men could stop paying attention to
danger. At the beginning, fear and paranoia drove them
to remain vigilant, guns armed and eyes keen. But after
days and days, the men could begin to lose their edge.
The constant grind of remaining watchful would begin
to wear thin. He had seen Guardsmen forget about covering fire, disregard flank security or forget to post
sentries. He worried that the extended operation made
his men almost contemptuous of their situation.
Baeder was determined not to allow that to happen.

As the men settled in, chemical fires were not per-
mitted, for fear of giving away their position. Gun pits
were dug and double sentries were posted. Baeder
voxed Angel One and gave the aviator clearance to fire
on anything suspicious. He made it clear that the overwatch flier should fire on anything that was not within
the camp perimeter. The battalion was on wartime
footing.

WHILE THE BATTALION rested, Baeder went to work.

He handpicked a ten-man squad of the battalion's
most light-footed Guardsmen. Back on Ouisivia, these
men had lived the lives of trackers, swamp huntsmen
or thieves. But here, Baeder needed their talents to
accompany him on a scouting mission, deep into the
Kalinga Curtain. They would sidle up close to their

enemy so they would know what they faced. Initially, Mortlock had protested Baeder's involvement in such a dangerous task. But the colonel had insisted. After all, he would be in command of the final operation and therefore would benefit most from firsthand assessment of the enemy positions.

The selected squad assembled on an assault lander at midnight. Their faces were darkened with ash mud and they had bathed in river water to scour away their heavy scent. They pushed out into the estuary and carved up a narrow channel towards the Curtain. On the map, the narrow canal was a shoestring artery that would carry them to within less than a kilometre of the Curtain, a perfect run for the scout team.

They made their way very slowly in order to minimise engine noise. Overall command of their scout operation was given to Corporal Schilt. Although there were two sergeants and a lieutenant present, Baeder made certain that no one in the squad would contradict the corporal's expertise. Schilt was by far the most experienced of them all. A ragged, skeletal man, Baeder knew Schilt had been a gun for hire in the port cities of Ouisivia. Why he chose to join the Guard, Baeder did not know and it was probably better not to ask, yet Schilt had already served in the regiment for three years. In that time, Schilt had accumulated more gretchin kills while patrolling the fens than any other Guardsman Baeder had known.

The little gretchin who infested the steaming wetlands were notoriously hard to kill; wily and elusive, catching them was likened to grappling with eels. During the hotter months, gretchin spread like an infection, swelling in numbers so great that they threatened the major trading routes between parishes. It took a special sort of man to be able to sneak behind a gretchin and strangle it dead, but Schilt was that man. He held a record of eighty-nine gretchin kills and two swamp orks, all without taking any return fire. Instead, he preferred garrotte wire.

Confident in his team's abilities, Baeder was content to let his men direct the course for once. It was a dark night, as was often the case during the wet season, with the moon choked by dark clouds. At all times, a Guardsman stood upright on the bow, scanning the canal banks. They did not want to run into an insurgent patrol so close to their objective.

Two kilometres out from the Curtain, the team powered down the outboard motor and laboured the vessel up onto the bank. Taking care to cover the inflatable with branches and sod, the team decided to cover the rest of the way on foot.

On land, the task at hand suddenly seemed far more real. The enemy would be close by. Fog clung to the ground in vaporous clouds. The team crouched amongst shrubby pinwheel flowers, bobbing from cover to cover. Schilt halted the team every so often to confer with Baeder's maps, the pace counters and team auspex. They kept up a murderous pace, shooting nervous looks at the sky for fear of dawn.

The Curtain loomed above them when Baeder's team encountered their first enemy patrol. 'Heads up!' Schilt had hissed urgently. He flashed the field signal for enemy. The team auspex began to chime and was switched off hastily in order to maintain their stealth.

Baeder went to ground along with the rest of his men. He peered intently into the night, holding his breath. He dared not open his mouth for fear that it would echo the pounding of his heart. He saw movement, like shadow puppets at first. Then, one by one, the enemy emerged from the dense fog. Baeder counted six. Six insurgents in rural garb, their silhouettes spiked with weaponry. Judging by the slump of their shoulders, the drooping of their heads and their lurching gaits, the men were tired. It was late in the night and it was probable that the insurgents had been patrolling for some time. Inexperience and weariness had dulled their alertness. Baeder aligned one of the insurgents with the ironsight of his lasgun and coiled his finger over the trigger.

Had Schilt chosen to, they could have wiped out the entire patrol. But that would have alerted the Archenemy. Instead, the team lay in wait, allowing the patrol to pass by no more than five metres in front. They waited until the last of the insurgents had disappeared back into the fog before they broke cover and continued on.

The team dared to press on until they spotted a chain-link fence intersecting the thinning jungle. They had finally reached the ex-PDF compound that occupied the Kalinga Curtain. Beyond the wire netting they could see the rocky scree slopes of limestone. Around the rocky slopes sprawled a military installation. Baeder immediately began to take notes in his fieldbook.

The Kalinga installation occupied a fenced rectangle of roughly a kilometre in length. Its perimeter followed the jagged contours of the Kalinga Curtain, making use of the natural rocky defences. It was a large installation with rockcrete blockhouses that studded the hillsides. Many had been laid open by repeated bombing attacks and the parade grounds at the fore were scorched and cratered. Despite the damage it had endured, the compound would be difficult to assault. The only opening that Baeder could see was a docking bay which stretched out into the Serrado Delta on the west side of the compound. It would be a perfect position for them to commit the 88th's water assets, but Baeder had no doubt the pier-approach would be well defended by hidden firing positions. Further up the Kalinga Curtain, Baeder could spot large openings cut into the rock face. It suggested that the siege-batteries had resisted aerial destruction because they were deeply embedded below ground. More than that, it confirmed the intelligence reports that the compound had an underground complex as well.

The team surveyed the perimeter as well as it could, sweeping the area with the auspex. They did not linger for long, as sentry towers spread out along the perimeter probed the jungle with sweeping searchlights. They flitted like rodents, snatching in and out of the trees, never straying far from the curtain of foliage. Fear of discovery was a tense constant and, while some worked feverishly to sketch rough plans and make auspex scans, the others kept watch with their lasguns. According to the auspex, Baeder noticed that no insurgents lingered above ground in the compound's external blockhouses, save for the sentries up in the towers. They probably huddled underground, manning the siege-batteries.

In five minutes they were done. On their way back, the team avoided another patrol of insurgents. But by now they had found their rhythm. They barely took any notice of the Archenemy patrol, going to ground and circling away from the undisciplined rebels.

The trouble did not start until they returned to their boats. By then it was almost dawn and the sky was a lighter shade of dark blue. The team piled into the inflatable and pulled on the outboard motor. Yet the motor would not catch, not even after the sixth or seventh pull.

'Chaos witchery!' Schilt spat, slapping the side of the motor.

'No, it's damn Ando Tate and his boys,' swore Baeder, thinking back to his conversation on base with his old friend the colonel. It seemed another lifetime ago. 'He never could fix a boat,' Baeder concluded.

It was a precarious situation. They paddled the boat out into the channel and Baeder began to work on the motor. Sergeant Asper, a former fen trapper with a good hand for maritime mechanics, added his expertise to the laid-open wires. They adjusted, shook and fiddled. Everyone else formed a defensive perimeter along the banks. They would have to stay alert. Dawn was creeping up on them.

As he dug around the wires, Sergeant Asper shook his head in wry amusement. 'Irony,' he said. 'I used to lay traps in the wetlands during the night. In the dawn I would begin to follow my trapping lines and collect the nets. Those rodents always looked at you with such terrified eyes. I often wondered how it felt to be snagged in the dark, knowing by morning, the huntsman would find you. Now I know.'

Finally, after a frustrating twenty minutes of the engine almost catching, sputtering and dying, Baeder gave up. The sky was a ruby pink and he was determined not to put the battalion at jeopardy so close to the end. Fear hunched the shoulders of the men around him. Not fear of death, Baeder knew, but fear that discovery would give away their only advantage of a surprise assault. Fear that they would die a pointless death out here without being able to advance with their comrades into the final fray. That thought resolved Baeder.

'We're moving out now,' he said, lowering himself into the chest-deep water. The early morning canal was shockingly cold.

The other nine slipped into the black water and with one hand on the boat, the other holding their lasguns above the waterline, they began to tread like pallbearers. The sides of the canal bank rose a metre or so above their heads and Schilt was the only one who sat in the craft. He crouched near the bow, peering above the bank onto the land so he could scout for possible enemy movement.

They had not been going long when two things seemed to happen at once. An early morning rain suddenly pummelled from the sky, so abruptly it was as if someone had turned open a tap above them. At the same time, Schilt clambered down from his perch and hissed into Baeder's ear, 'I see enemy movement along the shore, fifty metres parallel to us.'

'How many?' asked Baeder, suddenly shivering from the rain and enemy presence.

'I can't peep through the rain. I don't think they've peeped us either.'

Baeder passed the word along to the other boat pullers. Their speed increased dramatically, slogging double pace through the syrupy water, boots sinking deep into the tissue-like mud. If the Archenemy were to suddenly appear over the lip of the canal, there would be nowhere for the team to go.

Baeder closed his eyes and let the rain run over his face. Above the gushing raindrops against the canal he tried to listen for enemy movement. He strained for voices. The clatter of weapons. The sound of an auto-gun being cocked. He heard nothing. But although he heard nothing, Baeder trusted Schilt, and without question. He never second-guessed his men. Every man in the battalion was a combat veteran and what they said stood. It was something that many other officers over-looked.

It was a tense and tiring march. The muscles of Baeder's left arm and shoulder, pulling the boat, were soon throbbing with lactic build up. He felt as if every bone had been teased out of its socket. He could almost see waves of pain radiating out from his hands. The mud below denied them proper purchase, pulling at their boots, sinking them down and slowly draining their efforts. Schilt kept watch, ducking down every so often. It was to their misfortune that the enemy seemed to be following the canal as a patrol route. Baeder did not pray often. But he prayed to the Emperor that they would soon turn back before the rain stopped.

After an hour, the team had to rest. Their webbing was cutting their shoulders raw. Everything ached. Wallowing in the water, Baeder rolled his neck back on his shoulders and stretched out his muscles. He opened his eyes and sucked down several chest-expanding breaths. He looked at the overcast sky, still pouring with rain. What he saw made his heart skip.

There, in the clouds above he saw a winking light. Moving slowly towards them.

Baeder knew it would be Angel One, their overwatch pilot. He also remembered, instantly, that he had given Angel One clearance to fire on anything that was beyond the battalion's secure perimeter. No doubt the aviator, from his high vantage point, would see only an irregular man-made blip on his surface radar, moving

down the canal in the direction of the Imperial camp.
There was also no doubt that Angel One would consider them an open target.

Swearing, Baeder vaulted up onto the inflatable like
a surfacing fish. 'Schilt, vox-channel to auxiliary frequencies! Right now!' he hollered, slapping the side of
the boat for emphasis. All pretence of stealth was lost.

Schilt dragged the bulky vox-pack over to him and
began to key frequencies. Unfortunately, it was only a
small-squad level vox and Angel One's channel had not
been set into the system. They could not reach Angel
One directly. Rather they could only broadcast on an
open channel in the hopes that Angel One would be
monitoring. Angel One was not. They received no
response.

Baeder rocked back on his haunches and scratched
his head. He tried to remain composed in front of his
men. The team murmured in helplessness. They shook
their heads. It slowly dawned on them that the
Persepian aviator was going to hunt them down.

'Vox back to battalion. Have them reach Angel One,'
Baeder said. He breathed out hard, trying to maintain
control.

Schilt voxed but received no response. He voxed
again, still no response. The winking light was closer
now, dropping in altitude. Schilt adjusted the antenna,
daring to unfold it above the canal edge so that it could
be seen from the bank.

The vox suddenly blared to life, startling Baeder. The
volume had been toggled to its highest setting on their
previous desperate attempts and the response was unexpectedly loud. It cut above the rainfall and echoed across
the wilderness. Cursing, Baeder dimmed the volume setting repeatedly and snatched the handset from Schilt.

'Scout element, this is eight eight. Report, over.'

'Eight eight. We are trapped in Angel One's fire zone. Danger close. Give orders for Angel One to cease fire clearance, over.'

There was a pause at the other end. The pause became agony as the winking light lurked closer. The aircraft almost appeared to glide overhead, but then it rolled a tight turn and began to head straight for them.

'Scout element, this is eight eight. We can't do it, sir. Haven't been able to reach Angel One all morning due to heavy rainfall and dense cloud cover. You should be in range to reach Angel One on your vox, but we don't have range to establish contact.'

'Fine!' said Baeder, almost shouting. 'Give me his operational frequency.'

'Sir. Uh, we'll have to find it. It's written down in a book somewhere…'

Baeder almost howled with frustration. He slammed the handset against the receiver. The strike-fighter was so close now they could make out its silvery outline in the sky. The war cry of its engines was growing and it was dropping for a strafing run along the canal. Some of the team leaned back against the canal slope in resignation, still standing in the water. They began to take out tabac from soggy upper pockets and tried to light them. Sitting across from him, Corporal Schilt regarded him with a look of hatred that Baeder found difficult to reconcile.

'Sierra Echo. This is eight eight. Angel One op frequency is one zero niner, niner zero eight. Coordinate grid breaker-eight-bravo–'

Baeder cut the operator off before he finished speaking. They could hear the whine of the strike-fighter's engines, becoming louder. As Baeder keyed the frequency with trembling fingers, he could imagine Angel One arming his hellstrike missiles and locking them on target.

There was a click.

'Eight eight secondary, this is Angel One. I'm a little busy right now–' said a familiar voice.

'Angel One, cease clearance! Cease clearance!' Baeder screamed. 'Don't fragging fire!'

'Affirmed,' said Angel One.

The strike-fighter levelled out. It roared overhead, just two hundred metres above. Baeder could see the tips of the hellstrike missiles racked on the wings, primed for them. As an infantryman, he had never before felt so helpless in the face of complete and over-whelming firepower.

'Eight eight secondary, this is Angel One. Was that a friendly?'

Baeder lay down in the inflatable, his heart drumming in his chest. 'Yes, Angel One. Am I glad to hear your voice.'

The crackly baritone chuckled politely. 'You're always glad. When we mop up this mess, you owe me a mether.'

'Make that two or three, Angel One. Out.'

As Baeder lowered himself back into the water, amidst the backslaps and whispered cheers of his men, he could not help but wonder if the angels of prehis-toric scripture were all just aviators with prophetic call signs.

CHAPTER FOURTEEN

THE SIGHT OF a Chaos Legionnaire thunderous with anger was not something that bore thinking about. It was akin to witnessing an earthquake, or an avalanche of multi-thousand tonnage hurtling down a mountain. There was a paralysing awe to its scale that instilled a hopeless vulnerability in those who saw it. It made Mautista feel meek and fragile.

It was worse when two Chaos Legionnaires were as equally displeased as each other.

Gabre and Sau seethed darkly in their command bunker, their enormous frames perched atop thrones of sandbags. They were both stripped of their armour and clad only in loincloths. Every so often they would slam their fists as they muttered to each other in a staccato language Mautista could not understand. Their white-painted bodies twitched angrily, each slab of muscle separately laid atop another muscle like overlapping sheathes of hard chitin. Sitting there as they did, they looked like furious barbarian kings, ready to cast judgement.

Ready to cast judgement on Mautista, who knelt before them.

'The Imperials have entered our region of operations, you say?' muttered Gabre, his face deeply shadowed by the sodium lanterns that burned dim.

'Yes,' said Mautista, unsure of what else to say.

'Then the Lauzon Offensive failed to dislodge them from our sides,' said Sau to nobody in particular. He gripped his big, blunt fingers into the sandbag his arm rested on. It popped like a dry blister with no effort at all.

'Tell me again. What happened?' Gabre said, placating his brother with a hand on his shoulder. The two Legionnaires had been doing so since Mautista first reported his findings. One would drive himself into a furious anger and the other would calm him down to a level of coherency. Then it would happen again in reverse. The Pair had a strange, almost symbiotic relationship that unsettled Mautista.

'I took my warband out to the Mato-Barea Canton. We encountered Imperial soldiers in the night. Judging by their firepower, I would say at least one hundred or more. We were broken and chased back into the jungles where they did not follow,' Mautista said. He was too frightened to mention that they had spent the better part of the day pinned down by two rural custodians with shotguns.

The Pair rose up from their thrones. Although Mautista's chemical treatments had nourished another two centimetres of growth from his pain-wracked body in the past week, the Pair were still head and shoulders taller than him. They were also three times as broad and Mautista was sure at any moment they would strike out with their bone-stud knuckles and break him apart. But the Pair had no intention of punishing him. They had no further intentions of even paying Mautista any attention. They crossed over to their planning maps and began murmuring to each other in low, terse tones.

'It could be a stray Imperial patrol,' Mautista offered hesitantly.

Gabre waved him away. 'Never.'

'A patrol would never come this far inland, to do so would require extended fuel and rations. That would require planning,' Sau said.

'No doubt, Imperial elements this close to our region denotes a planned mission,' said Gabre.

'They are planning an assault on the Earthwrecker,' Sau concluded.

Of course they were. Mautista had twice visited the Kalinga Curtain, once when he was issued his recruit weapon, and the second time when he was ordained a Disciple. He had seen the enormous super-heavy cannon that resided deep within the hills. The enormous machine rested on rail-tracks and could be wheeled deep into the hillside caverns to prevent its destruction by Imperial bombs. On his second visit, Mautista had even been fortunate enough to witness the weapon lob a shell hundreds of kilometres out into the ocean beyond. It had delighted Mautista when the super-heavy weapon had fired a thirty-tonne shell from a barrel so big that he had only seen the tip of it peeking out from an opening in the hillside. The muzzle flame from its discharge was a horizontal cloud, orange and black, that was actually larger than the entire Kalinga

Curtain itself. The gas and smoke from the single shot drifted up into the sky and blotted out the sun for several minutes. For kilometres around, the earth trembled and the jungle fell into a hushed silence in the wake of its firing. With it, Mautista was sure they could win the war. It was little wonder that the Imperial Guardsmen were seeking to reclaim it.

'Brother Jormeshu will go and prepare the defences at Kalinga,' Mautista heard Gabre say to Sau.

'You will go too,' said Gabre, suddenly turning on Mautista. 'The Kalinga will need as many Disciples as we can spare to defend it. The insurgency will need leaders there.'

Mautista nodded obediently, glad to be given the chance to redeem his earlier failure. He rose from the dirt floor with a click of swollen knees and saluted, as he had been taught.

Gabre anchored a heavy palm on Mautista's shoulder. 'You no longer fear death, do you?'

'No, Gabre. I do not,' Mautista replied.

'Then we will have a punishment far worse than death for you, if you fail so thoroughly again.'

For the first time since he had followed the Primal State, Mautista became reacquainted with fear. It had become such a distant memory that he had forgotten its acidic, spiteful resonance. Not even with all the chem-treatments, mental conditioning and martial skill at his disposal, did Mautista wish to incur the judgement of the Four. He made up his mind, quite certainly, that he would rather die than fail.

By THE ONE hundred and forty-first day of the uprising, most of the Imperial cities had barred their gates to those of indigenous blood.

Never on Bastón had the enemy been so brazen as to besiege an Imperial city. But outside the walls of Fortebelleza, thousands of heretics and Carnibalès fighters had erected a makeshift camp. Their numbers grew every day, a swollen sea of protestors engulfed the city limits. From the walls, Governor Alton relayed to High Command – 'Never before have these natives displayed such bold disregard for Imperial edict. They dare to dissent within the gates of my city in utter contempt for the authority I indisputably hold.'

They erected shrines of worship. Totemic pillars of stone. The citizens of 'belleza declared that there were mutants among those heretics, horribly metamorphic beings changed by their worship of foul idols. Military Intelligence reported that insurgency support in the rural hamlets had spiked, Carnibalès numbers were believed to have quadrupled and incidences of raid and ambush had increased to the point where it was no longer prudent to send single platoons on patrol.

At Fortebelleza, a one hundred strong company of Riverine manned the walls but could do nothing. Without supplies, especially ammunition from the Persepian fleet, the Riverine vanguard could only remain effective for so long. Yet still the insurgency grew as the Imperium watched and waited.

JORMESHU SURVEYED THE blisters of low rock that formed Kalinga from his lookout nest. Before him the hills were strung out six hundred metres to his left and five hundred to his right. It was a long strip, rugged and broken. It would be difficult to assail the natural fortress, of this he was certain.

The plated giant was surrounded by Carnibalès veterans and painted Disciples, a retinue of forty or so who crouched or squatted around his armoured shins like scholam children. Dwarfed in his right gauntlet, Jormeshu cupped a data-slate. His left hand was bare and manipulated a tiny sliver of stylus, thick fingers sweeping angles and trajectory calculations on the display screen. The left gauntlet, segmented and bruised, was hooked to the tuille of his thigh-plate.

'The above-ground complex is poorly planned and not easily defensible,' he said, taking in the entire hill range with a sweep of his arm. 'The terrain is far too herbaceous, dense, covered. It will be no good.'

The external compound above-ground was a narrow ribbon of mesh fencing that housed multiple block-houses the PDF had once used as barracks and command posts. Due to the sloping gradient an irregular forest knotted the limestone. Small trees clung with their roots penetrating deep into the rock. The PDF who had constructed the compound had a poor grasp of siege strategy, Jormeshu lamented. Even with the past Imperial bombing scarring the area into a leprous, balding carpet of greenery, there were still ample trees to provide any assaulting force with cover to advance.

'We could attempt to fell some of the jungle close to the compound,' suggested a Carnibalès propagandist, a demure man in spectacles and grey rural garb.

'No time. The Imperials could attack at any moment,' Jormeshu countered. 'Besides,' he said, pointing towards the west, 'we could not properly deny the docking bay and hangars from enemy entry. This compound was not built to withstand a siege.'

The docking pier at the further western edge of the compound posed a defensive problem. It led straight from the Serrado Delta into wide-mouthed hangars which provided entry into the underground complex.

Jormeshu was a pragmatist. He would not attempt to hold what could not be held. Instead he would allow the Imperial forces to come that way and funnel them into the killzone within the compound.

'I have two hundred fighters in my warband. I can hide them well amongst the buildings and trees,' offered a shaven-headed Disciple by the name of Novera. He was one of the earliest Disciples; at least one of the surviving ones. He had received over four months of chemical treatments and it had ravaged his body, holes opening in clusters across his skin. All the Disciples who had been initiated alongside Novera were now dead, killed in fighting or dying to the mutagenic chemicals. Jormeshu valued Novera's leadership amongst the Carnibalès: he could not spare the man to die in the initial onslaught.

'No,' Jormeshu shook his head. 'Sixty men led by two other Disciples, no more, will be hidden in the above-ground complex. The rest will be needed elsewhere. Sixty will be enough to worry the Imperial assault and delay them.'

Booby traps too, thought Jormeshu. Pit traps, grenade rigs, mines. They would seed the entire hillside and docking bay with traps. Instead of allowing the Imperial forces the open fight they no doubt craved, Jormeshu would lure them into an abandoned complex filled with traps and hidden snipers. It would sap the aggression of an enemy when they charged ashore.

It would be below ground in the hollow belly of the Kalinga Curtain that the real fighting would begin… provided the Imperial soldiers made it that far.

In the warrens below, Kalinga resembled the inner belly of a fortress. Bunkers, storage units and winding tunnels. Jormeshu knew that, since Disciple Mautista had revealed that the Imperial force was still en route to the siege-batteries, the Carnibalès had been roused into renewed activity. Within the hill fortress the troops were preparing in their own way.

Jormeshu had never seen such fervent prayer to the Ruinous shrines. Many displayed their mutations proudly, no longer hiding them beneath leather bandages. Glorious mutation was rife and over thirty of their number had received the ultimate favour of the gods, transformed into Chaos spawn. Those beasts, all maw and tentacle, were now chained in the storage basements for release at Jormeshu's tactical discretion. Within the workshops, guns and explosives were manufactured at a double pace. The rural workers did not sleep.

Of the actual defences inside the underground, gun nests were erected at regular intervals within the tunnels. Ammunition caches were hidden in strategic locations. The rebels were possessed by a belligerent certainty. They were becoming bloodthirsty.

Despite this, in his heart Jormeshu expected the insurgents to be pushed back by the Imperial Guard. In the event that the Guardsmen made it inside the hill fortress in any significant numbers, Jormeshu knew that it would degenerate into bitter hand-to-hand fighting. He had lived war for centuries and held no illusions that even with superior numbers the rural rebels would not have great difficulty in a clash with the Guardsmen. They were Imperial Guard and, in Jormeshu's experience, those fighting men proved remarkably resilient and were capable of bravery that often exceeded his expectations. Jormeshu would not underestimate them. He kept these thoughts to himself. It would be folly to dishearten his minions.

'These Imperial warriors are hard fighters. Do not mistake their false theology for poor soldiering,' Jormeshu said to his assembled retinue.

Warlords of Chaos often disparaged the fighting ability of the Imperium, considering them weak and breakable. It was, in Jormeshu's opinion, a foolish thing to do. Belittling a capable opponent brought about nothing but complacency. Complacency brought about mistakes.

'Can they compare to us? We've been winning this war, have we not?' snorted Tsivalu, an insurgent veteran whose nostrils were pugnaciously bovine, with a sloping, knurled eyebrow ridge. The retinue chorused their agreement.

Jormeshu grumbled, a deep sound that echoed from the cavities of his expansive chest. He commended their bravado, but no amount of faith could account for the fact that even the most hardened Chaos veteran at his command had been fighting for no more than half of a year. The Guardsmen had been fighting for most of their adult lives, ferried from warzone to warzone. He did not doubt the aggression, ferocity and fanaticism of the Carnibalès, but he held no illusions as to their discipline and training.

'You will need every edge we can muster. Do not fall lax or the blood that bleeds will be mostly ours,' Jormeshu declared.

Within the tunnels, vox systems had been rewired to broadcast Blood Gorgon war prayers. He intended to fill the underground with the barking, pounding rhythm of drums and Chaotic incantation during the battle. It would disorientate the Imperial soldiers and drive his own forces into a trance-like fury.

'All of you,' said Jormeshu, taking the time to look every follower who was present in the eye, 'will lead your warbands within the fortress system. We cannot lose the siege-cannon. Without it, we will lose the insurgency and all hope of liberation. Die where you stand or may the Lords and Prince torment your undying soul.'

The assembly all bowed to him, touching their foreheads to the stone platform as a sign of affirmation. They commanded two thousand Carnibalès that Jormeshu had organised into a rough brigade-strength element. They were named the 1st Bastón Regulars. It was just a name, but it gave the rough-edged rebel fighters a sense of cohesion and purpose. They were dressed in a mix of scavenged PDF leathers and peasant attire. The leather jackets were most coveted and changed hands often; in a way their shambled appearance became a source of unifying pride for the 1st Regulars, irregular though they were.

Jormeshu had selected the title from an enemy he had encountered in his early days with the Legion. He had been a Gorgon youngblood then, two hundred and six years ago on the agri-world of San Cheval. He and his blood company had deployed for a retributive strike on the planet's surface, aiming for a kill quota of ninety-nine thousand kills to be paid in full. They burned and massacred, offering in the name of Chaos, without resistance. That was until the company had collided with the local soldiery known as the Chevilian Regulars. They were barely men: boy-soldiers. It should have been easy. It had not been. Jormeshu still remembered, quite vividly, how he had shot a Guardsman in the leg, taking his foot off at the ankle. The young man stumbled and fell. Another Guardsman had immediately appeared in the open to drag his comrade from further fire. The wounded soldier, heedless of his missing limb, continued to chip away at Jormeshu with his lasgun. It had so surprised Jormeshu that he had hesitated before killing both of them. That was the day he had formed a healthy respect for the fighting prowess of the common man. They had all died, of course, but that was beside the point. He hoped that the title could impart their discipline to his rebel force.

For all his preparations, Jormeshu knew the only thing that mattered was the rail-mounted artillery. Without it, Chaos would lose its influence on Solo-Bastón and his warband would lose a fertile ground of recruitment which had replenished their ranks since their inception. This was as much his home world as it was the insurgency's.

In the unlikely event that the Imperial force weathered the meat-grinding gauntlet he had orchestrated and reached the battery-cavern itself, Jormeshu was personally prepared. He would defend the hangar himself. He had spent the past six days fasting and in prayer to his Lords and Prince. He had anointed his bolter with warm blood. He had laid out his ancient arsenal of chainsword, maul, guillotine and sabre-sickle and blessed these too. The she-bitch daemon spirit of his power armour for once did not torment him. She had settled into a seething slumber, only crooning at the midnight hours.

Jormeshu could not trust the defence of the battery cavern to anything less. Of course, there would be a company-strength element under his direct command, but he was not concerned. They were a mere meat shield. Jormeshu expected that it would be his boltgun that would exact a heavy toll on any surviving Guardsmen.

* * *

'IT WILL BE a great pleasure to shoot these dogs as they come down the tunnel,' Mautista cawed. He crouched down behind the low rockcrete barrier, mimicking a rifle in his hands as he tested his line of sight.

'I've heard that Imperial Guardsmen are lobotomised. You can lure hundreds of them off the edge of a cliff with a ration pack,' said Canao as he stacked grenade crates packed with straw into their makeshift gun pit.

Another chimed in, not missing a beat. 'I've heard they are so big they can't run, the muscles on their legs won't carry them. That's why they need tanks and trucks,' he said seriously.

Mautista was not sure whether these stories were true. He surmised that many were fanciful tales sieved through the ignorance of rural farmers. Whatever the truth about the Imperial forces, he would not allow his Carnibalès to be the last to taste Imperial flesh. He had now, under his command, twenty-six Carnibalès and they held a stretch of tunnel two hundred metres long that connected the outer hill complexes to the bulk storage chambers close to the centre of the complex. It would be unfortunate indeed if he were not able to kill any Imperial soldiers, considering their advantage.

The tunnel was smooth and rounded, carved out of the porous limestone; its unobstructed length offered no cover for advancing forces while Mautista was well dug-in. Earlier in the day, Mautista had bartered for over twenty domesticated felines that Disciple Palahes had rounded up during a raid on an agri-village. It had cost him a sizeable portion of dried flesh but Mautista believed it had been worth it. They had boiled the felines alive and now strung them like bloated, white little ornaments in front of their rockcrete barriers for blessing. But not before the carcasses were squeezed to drain the cooked, curdled blood into a bowl. The congealed matter had been anointed to their various knives and bayonets, utilised as crude but spiteful poison.

Behind rockcrete barriers, his Carnibalès were going about their own rituals. Brother Jormeshu had ordered them to prepare for a protracted defence. Now many of them were praying to a small shrine they had erected to the Primal Gods. Inside a glass jar several human scalps had been placed. They were well tanned and shrunken and sitting in a solution of alcohol and oils. Each man in turn took a scoop of the liquid in his palm and slurped. They uttered incantations, kneeling down and praying. Some, the especially pious ones, had their eyes rolled back into their skulls as they swayed and chanted. Garlands of hill flowers surrounded the holy jar. As they prayed, others burned incense and bundles of human hair. The air was hot with the greasy smell of scorched protein and dry musk.

There was an excitement amongst his rebels, stirred from defeat by the prospect of killing. But it was nothing compared to Mautista's emotions. He could barely contain them. He sat cross-legged, away from the others. He uncurled a long strip of cured skin and began to wrap it slowly around his head, starting from the neck and working his way upward. Common insurgents had taken to hiding their Ruinous mutations with head garb. Mautista simply did it because it would put fear into his enemies. It dehumanised him and would not allow his enemies to recognise the familiarity of a human face. Ever since prehistoric man had gone to war, he had tried to terrify his foe with beard, or mask or sculpted helm. Warfare had changed but mankind did not.

Satisfied that his head was wrapped in an anonymous coil with only slits for vision, Mautista held the
loose end over his cheekbone. With one hand he held
a nail over the flap and with the other he drove the nail
with a rock. The pain was white hot and momentary.
He took up another nail, thin and pointed, and
repeated it, this time against the soft flesh beneath his
chin. Mautista did this nine times until blood wept
from the cracks between the cured hide. As he drove the
final nail into place, he could not help but remember a
single passage from an Ecclesiarchal Primer that he had
memorised as a young child. *'I am death, come for thee,'*
– a passage that the local preacher had forced him to
read. The words scrolled through his head, not in a
preacher's sermon, but in Mautista's own voice.

In the past days, perhaps weeks, he had not only
become accustomed to the idea of killing, but the very
concept of life-taking gave him a surge of euphoria.
Mautista was losing control. He knew it but there was
nothing he could do. The chemicals that distorted his
body and made him strong also sculpted his con-
sciousness. His hands tingled with the desire to
strangle, maim and pull a trigger. In fact, Mautista's
hands had grown large, his fingers tingling and stretching out as if in yearning. He was not quite sure whether
it was his subconscious that had rendered the mutation, or the mutations which had penetrated his
subconscious. Either way, Mautista so badly wanted
the Imperial men to come running down those tunnels. He would kill them with his lasgun and wrench at
their limb sockets with his enormous hands.

The mutations were a poison to him. Mautista knew
this too. It had occurred to him that very rarely did he
meet a Disciple who had been ordained at the beginning

of the war. At first he had assumed them to be casualties
of conflict, but then he had realised it was something
else. The chemically-induced mutations were unstable.
They ravaged their once human bodies. The mutations
that the common rebel often harboured were benign, a
gift from the gods. But the tremendous changes that
were induced in the Disciples were akin to a sacrifice.

Yet in his inevitable death, Mautista had also learnt
to see purpose. It forced him to impart his knowledge
upon the common Bastón-born in the few months he
had. He was a better combat leader for it, because he
did not think about the consequences of pain. Each day
was his last and, in the primal philosophy of Chaos,
there was no greater way to live. When the time came,
he would kill as many Imperial meat puppets as he
could. They would be terrified of him. They would
remember his visage for the rest of their days and,
when he died, he would ascend to an eternity alongside
the Lords and their Prince. Whichever way Mautista
looked at it, the killing would be glorious.

BAEDER LIFTED THE flap and walked into the officers'
tent, scrunching his cloth cap from his head as he did
so. All eyes fell on him expectantly. Baeder loosened his
collar against the stifling heat and nodded in greeting.

Seated or crouching around a foldout table were
Major Mortlock, Sergeant Pulver and the four company
captains. Captain Gregan of Serpent Company had suffered a thigh wound in the Lauzon Offensive. As a
result, he was feverish, pale and sweating, yet he leaned
on a fen-hammer as a crutch and insisted on being present.

Baeder laid down the scraps of notepaper on the steel
fold-out. He arranged them like a card dealer as the

officers leaned in eagerly to study them. Each note contained the scrawled intelligence he and the scouting
party had managed to scribble in their field books and
tear out. The tiny shreds of paper, containing sketches,
numerical data and observations were less than ideal,
but they were all Ouisivians and they could get by with
much worse.

'This is the Kalinga Curtain, a range of small hills
roughly three kilometres in length. A fenced, above-
ground PDF installation covers roughly a third of the
Kalinga Hills,' Baeder said, tracing a graphite sketch
with his fingers. 'It is our belief that the majority of
enemy assets reside below ground in bunker complexes, thus avoiding aerial bombardment for the past
several months.'

'Where are the fraggers hiding the big gun?' asked
Mortlock.

'There are firing ports cut into the hillside. We know
from the pre-mission briefing that the machine can be
moved by means of an underground rail network to
various firing positions. Follow the rail link and we'll
find it.'

'It's a one hundred metre long cannon for frag's sake.
How hard can it be to find?' shrugged Baeder.

'What entry points do we have?' Captain Gregan
whispered weakly. His leg wound had robbed the
young, athletic officer of his strength. Baeder feared
that Gregan would not be fit to lead his company in the
assault.

'Some of the structures in the above-ground installation must lead below-ground. There also seem to be
certain caves carved into the hill that lead into the
underground. These entry points are small, however.
The most likely entry point for a large force is here,' said

Baeder, tapping a badly drawn icon representing the installation's docking bays. 'These are riverside piers which lead into a large hangar that appears, from our observation, to connect directly into the underground.'

'Then that's where we'll hit them,' Captain Fuller declared. 'Hard and direct.'

'It's also where the Archenemy will expect an attack. They'll be waiting for us there,' Pulver said.

Baeder nodded in agreement. 'It's too obvious. I really would rather not fall into a well-laid trap, especially given the Archenemy penchant for deviant behaviour,' Baeder added lightly.

On Ouisivia, officers had been taught to ignore the most obvious approach to any given problem. More than likely the enemy would be prepared for it and any enemy commander would take steps to shore up their weaknesses. Illogical though the Archenemy were, Baeder refused to fall into a well-laid enemy defence due to predictability, and if the Traitor Legions truly had a hand in this, as Baeder suspected, then it would be all the more likely.

'Here, the docking pier is the most obvious approach,' said Baeder, jabbing a finger at the rough sketch laid out before them. He traced the metal docking bays that spanned a width of some two hundred metres. 'So we set the decoy assault here. The entire flotilla manned by skeleton crews will conduct an assault on the docking hangars. The enemy will expect us to land troops here. Instead, the entire flotilla will sit back and hammer them with support weapons. We deny them the assault they'll expect. Major Mortlock, I'll need you to lead this.'

Mortlock looked crestfallen. 'Sir? I lead the decoy? What about the major assault?'

Baeder took a deep breath as if the words pained him. 'The entire success of our mission will depend on the effectiveness of the decoy attack, major. We need the enemy to really feel threatened there. It will be a delicate task and, make no mistake, a dangerous one. I'm entrusting second command during the assault to Sergeant Pulver. I need you to do this Mortlock, I really do.'

Mortlock clenched his jaw and thought for a second. Finally, he nodded. 'You can count on it, sir.'

'Good,' Baeder said, continuing. 'The main assault will be dismounted infantry. We'll move inland, four hundred and thirty-five men. Once the river attack is distracting the enemy, we will secure the above-ground compound and split into company-strength elements, entering the underground through the large firing vents carved into the mountain.' Baeder indicated these on the map in turn. 'Once inside, we will follow the rail network that is used to transport the gun to its various firing positions. Remember, the battery can only traverse the rail networks so, if we follow these, we'll eventually be led to the battery. Once there, disable the battery with det-charges.'

The officers leaned back, their eyes gleaming with the thought of the final assault. They were not violent men by nature, but the past weeks of boredom and terror had made them feel like victims. Now, the thought of finally meeting the enemy barrel to barrel filled them with joy. It was a curious concept. In any other context, the thought of danger and killing was far removed from that of promise. But these were Imperial Guardsmen and war, at least to them, held a terrible allure. It gave them a chance to do the one thing they had trained so long and so hard to do. Kill.

'When do we go?' Pulver asked, ringing his dip into a spittoon.

'It's 09.00 now. We will rest and prepare. Have all companies ready to deploy by 18.00 tonight. We will break camp by 20.00 and ready positions by midnight. The attack will be 04.00 the next morning so we can make full use of the morning fog. I will give a full briefing in the afternoon, until then gentlemen, go about your business. Rest when you can. Dismissed,' Baeder said.

CHAPTER FIFTY

CHAPTER FIFTEEN

'BAEDER IS A stone-cold killer!' shouted a Riverine, slapping his knee.

'Yeh. Wouldn't tell by looking at him but that ramrod is a machine,' agreed another.

The word was out that the attack would begin at 04.00 and the Riverine camp was lively with cheer. The 88th Battalion had survived the long trek inland largely intact; the four companies were more or less at fighting strength and spirits were high. A leathery, grudging respect for Colonel Baeder was beginning to build amongst the Guardsmen.

Corporal Schilt, however, did not share those sentiments. He crouched in the soft leaf mould beneath the shade of a gum-sap, hugging his lasgun to his chest, and tried to keep out of sight. It was early morning and cumulus clouds gathered overhead, threatening rain again. It had been mere hours since Schilt had almost been on the receiving end of an Imperial fighter and his nerves were frayed. The clouds matched his mood.

In Schilt's opinion, it was bad enough that the battalion was led by a reckless maverick of an officer. It was worse because now Baeder had earmarked him as one of the battalion's best forward scouts and almost gotten him killed that very morning. Schilt had no intention of being selected for further special missions.

It was not that Schilt disliked soldiering. He liked it, for the most part. He loved his lasrifle and the notion of being in the Imperium's warrior caste. The uniform too seemed irresistible to women at ports of call and deployment. But Schilt had no stomach for being put in the gunsights of an enemy. What good were the benefits of being a Guardsman if he was not alive to enjoy them?

Schilt lit a tabac, content to warm his dark thoughts with lung-burning smoke, when Trooper Volk tramped through the undergrowth towards him. Volk was smiling, grinning widely to reveal the gaps in his teeth.

'What the frag are you so happy about?' Schilt murmured into his tabac.

Volk was a balding, bearded brute in his middle years, growing soft around his middle. Although he had spent almost sixteen years in the Guard, multiple infractions had demoted his rank. He was forever a rogue and, consequently, one of Schilt's most trusted in their gang of 'creepers'.

'It's a fine day today and we'll be fighting by tomorrow. It's a wonderful life in the Imperial Guard,' Volk replied, squatting down beside Schilt.

Schilt spat derisively, eyeing Volk with a hint of disgust. There were still at least eighteen hours before engagement and Volk was already prepped to go, his webbing cinched, his canteens filled and his autorifle oiled and cleaned. The old trooper had even patched the holes in his combat boots with plastek tape.

'Since when did you become one of Baeder's lap-dogs?' Schilt asked snidely.

'Ain't,' Volk replied gruffly. 'I'm getting ready now so I can catch some sleep before the afternoon.'

'You better not go eunuch on me,' Schilt said, suddenly serious. 'Not now.'

The face-splitting grin dropped from Volk's face. 'Why? What are you cooking up?' he asked.

Schilt stamped out his tabac and sniffed. 'I'm going to frag Baeder.'

'Before the assault on Kalinga?' Volk asked. Judging by the furrows that creased his forehead, he did not think it a good idea.

'Of course not now, you damn pushball,' Schilt snarled venomously. 'During the Kalinga assault. I'm going to finish him there, nice and quiet like that.'

Volk didn't reply. An uncomfortable silence settled between them. Suddenly Schilt shifted forwards on the balls of his feet and gripped Volk by the collar of his flak vest. 'Damn it Volk, if you're not playing on this one I'm going to put you out. I'm going to slice you here and no one's going to shed a damn tear,' Schilt hissed under his breath. A knife was pressed up against Volk's ribs, sliding just underneath the bottom of his flak.

Despite being the older and significantly larger man, Volk stammered. Schilt terrified him. He did not doubt Schilt's threats. Besides being an excellent gretchin stalker, Volk knew that Schilt had already killed a Riverine before. Once, two years ago on their home garrison, Schilt had drowned their platoon medic for refusing to supply him with pain stimms. The regiment had put the death down to natural causes but Volk and a handful of creepers knew otherwise. You didn't turn your back on Sendo Schilt.

'All right. All right, don't get so slicey,' Volk pleaded, pushing Schilt's hand away from his neck. 'I'm in.'

'Good,' Schilt said. 'I'm going to pop him in a firefight. Make sure you and the boys finish the job. Spread the word to the others.'

Volk sighed. Up until then, he had been looking forward to engaging the Archenemy in a firefight, barrel to barrel, steel to steel. Corporal Schilt had just robbed him of all enthusiasm.

'Give me some tabac,' Schilt demanded, as Volk turned to go. 'I'm all out and look, I'm all shaken up,' he said, holding up his trembling hands for Volk to see. 'Baeder almost got me killed last night on his fouled-up scouting run.'

Volk began to rifle through his webbing pouches, trying to forage some tabac for Schilt, but he couldn't do it. His hands were shaking even harder than Schilt's.

BEFORE THE SUN was high and the air grew hot, Sergeant Pulver made a roll call of each individual platoon. It took him the better part of dawn and all morning, time he could have otherwise spent resting for their attack on the morrow.

But the lack of rest didn't bother him. These Riverine were his sons. He went to each man and checked on their preparations. During his rounds, Pulver gave out the last dredges of his dip and tabac. He found out that Trooper Velder's lasrifle had a warped focus chamber. Unable to fix it, Pulver gave him his own lasrifle and checked out a spare weapon from the supply barge. It was an outdated T20 stem autogun; the trigger mech was stiff and the balance was poor. Pulver slung it over his shoulder without a second thought and went to make certain each and every man would be ready for the fight ahead.

BAEDER COULD NOT remember the last time he had had more than three hours of sleep in one stretch. He was running on the last wispy fumes of energy, an energy that only lingered because they were so close to the end. Since he had returned with the scout force and briefed the battalion seniors on the assault strategy, their temporary ennui had become electrified. Guardsmen who only hours before had sprawled or crouched in sleepy, silent huddles were now up and moving with vigour. Their jungle clearing erupted with the clatter of men preparing their battledress, shouting orders and relaying supplies.

Following their briefing, Baeder had returned to his bivouac and tried to snatch an hour or two of rest before afternoon preparations but found that he could not. He had lain awake; his eyes open as his mind swirled with thoughts of the coming fight. Finally, unable to sleep, he rose and donned his uniform. He shed the sour rags that he had not changed for the past several days and foraged up khaki officer's shorts and a shirt of Riverine swamp camouflage. The simple change of clothes would go far in conveying his confidence towards his men. Baeder then shaved with a dry blade, scraping the coarse stubble from his skin along with a rind of dark filth. There was a ritual to preparing the regalia of war that all Guardsmen found universally comforting. As one went through the physical movements, the mind subconsciously readied itself for the trauma that would follow in the hours to come. Slowly, savouring each motion, Baeder shrugged himself into his webbing, a ubiquitous H-harness hip webbing that had served in mankind's front trenches for thousands of years. It was not the complex chest rig of the Caliguans nor the slim, side satchels of the Persepians but his webbing was slashed with the tans and cream greens of Ouisivia, and Baeder would not trade it for anything else. With a roll of plastek tape, Baeder fixed the loosened straps and buckles which had bothered him for the past few days. Satisfied with his attire, Baeder checked his wrist chron. It was not yet middle noon and he decided to make a tour of the camp before his formal pre-mission briefing.

As Baeder emerged from his tent, nearby Riverine greeted him with a loud 'Oussss!' Baeder raised his fist and hooted back. The men were in high spirits and, for Baeder, there was no better sign. The nearness of danger changed men. It was unspoken, but all the men understood it – many of them would be dead by this time tomorrow. Even the youngest, most timid Guardsmen in the battalion stamped around like ursine predators, banging helmets together while chewing dip. There was no time for fear now. The Riverine replaced it with aggression. They jokingly called each other out, snorted with crude humour and shared a gruff, intimate brotherhood. It was not an act, Baeder knew, but a way to quell the fear.

Even those Guardsmen who had never gotten along found time to sit by one another and share their remaining tabac. As Baeder walked through the camp he overheard fragments of conversation that would have been out of context anywhere else, at any other time.

'...so I left her back home, what else could I do? I didn't want to be stuck dirt farming like my old man. I hope she's found someone who treats her fine. I still think you know...'

'...my little brother almost took my eye out with that percussion cap. It lodged there. You should have seen the look on my mother's face. I thought she was going to throw him into the water. I even cried to make it seem more serious than it was...'

'...I just wanted you to know that I always thought you were a good, solid ramrod. I just never said it before.'

'Same to you brother. I want you to have my tags if I die...'

Baeder continued on to the outer perimeters of the camp. At the edge of the water, Riverine had spread out a groundsheet held down by stones on four corners. Spread in the middle was a carpet of solid slug ammunition for autorifles. The Guardsmen sat and cleaned them by hand. Their diligence made Baeder's heart swell with pride. For soldiers who barely bathed and never shaved, they were wiping clean each individual round to reduce the chance of jamming in the middle of a firefight. Approximately one third of the men in his battalion had opted to take the LH Fusil-pattern autorifles instead of the lasgun. Each of these men would carry five magazines of thirty rounds into combat. That meant over twenty thousand rounds would have to be wiped and slotted into detachable box magazines. It was a thankless job and it made Baeder glad he was a commander of the 88th Battalion.

Behind the picket line of camp sentries, a makeshift memorial had been set up around the buttress roots of a tall green giant. On sticks staked into the ground hung helmets and metal ident-tags: one for each River-ine who had fallen since their inland campaign and not been given proper burial. Guardsmen came and went, saying their last goodbyes or asking their fallen friends to watch over them.

Baeder knelt down and placed his palm on a helmet. Beside it lay the tag for Corporal Cinda Frey, Three Platoon, Prowler Company.

'Corporal Frey,' Baeder said. 'You may be eager to see your friends in the beyond, but I'm going to try and keep them away from you for a while yet. I want to keep them alive and I'm sorry I wasn't able to do the same for you. One day I know we will all salute each other again, but hopefully not tomorrow. Oussss.'

As Baeder rose and turned to leave, he started to see the skull-face of Mortlock looking at him.

'How are you feeling, major?'

Mortlock cracked him a wide grin; the sight of the smiling ork skull on his face was ironically comforting. 'I'm going to kill me fifty insurgents. Just you wait and see. I'm going to tear one limb from limb and beat his friend to death with it. It'll be a new personal record.'

Baeder did not need to feign amusement, as he often had to during the major's outbursts. This time, Baeder laughed genuinely. 'Good to hear, major. I'm going to expect a full field report when this is all over.'

Mortlock's arrogance had often bothered him. When he had first met the man, Baeder had both envied and disliked him. In the mess halls, Mortlock was loud and supremely confident. But out here, in the thick of a combat zone, the arrogance was like an anchor for morale. Baeder did not doubt that the sight of the one hundred and fifty kilo major slinging his fen-hammer could rally them from the brink of surrender.

Lastly, Baeder strolled to where the battalion's boats were waiting on the water. Riverine were making the final mechanical checks on their steeds. Others were hauling the last crates from the supply barges. For a moment Baeder considered wading into the water to check on their progress but thought better of it. He wanted the men to know that he had absolute trust in their abilities. The sergeants and soldiers were commanding the resupply with clockwork efficiency, shifting rations, water and ammunition from the vessels and over to the squad and platoon leaders for distribution.

Finally, after Baeder made several rounds of the camp, he retreated to find solitude. He sat beneath a spiny bactris and stared blankly into nothing. This was the fight he had been waiting and training for. Not only during this campaign, but ever since he had joined the Guard. Now here he was, leading a battalion into the heartland of enemy country. They were surrounded and outnumbered by Archenemy fanatics. The success of the entire war could be contingent on the operative success of his battalion within the next twenty-four hours. Despite knowing all these things, Baeder was not at all scared. The only thing that terrified him was the distrust of his own men. He did not know what they thought of him, or whether they even cared for his judgement. That one burning doubt nagged him.

He knew that this doubt, in part, had hardened him. It drove him to do terrible things. He no longer cared who he killed or how he did it. Baeder knew he would shoot women and children if they threatened the safety of his soldiers. Every shot fired against his men was a personal attempt to kill Baeder himself. When it came down to this, everything was negotiable. His world was the battalion. Fight and win.

Briefly Baeder wondered what his father on Ouisivia would think of the soldier he had become. The man had been the medical administrator of their parish, an avuncular and widely read man. Most likely, he would have been disgusted. Of course his father would not have understood the plight of command no matter how many books he read. No one would, until they stood in his boots.

THE WATER LAPPED against the boat hulls. The flotilla of the 88th Battalion was on the move. From the stern of his swift, Major Mortlock could see a long column of combat vessels behind him as they manoeuvred towards the staging area. Usually, Mortlock's boat carried a crew of six men, but tonight it carried three – one to pilot the craft and two to man the support guns. Likewise, the other vessels were strangely empty to his practiced eye. Even the inflatable assault landers, usually loaded with a full squad of Guardsmen, were now guided by a single Riverine. In those landers, the squat silhouettes of backpacks were heaped to resemble the crouched forms of Guardsmen in the dark. They sailed in silence, to match the hushed, devious manner of their decoy assault.

By two in the morning, they reached their attack position. It was a sheltered cove shielded by trees like hanging gallows, just one and a half kilometres east of the Kalinga Curtain. The boats clustered tentatively there, waiting for a vox-signal from the inland assault force. The loud, steady chorus of chirping insects interspersed with the plaintive squeals of the nocturnal was the only sound to be heard.

Mortlock took stock of the men around him. In the dark, shapes coiled up behind mounted weapons.

Although he could not see them, he imagined they would be chewing dip, their nostrils flared and their eyes wired open to reveal too much white. They were ready. Although they had not been granted the opportunity to join in the main assault, every man knew the importance of their objective. Their feint attack would need to be real and damaging. Damaging enough to make the Carnibalès believe them. It was not glorious but it was entirely necessary. At first, Mortlock had been offended that Baeder had ordered him to lead the decoy. He had wanted so badly to commit to the major assault. It was to have been his own *Great Crusade*. But then, slowly, it dawned on him that Baeder had separated him for a reason. Casualty rates were expected to be high. In the event that Baeder was killed in action, the colonel had wanted Mortlock to lead the battalion on their return. Mortlock could not argue with that.

A Guardsman coughed in the darkness. Mortlock savoured the sound. He wanted to remember everything he felt before the battle. If he could not participate in the final push, then he would still have his fight on the water. He wanted to remember the syrupy fog of the night, the gentle lapping of the water. This was what Mortlock had trained to do. Fight and win.

The minutes ticked on. Baeder and the battalion would be creeping towards the Kalinga now, Mortlock thought. He imagined the companies crawling into position beneath the rainforest's tall emergents. Once the battalion reached their attack point, two kilometres out from the Kalinga Curtains, they would signal Mortlock to charge. The plan was for the boats to hit the docking hangars of the installation with hard firepower. It would draw patrols and manpower in the area, allowing the main assault to stalk close enough to the installation and mount a shock raid on the Arch-enemy. To do this, Mortlock and the vessels would have to put up a fight for over fifteen minutes, allowing enough time for the assault teams to cover the distance.

From inside the pilothouse, the sudden crackle of vox transmission made Mortlock jump with a start. He slapped the stern-mounted heavy bolter. This was it. He could feel the heat, a spring coil in his stomach begin-ning to build in tension. He flexed his hands and wriggled his fingers.

But the transmission was simply a test signal. Instead, they waited. The air grew still. Riverine began to mutter, their voices drifting softly across the river surface. They waited some more. The minutes rolled by and Mortlock looked at the sky anxiously. They had maybe one or two hours before daylight. He began to wish fervently for the assault teams to hasten their task.

The vox from the pilothouse crackled again, this time so loud it echoed a metallic ring across the cove. 'Mort-lock, this is eight eight. We are poised. Proceed with Operation Curtain. Over.' The voice was strangely laconic.

Their coxswain voxed something back but Mortlock could not hear the answer. The air filled with the sud-den, chainsword roars of motors. It was loud and vibrated back to his molars. Mortlock settled into a semi-crouch as the swift boat lurched in gear. Churning the river white with foam, the battalion column uncoiled like a snake and crossed their line of depar-ture.

THE SIGNAL WAS a faraway *crump*. Gunfire strobed in the distance, flashing orange against the black horizon. The faraway chatter of guns could be heard, like a solitary blacksmith clapping hammers in the stillness of night. Men were already dying.

Missile tubes put glowing breaches in the mesh fence. Platoons hurtled through the opening. There were no visible sentries although squads trained their lasguns on empty watchtowers. The sloping hills loomed before them, dark and solid. But for the crackle of gun-fighting to their west, the hills were strangely quiet, almost serene. The sparse, bomb-shocked trees looked like lonely skeletons. Some of Prowler Company began firing up into the empty trees but a squad leader snarled for them to be quiet.

'Lieutenant Hennever! Take that building!' Baeder commanded, indicating towards the closest structure, a boxy rockcrete block with high slitted windows.

Baeder pushed up the hill as the companies spread out into an open file advance. Despite the feint assault, Baeder had expected at least perfunctory initial resistance. But there was not a single gun platform, nor even a Carnibalès fighter in sight.

As the battalion advanced, Lieutenant Kifer's platoon consolidated their position behind an empty block-house. Baeder pushed the battalion line another fifty metres up the slope, their left flank anchored by Kifer's platoon. Baeder sprinted over to a heap of brick rubble, no doubt the result of an Imperial sortie in the preceding months. He crouched down behind a splinter of rockcrete and scanned uphill with his magnoculars.

'Where are they?' Baeder whispered to himself. Further up the installation, a string of five blockhouses surrounded the bowl shape of a vox dish. A berm of sandbags oozed down the hill like sand dunes, providing defensive positions, but there were no gunmen behind them. According to his tactical maps, the cluster of buildings provided an entrance point into the underground facility. Although the maps were blueprints of the facility during its tenure as an Imperial outpost, it was unlikely the Archenemy could so easily reroute the complex tunnel systems. Turning to his companies, Baeder gave them the signal to advance. As they had planned, the four companies dispersed. Prowler and Serpent split away, clattering off into the trees towards the eastern slopes.

They continued up, almost at a stroll. Baeder aimed his Kupiter autopistol at the undisturbed trees. For a few seconds, Baeder wondered if Mortlock's decoy attack along the river had really been so effective as to have drawn the entire enemy defences away. It was only momentary, as a slicing round stole his thought away. He dropped as a trooper advancing several paces behind him pitched over and rolled down the slope.

'Did anyone see the shot?' Baeder shouted.

'Contact at left flank! In those trees!' shouted Captain Fuller, indicating towards a stand of white barks which appeared unnaturally bright in the moonlight. Immediately, the advancing line erupted into a mad splintering of las-fire. Branches were whipped away and leaves burst into flame as the fusillade tore into them. Baeder was not sure, but he thought he made out the shape of a gunman drop from the tallest branches under the searing flashes of las-fire.

'Cease fire! Conserve your ammunition,' Baeder commanded with a chopping motion of his hand. He was thinking that the Archenemy were playing smart. They were digging in with hidden snipers, presumably because they knew that a head-to-head clash with Imperial forces would be too much to risk. Most likely

the Carnibalès were concentrating their forces at critical
strong points and leaving hidden gunmen to harass
them. In such conditions, even a single gunman could
be a force multiplier against an entire battalion advancing in open terrain. It was a shrewd decision and
Baeder would have done the same.

MORTLOCK'S LITTORAL ASSAULT powered up the wide
delta channel and banked hard towards the Kalinga
Curtain. Beneath the harsh roof lights of the docking
hangar, the Archenemy were lying in wait. A bombardment was launched from the pier by sentry mortars but
most of them fell short of the rapid Riverine vessels,
punching high geysers into the river. The hangar
appeared as a wide maw at the base of the hills, almost
one hundred metres wide. From within that maw,
twenty ex-PDF cutters and a shoal of insurgent spikers
spread out into the river basin, crackling with weapon
fire.

The Riverine met them head on and engaged three
hundred metres out from the piers. Mortlock ordered
his forces to scissor into and through the Archenemy
squadrons, diluting their forces into a mingled dogfight. In doing so, Mortlock denied the Archenemy a
clear line of fire from the manned guns and troops
lurking within the cavernous hangar. Mortars and autocannons barked loudly regardless.

Vessel fought vessel, swirling and circling like fighting fish. The improvised spikers were no match for the
rugged swift boats but their numbers were telling. Las-
fire slashed in every direction and lit the night into a
coloured display of pink and white. The firepower of
support weapons pounding each other from point-
blank range shook the river. Muzzle flash touched and

turned into columns of clashing flame. An ex-PDF cutter flanked Mortlock's swift boat, wedging it between two frilled trawlers. The trawlers poured las-fire up into the stern, ricocheting off the railings as Mortlock ducked behind the mantlet of his bolter. Behind them, the cutter aligned the swift boat under the sights of its turreted autocannon. Out of the night, another swift boat rammed the cutter's portside, throwing its aim. A Riverine gunner tossed three grenades onto the cutter's deck. The explosion was swallowed by the chatter of guns. Beneath the light of predawn the boats continued to fight, jinking, ramming and burning.

It took Sergeant Major Pulver seventeen minutes to breach an entrance point and lead both Prowler and Serpent Company into the underground complex. During those minutes, he lost thirty of the one hundred and eighty-five men under his command and they had not even engaged the bulk of the Archenemy yet. Rather, the ground had been seeded with spike pits and shell mines. Hurried boots in the dark could not discern the freshly-laid traps from solid earth and the traps had claimed many of his boys.

Pulver grabbed the vox handset from his vox-officer's backpack. 'Breached! Serpent and Prowler are in,' he said, as he eyed his surroundings warily.

They were in a sub-ground hangar of the Kalinga Complex, a domed belly hewn into the limestone. The space was large and white grid markings on the expanse of concrete ground suggested that the sub-hangar had once been a motor pool for the PDF garrison. Overhead, extractor fans thumped and ventilated air into the multiple exit tunnels that led out deeper into the underground installation. According to his memorisation of the blueprints, it would be a two thousand three hundred metre distance to reach the facility's central core.

With Lieutenant Fissen's platoon spread out for covering fire, Prowler Company moved towards a large ovoid tunnel. A railed conveyance track was laid into the floor of the tunnel, stretching away to disappear out of sight. Captain Buren led Prowler Company away, stalking the railed track like a huntsman tailing spoor.

Pulver checked the schematics on his data-slate before forming up Serpent Company into three full platoons with at least twenty Riverine each. Emergency sirens were braying, while flickering hazard lights alternated brief moments of darkness and neon yellow.

'Leap frog on alternating sides of the wall,' Pulver commanded.

The three platoons crossed the sub-hangar and entered a carriage tunnel that sloped at a downward angle. The railed track-line down its centre had obviously been used to cart supplies and a pulley wagon had been abandoned halfway down the tunnel. The platoons bounded each other, one moving forwards, while the other two provided covering fire from opposite sides of the limestone walls. Of the Archenemy, there was still no sign. Pulver was sweating in sheets. Partly, it was due to the dry, artificial air, but also because the lack of resistance gave him the churns. He felt his heart fibrillating rapidly yet weakly in his chest. He had never before felt so acutely vulnerable in a combat zone.

His fears were not unfounded. The company had bounded down half the hallway before Lieutenant Hulsen signalled for them to halt. At first, Pulver felt a spark of irritation. Why the frag was Hulsen calling for a halt when they were stranded in an open tunnel without cover? But then he remembered that these men had been blooded before. They were not rawhides that needed minute management and he needed to trust their judgement. Pulver called a halt and sprinted at a low crouch towards Hulsen and his forward platoon.

'Report!' he snapped, wasting no time.

Hulsen pointed at the pulley wagon abandoned on the rails with a hunched, mischievous demeanour, almost like a boy who had found a guilty secret. It was a boxy, slate-grey six wheeler with a carrying capacity of half a tonne. Around it, a web of wire had been arranged to form a complex lattice that stretched from wall to wall. Under the flashing siren lights the wire glinted as fine filament. There was no doubt the half-tonner would be rigged with explosives.

Pulver's eyes widened. 'Get back!' he shouted, rising suddenly. 'Back! Back!' he waved. Serpent Company rose unsteadily from their positions and began to back pedal. In withdrawal, the men were confused but nonetheless obedient.

That discipline saved many lives. A squad of Carnibalès fighters clattered into the far end of the tunnel, shooting up at them. Their faces, distorted by the heavy brow and slit grin of mutation, glowed in the wash of their muzzle flashes.

'Find cover!' Pulver shouted, shooting as he retreated. 'Keep moving!'

The Carnibalès were firing at the rail wagon in an attempt to trigger the explosives. Each shot rocked the carriage on its suspension, lurching it and denting its thin metal hide. With each shot, Pulver flinched inwardly, expecting the carriage to detonate. The cluster of insurgents now solely concentrated their fire on igniting the det–trap, pouring las and solid slug into it.

From his experience, Pulver knew that even two hundred kilograms of poorly mixed det-powder would likely collapse the entire carriage tunnel.

Serpent Company had only moved sixty metres back up the tunnel when a las-round finally caught the det-trap. It erupted. A tidal wave of concussive force, heat and sound tore through the tunnel. Pulver was bowled onto his back, his eardrums popping with agony. Fragments of limestone peppered his face and for a moment Pulver thought he was dead. He rolled onto his side but quickly found that he was intact.

Smoke filled the tunnel. It burned his eyes and seared his throat. He tried to clear his vision by rubbing his eyes but only succeeded in smearing ash into them. He began to wonder if perhaps everyone else had been killed and he was the only survivor. Slowly the smoke began to settle. Pulver blinked and his company came into view. The familiar shapes of Riverine, swaying and groggy but otherwise unscathed, rose into sight.

'Serpent Company. Report injuries!' Pulver cried hoarsely. His throat was seared and his voice raspy and weak.

It was a small miracle, but the men only grunted. There were no screams of pain or wailing reports of casualties. Pulver had been furthest at the front and therefore the closest to the blast. Serpent Company had survived the first attack of Operation Curtain. The thought had barely registered when las-fire stitched into the limestone overhead, eliciting a downpour of rock drizzle and dust.

Suddenly, Serpent Company opened up, the bounding platoons pouring their fire at the Carnibalès at the far end of the tunnel. The tunnel was still smoking and beams of las seemed to flash out from the clouds. Pulver hammered a series of blind shots in the opposite direction. Trooper Kleiger took aim next to Pulver and racked off a trio of grenades from his launcher, the drum magazine cycling with a hollow *foomp foomp foomp*.

BAEDER AND SEEKER Company progressed steadily down Kalinga's main service shaft, following the wide rail tracks that transported the siege-battery. The service shaft was thirty metres wide, its cavernous roof buttressed by girders. From these girders, the Carnibalès had hung row upon row of poorly cured human scalps, which hung like a colony of rats. From all directions, speakers grated out the electric beat of drums, fast and pounding. The sound was distorted so it sounded like the rhythmic barking of hounds. The unwholesome sounds unsettled their focus. Their temples pounded with a distracted urgency.

The company moved in squads, bounding from girder to girder behind cover. Baeder moved with a platoon of twenty-six, leading them on with his fen-hammer. For twelve straight minutes, they encountered nothing in the service shafts, nor movement in the winding sub-tracks. They checked and rechecked their auspexes, cross-referencing them with their tactical maps every fifty metres. Following the service shaft for a full kilometre would take them halfway to the inner core and the way was eerily clear. Baeder was beginning to believe they were being lured into a trap. The waiting was intolerable.

Then, without warning, the Archenemy opened up on them. From behind sandbagged cubbies embedded into the alcoves, tracer snapped at Seeker Company. Caught in the open, six Riverine buckled and collapsed.

Under the splinter of fire, others ran out to drag them behind the rockcrete girders.

Suddenly the Archenemy seemed to be all around them. The Riverine, squatting beneath the wide support beams, traded shots in multiple directions. The Archenemy were thoroughly dug-in and had been waiting. Huddled down next to Baeder, Corporal Velson dared to lean his upper body out from behind the girder and fire a shot from his autogun. He swung back behind cover as the enemy answered with a salvo of shots, crazing the rockcrete near his shoulder with puffs of dust. Then a las-shot coming from his exposed right side tore out his throat.

Velson's legs swung out and he slid down into a sitting position; his chin dropped into his chest and his helmet rolled off his head. Baeder swore and fired his pistol in the direction of Velson's killers. The Archenemy had outmanoeuvred them through a sub-track along the main shaft. They had drawn them into a killing zone. Above his men the drums continued to pound.

They were saved only by discipline. The company held their positions, laying down defiant counter fire. Lieutenant Hulsen's platoon fixed bayonets and charged an enemy emplacement with a barrage of grenades. They ousted the Carnibalès like rodents from a burrow, stabbing and kicking into the emplacement. Under the determined cover fire of their company, Hulsen's platoon moved on to the next nest of insurgents. Hulsen himself was shot in the arm and chest but he kept standing, ordering his men onwards with his remaining arm. It took more than twenty minutes to clear the service shaft of Archenemy defences and, even then, lone Carnibalès continued to harass them.

Lieutenant Hulsen collapsed at the end of the skirmish, finally succumbing to multiple shot wounds. Although Hulsen was not the only casualty in that engagement, his platoon tried to drag his body with them, refusing to leave him behind. An officer from One Platoon finally had to order them to leave Hulsen's body, citing that it would not be fair to all the others that had fallen.

SERGEANT PETERO SLATER was the oldest man in the battalion, if not the regiment, at the age of sixty-eight. His beard was silver and the knuckles and joints of his trigger finger were rigidly fixed in the coiled position, a result, he often said, of a lifetime behind the lasgun. Slater had joined the 26th Founding of the Riverine when he had been a slum youth. He fought and bled with his comrades on the beaches of Bilsbane to the outer reaches of the Canis Cleft Sub. For forty-one long years, he fought with the 26th Riverine, watching his friends die one after another until there were less than a company's worth of men surviving. The old veterans were retired from service in the Austral Subsector and Slater had scrimped his savings to purchase a voyage back to his home of Ouisivia. It was every Guardsman's dream to survive his service and one day return home. But upon his return, Ouisivia was a strange and foreign place. The only home he knew was with the Guard. Old, tired but seeking purpose, Petero Slater reenlisted with the Riverine and joined the 31st Founding.

The solid slugs gouging craters in the rock around Slater brought serious doubt to the wisdom of that decision. Ghost Company led by Captain Steencamp followed a railhead that merged into a sub-track, parallel to Seeker Company's advance. Unlike the other companies, Ghost had suffered heavy fighting upon first entry. The Archenemy waited for them at every corner.

At one particular intersection, the Archenemy had erected a catapult that launched the rotting corpses of PDF soldiers at them. For Slater, being crushed by a blackened hunk of flesh was worse than a shot from a lasgun. But Ghost Company pressed on, desperate to keep pace with Seeker Company only fifty metres ahead, yet separated by impenetrable walls of rock.

Likewise, Slater fought to keep pace with the younger men. His joints were not as young as they used to be and a blade wound from an eldar pirate in his thigh had never healed properly. As a result, Slater moved with a galloping limp.

The Archenemy appeared in small, fragmented groups, barrels firing at them from corners and then disappearing. It was almost as if the Carnibalès were baiting them to give chase. Sergeant Slater was wary of this and warned Captain Steencamp. Slater had wanted to adopt a more wary approach. The eldar pirates on Sumudra had employed similar hit and run tactics against the superior grinding advance of the Imperial Guard. Entire companies of Guardsmen chased those stick-like creatures, snatching at shadow puppets, only to be lured en masse into clever, wicked ambushes. But Steencamp had not relented. Seeker Company might need mutual support in adjacent tunnels and Ghost Company had to keep pace.

In their haste, the company never saw the insurgents lurking on gangways built into ledges of the limestone above them. Slater noticed movement above, even felt the prickle of heat on the nape of his neck, but it was too late. As the Riverine swept down the track, the

enemy upended vats of boiling tar into the narrow sub-
track below. A torrent of bubbling pitch cascaded down
onto the heads of the forward platoon and flooded
down the sub-track. Steencamp withdrew his remaining three platoons as the resinous sludge chased them
back down the corridor. He had no choice but to leave
his first platoon, their cries merging into one keening
scream as their skin and fat cooked off them. Above the
clash of drums and screams for mercy, the insurgents
laughed mockingly at their suffering.

Sergeant Slater died slowly. He clawed at the scalding
pitch but only tore away strips of skin and resinous uniform. His only comfort was knowing that, this time, he
did not outlive his young comrades of the 31st Founding. It would have been a terrible shame if he did.

CHAPTER SIXTEEN

Eighteen minutes after the Riverine entered the porous stronghold that was Kalinga, the Archenemy began to suspect the water-borne assault against the docking hangar contained no landing elements. Pale-faced Disciples decided it was a decoy and abandoned their meticulously rigged traps and carefully measured firing lanes. They immediately withdrew their troop strength from the docking piers to join the heavy fighting within the complex itself.

The short delay was all the Riverine had needed. The 88th Battalion had lanced deep into their heart. Seeker and Ghost were stalemated at the inner core of the stronghold, fighting barrel to barrel amidst the former PDF barracks and mess halls that were now desecrated by the enemy. According to their auspexes they were less than fifteen hundred metres from the central belly that contained the siege-batteries. Yet the gridwork of the tunnels had been constructed as a maze by defensive design. Even with the aid of navigation tools and maps it was utterly disorientating. It would be the longest fifteen hundred metres of tunnel that any man would travel. Meanwhile, Prowler and Serpent in the western rail network found themselves pincered by dug-in Carnibalès to their front, and more insurgent reinforcements withdrawn from the docking hangars from behind their advance. The enemy pushed before them wheeled heavy bolters and replicate guns on treaded tires. Despite their dubious workmanship, the guns tore chunks out of the limestone with their spread of fire, pinning the Riverine elements into cover.

In that sudden, violent spike of fighting, Seeker Company lost both commanding officers to a single, tragic missile attack. Captain Fuller and Lieutenant Kifer had been working the company vox when the warhead blew out the pillar they had been crouched behind. Had it not been for Colonel Baeder, who strolled upright amidst the snapping rounds, rallying his men to hold, Seeker Company would have lost all sense of order.

CORPORAL SCHILT CREPT low amidst the long, empty barrack halls. Rank upon rank of bunks, four stacks high, lined the long hall. Yellowing papers full of text caked the walls like papier-mâché. Their seniors ordered them not to study the text on the walls, but Schilt had a good look anyway. They were prayers to the Ruinous Powers, written in a basic Low Gothic. The words were soothing and easy to memorise. Once Schilt read a sentence, he found it hard to shake it off. It was as if the words were like a melody he could not stop chanting in his head. The rhythm was intoxicating.

It took no small measure of willpower to focus himself on the task at hand. Schilt wiped his forehead with the back of his hand and pushed the wad of dip beneath his upper lip. The enemy were in front, and the enemy were behind. Stripes of las-fire left searing afterburn in his vision and he blinked them away. Carnibalès bolter teams pounded them with support fire, forcing the Riverine into huddled clusters, seeking shelter behind whatever they could put between themselves and the enemy. To Schilt's direct front, squatting behind wadded stacks of propaganda crates, a squad of Riverine returned fire with a heavy stubber. With a flash, an enemy missile streaked in from the darkened corridor beyond. It exploded above the squad, hitting them with shrapnel and a wave of concussive force.

The men were dazed. Seizing the advantage, a warband of shrieking Carnibalès swarmed over the squad. Schilt saw the flash of machetes and sprays of blood. A Carnibalès leader whipped his skeletal limbs back and forth, laying about him with a scythe-bladed sabre. Schilt was paralysed with fear as he watched the entire squad being systematically dismembered. The wet thud of metal on flesh could be heard above the clatter of small-arms fire. Then, out of the pandemonium, the Carnibalès leader locked eyes with Schilt from across the hall. His face was white and equine in length, his eyes and mouth blackened like empty pits. The Carnibalès opened his mouth, displaying pearly white teeth. Schilt turned and ran.

With his back against a bulbous copper heating furnace at the centre of the hall, Baeder continued to direct his retreating squads into some semblance of a counter-attack. 'Sergeant Galhorn, lead your men up to that alcove. Hold position and pin the bastards in

place!' Baeder shouted, pointing towards the Carnibalès.

Fifteen metres to Baeder's right, Galhorn and two
squads of Guardsmen were lying down miserably
behind a row of metal bed stacks. They clutched their
helmets as if trying to force their heads deeper down
into their necks as gunfire whistled above them. Galhorn looked at Baeder in disbelief. It was not that he
was disobeying the colonel's order, but his face was
locked in such blank shock that the sergeant did not
respond.

'Frag it!' Baeder shouted. As calmly as he could force
himself to, he walked out into the open towards
Galhorn. A las-shot fizzled on the ground before him.
A bolter shell kicked out a chunk of limestone on the
ceiling above. Baeder's instincts screamed at him to
scamper back into cover but he focused on placing
one boot before the other. 'See, sergeant,' Baeder said,
as he finally reached Galhorn's position. 'These
fizzheads couldn't hit the wall of a hangar if they were
inside it.'

Spurred on by Baeder's contempt for the Archenemy,
Galhorn and his men picked up their weapons and
surged towards the direction of flashing muzzles. They
dropped into position after a short thirty-metre sprint
and began to return enfilade fire along the advancing
enemy flanks. Carnibalès fighters were caught in a
crossfire and fled from the long hall back up the corridor, leaving behind the mangled husks of over twenty
insurgents.

'On! On!' Baeder urged. 'Don't give them breathing
space!' At his command, a platoon clattered down the
hall under Riverine covering fire and entered the
enemy-held corridor with bayonets fixed. There was a

grenade flash followed by the grunts, exertions and clash of body on body.

'He's going to get us killed,' Schilt muttered under his breath. From his position at the rear of the Riverine advance, all he could see were the lurking shapes of Carnibalès, and Riverine pushing forwards against the hail of enemy munitions. As a Riverine fire-team sprinted forwards, an autocannon round erupted in their midst, punching a jagged spear of limestone into the air. Bruhl and Drexler literally fell apart at the joints. Fragments of stone and metal shredded Daimler's flak vest from his torso along with much of his skin. Daimler skidded onto his rear, clutched his bleeding upper body with his arms and began to scream. Half of the squad halted and returned to drag Daimler by his boots. The Archenemy had expected this. They landed another autocannon shell in the exact same position. Haber, Landau and Riese disappeared in a mist of red.

Carnibalès rushed back into the barracks room, spraying wild gunfire. The fire-team closest to the corridor entrance faltered. Sergeant Ohm and Trooper Vasmer crumpled, spurting blood across the floor. Schilt never ceased to be amazed by how much blood the human body could leak. He saw Zermelo manage to fire back with two shots before a wraith-like commander of the Carnibalès chopped him from shoulder to sternum with a machete. The Riverine advance was blunted. It looked like the slight gain they had pushed for would be lost.

Then Schilt saw Baeder bring up the remains of Lieutenant Kifer's platoon. 'Don't fall back one step!' he bellowed. 'Bruhl and Drexler didn't die so you could fall back!' Baeder palmed a rushing Carnibalès in its face so violently that the insurgent's upper body folded backwards at ninety degrees. Combatants fired their rifles directly into the faces of their enemies. Bayonets clashed with machetes. A grenade went off, blowing apart Riverine and insurgent alike.

Schilt had had enough. In his opinion, Baeder was pushing them into a meat-grinder, churning able-bodied Guardsmen into loose shreds of uniform and gore. He lurked behind a stack of paper crates well behind the main thrust of advance. Inside the crates, there were pamphlets depicting a rosy-cheeked rural boy with the stencilled words – *'Question Imperial authority'*. If Schilt stared too long at the boy, the picture seemed to melt softly and blur, the boy's soft cheeks whitened and his eyes became dark holes. It was either a trick of the light or foul magic.

Spooked by the prophetic symbolism, Schilt crawled away from the crates and lined up his lasgun on Baeder. The melee was now a heaving scrum of heated gun barrels and flashing blades. Schilt saw Baeder plough his power fist into the Archenemy pushing down from the corridor. The colonel had established a solid brawling stance with his legs staggered, throwing looping punches from the hip. A Carnibalès rushed at him with a raised machete and the colonel put him down with a wound-up punch. Two more insurgents charged forwards and Baeder crushed their sternums in rhythmic succession, one – two. Schilt lined up Baeder's back with his cross hairs. He breathed out, releasing all the tension through his nostrils.

'Snap. I got you, you fizz-headed fragger.'

And with that, Corporal Schilt clenched the trigger.

* * *

MURALS ON THE mess hall walls had once depicted PDF soldiers standing side by side with Bastón natives as a symbol of solidarity. Now they were smeared with the blasphemous runes of Chaos. Dark daemonic shapes had been painted into the original artwork, wraith-like apparitions that seemed to shift and move if one looked upon them for too long. Steencamp ordered flamers to be put to the walls, peeling and blistering the murals from the rockcrete. Some Riverine swore that the walls screamed as they were torched.

The fighting had ebbed and floundered in their advance. Steencamp consolidated his remaining men, just over sixty Riverine, in the empty mess hall. The Carnibalès had been filthy, carpeting the entire floor space in refuse. Gnawed bones, rations wrappers, crockery and plastek had been mashed into a splintered carpet of detritus. Steencamp thought he saw a human fingerbone amidst the mess and hurriedly kicked it away. He set up fire-teams on the three double door entrances and reorganised his battered company.

From vox reports, Baeder and Seeker Company were mired in heavy fighting in a barracks facility just two hundred metres west of their position. Supposedly, they were close to the core and the Carnibalès were throwing up a stiff resistance. Prowler and Serpent Company were bringing up movement to their east, lagging several hundred paces behind in the bowels of sub-tunnels. Those companies were drawn into a savage firefight with Carnibalès elements flooding up the tunnels behind them. According to reports, the enemy reinforcements were troops withdrawn from the docking hangars away from the decoy Riverine assault. Steencamp noticed that, for the first time, the vox-officers referred to the Archenemy insurgents as 'troops'. If anything, this hellish fight in the rail tunnels had earned the rebels a measure of bitter respect.

Steencamp recharged his lasrifle with a fresh clip and tucked the spent one under his flak vest. 'All right, ram-rods,' Steencamp drawled in his vowel-heavy Ouisivian accent. 'Colonel Baeder and Seeker are close to the Earthwrecker. The Carnibalès are soiling their rags now and throwing up everything they have left. We're going to move in and support them. Prowler and Serpent are going to defend our rear.'

Steencamp led the sixty men off into the darkened tracts which fed into the core of the subterranean fortress. Murals were there too. The Archenemy had painted depictions of their idols into the brickwork – wispy, daemonic faces that danced and leapt and whirled. The overhead luminite strips gave the paint-work a surreal backlit quality. Their world seemed to consist of only three colours: black, crimson and ruddy ochre.

As the company pressed on in squad order, Steen-camp could not help but stare at the paintwork. As a child, he had always been frightened of particularly realistic portraits of stern ancestors that dominated the hallways of his family home. He had been convinced that those stern oil painted features would move, and those hands, clasped so demurely in their laps, would lunge out to seize him. Now, in the intestinal depths of the Archenemy lair, those fears suddenly seemed very real. So real, that when the paintings began to shift and move, Steencamp refused to believe it.

The paintings peeled away. The shadowy forms came unstuck from their two-dimensional moorings and moved towards him. Steencamp was paralysed by fear.

'Sorcery!' screamed a Riverine. A las-shot cracked out.

The snap of gunfire broke Steencamp's stupor. It was Archenemy magic indeed. He had never seen it, but he had heard the Ruinous Powers were certainly capable of such things. Carnibalès fighters seemed to melt from the walls, camouflaged amongst the paintings. They were daubed in blacks and reds and ochre chalk to blend in with their surroundings. Heretic sorcery had done the rest. It was an ambush that no textbook in the Guard Primer could have prepared him for.

Carnibalès troops crashed in on both flanks with the tools of close combat. Blades rose and fell. The company fell into disarray. Dozens of Guardsmen were run through before they could react coherently. Steencamp's nightmare was now reality. Where there had been a particularly obscene painting of a red tribal dancing with a black daemonette, a Carnibalès wielding a machete materialised in its place. The heretic was naked, his skin reddened with inks. When he smiled, he showed the whites of his teeth and eyes.

The captain brought up his lasrifle, but the heretic jammed the rifle at chest level with his machete. Something surged into him from behind and Steencamp lurched towards the red fiend. They fell against the wall, clinched up, lasrifle locked against rusty blade. Another Carnibalès appeared at his side, this one entirely black and wielding a scythed sabre that resembled the crooked claw of the painted daemonette. Steencamp screamed as the sabre carved into his lower back. His vision dimmed from the pain. The metal plunged into his side was shockingly icy. Another blade hacked into his upper legs. Steencamp crumpled into the swarming press of bodies. Painted fiends looked down on him as his vision tunnelled. More blades stabbed downwards. Just like that, the paintings swallowed up Ghost Company.

'SCHILT! DON'T DO it!'

A boot kicked Schilt's perfectly angled elbow from its shot. The lance of las-fire went wide. Colonel Baeder continued to fight, unaware of how close to death he had come. Schilt snarled and rolled onto his back and, for once, it was he who was surprised.

Standing behind him, eyes still wide with surprise, was Volk. The big man seemed to be awed into disbelief by his own actions.

'Damnit, Volk. Why'd you have to go and spoil it?' Schilt growled.

The dissident Riverine, usually foul-mouthed and pugnacious, stammered for the right words. 'You can't kill our colonel,' Volk finally replied.

Schilt narrowed his eyes. It was a familiar experience. It slitted his face into a serpentine glare. '*Your* colonel?'

'He... he's not that bad, Schilt. I didn't join the Guard to duck fighting. A bad officer can get us killed, I'll throw my hat in with that. But Baeder, he ain't so bad. He's a gambler, but he does the job.' Volk took a deep breath, as if summoning words that had been bottled up inside him for a long time. 'Schilt,' he said, exhaling, 'you've got your priorities all messed up.'

Schilt's expression softened. It was a strange contrast to the roaring gunfight around him and the pounding drums of the Archenemy. He stood up and pulled Volk behind a support column as stray shots whined past them. 'You're right. I'm a Guardsman. Damnit, what was I thinking?'

'You weren't!' laughed Volk in relief. He slapped Schilt on the back. 'If either of us get out us this alive, you'll thank me.'

Schilt leaned in and smiled. 'I know *I'm* getting out of this alive.'

Volk's eyes widened. Schilt had already stabbed him in the chest. Volk gurgled. His eyes bulged. The stub gunner tried to push away, but his left leg began to spasm. Schilt leaned in with his blade and twisted. After more seconds of trembling, Volk stopped struggling and sagged towards the ground. Schilt laid him down in a seated position, well hidden behind the column. He wiped his knife clean on Volk's uniform and resheathed it.

Warily, Schilt peered around the column to see if anyone had witnessed the killing. No one had. Fire-teams were clattering towards the corridor. A squad sergeant spotted Schilt and waved him on. 'Leave him, he's done for,' commanded the sergeant, pointing at Volk's body.

In the smoking aftermath of their skirmish, Baeder had broken the stalemate at the corridor and the company was moving up to support him. The shooting had finally subsided. Still cursing the misfortune of his spoiled shot, Corporal Schilt picked up his lasgun and ran to join his company.

PULVER DIDN'T FEEL like the aggressor. It certainly did not seem like the Carnibalès were fazed by the suddenness of their assault. The Archenemy had reeled like a wounded ogre stung by a needle, but they had rallied swiftly and were now mauling them, lunging and trapping them from all directions.

The sirens were whooping. Emergency lighting flickered. The tunnels were hot with the shimmering haze of flame. Pulver's Serpent Company became lodged at a main carriage tunnel, pinned ahead by emplacements dug into the railhead and assaulted from the rear by reinforcing units. They simply did not have enough guns to cover all areas. The Riverine clustered in the open. Las-fire scythed down dozens of men, each of whom Pulver knew by name and had served with for many years. A bolt shell glanced off Trooper Freige's leg at the shin. Freige fell on his backside, swearing at the enemy who had just changed his fortunes forever. Corporal Klader ran to put himself between Freige and the enemy line of sight as Medic Lowith tried to stem his blood loss. Freige swore at Lowith and he swore at Klader. 'Roll me onto my stomach and give me my gun you fraggers,' bellowed Freige. Klader did as he was told and Freige began to bang shots down the tunnel at the enemy. A grenade exploded overhead and Pulver lost sight of them all in a dense shower of smoke.

Baeder had voxed them and ordered them to hold their position. Seeker Company was close to their objective, Baeder promised. He just needed Pulver to halt the Archenemy for another fifteen minutes. Pulver had spat. 'I'll give you thirty,' he had said.

Pulver simultaneously led the fighting on both fronts. He directed fire-teams heavy with flamers to hold the Archenemy at bay to their rear, while he assaulted the railhead to the fore with bayonet.

At two metres tall, Lieutenant Vayber led the charge, crashing his fen-hammer into the Archenemy barricade. The Carnibalès shot at him as he ran, but big Vayber did not fall down. The enemy lost heart and fell back. Once they claimed the railhead, Vayber folded to his knees and allowed himself to die.

Pulver surveyed the carnage. A landslide of bodies littered the sloping carriage tunnel they had come down. Riverine and Carnibalès alike were twisted in the stiff-armed poses of the dead, their legs straight and stiff while their arms were locked up, some pointing upwards, others reaching out for something. The air stank of blood and faeces. The Riverine were taking up defensive positions at the railhead, kicking and rolling bodies off the barricades and firing points. Pulver jammed a wad of dip into his mouth in preparation for the inevitable counter-attack. Just thirty more minutes, he thought. Thirty.

THIRTY-ONE, THIRTY-TWO, THIRTY-THREE...

Trooper Kesting counted the dead felines the Archenemy had such a fondness for stringing up. It kept his mind off the grinding fear of death. The deeper Baeder led them, the heavier the fighting had become. A crackle of shots lit up their front.

The column stopped and Guardsmen scrambled for cover. Kesting followed his squad behind a stack of locomotive machinery. Support weapons spilled out to cover the various angles of approach. The entire company fanned out before a blast door, wide enough to accommodate the girth of a super-heavy artillery piece. The grid-toothed shutter that towered above them was half open like an iron jaw, inviting them in. From side tunnels, Archenemy troops fired sporadically. Kesting watched rounds shatter off the limestone with an almost bored detachment.

This was it. The final push. The Earthwrecker, by all accounts, lay dormant beyond those blast shutters.

I wonder if they've sacrificed more felines in there, Kesting mused. A las-shot skimmed his helmet, the

kinetic force slapping the top of his head as if remind-
ing him to keep behind cover. It was absurd but Kesting
was not at all frightened. They had come too far to be
panicked. Even the lurking enemy gunmen, sniping
from their posts, no longer really fazed him. He looked
around. The enemy fired at him again, this time missing by a wide margin. Kesting spotted the muzzle flash
and calmly pointed it out to Ruslet who carried the
squad's grenade launcher. Ruslet plopped a round into
the distance and settled back, quite pleased with himself.

This war is absurd, Kesting decided. A missile shook
the chamber. The Riverine answered back with heavy
bolter and stubber. As they did, Kesting rocked on his
haunches and thought about felines.

'ALL COMPANIES, THIS is Seeker. We are in. Push towards
us and hold the Archenemy reinforcements off our
backs,' came Baeder's command over the vox.

Pulver fired a shot with his autogun in one hand and
gripped the vox speaker with the other. His lasgun,
spent of all clips, lay discarded by his feet. 'Seeker, this
is Serpent. Prowler and Serpent are holding the tunnels
to your direct rear but we are low on ammunition.
Enemy presence is thick.'

'What about Ghost Company?'

Pulver hesitated, surprised that Baeder did not know.
'Ghost Company are gone, sir. They were ambushed in
the main carriage tunnel parallel to your position
about a quarter hour ago. We've since lost contact.'

'Hold position, sergeant. We're in,' Baeder repeated
before static swarmed the channel.

Pulver dropped the handset and edged his head
above the ridge of sandbanks. Carnibalès elements

ghosted in the carriage works, less than forty metres away, flitting from shadow to shadow. The fighting had waned to a drizzle of half-hearted las-fire. The Carnibalès were sending four- and six-man teams down the tunnel, probing their strength, testing their resolve. The Riverine dug in behind their captured fighting positions to conserve ammunition. They could see the Carnibalès out there were gathering, swelling for another surge.

Sliding a new clip into his laspistol, Pulver made a mental checklist of what he would do in the final delaying action. He had one spare clip in his webbing and a half clip he wedged into his harness strap. A missile launcher was propped against the sandbag within reach, two warheads laid out beneath it. His tools were rudimentary, but the hand administered to him dictated the result. He would try to kill as many of them as he could before they killed him.

It was an ammunition bunker adjacent to the core where the Carnibalès walled up the fiercest resistance. Amidst the stacks of Earthwrecker shells, Archenemy fighters laid down a furious web of las. Resembling coned silos, they stood ten metres tall, enamelled in the pitted black of a ship's anchor. Ordnance stood in rows like sentinels, dozens and dozens of them.

Within the maze, Baeder directed the remaining squads of Seeker Company. Las hissed into the munitions, rounds ricocheted off the thick black skin. Baeder flinched inwardly every time one of the shells was struck. These were not simple ordnance but self-propelled rockets capable of long-range ballistic trajectory, each carrying a fission charge. It would only take one ruptured shell to devastate the entire bunker.

Perhaps that was what the Archenemy were trying to achieve, he thought.

To his left, Sergeant Bering's squad was getting hit hard. A Riverine was bleeding out on the floor as Bering and the medic fought to clip the artery. The squad huddled around them were sprayed with blood. Distressed, Trooper Tuton crept around the cover and squeezed off a long burst. A bolter round exploded from his lasgun. The broken weapon flew off in one direction and pieces of his hand sprayed out in the other. Tuton fell back to his squad, clutching the stump of his wrist.

To his right, Baeder saw Corporal Helvec's squad pinned out in the open. Carnibalès trapped them in three directions. Rounds popped at them, slicing between the Riverine, over their heads, around their shoulders, glancing off the ordnance with metallic rings, punching smoking holes into the enamel. It looked as if rain was kicking up chalky clouds of lime-stone around their feet. Helvec held the platoon together by example alone. He stood up in the firestorm and coordinated his men to fire in disci-plined volleys.

Baeder was aware that if they did not advance their position, the Archenemy would pick them apart and overwhelm them. He spotted an enormous locomotive carriage on the rail grid that ran the length of the bunker into the tunnel beyond. It was a payload trac-tor, a flat-nosed hulk of yellow metal and railing that carried six Earthwrecker shells on its flatbed. If he could get at least one platoon behind that thing, they could drive it before them as cover. To reach it, however, they would have to expose themselves in the open. As Baeder considered his decision, he saw Corporal

Helvec picked off his feet by a bolter round. The shot slammed him backwards and left a smear of blood on the shell behind him. Baeder's mind was made up.

Baeder lifted his power fist. 'Three Platoon, on me! Go!'

Baeder broke cover and ran. He could feel his legs shaking from fear. He squinted into the line of Archenemy muzzle flashes. Some of them definitely were not human any more. Their faces were mummified in strips of leather and some bore inhuman appendages. These were not peasant rebels. At least not to Baeder. He expected to be pole-axed by a well-aimed round, but the killshot did not come.

Instead, Baeder ran into the rail tractor so hard he clashed his elbows into the rear of the machine. Three Platoon piled in behind him, shooting in all directions.

'Release the braking system!' Sergeant Melthum yelled hoarsely. Several troopers put their weight against a rusting track lever that locked the tractor in place. Shots whipped into the platoon, dropping three men. The lever would not give. Archenemy troops scurried into the open, dozens at a time, firing volleys and then ducking back into cover. Still the lever would not give. The Archenemy reappeared, ready to catch them again. This time the platoon's heavy stub gunner was waiting for them. He emptied what must have been an entire drum of rounds in their direction, firing long after they had rushed back into hiding.

In those brief few seconds of respite, Baeder tore away the track's braking pads with his power fist. He gouged them away with his armoured fingers, tearing off strips of metal like strings of melting rubber.

'Get up, ramrods!' Baeder ordered. Sergeant Melthum was already in the cab by the time Baeder clambered aboard. The rest of the platoon piled onto the flatbed or stood on the running boards with one hand on the side railing and the other firing their lasguns. Melthum roused the gas engine. The tractor jolted and began to pick up a grinding, steady speed. A shot crazed the cab windshield. A Carnibalès insurgent with a flamer ran out into the open and aimed his flickering ignition flame at them. Baeder leaned out of the open cab door and flattened him with a burst from his autopistol. As the tractor advanced, the rest of Seeker Company fell in behind the locomotive.

The tunnel loomed ahead. That was when the killing started.

It began with a roar. A bestial yell that temporarily silenced even the stutter of weapons. The sound rebounded off the walls in waves.

Heavily mutated Carnibalès fighters surged down the tunnel. Warped, their features melting, skin sloughing, bodies scaled, horned or fanged. They appeared barbaric in their looted leathers, many draped with chainmail surcoats or bolted with oblongs of beaten iron. Baeder gathered that these would be veterans – such a level of warp-touch required lengthy devotion to the Ruinous Powers.

A shadow darkened the corner of his vision. There lurked a phantom, solid in his plate like a citadel given human form, a heretic of the Traitor Legions.

It issued its challenge, that same resonant roar. A comb of membranous spines flared from its helmet. The crest raised up, trembling and fearsome.

Riverine redirected their fire onto it. Burning flashes radiated from the Traitor Marine's armour where nearby Guardsmen shot at it. The monster appeared unfazed. It raised a boltgun and fired six shots. The first gauged its aim. The subsequent rounds chopped down five Guardsmen off the tractor running board.

Then it was on them, ploughing into the side of the tractor cab. The chassis crumpled. Glass exploded. The metal punched inward. Riverine shouted. The monster snorted like a raging bovine. Baeder backed away from the buckled left-side of the tractor cab. A Riverine leapt off the running board and fired up at the Traitor Marine's armoured back. The Traitor torqued its immense torso and chopped out with a crescent blade the size of a harvesting combine's industrial cutter. The Riverine was cleanly separated with a curious puffing sound.

Baeder drew his bayonet, unsure of what he hoped to achieve with it. He clenched his power fist with the other hand. This would be it, he realised. If he hesitated now, then he could never look his men in the eyes again. He could never give an order or be saluted. All the privileges of command would now be repaid. Biting down on his tongue, Baeder leapt out of the cabin and drove his fist at the Legionnaire's chest.

JORMESHU SLAMMED HIS weight into the tractor cab, rocking the multi-tonne locomotive. Through the splintered glass, Jormeshu's ancient helmet focused its visual scanners on the rank slides of their occupants. If his knowledge of Imperial soldiery did not fail him, one was a squad-level leader and the other was the force commander. Punching his fist through the windshield, Jormeshu screamed into the cab with the sonic blast of his chest speakers. The door of the cab was too small to facilitate the width of his shoulders and the Legionnaire peeled off chunks of twisted metal in his fury to get at the Imperial commander. The man was terrified. Jormeshu's olfactory glands could already smell the sour spike of fright musk.

Jormeshu reached out with a gauntlet, the clawed tips of his glove plucking at the soldier. The man recoiled. A peal of laughter escaped from Jormeshu's vox-gills. Imperial soldiers had never been much sport for a Traitor Marine. The only time they had threatened his existence had been nine decades ago when Jormeshu and his gene brothers had fought a regiment known as the 'Valhallans' on some wastrel's ice-world. Those tenacious long-coats had actually forced the Blood Gorgons into retreat down frozen slopes. Still, the Blood Gorgons had wiped them out within the hour and their bones were now entombed in some forgotten glacier. As empires went, the Imperium's standard of soldiery was woefully incapable when compared to a Traitor Marine.

So it came as a great surprise when the commander launched himself at Jormeshu. Caught off-guard, the commander's power fist rammed into his chest. Sparks lashed out from his ruptured plating. The armour's daemon spirit shrieked in shock. Bones in his chest cavity snapped. A rib punctured his secondary heart. The visual read-out on Jormeshu's helmet flickered and hazed as its spirit voice cursed him for his carelessness. The Legionnaire staggered, the columns of his legs churning for purchase as he lurched off the tractor.

A Guardsman shot him in the side. Without looking, Jormeshu fanned out his sabre to the left and silenced him. The Imperial commander actually had the gall to follow him off the tractor and strike him again while Jormeshu's nervous system was stabilising the shock trauma in his secondary heart. Jormeshu turned with the punch and the power fist pounded a crater into his shoulder pad. Furious, yet stunned, Jormeshu simply threw his weight into the commander. With five hundred kilograms of post-human sinew and augmetic plate, Jormeshu collided with his opponent and ran him into the ground. A volley of las and solid slugs drummed against his chest and bit shrapnel off his helmet, forcing him backwards before he could deliver the deathblow.

Then the Carnibalès veterans rushed onto the tractor, attacking the ponderous yellow beast like a swarm of tiny predators. The Imperial soldiers fanned out to meet their charge. To their credit, the soldiers held a thin line bristling with bayonets. Veteran Carnibalès fighters pushed forwards in a solid block, thrusting behind tower shields of cold forged iron. The clashing forces resembled warrior formations of prehistoric Terra, metal rasping against metal, shouting to be heard above the crack of splitting bones.

With only sixty-odd men in the company, the surging Archenemy spilled around them and viced their flanks. Face to face with the Guardsmen, the Carnibalès howled and spat from fish-toothed maws. They threatened to eat the livers of the Imperial fallen and put their spines in soup. The Guard struggled to hold their line, thrusting bayonets or hammering out with the butts of their rifles. A heavy bolter opened up at point-blank range, flattening a semi-circle of Carnibalès fighters before the crew were wrestled to the ground, hacked, stabbed and swallowed by the crushing advance.

Bruised and shaken, Jormeshu cursed. In the press of combat he had lost sight of the enemy commander. Never in his centuries of service to the Legion had he ever not been able to kill what he set his focus on.

Furious, Jormeshu discarded his bolter and whirled his sickle-sabre two-handed. He waded through the press, shearing limbs and bisecting torsos with a horrible, fluid ease. The sickle winnowed as he looped it back and forth. Guardsmen fled before his warpath, the line folding in panic.

FEAR, WARM AND tangible, ran down his legs. Corporal Schilt sagged to the ground as his throat constricted from panic.

Schilt considered running, but there was nowhere to hide. Instead he curled himself down and began to drag a corpse over himself. The body was that of Trooper Eschen, a rifleman of Eight Platoon. Eschen was still largely intact except for a bite wound that had separated most of his right cheek and forehead from his face. The blood rolled onto Schilt, still hot with vitality. Closing his eyes, Schilt tried to imagine he was somewhere else. Anywhere else but here.

'FIGHT AND WIN, ramrods! Fight and win!'

Even as the words left Baeder's mouth, they felt hollow and devoid of conviction. In the tide of combat, Baeder had been knocked into the rear lines, lurching as he tried to regain his bearings. The colours of the fen were on all sides of him, Riverine with their bayonets braced like spears. Rising like a leviathan above the sea, the Traitor Marine raised his reaping sabre. Blood drizzled off the slick surface.

Baeder raised his autopistol and emptied the entire clip at the Traitor Marine from a distance of twenty paces. Although a dozen skirmishing bodies separated him from his target, every shot found its mark on the Traitor Marine's chestplate. Yet the shots did nothing. Most ricocheted away from the ceramite slab and the sparse few which penetrated opened up pinprick wounds on the expansive pectorals. The Traitor Marine did not even spare Baeder an irate glance as he continued to chop his way through the Riverine.

CAPTAIN BUREN AND the last twenty-eight of his one hundred and twenty man company limped into the ordnance bunker to the sounds of throbbing combat. The bunker was high and wide, Earthwrecker shells lining the walls like monument stones. The sounds of fighting climaxed to such intensity that even those stoic black sentinels began to shiver, warheads shuddering rapidly against one another. The very ground seemed to shake.

'Forward, men. Not long to go now,' said Buren with renewed vigour. The Riverine, beards soaked in blood, uniforms hanging off their slumped shoulders in loose shreds, jogged forwards, suddenly alert.

At the opposite end of the bunker's cavernous womb they could see Seeker Company fighting to the last, a ragged fighting circle anchored in the centre by a rail tractor. Heavily armoured Carnibalès fighters assaulted them from the front, while Carnibalès regulars engaged them from the rear. They could not see much of the Riverine, except for brief flashes of swamp camouflage. The Carnibalès were all over them, a heaving, swarming, disjointed mess.

Buren, the youngest of the company's captains, was a stranger to warfare so ugly. He had been an academic in his youth and had served his early years as an artillery officer with the regiment's floating gun-barges. His expertise lay in trajectory, range-finding and the variable gravity of planets. The violence of close combat frightened him.

It was precisely his fear of a hand-to-hand engagement that had forced Buren to salvage the support weapons of their decimated company. The men clattered, not only with their own small-arms but with spare barrels and disassembled heavy guns. Those who did not strap a spare weapon to their backs were draped with coils of ammunition or hung hands of warheads like fruit from their webbing for those who did. Buren's prudence now proved its worth.

With great haste, Prowler Company uncased their missile tubes and unwrapped stubbers from canvas cloth. Bolt belts were connected to bolter feeds and arcs of fire established. Buren put his expertise to use, directing missiles into the rear of the Carnibalès formation, dropping the warheads just short of the melee so they lacerated the Archenemy with shrapnel and flattened them with the force of explosion. Meanwhile, three grenade launchers pumped forty millimetre rounds in curving arcs, dumping their payloads into the Archenemy shield formation at the fore. Concussive bursts split the tightly-packed heretics so hard that shields flipped high into the air. Four heavy stubbers drilled cyclical fire, chopping Carnibalès' legs out from underneath them. Prowler began to carve a path towards the beleaguered Seeker Company.

The Carnibalès assault began to disperse under the sudden salvo of heavy munitions. Carnibalès broke away, scurrying to avoid the relentless bombardment. A missile misfired and exploded against an Earthwrecker shell; its thick skin unperturbed, the shell toppled onto a rank of shield-bearing Archenemy fighters. Shrapnel whistled through the air like buzzing silver hornets. In the mayhem, Buren began to appreciate the brutal artistry of his craft.

THE FIRST BARRAGE hit the outer lines of the Archenemy and rippled panic through their ranks. With the certainty of slaughter suddenly denied to them, their barbarous ferocity weakened. Baeder climbed aboard the wrecked tractor and raised his power fist like a standard, its energy field shining outward in a perfect circular halo. 'The fury of Ouisivia renewed! Let's quash these heretics under a soldier's boots!' bellowed the colonel, reciting a line from a folk poem of the fen.

Less than forty men were able to drag themselves, bleeding and bruised, around the colonel. They discharged the remaining rounds from their rifles at the retreating foe. Rocket and fragmentation erupted around them, dangerously close, but they held firm.

As THE ARCHENEMY receded, Schilt rolled out from beneath the corpse of Trooper Eschen. The Archenemy left their dead in trampled piles. The Traitor Marine, wounded and bellowing in rage, knelt amidst a tumble of dead Carnibalès heretics.

Schilt edged towards the Traitor Marine slowly. Both its legs had been shorn away at the kneepads, the jagged ends of his ceramite scorched by rocket flame. Numerous gunshot wounds punctured its upper chest and arms, a mixture of syrupy blood and black fluid leaking from the gaping holes. In between its brays of outrage, the Traitor Marine's breath was ragged and irregular. Electrical sparks spat from the gargoyle vanes of its powerpack.

Despite its weakened state, the Traitor Marine was still dangerous. Schilt circled warily until he was behind the armoured beast. Despite Schilt's notable stealth, the Marine snapped its head around. The helmet had been worked into the shape of a long-faced female with a harlequin's grin. The mask regarded Schilt with a frozen, long-toothed smile. It snorted a metallic chortle through its vox-gills.

'Well done, Emperor's soldier. Your commander has outplayed me. But I am just one Legionnaire. How many of your friends have I killed today?' it rasped.

'They weren't no friends of mine,' replied Schilt through gritted teeth. He raised his lasrifle to his shoulder and aligned the ironsight on the Traitor's helmet.

The Traitor Marine grunted in resignation. Schilt savoured that. The monster that had robbed him of his dignity had now been reduced to Schilt's mercy. He squeezed the trigger. Automatic las-fire whined from his muzzle in whickering, white flashes. Molten droplets fanned out like a welder flame to iron. Slowly, the faceplate deformed and split, flesh parted to fortified bone. The bone gave way and finally the Traitor Marine slumped.

'Corporal! It's done! It's dead. Let's move!'

Schilt spun and saw Baeder waving him on. Seeker and Prowler Company had formed up and were following the track bend out of the bunker before the Carnibalès could regroup. Stray rounds were already hissing towards them from behind the cover of Earthwrecker shells. They did not have the luxury of time.

'Yes, sir,' Schilt replied, breaking into a jog. 'You're next,' he added under his breath.

THE EARTHWRECKER WAS an ugly behemoth. It was sixty metres of barrel supported on an arachnid grid of gas valves, shock dispersal coils and pistons the size of cathedral columns. The entire weapon was self-propelled on a locomotive engine of heavy steel and grease. Structurally the interlocking support beams had to withstand the pressure of seven hundred tonnes. The Earthwrecker, Baeder decided, was a monument of destruction.

It was dormant now in its firing station, the muzzle locked into a crane system that delivered shells down into its iron gullet. Eight vertical apertures carved into the circular chamber allowed the Earthwrecker to steam forwards on a U-shaped rail track, once loaded, and slide its cannon barrel into a balistraria. The view from the apertures was shockingly beautiful: a broad vista of the jungle canopy below, a flat pane of green that reflected the rosy hue of dawn.

The survivors of Seeker and Prowler Company were laying a web of detonation cord and clamp charges on the war machine under the direction of Trooper Leniger. At thirty-eight, Leniger had been a bridge builder back on Ouisivia before he mustered for the Guard. The man often referred to himself as a mechanic of the landscape, laying down bridges, roads and swamp crossings. In Baeder's experience, Leniger was as good as if not better than combat engineers from more specialised regiments. Under his supervision, the Earthwrecker would not fire another shell.

Baeder climbed the ladder to the loading gantries as the few remaining officers of the 88th climbed after him. From the upper gallery of the circular chamber they trained their weapons on the blast doors, expecting one last Archenemy push. But none came.

'Sir, it's done!' Leniger shouted from below.

As the charges were placed and timers set, the Riverine evacuated the chamber. Baeder was the last to leave.

He took one last look at the Earthwrecker. He tried to envisage the immensity of its recoil, threatening to split its structural girders. He imagined the cranial-pounding roar of its gun as it was fired in the confines of that chamber.

'Sir!' Leniger repeated. 'We have two minutes, sir. This chamber is rigged to collapse.'

Baeder lingered, casting the Earthwrecker a final look. A look of equal parts awe and hatred. The machine was silent in its execution, indomitable and unmovable.

'Can't hate the gun, sir,' Leniger said, tapping Baeder by the elbow. 'It didn't kill the men. The gun didn't send us alone into a meat grinder. The Ecclesiarchal fizzheads did.'

Leniger's accusations shocked Baeder. It was borderline heresy and, by all rights, Baeder should have given him *the heretic's court martial*, four rounds to the body forming the points of the aquila. Yet, startled though he was, Baeder could not find a reason to disagree.

ALL SOUND WAS drummed out by the tectonic quaking of earth and tunnel. The Earthwrecker was dying, consuming in its pyre the exposed shells. A chain of explosions trembled the stronghold. Carnibalès tried to gather their shrines and flee above-ground like drowning rodents.

Seeker and Prowler retreated to the docking hangars, passing the abandoned war machines of the rebels. Aimed at the landing piers were quad-linked support guns and a dozen missile batteries. Facing the mouth of the hangar, an Earthshaker cannon was aimed squarely out towards the water. It was only then that Baeder recognised the wisdom of his judgement. Had the 88th

Battalion elected to storm the exposed pier as expected, the waiting enemy would have decimated them.

Major Mortlock and the flotilla waited for them thirty metres from the shore. Of the 88th Battalion's five hundred and fifty men, ninety-six remained. Ghost Company had been entirely lost. Casualty rates had exceeded even initial estimates and stood at eighty per cent. So decimated were they, that fully two-thirds of their vessels were abandoned for lack of crew. The survivors were feverish with infection and malnutrition. As adrenaline drained away, the last fumes that had propelled their weary frames deflated.

Baeder was the last one onto the boats. He waded through the water and had to be pulled up onto the vessel by others. He simply lacked the strength. They were paper soldiers now, thought Baeder as he passed out on the deck of his swift.

The 88th who sailed down the Serrado, victorious though they were, sailed with the dreadful silence of the defeated.

CHAPTER SEVENTEEN

THE PERSEPIAN NAUTICAL Fleet sailed into Union Quay like silver blades against the flat grey pane of ocean. They were greeted by the great fanfare of the local administrates, docking for the first time in months amidst multi-coloured blizzard streamers and the pomp of brass bands playing Vinevii's *Hail to the Cavalry*. Imperial citizens who just days ago had been hiding in their habs now flooded the dockside in force. Mothers carried toddlers who waved paper banners. Acrobats vied for attention alongside preachers who praised the grace of the Emperor in righteous bellowing voices. The clap of fireworks painted streaks of pink, green and yellow into the sky.

The festivities were cut abruptly short. Military command was in no mood to rejoice. Admiral de Ruger ordered the port cleared of all civilians for the disembarkation of the landing forces. Thousands of stern-faced Guardsmen, hungry for combat, were released onto dry land. Columns of Chimeras churned down the eastern viaduct of the city, the graffiti of the previous week's rioting covering the damaged structures that towered above them. Loyalists stood on the streets and leaned out of windows to watch the Guardsmen pass by. Tall shaven-headed soldiers rode on the roofs of their armoured transports, their faces expressionless. The population of Union City was convinced that the insurgency would soon be over.

Within two hours, twenty thousand Motor Rifles had rolled into the rainforests of Bastón. Hamlets were crushed under the treads of APCs while truckloads of dismounted infantry chased down the villagers. It was like a hunting of vulpines by ancient Terran nobles, the Guardsmen crushing their way into the forest and shooting down anything that fled from the disturbance. No distinction was made between loyalist and heretic. In the eyes of the Ecclesiarchy, they were all tainted. According to Montalvo, it simply made for an effective military strategy.

Persepian Poseidon-class patrol boats, off-shore combat vessels forty metres long from bow to stern, were released into the river systems under orders to 'reclaim the waterways'. Beyond that, orders were flexible and the Persepians rampaged in the coastal estuaries, volleying broadsides into river villages. Their destruction was only restricted by shallower waters further inland.

Despite this, insurgents continued to fight. Mortars, preceded by hit-and-run, were the preferred method of engagement. Small groups, sometimes as little as two or three Carnibalès, harassed the grinding Imperial advance. By afternoon, the Guard reported an estimate of two hundred dead enemy combatants. Yet they also reported forty-five Caliguans and three Persepians killed in action. An Orca was further immobilised by a mortar round and grounded its keel in the muddy Serrado. As the advance continued inland, casualties were expected to escalate.

THUNDER ROLLED ACROSS the ocean, its approached heralded by tides crashing against the quayside. A strong gale dragged a sheet of darkening clouds overhead, pulling black and grey over the blue sky. On the harbour, the deployment continued. Wind lashed and pulled at the Guardsmen as they guided trucks and Chimeras off the carrier ramps. They thought this a bad omen and pointed their thumb and smallest finger towards the encroaching storm, shouting '*Misfortune and mischief, away away*' as the keening wind stole their voices. It was only an infants' nursery rhyme, but it seemed to give the Guardsmen some comfort.

Lieutenant Duponti clambered down the side of his Lightning and sucked the cold, un-recycled sea air into his lungs. It was a welcome change, after having spent the majority of the previous weeks in the pressurised cockpit of his strike-fighter. But finally the 88th had broken the stalemate. Duponti's duty, for now, was fulfilled.

The flight deck was empty except for a small huddle of officials waiting to greet him. Duponti was in no mood for ceremony. His limbs were stiff from poor circulation and the stimulants were intoxicating his system. He felt giddy and light-headed. As he approached the group, Duponti's heart sank. It was an Ecclesiarchal gathering, no doubt ready to save his soul when what he really needed was for them to have saved him a shot of dramasq and some eggs and ham.

Cardinal Avanti stood in the centre, flanked by two altar bearers, regarding him with cold, flat, watery eyes. A cope of gold thread bound him together and kept the wires and machines that sustained him hidden from view. A mantle of sea-bird feathers was draped across one shoulder and embossed rings of blocky gold lined his well-manicured hands. The altar bearers wore only tabards of parchment despite the storm winds, their chem-nourished arms oiled and scraped. As much for intimidation as they were for clerical service, one bore the cardinal's sceptre of authority and another a gilded trident.

'Let me be the first to commend you on exemplary conduct in the course of your duties,' Avanti said, spreading his bell-sleeved arms.

It sounded like rehearsed babble to Duponti. The aviator eyed the cardinal warily. He had defied the admiral's orders and he doubted the cardinal was unaware of this. It was common knowledge amongst the Persepian soldiery that the cardinal's attention was best averted.

'The Emperor and His saints have smiled upon you. Surely were it not for them, you would not have succeeded in this arduous task,' Avanti continued, clearly enjoying his own impromptu sermon.

No, Duponti thought, it was a dangerously high amount of stimms and my own brass balls that got the job done. Yet he bit his tongue and nodded, forcing up a thin smile.

'The 88th's sacrifice in allowing my campaign to proceed will surely earn them the Emperor's forgiveness. In fact, I myself may give personal respect for their deeds,'

Avanti continued, seemingly addressing an audience of thousands rather than a lone weary aviator.

'Of course. Your respect is invaluable to front-line Guardsmen,' Duponti said.

Avanti dropped his glacial stare level with Duponti. 'How tainted were the 88th by the end of the mission? I expect them to be turned stark raving mad by the Ruinous Powers after having been in such close proximity.'

Something was not right. A sudden menace crept into the cardinal's cold, detached manner. Duponti decided to pick his words carefully. 'No, sir. They were coherent and unaffected. I can attest to that as we maintained vox contact up until twelve hours ago.'

'No. The Ruinous Powers would have changed them, just as they have changed the people of Bastón.' The cardinal spoke with a knowing tone that foreclosed any further argument.

Duponti gritted his jaw. Who was this Ecclesiarchal bureaucrat telling him what he knew? He had been out there in the field flying through flak while the cardinal had been pampering and manicuring himself in a stateroom.

The cardinal laid a palm on Duponti's heart. 'My poor child. It seems your judgement has been clouded by your close proximity with the Ruinous Powers as well.'

There was something in his voice. Something that suggested Avanti was playing a game with him. That the outcome of their conversation was predetermined and the cardinal was only going through the motions.

'I'm fine,' Duponti said, suddenly trying to walk around the trio. He was too tired for this.

'You are not. Do you hear voices and daemons?' Avanti asked, his voice raising several octaves and his eyes widening.

Duponti stepped backwards, knocking the cardinal's hand from his chest. He was being played with, he was sure of it. Something was conspiring against the 88th, and his insubordination had drawn him into it. Duponti darted his eyes about, hoping to see a fellow Persepian, but the wind howled across an empty flight deck.

'What do you hear?' Avanti repeated, eyes wide as he glided forwards.

Before Duponti could speak, the altar servant with the sceptre swung at his neck. Four kilograms of solid bronze landed with a jarring crunch on the top of Duponti's spine, whiplashing his head and sending him down.

'He is possessed, the poor child,' Avanti said with genuine concern. The altar servant with the sceptre continued to pound down with the holy relic as the aviator tried to shield the blows with his arms. The sceptre continued to rise and fall, breaking his forearm and forcing a scream from Duponti that was muffled by the buffeting northerly. Droplets of blood danced in the air, the wind carrying them into Avanti's face. The altar servant laid about, heaving and spitting with exertion until Avanti commanded him to stop. By then, Lieutenant Duponti was no longer moving.

'Give his daemonic soul to the sea. Let him drown for eternity,' Avanti said. He watched his servants tip Duponti's unconscious body into the waves. Satisfied, Avanti gave praise to the Emperor and wiped the blood from his face and his vestments.

* * *

IT HAD BEEN less than one week since the Guard had landed on the inland and already the Dos Pares cause was on the verge of collapse. Somewhere in the forest, Mautista heard the rustling snap of a felled tree, and the steady grumble of engines.

Mautista peered through a thicket, keeping amongst the leaves. He could see nothing in the distance. His eyesight had deteriorated in the past days, blood spots blanketing his vision. He knew his veins were haemorrhaging. His body had continued to warp, tearing and re-knitting his muscles. Most painfully, his bones had grown barbs, the tiny growths puncturing his skin like translucent quills. The internal bleeding was hazing his eyesight and swelling his flesh. It was agony to simply walk upright, let alone navigate the jungle.

His warband squatted miserably at his feet, wrapped in blankets of beaded fabric and dirty sheets of plastek. They had spent the last several days wandering from village to village in search of food. What they found were abandoned settlements as the Bastón fled before the march of the Imperial army, spurred on by tales of massacre along the coast and river regions.

The insurgency had relied on the support of the native population. It drew its strength, its resources and its powerbase from those native provinces. Indeed, its survival depended on the anonymity afforded by a network of Dos Pares agents seeded within the civilian population. But the Guard were razing and burning them, uprooting the insurgency from the ground. Just two days ago, Mautista tried to negotiate for ammunition from a local Disciple based in Manecal province. But word had arrived that their Disciple had perished and already been buried. The mutations had finally killed him. He had only been in service of the Dos Pares for forty-six days.

Worse still, when Mautista led his warband to seek medical supplies from the village of De Pano, they found an empty ghost town. Bodies of Bastón-born littered the streets, stiffened with their arms up to ward off their murderers. Province by province, the insurgency lost their network of influence. Where once there had been well-established lines of supply there were now scorched blisters of wasteland.

Communication lines had broken down throughout the network. Rumours were abounding that Carnibalès fighters were withdrawing from the coastal provinces to consolidate inland. Conflicting rumours suggested that other Dos Pares warriors were going to face the enemy head on.

Thus far the only tactical advantage possessed by the Carnibalès was their mobility and knowledge of terrain. The Four directed the warbands to avoid the Imperial combat elements and harass their supply lines. The inevitable tail of fuel trucks and logistics trains that followed the wake of the motorised divisions was firebombed and ambushed. Yet the war could not be won that way and, in six days, the Imperial Guard had reclaimed provinces almost two hundred kilometres inland.

'Mautista, do we flee or do we fight?' asked Canao, tilting his sloping cranium and clicking his mandibles nervously.

His question was punctuated by a sudden burst of cannon-fire. It sounded close, the rolling blast sending a burst of birds into flight. It was followed by flutters of small-arms. If Mautista strained, he could almost hear the agonised shouts of men.

'There,' Mautista said, pointed into the tangle of jungle where the river met the trees. 'There is fighting there.'

The rebels threw off their blankets and rose to their feet wearily. They cocked their weapons. Mautista did the same. 'We should join the fighting,' he said, but there was no need. The rebels were already slinking into the undergrowth.

THE RIVER STRETCHED out like a soupy brown thread towards the coast. Behind them, the dog-toothed silhouette of the Kalinga Hills faded into the distance. Monsoon season was fading too, yet the morning showers lingered reluctantly, desperate to exert the last of its sodden influence over the canopy.

The 88th travelled west, branching away from the Serrado river. By all accounts a Persepian naval picket had deployed Guard forces into the western seaboard. It was only a three day pass from their original route and an Argo-Nautical would pick them up. The thought of extraction was the only thing that kept Baeder's ailing body going forwards.

He dreamed of a scalding shower to dislodge the dirty crust from his body on board the Nautical's hygiene facility. Perhaps a full breakfast with extra servings of ham and eggs in the officers' mess. He reasoned that he could fall asleep in the infirmary while medics attended to his accumulated cuts, bruises and tropical agues. He would sleep for a long time.

Until then, Baeder instructed the 88th to remain alert. The Carnibalès were desperate now, cornered and wild. Although the region was dominated by the presence of an Argo-Nautical just off its shores, the threat of ambush was ever persistent.

By afternoon, when the heat extracted steam from the rain-slick surfaces, a forward scouting swift boat reported sighting a Persepian Nautical picket at a fork in the river where the ocean currents branched out into twigs of minor rivers.

'We've broken the stalemate, men. The 88th ended this,' Baeder proclaimed on the battalion vox. There would be a time for speeches later, for now it was a simple congratulatory remark that lifted a burden of tension from their shoulders. Riverine appeared on deck, embers of tabac hanging from mouths. They sagged against the gunwales, craning to catch a glimpse of the Persepians like lost sailors sighting land.

The last boats of the 88th linked up with the waiting scouts and rolled in to announce their arrival together. Baeder watched the men of the 88th gather on their bows. They looked less than human, like badly-drawn outlines of men. Wild dreadlocked manes and beards that appeared ridiculously leonine upon their slouching bodies. He could see Mortlock too, his head wrapped in gauze from where a bolt-round had bent his ship's rear railing in half and sent tiny particles of it into his scalp.

There was no cause for celebration. Instead, as they neared the extraction point, the 88th mourned. They remembered those who had set sail but not returned. Pulver, Steencamp, Vayber and hundreds of men they had known for years. It was doubtful that the 88th were even a functioning battalion any more. They were done. The war, at least for a while, would not include the 88th.

Closing the distance, a Persepian Orca-class patrol boat broke away from the picket. Long and lean with a towering cluster of vox-masts and auspex sweepers, it was larger than five swift boats in length. A trio of twin-linked autocannon turrets was tiered on the vessel's short streamlined superstructure.

It hailed them on a direct vox broadcast. 'Halt your position. On orders of the Imperial Guard.'

'This is eight eight battalion. We're coming in for extraction,' Baeder replied into his handset.

The Orca continued its path towards them, not appearing to slow. In the distance, another Orca peeled away from the picket and sailed towards their flotilla.

Baeder tried again. 'This is eight eight. Do you receive? Over.'

The first Orca was less than one hundred metres away and still closing fast. It split a frothing bow wave, breaking the smooth pane of brown water with its momentum. The men grew uneasy. Hesitantly, with no small amount of confusion, some of the Riverine settled behind their bow guns, unsure of why they were doing so.

Finally, the vox clicked and the Orca transmitted. 'Colonel Baeder, this is Lieutenant Commander Nemours of the Persepia 17th Patrol Group. I'm sorry. Soldier to soldier I'm sorry. But the cardinal's orders…'

The Orca smashed into the front rank of the flotilla, the sharp prow tilting airborne as it sliced into a swift boat, spilling Riverine into the churning water. The larger vessel's bulk landed like an ursine amongst pack dogs. Once it had entered the formation the Orca's turrets thudded, slashing 25mm rounds in a wide fan. Plumes of water misted the air, Riverine vessels broke apart, blood and debris fluttered down like an autumnal gale. Baeder stood still, for how long he did not know. After his ordeal, his mind did not comprehend the reality of what he saw.

The Riverine responded aggressively to the carnivore in their midst. Several missile tubes clapped, and warheads blossomed against the Orca's blue hide. A gun-barge drew parallel with the larger vessel and began to wash the length of it with a heavy flamer, fanning its weapon up and down. An Orca turret swivelled and unleashed a loud burp at the gun-barge, igniting its fuel tanks. The resultant explosion crumpled the Orca's starboard and it listed, the jagged wound taking water rapidly.

Regaining his senses in the white-hot fury of the explosion, Baeder pressed the handset to his mouth. 'Turn and move! Disengage upriver!'

Speed and manoeuvrability were the only things that would keep them alive as the second Orca surged in, with a third and fourth chasing its tail. The flotilla reversed direction rapidly, stern guns chattering defiantly. Three tubby gun-barges, all flamer vessels, intercepted the lead Orca to buy the other vessels time to escape. Smaller and faster, the barges circled the Persepian craft like piranhas worrying a sword-snout. They spat spurts of flame as the turrets swung in to track them. It was a brave but sacrificial gesture as more Persepian vessels flanked them and locked on with their targeting systems.

As the 88th fled from the Persepian picket, the flashes of the burning gun-barges shone orange on their backs. Their triumph burning away to tragedy, Colonel Baeder led his survivors inland. There was nowhere else for them to go.

BRIGADIER KAPLAIN WAS lying awake in his tent when he heard the first shots. Wary, yet curious, he tugged on his boots and slung his chest holster over one arm. The single shot crackled into a sustained splinter of gunfire that echoed in the still night. Shouts, sirens and then an explosion. Sweeping up two loaded pistol clips from his writing desk, Kaplain lifted the flap of his command tent.

Riverine Base Camp Echo was in a state of panic. Guardsmen sprinted in their undershirts to man battle stations. A storage hangar was up in flames. The klaxons were whooping on double-time, signifying red alert. The base camp was under attack.

The enemy were already among them. He could see shapes, backlit by vaporous curls of flame and smoke. In the distance, he saw the outline of a Rhino-pattern APC shooting bolter rounds like star clusters into the barrack lines. Kaplain strode into the path of a sergeant running towards the flames with a canister of compressed extinguisher. 'Report, sergeant,' Kaplain commanded in a soft even tone.

'They're in the perimeter, in amongst us,' gasped the sergeant, coughing between words on smoke-clogged lungs.

Kaplain remained calm. 'Who? Who is amongst us?'

'Adepta Sororitas entered the camp. Sentries had no reason to deny them entry,' the sergeant replied. As he spoke, his eyes flickered about in fear. A crackle of lasfire lit up the western perimeter of the base camp, just beyond the boat sheds.

'The Adepta Sororitas?' Kaplain echoed in confusion, his composure fracturing for a second.

Before the sergeant could reply his head disintegrated in a puff of blood, following the distinct report of a bolter. Kaplain blinked the red back from his eyelids. Tiny, clustered dots of blood fanned out in a circle ten metres wide.

'Brigadier,' said Palatine Morgan Fure, rising like a phantom out of the dense smoke pall. Five, ten, twelve battle-sisters followed her from the smog, marching in unison like automatons. Kaplain felt hopelessness when he saw them, a sheer weakness that he had never felt before. The Ecclesiarch had ordered the death of him and all his men. He was sure of it.

'Brigadier, we've come to take you. Do not resist us,' said Palatine Fure. Her sisters clacked their bolters into place against their shoulders like a firing squad. Each was shod from helmet to sabaton in plates of iridescent pearl that caught and reflected the flames like burning oil. The armour of their torso had been shaped into rigid corsets, studded lamellar plates that gave them feminine form, yet there the humanity ended. Their full helmets had visors worked into the hook-nosed grimace of Ecclesiarchal gargoyles. Crease-heavy cloaks of lavender velvet trailed from bulky power-units on their backs, fluttering like banshees. Their bolters, lacquered in black panelling, were tangled with coils of piety beads.

'You cold bitches. These men you're killing would have given their life for your damned cardinal,' Kaplain said evenly.

'No they wouldn't, brigadier,' said Fure with a smile. 'Your men and yourself are tainted by the dark influence of the interior. We can't afford the risk.'

'That's grox shit and you know it,' Kaplain said, reaching into his pocket for a tabac. The sudden movement caused the sisters to thrust their bolters meaningfully. Kaplain slid the tabac stick out without missing a step and lit it with a clink of his igniter. 'I suppose I'm not surprised the cardinal would do something. I just didn't think he'd be so brazen.'

'He is the Emperor's authority,' Fure said in a tone that suggested rote learning.

'What's the real reason. The 31st were a liability? We landed on the mainland as a self-sustaining vanguard and as soon as the cardinal's men arrive we become a liability. Shoot us all while we sleep and be done with it. Is that it?' Kaplain said, blowing smoke in Fure's face.

'We are cleansing the mainland. You would have refused,' Fure added, suddenly hesitant. 'Wouldn't you?'

'Yes. I would have refused,' Kaplain said, with a hint of pride. In the distance the ammunition stores cooked off in a great mushrooming cloud of white flame. Kaplain swore and slowly, steadily, put a hand to his pistol.

'Don't do it,' Fure warned, raising her bolter.

He drew it out a centimetre, as if daring the sisters to shoot.

'Last warning, Kaplain. The cardinal prefers you alive. It doesn't matter to me.'

Kaplain, in agonisingly slow fashion, unsheathed the autopistol from his holster. Fure and her line of white-clad executioners fired. Kaplain died instantly, pulled apart under a volley of bolt shells.

FOR A FULL day following the failed extraction, the 88th Battalion fled inland on foot. They abandoned their vessels sixteen kilometres east of their extraction point as arrowheads of Persepian aircraft shot overhead like migrating flocks.

The rainforest near the coast was a humid wilderness of sagging trees and mossy emergents. Without the use of machetes, the Riverine sawed their way through the vines, branches and entanglement with their bayonets. Sprightly, simian forms watched their piteous advance from the treetops. Palm-sized beetles vibrated their wings in a dry, clicking chorus and the air smelt of mildew and soil.

The last sixty-five men of the 88th Battalion slumped in a single file. Some of the troopers were so sick they could no longer walk without the support of a comrade. Finally, as exhaustion became total, some Riverine began to shed their support weapons, leaving them to rust in the jungle as they clawed their way forwards.

With his head down, speaking to no one, Colonel Baeder began to think. He thought first of the Imperium, of the empire that his men had died for. He was a soldier of the Emperor and he had given his entire being to serving His Grace. Yet in his finest hour of service, the Imperium had abandoned him. No, they had betrayed him. Even then, betrayal could not encompass what had occurred. The Imperium had tried to end him as if he had never existed.

It dawned on Baeder that, for his entire life, he had been fooled by the Ecclesiarchs, the historians, even his fellow officers, into believing the Imperium existed as a bastion of 'good' against the evils of the universe. There was no such thing as good or evil. There was just perception. Various, multitudinous, infinite modes of perception. That was all. Moreover, the death of his men had shown Baeder that the Imperium's perception of reality was not infallible.

Under the vastness of the rainforest, he saw himself as a lone individual whose perception had been pressured and sculpted by the Imperial system.

The rainforest thrummed with life, breathing as one vast organic mass. Each part was the constituent of a whole: the mammals could not survive without the nourishment of the wild, the greenery would not flourish without the seeded droppings of birds and herbivores. Even the mighty carnivore could not live without the insects, moss and microorganisms that sustained the lowliest of prey. Just as Baeder could not survive without his men, the battalion existed as a single, living beast. Where the Imperium fit into that equation, Baeder did not know.

He began to understand why the Bastón-born fought against them. The ferocity of their resistance seemed apt now. The way rebel provinces formed a network to shelter, provide and recruit for the insurgency. The way they willingly sacrificed their rural sons to fight trained Imperial soldiers. They fought for their right to existence. Their right to live or perceive the world as they chose to, not the perception that the Imperium imposed upon them. They had nothing to lose beyond that.

There was no good nor was there evil. The Ruinous Powers were the Archenemy, but they were not *his* Archenemy. As far as Baeder could discern, the only true enemy were the ones who fought to deny Baeder's right to existence. As that Orca had ploughed into his men, rewarding their triumph with an ignoble, shameful execution, Baeder had come to hate the Imperium.

The colonel tore the silver Imperial eagle from his lapel and cast it into the deepest hollows of the undergrowth. He stripped the rank slides from his epaulette and discarded those too, crushing them into the mud with his boots. Cursing, he stumbled forwards, lurching only through the forward momentum of his slumping head.

SOMETHING WAS CRUSHING his chest from above. Baeder could not move, could not even snatch open his eyelids. The weight on his chest was nauseatingly large in measurement. Hundreds upon hundreds of kilograms. The thought of trying to imagine the scale gave him a curiously sickening feeling in his stomach and made his temple throb.

Someone had taken the Earthwrecker, barrel and all, and then balanced the entire machine on his sternum. It compressed the blood from his torso out into his limbs, pulsating pressure into his fingertips. Baeder tried to force his eyes to open. He tensed his muscles, coiling them for one almighty push.

Baeder spasmed. He awoke from his fever and rolled onto his stomach. Phlegm clogged his chest and he gagged, dry-retching to clear his airways. Even the task of coughing fatigued him. He was slick, almost slimy with sweat and blackened grease. It dampened his clothes and made him shiver with cold, yet his head was searing with heat. Every breath he took, he felt as if were breathing pure steam. He dry-retched again.

Night was falling. He was in a clearing of sorts: a dell created by a depression between the tendril roots of tall blackspurs. A festering pool of water had collected in the hollow, its unmoving surface waxed with a dirty film. The waning indigo sky was fading between the blackspur canopy above.

Baeder could not remember, but it was likely they had chosen to rest here in search of water. The remnants of his battalion lay slumped, supine or curled up. They looked like battlefield dead, collapsing in a jumble of fatigued heaps. Major Mortlock lay next to him, his chin slumped into his chest, the bandages on his head dark red. Baeder thought he was dead until his eyes popped open.

'Sir,' Mortlock croaked. His lips were cracked from fever, peeling his tattooed ork's teeth into bleeding scabs. 'What now?'

It was a loaded question. *What now?* It asserted how directionless and devoid of purpose they had become. Baeder shook his head. 'I'd like to say we die fighting against the bastards who did this... but I just don't have the strength any more.'

'Who do you think will get us first? The Carnibalès or the Guard?'

Baeder knitted his brow in concentration. 'I'd rather die to the heretics than be killed by our own,' he decided.

'Can you imagine the memorial at Centennial Park back home? *In the memory of the 88th Battalion/31st Riverine Amphibious lost in action to fellow Guardsmen. May we forget them.*' Mortlock sighed. 'What a way to die.'

'They think we're tainted now, don't they? I don't think they erect memorials for renegade mutants,' said Baeder.

Mortlock suddenly held up a hand. 'Do you hear that?'

'No,' Baeder said.

Mortlock held a finger to his lips and motioned for silence.

Baeder sat very still, trying to make sense of the croaking, chirping choir of insects and amphibians with his feverish brain. Then he heard it. The heavy rustle of undergrowth, boots trampling the crisp stalks of tropical succulents. There were voices in the twilight. Then the distinct, echoing clack of an autogun being chambered.

A figure emerged over the crest of the dell, peering down at them. A face mummified in shreds of coarse leather. Loose canvas clothing. A lasrifle of raw metal.

Baeder closed his eyes. The Carnibalès had come for them. Some of the Riverine stirred, groping for their weapons. Strangely, Baeder felt neither fear nor panic. His temples were throbbing and that bothered him more than death.

They crashed down the slope, sliding and slashing through the foliage. Baeder clenched his power fist but realised the fusion generator was depleted, its display screen chipped and clouded with water. It was dark but Baeder could see the Carnibalès surrounding them, weapons drawn. The babble of foreign dialects hurt his head.

'Put down your arms,' commanded their leader. It hardly needed to be said. Caught off-guard, the Riverine had no fight left in them. Some looked up despondently and surrendered with their hands in the air.

The Carnibalès picked his way over to Baeder. 'I smell the musk of a leader in you,' he announced, pointing a finger at him.

Their commander had the characteristic corpse face and long-shinned bones of a Carnibalès warlord. He was tall, so very tall and thin that he seemed like a shadow thrown out by a setting sun. He wore the husk of ex-PDF leather with small discs of metal riveted over the torso and upper thigh. Black, swollen veins pulsated across white forearms in stark contrast. The moonlight reflected off the flat, angular planes of his face. Mutations had distended his jaw so that it jutted downwards and into a point, revealing long equine teeth. He couched a long-barrelled autorifle upright against his shoulder.

'I am,' said Baeder calmly.

'You are Fyodor Baeder. We have been looking for you. I am Mautista.'

Those words cut through Baeder's sickened state with startling clarity. He suddenly rose to his knees. 'How do you know my name?'

'It doesn't matter,' hissed Mautista, suddenly springing forwards into Baeder's face. 'You and your men will come with me now.'

'Just kill us here and be done with it,' Mortlock interjected with his head still sagging.

'Believe me, I want to eat your livers here while you squirm,' said Mautista. 'But the Dos Pares command otherwise. Come with me.'

'Why?' Baeder asked.

'I can't answer that. The Dos Pares see things that others cannot see. Gather your men and come with me.'

Several dozen figures loomed over them, guns drawn like spears in the fading light. Baeder thought about the Carnibalès's words. Surely, if they had wanted him dead, they would have killed him already. But they knew his name and evidently needed him for a purpose. He had no choice. He could not think of anything worse than being still alive while heretics chewed at his organs. At least playing along with them would give them all a chance to avoid that fate.

'All right.' Baeder rose unsteadily to his feet, feeling faint.

Mautista nodded. 'I will say this now. The Four have called for you. I have not. I will not hesitate to kill all of you if you try to harm me.'

THE GOUGE HAD many names – *Machanega* in the indigenous tongue, the earth's scar, split valley, although Imperial cartography referred to it simply as a gorge. Like most fluvial landforms, it was the product of prehistoric erosion, a deep canyon in the heart of

Bastón mainland. A narrow cleavage, eighty metres deep and almost one kilometre in length, it resembled a mouth in the landscape. A ridge of forest emergents formed its outer maw and stunted, hardy tendril growth lined the rocky interior. Dark and sheltered, the gorge festered with spore-bearing growth, polyphore and stalked fungi fighting for nutrients with horse root and flowering creepers.

There was history here. The earliest footsteps of mankind on Bastón were fossilised upon the mud. The early tribes believed the gorge had been caused by the crash of Dark Age exploration craft, the ancestors who had raised a human colony on that wild planet.

Petroglyphs depicting the creationist myths were carved in varying sizes into the sandstone. Anything from pictorials chipped into pebbles and discarded in the quarry, to carvings cut into the gorge face soaring sixty metres up.

Millennia later, the Bastón warrior-king Machad had united the kin groups in the fabled forty-year war against a band of alien pirates from the sky. Although the fey-like aliens had been few in number, they inflicted thousands of deaths upon the Bastón, until finally, with club and machete, the indigenous tribes trapped the aliens in the Gouge and starved them. Chalk paintings of stick-like creatures with leering pointed faces cavorting with spiked rifles, fighting ranks of ancient Bastón huntsmen, spanned five hundred metres of rock shelf. The paintings imparted legend into the history of the Gouge and, indeed, into the history of all the Bastón archipelagos.

It was here that the Dos Pares rallied their fragmented cells and prepared for their major counter-offensive. From across the mainland and its satellite islands, insurgent warbands gathered in the Gouge. But it was not only Carnibalès fighters that collected there. Refugees, many Dos Pares sympathisers, were there too and they aided the fighters in the industry of war. Crude munitions workshops set up in rock niches produced pipe bombs and fyceline. Production lines rushed to press-stamp lasgun components throughout the day and night.

All told, the Carnibalès fighters mustered a force of four thousand, many of them veterans from the previous months of conflict. At least one hundred were Disciples of the Four, their unstable mutations afflicting them with such physical pain that they raged and slavered, eager to die for the Primal Cause. The Four were also present, although now there were only three: Sau, Gabre and Atachron. Their very presence emboldened the Carnibalès. Every night, both fighter and tribal sacrificed livestock and rodents in their honour, spraying the blood against totem shrines. Even the children vied for favour by catching beetles and winged flies, dissecting them and pinning their wings onto the totems.

Despite the inevitability of the Imperial conquest, the Pair and Atachron promised them victory. They swore solemnly upon the great Ruinous Powers that Bastón would not fall again to the Imperial colony. Not even the pounding artillery of Persepian fleets, nor the avalanche of motor infantry crushing through the rainforest, could convince the Carnibalès otherwise. The Blood Gorgons had spoken and their word was as good as the word of Khornull, of Slaan'esh, Ni'urg and of the great Changer in the Sky.

* * *

THEY MARCHED FOR three nights, hiding during the day. Baeder, the survivors and their captors followed an unmarked trail through thick walls of thorny bromeliaceae and barely navigable trees so densely packed they formed curtains of mossy wood.

Baeder counted three dozen captors, all men who hid their facial mutations beneath swathes of leather binding. Although they did not attempt to tie or restrain the Riverine, they had confiscated their weapons and marched both in their rear and front. They did not speak, but gestured their directions and intent with the thrusting of lasguns.

During the day, they smeared their bodies in mud and wedged themselves in the thickets to sleep. In the distance could be heard the pounding of Imperial artillery, the low moan of engines and thudding flight of Vulture gunships. Many times Baeder awoke to hear Caliguan Guardsmen on foot with tracking hounds, hunting ahead of the motor columns. Those were moments of tense, terrifying silence as boots *crumped* closer and each bark of a hound elevated his heart rate. But the wet mud hid his scent and the barking would fade, leaving Baeder to drift back into fevered dreams.

At night, the going was difficult and taxed the frail constitutions of the 88th survivors. Three men died on the first day, falling down and no longer rising. To Baeder's surprise, their Carnibalès captors began to treat their tropical agues and infections. The insurgents pounded foraged roots and berries into salves, oils and powders, tending to his men in a rough but thorough manner. Some of the Riverine refused treatment from the heretics, believing it to be Chaos sorcery. Baeder did not blame them, but he reluctantly accepted a slimy paste of gum-sap and bitter roots to smear into the festering wounds on his skin. As he awoke on the third night, he expected horns to sprout from his brow but, to his astonishment, found his forehead cool for the first time in weeks. Even the wracking pain in his joints had receded.

Although the indigenous medicine had alleviated his fever, his fatigue was total and the lack of full nourishment did not abet his condition. Baeder's left arm had developed an uncontrollable twitch and the sweat rash on his chest had become so severe the upper dermal layers were peeling off in filthy, brown strips. His stomach was empty but for phlegm. The Carnibalès had pilfered the rations from their webbing and distributed meagre quantities before dawn as they prepared their hiding places. Those who were sick, much sicker than Baeder, were given larger quantities and even supplemented by broth from a kettle. It occurred to him that the heretics were keeping them alive.

On the fourth dawn, as Baeder was slathering cool mud over his limbs, Mautista came and stood before him. In his segmented fingers he held a cold gruel of cereal, tinned meat and jellied broth. His face, constantly split by a mad daemonic grin, was unreadable, yet something in the way he stood told Baeder that the heretic wanted to speak to him.

'I should hate you for what you've done to my home,' Mautista began, 'but I don't. Every thread of your fate has already been designed by the Great Changer. I cannot hate you for what you've done, for those are the plans.'

Baeder didn't touch the food. He simply stared at Mautista, unsure of the heretic's purpose.

'But I do hate you when I see you. You *Guardsmen*. You have tried to kill all my people and take our land.'

'We did not participate in genocide,' Baeder said, rising. 'That was the Caliguans. We were raised with more manners than that.'

'Yet you stood by and did nothing. That makes you just as accountable as those who carried out the executions,' Mautista declared. By the tone of his voice, Baeder knew it was something that the heretic had carried on his chest for a long time. He had wanted to say it ever since he had laid eyes on Baeder.

'I thought you said our actions are devised by the Great Changer. Everything is simply a thread of his plans.'

Mautista smiled, unnaturally splitting his face from ear to ear. 'Your perception is very good, colonel.'

Baeder sat back down, suddenly very tired. The blasphemy of his words shocked him. Before the insurgency on Bastón, such an insight would have been sacrilege. But his world had changed now. Everything was different, somehow. He no longer felt confined by dogma or Imperial law. Despite his pitiful state, lying in rags on the forest floor and held captive by the Archenemy, Baeder had never felt more liberated.

CHAPTER EIGHTEEN

THE SKIES BELONGED to Nautical Aviation. Lightnings and Marauders dominated the troposphere while Vulture gunships hunted above the canopy. The drone of engines became a constant, interrupted only by the pounding of bombs. With the Argo-Nauticals now anchored off the coastal mainland, sorties increased twenty-fold. No longer were they restrained to long-distance probes. With fuel stations and rearmament well within flight range, de Ruger was able to conduct the sustained aerial campaign he had craved.

By the one hundred and sixtieth day of the insurgency, the Imperial ground advance had secured one-fifth of the Bastón mainland, no easy task considering the choking terrain. The coastal Imperial provinces previously threatened by rebel attack were declared green zones of safety. Along the northern coastal tip, the provinces of Fontabraga, Fuegos,

Uventin and Mentulo were secured by elements of the
Caliguan 2nd and 10th Brigades. Likewise, the littoral
channels and port city of Dellavio were held by
Persepian Orcas, while the roads were blockaded by
Caliguan sentries drunk on pilfered liquor.

Every indigenous village encountered was put to
flame. Charred rubble was reconsecrated by preachers
who followed the Imperial advance, rendering the
bone-rich soil ready for replanting and immediate
resettlement.

Insurgent junk fleets retreated to the inland estuaries
where the larger Orcas and Persepian naval hunters
could not follow. Many other Carnibalès were driven
underground into their system of fighting tunnels. Initially, Caliguan foot troops sent forays underground
but traps hidden within the labyrinthine tunnels soon
convinced them otherwise. Rather, the Imperial Guard
were content to collapse the hidden entrances when
they stumbled across them. Imperial intelligence estimated the war would be won in five weeks.

ON THE SIXTH day of their march the 88th Battalion
reached the Gouge. From afar, the knitted tree line
dropped away suddenly into an almost vertical decline.
Yet deciduous growth defied gravity and continued to
grip the rock with horizontal roots, their branches bent
and twisted as they struggled to reach the sunlight. It
was only the purchase afforded by the stunted, multi-
stemmed trees that allowed the 88th and their captors
to descend into the gorge.

On the valley floor, the gathering war camp resembled a barbarians' mustering army mixed with equal
parts refugee exodus. White canvas tents were mixed
with lean-tos of flapping plastek sheets. Carnibalès

fighters and leashed canines picked their way between
the huddled rags of non-combatants. Forges embedded
in rock shelves smelted and hammered. Villagers
stirred cauldrons. The tents formed circles, cowering at
the base of totems that towered like monoliths. The
stony obelisks were festooned with offerings of dried
human remains, bones and plundered Guard equipment. Judging by the campfires, Baeder guessed five or
six thousand were settled here.

At the centre of the camp, rising thirty metres into the
sky, was by far the largest totem. The stone was roughly
hewn at the base, blending into a colossal human face
at its upper portion. Androgynous and smooth-
skinned, the face had no features but square-cut
cheekbones and a sharply-pointed chin. The broad,
sweeping panes of granite gave the totem crude, powerful dimensions. Bloodied Imperial Guard helmets
were stacked a dozen high around its base: Persepian
pickelhaubes, padded Caliguan R-61 anti-ballistics,
cloth-covered FEN-Cam helmets of the Riverine. Along
with the helmets were shreds of torn fuselage, the turret of a burnt Chimera and even a string of severed
hands.

It was under the central totem that the 88th finally
met the Dos Pares.

Three armoured superhumans, the tallest almost
three metres in height, waited for them. Like the totem,
there was a broad, uncompromising presence to their
frames. Their power armour was blackened umber with
a glossy carmine sheen that caught the morning light.
Each panel was etched and worked into the organic,
stylised texture of flesh. Bronze charms, monstrous
talons, opalised jewels, braided scalps and trophies
from untold warzones hung from the armour plates.

Their helmets, like their armour, were individually
unique in design. They resembled commedia masks
with furrowed foreheads, wickedly-beaked noses and
warped venting grilles that symbolised howling
mouths. Baeder knew they were Archenemy, yet the soldier in him was humbled by the might of these
superhuman warriors.

Mautista halted them at a respectful distance from
the totem. The Riverine were silent. They settled
around the totem with wide-eyed expressions. Carnibalès began to light incense from iron braziers, fanning
the smoke with dried palm fronds. Mautista
approached the Archenemy warriors alone. He opened
his arms wide with his palms facing the sky and knelt
down. The shortest of the warriors plodded forwards.
He was slightly taller but many times wider than the
rake-thin Mautista, with antlers that branched wide
from the brow of his helmet. Reaching down he
gripped Mautista's throat in his gauntlet and said
something to him that Baeder could not hear. Mautista
smiled in glee, despite the fist encircling his crookedly
narrow neck. Baeder guessed it was some sort of a greeting ritual.

The antlered warrior withdrew his hand from
Mautista's neck and pointed at Baeder. 'Come forward.'

The voice was soft and sonorously rich. It was startling. Baeder stopped several paces away from the
antlered one and swore he would not kneel. The
antlered one stared at Baeder with black visors like
deeply sunken eyes. Suddenly, without realising, Baeder
found himself sinking down onto his knees. It was not
even a conscious effort.

'Fyodor. I know your name and it is Fyodor Baeder.
May I call you Fyodor? Good. You may call me Gabre.'

'Yes,' Baeder said, not finding the words to say anything else.

Gabre gestured at his fellow warrior who had a helmet visage that resembled a lamenting crone. 'This is Atachron the Old.' He turned and pointed at his other side, at the last warrior with torso armour that was worked to resemble a black-faced daemon with a flat nose and a thin, darkly secretive smile. 'This is Sau, of Poisoned Mischief.'

'How do you know my name?' Baeder asked, immediately feeling weak for doing so.

'We have had visions of you, Fyodor,' replied Atachron. 'You are a great man. An admirable man. The gods show you unprecedented favour.'

Baeder rocked back on his heels, unable to comprehend what they were saying. The fever was throbbing in his sinus cavities.

'You must be tired,' Gabre said.

'Yes,' croaked Baeder, nodding weakly.

'Do you wish to feed and water your men? Perhaps have us tend to their wounds and ailments?'

Baeder nodded.

Upon his assent, Baeder's men were led into a shallow cave at the edge of the camp. The Guardsmen went mutely, whether silenced by exhaustion or fear of the Chaos Marines, Baeder did not know. The cave was wider than it was deep, a gap of shade at the bottom of the canyon. Beards of climbing creepers drooped across the sandstone entrance.

Inside it was cool and sheltered from the tropical heat. The temperate clime instantly felt soothing on Baeder's blistered skin. Rush mats were spread out on the rocky ground. Someone had prepared for their arrival and incense smoke wafted from wood lanterns.

Without being told, the Riverine lowered themselves
onto the rush mats, hushed and expectant. The Carnibalès brought them pails of sloshing water and set
them around the rush mats alongside strips of washing
cloth. The sight of the clear water almost made Baeder
give thanks to whatever Dark Gods the Carnibalès wor-
shipped. Despite their fatigue, the festering state of
their bodies warranted immediate attention. The Riverine clambered for the pots, dredging up slopping
handfuls onto their faces. Baeder clawed at his skin,
scraping away pieces of dried dirt with his nails. The
cold water on his heat-rashed skin took the edge off the
stings, the itches and the prickling burns. Scabs, gore,
mud and sweat all fell away from them like a layer of
hardened clay. Some scrubbed so hard their skin began
to bleed. The pails of water soon turned black and were
replaced with fresh ones.

When the Carnibalès finally took away their pails,
they distributed jerry cans full of distilled spirits that
smelt strongly of kerosene. The men tipped them into
their mouths, alcohol spilling out and down their
fronts. After having taken their drink, some sat around
in a stupor with their eyes closed in a state of half sleep.
Baeder dabbed some of the spirits onto the infected
cuts that criss-crossed his body. He did not remember
sleeping, drifting off with the wash rag in his hand. He
simply woke up fitfully to the smell of incense several
times. The Riverine were sprawled on the mats around
him, in various states of intoxication. Some were laughing incoherently. Trooper Roschig was squatting over
an incense lantern dragging deep, chest-heaving inhala-
tions. His eyes were rolled up to the whites and he was
babbling. As an officer, Baeder wanted to get up and
wrench Roschig away from the incense. But his limbs

wouldn't respond. He closed his eyes and didn't remember falling back asleep.

THE SMOKE ROSE and fell in coils of purple. Outside the air was filled with the chirp of valley beetles and birds shaking off the morning rain. Sun spilled through the cave mouth onto mats and smoke and bodies.

In the furthest corner, away from the others, was crouched Corporal Sendo Schilt. He breathed short gasps through his mouth, trying to inhale as little of the incense as possible. The fumes were dark magic, perhaps even spirits trying to invade his body. Some of the Riverine were going mad. Schilt was sure of it. They lay on the mats, giggling in childish glee.

Schilt would not damn his soul like those fools. Perhaps the Ecclesiarchy had been right about Baeder. Maybe the mainland had tainted him. Perhaps the entire battalion had been tainted. But he was not, and he would not be damned with them.

Schilt gnawed at his nails as his mind tried to find a way to keep him alive. Perhaps if he brought back proof he had killed Baeder, the Ecclesiarchy would pardon him. Surely Cardinal Avanti would reward him for his piety? Perhaps a dog tag and an ear would suffice? Yes, thought Schilt, that would buy him his pardon.

He would wait until nightfall. Then he would strangle the bastard colonel in his sleep. Schilt had strangled many living creatures to death and it never bothered him. He would have to bite off Baeder's ear too, for the Carnibalès had taken his blade, but that didn't bother him either. The hardest task would be escaping the Archenemy camp. But he would come to that when the moment arose. The incense was making it hard to think. Schilt just wanted to lie down and close his eyes for a while. When he did, the backs of his eyelids were illuminated in complex spirals with a mathematical significance that Schilt didn't understand. Outside the cave, he began to hear chanting. The shapes in his eyes pulsated and oscillated in sync with the chants.

He would kill Baeder after he rested, Schilt decided. Then he would be given the Emperor's Forgiveness.

AT NIGHT THE war camp was still. The campfires were put out to prevent aerial observation and not a sound was heard. Noise discipline was absolute. The shadowy outlines of Carnibalès sentries and their canines patrolled the upper edge of the Gouge.

It was during this period of darkness and quiet that Mautista came for Baeder. They woke him from his slumber and marched him foggily back to the central totem. A large Munitorum-issue tarpaulin had been stretched around the monolith, with the totem providing central support to form a circular tent.

Inside, the air was dry and stale. Nothing moved. Even the motes of dust that flitted before the sodium lamps seemed suspended. The ground was layered with rugs of woven wool, exotically off-world and, judging by the faded tones, very old. The offerings of dead Guardsmen were still stacked around the central pillar, although now other items adorned the room, items that Baeder had never seen before. A yellow Astartes helmet hung from the roof, a round shield of layered bone and iron was hooked on the wall, even the fanged skull of a xenos creature two metres in length was anchored against a support beam. There were other trophies too, but these were just unfamiliar outlines lost in the shadows of the great tent.

Beneath the sodium lamps stood two Chaos Marines. Baeder recognised Gabre and Atachron. The two stood in the thick shell of their armour with their helmets curled beneath their arms. Their faces were bare and chalked in white. Lips and eyes smeared in kohl gave their features an unnatural depth. In the pale light their faces were all cheekbones and stern jawlines.

Baeder knelt this time, if only out of neutral respect to their martial prowess.

'You don't have to do that,' Atachron intoned.

'Rise please. We only want to talk between soldiers, as equals,' said Gabre.

Baeder knew as soldiers they were anything but equal. The presence of leadership radiated off them, instilling calm and confidence with every slightest gesture or tonal inflection. He remembered the Chaos Marine who had ambushed Seeker Company at the Kalinga Curtain and the raw measure of its combat power. Baeder had hated the Chaos Marine for killing his men. But in retrospect, he had been acting only as he would have done, protecting the men under his command. Perhaps in a strange, indirect way, they were indeed just soldiers.

Baeder rose. Gabre picked up an autopistol from the trophy stack behind him. It was a Brickfielder-pattern, a local replica used by Bastón PDF officers. The body was finished in contrasting wood grains of gum-sap and blackspur panels with a frosty black parkerising on the exposed metal components. Gabre released the magazine, checked that it was fully loaded and slammed it back in. He racked the slide. Holding it barrel first, he handed the weapon to Baeder. No soldier could be whole without his weapon. It was a gesture of absolute trust. Either that, thought Baeder, or the

Chaos Marines were so confident in their abilities that even armed he would pose no threat. Whatever the gesture signified, it humbled the colonel.

'The Imperium has betrayed your men. How does that make you feel?' Atachron asked.

Hopeless, utterly hopeless. But Baeder kept these thoughts to himself. Instead he remained silent.

'The Ecclesiarchy has condemned your regiment to death. We offer you a chance to keep your soldiers alive. But let me make this clear, we do not need your alliance. It is a privilege we grant you.'

Baeder stiffened. He was speaking to the devil, he realised. They were asking him to damn his soul. Baeder had always imagined the lure of Chaos to be seductive, but he never before thought how.

As if reading his thoughts, Gabre chortled. 'We are not inviting you into our way. We are allowing you to fight your enemies. An enemy of my enemy is another sword at my side.'

'It is simple, Fyodor,' said Atachron. 'We are going to end this war now. Solo-Bastón will be reclaimed in our name, no matter what role you play. But we are letting your men, betrayed and sacrificed, exact revenge.'

'The end justifies the means?' Baeder asked, mostly to himself.

'Ask yourself this. On what basis, by what authority do you decide your moral prohibition or ethical imperatives?' said Gabre.

Had he been asked that question before the insurgency, Baeder would have answered '*the Emperor*'. 'None,' Baeder began, but halted his words and corrected himself. 'Or rather, my own. As an officer to my battalion.'

'The authority of human reasoning thus replaces high authority. A prehistoric philosopher said that,

Iman Kant, I believe. I ask you again, what prohibits you from keeping your men alive?'

'Nothing,' Baeder found himself saying. 'I...'

'Fight with us, Fyodor. We have seen things you have not.'

Baeder took a step away, shaking his head. 'Why did you invade this world? It was Imperial territory. Your actions brought about the death of thousands,' he said.

Gabre seemed slightly amused. 'We did no such thing.'

'It was the Imperium that instigated this,' Atachron said. 'The Ecclesiarchy began removing kin tribes from their native land, herding them into work camps so their soil could be tilled by Imperial agriculturalists.'

In truth, Baeder had suspected this. But it seemed like everything he had known had fallen apart over the past few months. His loyalty to the Imperium; his faith in the God-Emperor. Now he clung to the last vestiges of his reality. The new truth that these Chaos followers showed him was overwhelming.

'The Bastón fought back, but against PDF guns and machines, they only escalated the violence,' said Atachron.

'What they did not know is that Solo-Bastón has long been one of the recruitment worlds of our Legion, ever since the days of the Fragmentation. We came to the aid of our benefactors.'

'Just four of you?' asked Bader, suddenly drawn to the narrative.

'We did enough, didn't we,' snorted Gabre.

'Avanti is a sick, cruel little man. He embodies the corruption of the Imperium. Exploitation, hierarchy, materialism, all hidden under a veneer of Imperial benevolence.'

It was enthralling to hear such physically powerful beings belittle the cardinal. These were thousand-year-old warriors, mocking the desiccated puppet master of Imperial Bastón. There was a righteous, natural law to their judgement. Baeder could not help but agree.

'You are at a crossroads, Fyodor Baeder,' said Gabre, using his birth name.

'One road, you can fight for your men again. Avenge those who have fallen and impel those who still yet live with purpose. We can give you this.'

'The other road,' Atachron intoned, 'the other road leads you to an anonymous death, dying for a cause that has betrayed you, and holds no meaning.'

'Will I need to worship your gods?'

'You do as you wish. Piety is witnessed through action, not in scripture and cathedral stone.'

Baeder held out his hand. The great, segmented gauntlet folded his within its palm. 'I will fight side-by-side as long as only I command my men and no one else,' said Baeder.

HE WAS NOT the only one. Riverine turncoats were getting rounded up. The Carnibalès had learned to ghost on the trail of fleeing, desperate Guardsmen.

Along the banks of Serrado Minor, the remains of Sierra and Bravo Company 31st Riverine were overrun by forward elements of the Caliguan 6th Motored Regiment. The Riverine fought a desperate last-ditch engagement from between the trunks of a rubber plantation. Despite forcing the Caliguans to dismount, the Riverine were vastly outnumbered by some two thousand Calig Heavy Infantry. It was only the timely flanking interference of a Carnibalès warhost that drove the Caliguans out of the plantation. Missiles wove between bowers, mortar fragments whistled through leaves, breaking the Caliguan formation and forcing them into the river.

In the aftermath, the Riverine Sierra and Bravo were extended a temporary alliance by Disciple Thaleis. Captain Thorn, the stiff-backed commanding officer, refused, declaring stoically that he would rather die at the hands of fellow Guardsmen than dance with the devils of Chaos. Following his wishes, the Riverine shot him and offered Thaleis their allegiance. Pragmatically, if the Ecclesiarchy had accused them of taint, the Riverine would not die trying to prove them wrong. Tainted they would be.

Three hundred kilometres away, a swift boat squadron led by Sergeant Gamden was trapped by a blockade of Persepian littoral vessels in the channel and ambushed by Caliguans from the bank. They lost three boats to the Chimera-mounted autocannons before the enemy fire slackened and seemed thrown into disarray. To Gamden's astonishment, Carnibalès fighters exploded from the tree line. Firebombs splashed in fiery liquid rivers across the Chimera hulls and Caliguan infantry were cut down from behind by sustained las. Trapped in a crossfire, some Caliguans threw themselves into the water and attempted to swim upstream. Gamden ordered the flamers onto the water, bringing the temperature to a rapid boil.

The Carnibalès insurgents signalled for ceasefire from the land. The Persepian blockade closed in, turrets traversing for range. By then, Gamden had little choice. He had no food, no water and sparse ammunition. To keep his men alive, he went inland with the Carnibalès.

Up and down the coast, the hunted remnants of massacred Riverine base camps were offered a second chance by the Disciples of the Two Pairs. Some resisted, others regressed to outright hostility, answering the offers with bullet and bolt. Many entered an alliance with the Archenemy, a heretic pact of desperate, hopeless men.

IN THE MORNING, Baeder returned to the cave and brought with him kettles of food. Clay pots of rice, stirred with lard and salt. Whole birds stewed in a clear broth. Then came trays of raw, diced onions and leafy, bitter herbs floating in dipping vinegar. The Guardsmen stared at the food as it was arranged on the rush mats as if their extended period of famine had made them forget how to eat. Baeder had to command them to eat before they began to dig at the food with their bare hands.

Hot and greasy, the food plugged the cold, painful void of their stomachs. The Riverine ate in silence, intensely focusing on the bowls of food in front of them, careful not to drop a single grain.

Schilt could smell the food, the savoury aroma cutting through even the constant smog of incense. Yet he refused to eat. He did not trust the fruits of the Archenemy, or Baeder for that matter. He had, however, risen to retrieve something from the food kettles. A serving fork.

Now in his corner of the cave, Schilt nursed the eating fork to his belly. It was a fork of long and narrow design to spear food from scalding cauldrons. The two tines were five centimetres in length, protruding like clawed fingers from a wooden handle the length of his forearm. He hid the utensil from the others. It was to be his pardon.

Schilt had always been a survivalist. As a young ganger in the wayside drinking dens of the bayou he had purposely sought trouble to hone his gutter-fighting skills. Those watering holes, filled with fen labourers, juve gangers and the surly, wasteful outcasts of the swamp had been tinderboxes of aggression. Fights erupted over bumped shoulders and men were stabbed over spilt briner. As a lanky pubescent amongst burly men, Schilt had not only survived but became feared in many establishments for his murderous intent. They quickly learnt not to pick a fight with Sendo Schilt. He was the sort who could receive a thorough gang beating, but unless his attackers managed to kill him, Sendo would eventually be waiting around the corner with a hammer for the knees or a shiv for the neck. No one ever got the better of an engagement with Sendo Schilt.

Slumping against the cave wall, Schilt fell into a fevered, delirious dream. The memories of his youth on Ouisivia filled him with determination. He would kill Baeder and escape from the Carnibalès. They would not find him for he was Sendo Schilt. The cardinal would personally commend him for his actions, perhaps even award him with the Saint Tarius Cross. Perhaps he could even buy his freedom from the Guard and return to Ouisivia.

'LISTEN UP, RAMRODS,' bellowed Baeder.

He crouched amongst the feeding Guardsmen and scrutinised each and every one of them. The survivors now looked at him expectantly. Despite their grease-slick beards and dishevelled uniforms, they had the air of soldiers waiting on the parade ground. The resentment and distrust that Baeder had feared was gone. At some point during their ordeals, they had put their lives into his charge.

Just months ago, Baeder would have been hesitant to issue the slightest commands. He had not even dared to press for uniform infractions for fear of aggravating the notoriously roguish Riverine Guardsmen. But now, he wielded absolute command. The Guardsmen obeyed simply because they respected his orders. Baeder treated his battalion as an extension of his body, as one would preserve one's own fingers or limbs, not as anonymous units to hurl into the meat-grinder.

Colonel Baeder nodded to himself. 'Men. Gather your arms. The cardinal has written us off, so let's remind him what we can do.'

Mortlock grinned his skull-faced grin. Most of the Riverine nodded. Others simply gazed at him with blank expressions. They were prepared to follow.

'The Carnibalès insurgency are consolidating for a counter-attack against the Persepian flagship *Emperor's Anvil*. We will fight, not for them, but alongside them. I will maintain full command of Riverine elements. Any objections?'

There was a moment of silence. Some smiled amongst each other, suddenly motivated by the purpose it gave them. Many others seemed too spent to care. 'The Ecclesiarchy have excommunicated us as damned souls. What more have we to lose? It's better than dying from starvation,' said Mortlock, breaking the silence.

'Heresy!' came a weak lonely voice from the rear of the cave. Shaking his head and muttering, Schilt stood up. He had never been a brave man but he acted now, without thought. 'Heretic! I am a soldier of the God-Emperor. You will not sin!' he shouted. Froth gathered at the corners of his mouth. The whites of his eyes surrounded his contracted pupils.

As a boy, Baeder had often accompanied his father in the medicae clinic. He remembered that once a mad man had been brought in to see his father. He was bound at the hands and had to be held down by three strong fishermen. The patient had been stabbed by a gretchin spear when their fishing boat had wandered too far out into the uncharted fens. The wound had become infected and the man had fallen into a howling, delirious madness. There was nothing his father could do for the man and the fishermen took him away. When Baeder was much older, he learnt that the fishermen had taken their friend out to the bayous and drowned him to end his misery.

'The cardinal will pardon those who prove their worth. We can survive this,' Schilt ranted, wiping his mouth on his sleeve. He approached Baeder, murmuring under his breath in rapid yet incoherent syllables.

'Corporal Schilt. The Imperium, the Ecclesiarchy, they treat us as meat puppets. We survive as a battalion or not at all,' said Baeder.

Schilt came closer. He pushed the other Riverine aside with his hands but his eyes were transfixed on Baeder. 'The Archenemy killed my friends. They tried to kill me.'

'No,' Baeder shook his head. 'The Carnibalès fought for the same reasons we did, to protect their comrades and their homes. We are not so different. It was the Imperium who condemned us all.'

Schilt moved to within an arm's length of Baeder. His skin smelled of rot. Raw, bleeding blisters covered the corporal's face. He was a very sick man, Baeder realised.

'The cardinal can forgive us,' Schilt rasped. 'But not you. Never you,' he spat at Baeder.

Suddenly, Schilt uncoiled his right arm. A flash of metal glinted. He stabbed hard at Baeder's heart. Acting on instinct, Baeder burst forwards, jamming the stab with his left forearm. Pain exploded all the way up into his left shoulder. Although unarmed, several nearby Riverine made ready to lunge at Schilt.

'Stand back!' Baeder ordered as Schilt stabbed at him again. The Guardsmen paused, hovering in a circle around them but staying at bay.

Schilt was practised in knifework. The corporal adopted a low gutter stance and darted forwards with a double stab. Baeder circled away, maintaining distance by footwork alone. The long carving fork in Schilt's hand was already glistening with red. Baeder's left forearm was feathered in rivulets of blood. Despite Schilt's decrepit state, he fought like a cornered rodent.

'You condemned us, Baeder. I just wanted to live but you won't let me!' Schilt accused, almost plaintively. He lunged forwards like a fencer.

'Trying to keep you alive was all I did,' growled Baeder as he stepped into Schilt's thrust. He jammed the fork into his arm again. This time the tines sank deep. Gritting his teeth against the electrical pain, Baeder wrenched the blood-slick fork away from Schilt's grasp. The tide of the fight changed abruptly. Terror replaced Schilt's maddened grimace.

The corporal back-pedalled, almost stumbling. In the shadows of the cave, it seemed Baeder's presence grew. He was not tall, nor broad, but there was a change in the way he moved, a slight stiffening of his shoulders and a rolling menace in his gait. Advancing, he cut off Schilt's retreat and flattened him with a left hook.

Schilt scrambled away, clutching his jaw. Baeder stalked forward, slowly. His shoulders were rounded and his fists raised like a pugilist, circling his downed opponent. Schilt reached out and seized a wooden lantern, hurling it at Baeder's head. Side-stepping contemptuously, Baeder followed up with a knee to the side of Schilt's head. The corporal folded over. Baeder did not relent. He followed Schilt down to the mats and dropped hammerfists to the side of his head. Schilt tried to turtle up, curling his arms over his head. Baeder began to stamp on his ribs. Schilt squealed. To the watching Riverine, Baeder was possessed. His methodical assault on the corporal was animalistic.

As Schilt struggled to rise, Baeder caught him in a reverse headlock. He arched his back up high, cranking Schilt's neck, guillotining his throat with his arm. There was a snap that echoed in the cave. Schilt's neck broke. Baeder had killed one of his own, in order to protect the rest. In keeping his battalion alive, everything was negotiable.

As Schilt died, the Riverine were up and shouting. They were shouting for him. The men chanted his name. There was respect, but now Baeder saw something else. The same thing that the Carnibalès showed in the presence of the Chaos Marines. There existed an unmistakable widening of the eyes and tense shoulders of uncertainty. Fear. His men feared him.

CHAPTER NINETEEN

Union City governor's palace was like many colonial estates on Bastón, or any other remote Imperial outpost. It stood in stark contrast to the environment, floating pale and sharp against the sea of green.

Rising above the warren of shanties and concrete hab-blocks that spilled down the harbour side, the palace was a sixteen-storey artifice of Latter-Orient Gothic architecture. Wide, open-aired mezzanines and over a hundred interlocking balconies afforded a panoramic view of Union Quay harbour. In order to dispel the tropical heat, cold cream tiles covered every surface, each piece individually painted with flower and beast by off-world artisans. Gated awnings were unhinged over windows and fanned by native servants to induce airflow.

The central reception hall was small but neatly ordered for the purposes of business. Pink gauze curtains filtered the sun through open windows, muffling the sound of Guardsmen assembling on the parade grounds below. A small gilt table laden with imported teas and chilled cream was carefully arranged, surrounded by caquetoire chairs at neat angles. The sacred armour of a Kalisador casually adorned the wall alongside a chalkboard of teatime menus. In the soft, rosy haze, Cardinal Avanti lounged with a collection of rogue traders, subsector trade barons and starch-collared representatives from investment holdings.

Despite the hushed civil tones, the meeting was a subtle war of words. Solo-Bastón was being carved up, each fertile piece of land being wrangled, negotiated and traded, with Avanti at the head of the feast. Opposite him sat Octavus Sgabello, most esteemed of all the rogue traders present. Sgabello held trade charters from the Bastion Stars to Medina and back to the Lacuna Stars, earning him the title of Tri-Prince. He sat cross-legged in velvet hose with one pointed slipper bobbing jauntily.

Next to him were the trade barons. Stiff, humourless men ruffled in finery – slashed and puffed sleeves, periwigs and hundreds of yards of ribbon. For these men, the domain of anything exportable – fabric, spice and even wood pulp – was theirs and theirs alone. Such was their influence on the subsector that the wealth of planets relied on the accuracy of their calculation servitors and the shrewdness of their minds. Accompanying these oligarchs were the mercenary-explorers of the Weston-East Phalia Holding Company. Jack-booted and moustachioed, the explorers were represented by Commandant Amadeus Savaat. Resplendent in their frock coats of reds, blues and yellows, bastion loops lacing their chests and pewter buttons on their cuffs, the mercenary-explorers each bore a lance with their company heraldry.

Amadeus Savaat, loud and militant, had been by far the most vocal of the group and it was he who protested the most. If anything, Avanti would have preferred to have had the man shot for his insolence, but such an undiplomatic act would not go down well in negotiations.

'We have heard rumours that the inland is tainted by Chaos,' Savaat rasped. He touched the laspistol at his hip to ward against bad luck before continuing. 'If this is true, then not even with all the Chapters of the Astartes will I send my expeditions into the jungle.'

'Simply not true. Local superstition,' Avanti dismissed flippantly. 'If your company maps and charts the inland, then the Ecclesiarchy is prepared to offer you a sum of sixty-four million credits, half to be paid in advance.'

'There could be an appreciable risk,' Savaat countered. 'Sixty-four million including a right to levy slaves from the indigenous population. A quota of forty thousand males and twenty thousand children, cardinal. That is my final offer, my company knows where we stand.'

'It's only fair,' chimed Rogue Trader Sgabello. 'There is after all, an appreciable risk,' he said, smiling with his laminated teeth.

Avanti transfixed Sgabello with a stare he reserved for the most unrepentant of sinners. He knew the only reason Sgabello supported Weston-East Phalia was due to the fact that any slaves gained would require transport on Sgabello's fleet. Such transport would likely net the rogue trader a ten to twenty per cent cut of slaves on top of transit fees. In response to Avanti's withering attention, Sgabello looked away, still smiling although with much less mirth than before.

'That's out of the question,' murmured Baron Cuspinan in between sips of his tea. 'I have already invested a sizeable amount into agrarian land once the jungles are cleared. We will need slaves to till the soil and I can't have you shipping them all off-world, Master Savaat. The pinseed is not going to pick itself.'

'And your trade blocks will need our logistic expertise in order to establish and build your farms and mills,' Savaat snarled aggressively. 'Unless you are willing to compromise.'

Cuspinan sighed and put down his teacup with a rattle. 'You can enslave all the children you want. Their little hands are terribly labour inefficient. I am also prepared to sign a ten-year treaty guaranteeing you five per cent of all agricultural stock on the southern mainland payable in bond.'

Savaat grunted, apparently satisfied.

Avanti clapped his hands. Although a five per cent cut to Weston-East Phalia meant a five per cent reduction to the Ecclesiarchy, the Imperial church would still hold forty-five per cent of all rural profits on Bastón. Indeed, it would be a new age of enlightenment and civilisation on the world. Avanti was still bathing in the glow of his triumph and the afternoon sun when a Persepian aide appeared at the accordion door and bowed.

'Your grace. We have intercepted a vox transmission from the renegade Riverine forces.'

Before Avanti could respond, Savaat swore aloud. 'Renegade? You promised us no threat of Chaos taint.'

Suddenly, the trade barons and investors all looked to him expectantly. Avanti cursed the stupid aide for being so candid. Undermining investor confidence now would be disastrous. He would have to choose his words very carefully.

'Explain the situation,' Avanti ordered the aide calmly.

'At 14.00 today, Persepian vox-officers intercepted a broadcast from one Colonel Fyodor Baeder of the 88th Battalion, 31st Riverine. He claimed to be the highest ranked surviving officer of the Riverine and issued an order for them to rally to an unknown location. They used Ouisivian slang or local dialect and we were unable to discern the location.'

'You never mentioned that the Guardsmen turned renegade,' Savaat cut in. Sgabello mewed in agreement.

Avanti sighed. 'It was not worth mentioning. The Riverine only comprised a smaller section of the overall campaign force, roughly eight thousand in number. They were disobedient and a raucous lot, complete savages. Their superiors had disagreed with the conduct of the campaign and we dealt with them accordingly.'

Turning back to the aide, Avanti waved him away. 'This is such a minor, inconsequential threat that it requires no pre-emptive action.'

The Persepian junior officer shifted from foot to foot, wringing his hands. 'But your grace, the Riverine are gathering and reassembling. Intelligence estimates that anywhere between one to three thousand are unaccounted for amongst the Riverine war dead. It is a matter my superiors would like clearance to investigate further.'

Outwardly, Avanti smiled at his guests. 'One thousand? That's nothing. We broke them. The Riverine are scattered and directionless. What could they possibly do?'

By now the assembly no longer cared. Indeed, they seemed to share Avanti's opinion that the matter was trivial. The trade barons had lost interest in military matters and now talked of output data and statistics amongst themselves. Sgabello nibbled on a biscuit and laughed quietly amongst his rogue trading fops. Only Savaat and his damned explorers seemed to be paying any attention.

'My expedition will not fight rogue Guardsmen. That would incur a greater risk, cardinal.'

'So few remain and they will all be swept from the mainland well in advance of your endeavours. Take my word for it, commandant.'

Rising from his seat, Avanti clapped his hands for attention. 'To assure your interests are secure, I would like to invite you aboard the Argo-Nautical *Emperor's Anvil*. The Persepian fleet spearheads the campaign on Bastón and will remain long after the war is done in order to protect your investments.'

With that, Avanti left the chamber and the assembly rose to follow. Indigenous house servants wearing liveried tabards swept in from adjoining chambers like clockwork birds in waiting. The dishes were cleared and the furniture polished as the self-appointed rulers of Bastón left, leaving crumbs in their wake.

A COASTAL INLET, thirteen kilometres south-east of the docked Persepian fleet, was the weakest and most viable approach. The system of saltwater estuaries fed into the ocean where the Persepian flagship *Emperor's Anvil* was anchored ten kilometres off Union Quay. That was where Baeder planned to strike.

In the days subsequent to his vox broadcast, Riverine emerged from the rainforest as skeletal wrecks bearing with them stories of massacre and Ecclesiarchal betrayal. They joined the gathering Carnibalès war camp, their spirits resurrected by the prospect of revenge. In all, they formed a force of eight hundred able-bodied Riverine and four thousand Carnibalès veterans.

On the one hundred and seventy-sixth day, Colonel Baeder stepped onto his swift boat and cast away from the riverbank. The last survivors of the Riverine deployment, Guardsmen whittled thin and sharp by experience, followed him in a convoy. They were feral soldiers in the milk green and tan fatigues of the swamp, their weapons freshly oiled and clean in stark contrast to their barbaric appearance. Behind the fleet of Riverine combat vessels came a mixed flotilla of Carnibalès spikers, commanded by the architects of the insurgency, a trio of Traitor Marines. Those insurgents were also the veteran survivors of war. They hid their mutations under coiled face-wraps, yellow eyes peering from within the folds of their bindings. These were not rural rebels any more, but Archenemy warriors in leather armour and chainmail, holding lasrifles at the ready.

In the centre of the column were over two dozen spikers, stripped of their armour and any excess weight. The vulnerable vessels were hemmed in and escorted. Each carried a payload of raw, crudely manufactured explosives. Their pilots were martyrs, a single Carnibalès who would ram the spiker to a glorious death. Some were insurgents, their faces wound in strips of scriptured cloth and prayer seals. Most were Disciples already dying; their physical bodies deteriorating as

Henry Zou

their mutations spiralled, shedding their skin, hardening muscles, melting their organs.

The combined fleet embarked under a supernatural storm, its ferocity blackening the skies with cloud and thunder. The tongues of lightning and sleeting rain were not a coincidence. There was Ruinous influence at work, and even the Riverine knew this. They could feel its ominous presence in the air, like spirits watching them from afar. The clouds had boiled so black that they resembled ashen smoke. Rain curtains smeared visibility to a grey blur.

The fleet dispersed into the smallest littoral channels, its advance masked by the clashing storm which did not abate. Once they reformed out from the inlet, the flotilla emerged warily onto open waters, circling wide to avoid coastal patrols, and began a hard two days' sail towards Union Guay.

In their maritime tradition, the storm was a bad omen to Persepians. The clouds were so dark and so heavy, they dragged with them a sinister presence. The rain was a constant torrent of water from above, clattering the ships' decks like a tin drum. It confined the coastal patrol Orcas to sheltered ports and threatened aerial patrols with such ferocious gales that bombing sorties were temporarily suspended. Whenever that thunder rolled, Nautical armsmen touched the iron tip of their helmets and made the sign of the aquila.

On the one hundred and eighty-second day of the Bastón Insurgency a bridge operator on board the *Emperor's Anvil* noticed a suspicious blip on his radar. The blip soon turned into two, then a dozen, then several dozen. Within a minute, the radar screen showed a mass of several hundred green pixels sweeping in on

Union Quay. An alert was sent out two minutes later on board the *Emperor's Anvil*, and relayed to the only other Argo-Nautical docked at Union Quay, the *Barbute*.

Six minutes after initial contact, Admiral de Ruger, aboard the *Emperor's Anvil*, ordered all personnel of both ships to their respective stations. In anticipation of impending attack, gunners peered from behind autocannon turrets, while torpedo crews and deck gunners gathered at their battle stations. Range-finders leaned forwards into rubberised eyepieces, trying to make something out of the rain.

Lightning strike-fighters were scrambled despite the high-pressure wind, yet there was no time for them to respond with any measure of effectiveness. By the time they took to the air, the Carnibalès were within bolter range of the Argo-Nauticals.

It all happened so quickly. Out of the crashing storm, a swarming fleet of river vessels bobbed on the swollen waves. The coastal patrols, pressured by the storm, offered no warning.

The range closed on the radar. The *Barbute* sighted a spearhead of Riverine gun-barges to starboard, materialising from the rain well within range. The deck-mounted storm bolter batteries drummed out a salvo of ranging shots, throwing glowing tracers over their heads. Both Argo-Nauticals opened up with broadsides, 254mm naval guns sending a curtain of shell-splashes into the sea. The gun-barges sailed on in a widely dispersed formation, the heavy shells crashing between the skirmishing Riverine vessels. Yet the ordnance which found their mark tossed gun-barges upwards on towering geysers of steam. In a futile effort, gun-barges bounced heavy bolter, autocannon and bursts of flak off the Argo-Nautical's thick hide.

Although it was afternoon, Persepian searchlights groped out into the cauldron sea in order to illuminate the storm. From behind the gun-barges came a flotilla of brown water vessels. Some were Riverine combat boats but many were the improvised Archenemy spikers. They spread out and around the Argo-Nauticals like shoals of carnivorous fish. The Persepian main cannons were not meant for tracking such small and fast-moving targets. Instead, deck gunners sprayed the ocean with waves of smaller calibre weaponry. Hundreds of men died within seconds, their corpses swallowed by undulating crests of water. It seemed the enemy attack was suicidal. Their small-arms could not penetrate the 280mm skin of the Nauticals. Commander Stravach gave the order to conserve ammunition and 'pick the bastards off in our own time.'

At that moment, over a dozen spikers broke away from the main formation, surging ahead. Unbeknownst to the Persepians, each carried a volatile cargo of compound explosives towards the *Emperor's Anvil*. As they neared, deck gunners tracked their approach with tracer, lashing out at the approaching spikers. Two were hit, igniting and exploding in blossoms of superheated gas and flame that far exceeded the size of the vessels. The Persepian officers on deck immediately realised the error of Stravach's judgement. The incoming vessels were burdened with explosives, although by then the revelation was entirely too late.

Five collided simultaneously into the hull of the *Emperor's Anvil*. Explosions bloomed with such force that tonnes of seawater crashed onto the decking. The silver corpses of fish floated up for a hundred metre radius. After the clouds melted away from the ocean surface, two gaping wounds were exposed in the

Nautical's midship and several minor scars opened her blunt-nosed bow. Water filled the wounds, listing the great ship to port. Into the breach, assault landers and spikers surged along with the flooding tide.

THE BULKHEAD WAS flooding with seawater and oil as the Argo-Nautical continued to list. Baeder leapt off his swift boat into the chest-deep water. Pieces of flesh and charred Persepian uniforms floated with twisted steel debris. He found himself in the hull's bulkhead, support girders ribbing the steel compartment. The bulkhead door with its wheeled lock was blasted off its hinges and inside could be seen service elevators and the tubes, piping and gas valves of the ship's corridors.

Baeder splashed his way to the door and took a knee. Shaking his lasgun free of water, he aimed the weapon out into the corridor. Major Mortlock crouched down next to him, slinging a fen-hammer across his shoulders. Behind them, assault landers poured into the breach, disgorging mobs of Riverine, creating a jam of empty vessels which the flooding tides pushed away. There were no platoons, nor were there companies. Their only objective was to rend their way into the ship's superstructure, inflicting as much destruction as they could.

Baeder crossed the corridor into the next partitioned chamber and met Persepian Nautical infantry running towards the breach. Spike bayonets polished to a gleam, they lowered their lasguns and fired a volley. Baeder swung behind a bulkhead frame as las-shots punched the ventilation pipes, spurting cones of steam.

'Isn't this what we came here for?' Mortlock shouted to Baeder as he ran past into the open. Flexing his arms, he wound up and hurled a fragmentation grenade into the Persepian position, scattering the firing line. The resulting explosion sounded like a pressurised clap and a burping gurgle of water. Seizing the brief seconds of respite, the rebels charged down the corridor, heavy stub gunners running point with cones of suppressing fire.

With the way cleared, the Riverine advanced into the next compartment. The retreating Nautical infantry, a platoon-sized element, waited for them in the valve chamber beyond, now reinforced by more of their number. The hatchway created a bottleneck and four Riverine were shredded by las-fire as they attempted to enter.

'Shoulder charges!' Baeder bellowed as he strode towards the hatch where the Nautical infantry sought shelter. Troopers Fendem and Olech clattered forward with missile tubes pressed against their shoulders. Fendem took a knee and put a hand to the trigger spoon. A Persepian round zipped out from the doorway and blew out the back of his head before he could aim. In turn, Olech managed to fire before Fendem had hit the decking. There was a deafening back blast as the missile hurtled less than twenty metres into the compartment beyond. It was such a close range shot that Olech was caught at the hatch and torn apart by an explosion of super-heated gas. From where Baeder leaned against the partition, the metal warped outwards from the force.

Mortlock tossed two grenades inside for good measure before Baeder led the charge into the compartment. Slumped against walls or thrown across the room were the charred corpses of Persepians, fused to the melted, waxy fibre of their blue uniforms. A Nautical officer had been tossed face first into a corner, his back twisted at an obtuse angle. He moaned as Baeder stepped past. Halting, Baeder turned back and fired a clean shot through his head. The man was dead before Baeder realised what he was doing or why he did it. He had always been a calculated thinker, but now he was falling more and more often into wild, frantic lapses of control. The reason and restraint which had made him human now seemed replaced by an animalistic urge. He did as he wished, and it filled him with a euphoria that started in his chest and spread to his limbs. Spraying a side compartment with las-fire, Baeder moved on, leading the column deeper into the *Emperor's Anvil*.

MAUTISTA ENTERED A rent in the bow and fought his way abaft of the collision bulkhead. He led fifteen Carnibalès fighters into the dry provision stores and began to burn the rations with flamers. In the pandemonium, Mautista had linked up with eight Riverine and pressed on.

A large number of transverse, watertight bulkheads extended from the outer shell of the vessel to the deck compartments. There, groups of crew ratings fought to keep the pump valves working in order to counter the seepage of water. Unarmed, almost forty of them surrendered to Mautista. The Carnibalès executed every one and Mautista had to physically restrain some of his men from carving strips of flesh from their enemies. There would be time for trophy taking later.

In the ship's berthing spaces, damage-control parties were hosing down oil fires with compressed air pipes. Ratings with buckets tossed up water from the rising pools into the flames. Mautista shot down three of them before they realised where the shots were coming from. The rebels massacred their way onto the third deck before meeting concerted Nautical resistance at the junior officers' quarters. From within the cabins, pockets of Nautical infantry and provosts savaged them with heavy support weapons.

Mautista dove into a cabin as a bolter round chopped down Mader, a former Kalisador. The cabin was cramped, with a single foldout cot on the far wall and a footlocker. A pair of socks lay on the pillow and a framed photolith of a girl with a high forehead and a single braid wound in her hair sat on the footlocker. Mautista peered around the cabin door and dared expose his upper body. He fired a sustained burst at the Imperial positions. It was a reckless move, but Mautista no longer cared; his heart pumped poison into his bloodstream and the agony had become constant. He knew he was not long for this world.

A shot sheared away his forearm. The limb, including his gun, skidded away down the corridor. There was no pain. Falling back into the cabin Mautista looked at it curiously, even probing at the exposed bone. Blackened, curdling blood leaked weakly from what should have been a shocking wound.

A Riverine sergeant sprinted into the cabin with Mautista, tearing at a gauze pack from his webbing. 'Critical grade four injury here!' bellowed the Riverine as he fumbled out a coagulant powder from his med pouch.

'I'm fine, I don't feel it,' said Mautista, staring at the stump of his arm. The mutations that tortured his body from the inside out numbed him to external pain. He looked up from examining his wound to see the Riverine's mouth agape in horror.

'What is that?' the Riverine asked in hushed, drawn out tones.

'It is the lifeblood of a Chosen Prince,' replied Mautista.

Blood continued to dribble from the stump, pouring like wine from a gourd when Mautista lowered his arm. Daemon's blood. The very same which had been injected into his veins for the past months of his induction.

'You are a daemon?' shouted the Riverine, suddenly startled. He backed away, almost falling out of the cabin door into the splinter of enemy fire. The sergeant dropped the bandages and touched the metal of his belt buckle.

Mautista shook his head sadly. 'I am a human. But we humans cannot contain such noble blood. It eats away at us, finding a way to claw out of its flesh vessel. But it is a worthwhile sacrifice for the fleeting clarity of vision and strength it gives us.'

The Riverine seemed puzzled. His knitted eyebrows showed he did not understand. But Mautista no longer had any time for him. He unsheathed an eighty-centimetre-long machete from a scabbard on his back and shouldered past the sergeant, back into the fight.

BAEDER AND MORTLOCK cut their way through the bulkheads and structured compartments, driving the Nautical defences back through the navigators' stores and into the torpedo bays.

'What's beyond, sir?' Mortlock asked.

Baeder craned to look over a fire control panel as stray las snapped the air. Beyond could be seen a hatch and a corkscrew staircase that spiralled into the upper decks. But before that came a block of Nautical provosts. They wore grey, fire retardant overalls and

Persepian pickelhaubes. The provosts fought in two-man teams, one bearing a full-length oblong shield while another fired around it with a shotgun.

'Ship marshals and shotguns,' Baeder replied. 'We need some heavy support fire down that way.'

'Save the big guns for later, sir, we'll need them,' Mortlock said. He patted his fen-hammer. 'Give the order to fix bayonets.'

At first Baeder hesitated. A frontal assault without cover into well-defended Imperial positions would be suicide. But he had also come to know the importance of trusting his subordinates when they were sure. He owed them that much. In any event, Mortlock did not attain the rank of major by making mistakes.

'Are you sure?' Baeder asked.

'Ship marshals aren't Guardsmen. This will be too easy,' said Mortlock.

'All right. I'm coming with you,' Baeder said. 'Fix bayonets!'

Mortlock swung out from behind cover and swung his fen-hammer in a wide arc. Baeder signalled the advance with his power fist. The Riverine roared, pouring towards the partition. The ship's emergency lights caught the flash and glint of naked steel.

The Nautical provosts gave out and broke. Not a single shot was fired. The sight of the wild men clattering towards them with drawn steel had overwhelmed them psychologically. As Baeder chased down a fleeing provost and clubbed him down with his power fist, he smiled. A drill sergeant had once told him that an officer was only as great as the men around him. Only now did Baeder realise the truth of his words.

CHAPTER TWENTY

THE PENITENT ENGINE activated with a squeal of hydraulics and hosed the boiler room with cones of flame. Riverine scattered at the machine that had arisen in their midst, falling away in all directions. Fire blistered paint from the walls and churned the ankle-deep floodwaters, boiling up a solid curtain of steam.

'Heavy weapons! Heavy weapons on target!' shouted Baeder as he bounced shots off the Engine's frame with his autopistol.

Three and a half metres tall, the Penitent Engine had collapsed its hydraulic legs and crouched amongst the generators, purifiers and compressors of the boiler deck. It had hidden there, camouflaged amongst the raw metal machinery.

When it rose, the Penitent Engine rose as a solid walker frame, its hard-wired pilot crucified across its central chassis. From afar, it resembled a hybrid between an industrial servitor and a chapel organ. Banks of pistons powered its theropod legs and smoke stacks were arrayed along its upper back. Tilt cylinders engaged the use of its upper appendages, both ending in flamers.

Trooper Gresham managed to circle off behind the Engine and squeeze off a long burp of his heavy stubber. The solid slugs had no visible effect. Shuddering on stiff, rotary joints, the Penitent Engine about faced and fired. Gresham disintegrated under a sheet of white heat, his black outline visible for a split second beneath the fire.

Baeder knew they were in trouble now. The boiler room was packed tight with the ship's vitals. Silo furnaces dominated the chamber and what little space remained had been devoted to nests of piping systems and bulky, thrumming generators. The main Riverine assault was now bottlenecked with no space to utilise explosives or armour-piercing rockets. The flamers of the Penitent Engine were devastating them in those confines. Tactically, it was the worst possible position for them to be in.

'Sir!' cried Mortlock.

Baeder flinched. He recognised the panic in Mortlock's voice. He had also come to know that anything which could panic the indomitable Major Mortlock was probably very bad indeed. Baeder turned around and froze. From the space between two welded air compressors, a second Penitent Engine clawed up from its dormant state. A third was cutting off the boiler room entrance, suppressing the hatch with its twin flamers.

It was as if Baeder's rational mind chose that very moment to shut off. His mouth roared a war cry that he didn't hear or understand. He vaulted over a turbine

generator and rolled directly into the path of the first
Penitent Engine. Baeder tried to get inside the Engine's
flamers, looking to trade blows at close range. Industrial chainblades, painted with yellow and black hazard
stripes, underslung each flamer. They revved up into a
high-pitched whine and swung in a rhythmic, clockwork pace.

Baeder bobbed underneath, as he had drilled often
in the regimental boxing yard. He lunged with his
power fist but the Engine back-pedalled with a speed
that was at odds with its size. Piston banks pumped its
bird-legs backwards as Baeder doubled up on his
punch. The chain fists snapped together like scissors.
Baeder ducked low, almost bending his knees into a
full crouch. A coxcomb of sparks splattered down over
his shoulders as the chainblades collided.

In the corner of Baeder's vision he saw a second
Engine thud towards him. The remaining Riverine in
the boiler room were now trapped by the marauding
machines. The men aimed at the Engine's exposed
pilot, a female in a white shroud racked into the
machine's frontal chassis. Yet even with their lasguns
set to the highest output, punching cauterised holes in
the pilot, she continued to shriek and babble in
pseudo-prayer.

Baeder knew the Ecclesiarchy was not above the use
of chemical drugs. He was reminded of the time his
tutor had taken him to witness a public execution that
the Ecclesiarchy had staged in a local theatre near his
scholam-house. The brutality of the punishment meted
out by the preacher had stunned his young mind. By
the time the man was limbless and screaming for
penitence, Baeder had been retching bile. The preacher
then shot him three times in the chest with a

pneumatic stake and declared the exhibition over. However, Baeder never forgot the look in the heretic's eyes as they snapped open and he shrieked even louder. Through bubbles of blood he asked why the preacher had not allowed him to die after his penitence. The preacher fled the stage in a fright. Chemicals had kept the victim's heart pumping despite the horrendous trauma. He saw that same glazed look in the eyes of the hard-wired pilots.

The Riverine had nothing to match them.

Baeder was pincered between two Penitent Engines, their chainblades buzzing from every direction. He was alone. There was no room to escape. Pipes and ventilation tubes caged him. He dived low as a chainblade soared over his head. When he came up his heart was pounding hard. Somewhere in the thin pool of water he had dropped his autopistol. Yet still he raged. It was a volcanic build-up from months of carnage and mental anguish. He physically felt his veins swell in hot, angry flushes. His power fist suddenly felt light. He was no longer in control of his own body. Baeder hurled himself at the Engine to his left and reached for the chainblade with his power fist. The fist's disruption field collided with the whirring chain teeth. The external generator on his wrist spiked in voltage and snorted a plume of sparks. Violent tremors shook Baeder all the way up to his shoulder socket. He wrenched the Engine's left appendage away with a squeal of twisted metal and wire. As he did so, the corona of energy around his fist flickered and died. The power fist was spent.

Baeder stood very still. The battle rage ended, whisked away like a shroud from his head. Rationality set in. As the Penitent Engines raised their arms in execution, Baeder could only think that struggling as he died would be an undignified death. He wondered if he would truly be damned to the warp for all eternity.

The Penitent Engine to his rear was suddenly smashed aside. Chips of metal pelted his back. He felt the force and sound of a locomotive collision. Turning, Baeder saw the Penitent Engine lying on its side, embedded into the dented heap of a purifier tank. Atachron straddled it like a triumphant wrestler, hammering away at its chassis with strokes from a double-headed axe.

'Down, Fyodor!' shouted Gabre as he wedged his enormous shoulders through the boiler hatch entrance. Acting on instinct, Baeder threw himself flat onto the decking. Gabre released a tentacle of thermal rays from his meltagun into the one-armed Engine at Baeder's front. The Engine's pilot began to steam as the molecules of her body cooked off. It collapsed to one leg as the metal bubbled and warped, crashing the machine out to the left. Gabre continued to play his meltagun over the wreck until it had fused with the metal of the decking, spilling out in wide, molten slags.

'I owe you a blood debt,' Baeder said as the Chaos Marines approached him.

'Everything will be repaid in full,' replied Atachron, his voice meaningfully passive.

Baeder wanted to ask what he meant, but Atachron waved his great axe onwards. 'The gods tell me our prey lies beyond these hatches. Your men will need you to lead them. The cardinal has much to answer for.'

Stripping off the inert power fist, Baeder pried a fen-hammer from the fingers of a fallen Riverine. It was a weapon that he was not familiar with. Yet the striking head gave the hammer a sturdy weight and the padded grip felt good in his palms. It felt right. 'Let the cardinal answer to this then,' said Baeder. He looped the hammer over his head like a drill sabre and advanced at the head of his Riverine.

ADMIRAL DE RUGER was indignant. His grand ship was being sunk by filthy indigs and estuarine corsairs. The greatest pride of his entire fleet was being invaded by barbarous heretics who had no right to tread on its hallowed deck plating.

'Sir, we have to abandon ship,' shouted one of de Ruger's aides. The bridge room was tilting at a twenty-degree slant. Console displays were flashing urgent red warnings. The smell of burning petroleum was on the air, cut with the dry aftertaste of sea salt.

De Ruger tried to protest but he had no more ideas. For all his political wit and cleverness, the admiral became stricken with fear. 'These filthy, landless thieves are sinking my ship,' he repeated in disbelief.

'Sir, they're boarding us. We have to head for the preservation rafts now,' the aides insisted.

'Come then,' de Ruger said, waving them on. 'Before they fall upon us.'

His three aides led the way through the compartments which were rapidly filling with smoke. The three junior officers had discarded their frock coats and boots, rolling their jodhpurs up to their thighs as they waded through the rising flood. De Ruger followed behind, weighed down by his silver chestplate and lobster tail tasset. His black riding boots filled with water and the blue and white ostrich plumes on his burgonet wilted with moisture.

By the time they reached the deckhead, the battle had caught up with them. Nautical infantry jammed the wide corridors in their bayonet formations, bristling outwards in a phalanx of lasgun and boarding pike. The insurgents seemed to be attacking from all directions without any sense of order, appearing only to inflict random damage. The way onto the deck was blocked by heavy fighting.

De Ruger drew his sabre, a basket-hilted briquette, and waved his aides into the fray. 'Go on! Make a path!' His only means of escape was a cage elevator at the end of the service corridor, but a melee between ten Persepians and a handful of rebels degenerated into a mauling close quarter fight before him.

'Sir! Beware to your left!' shouted an aide as he tried to pushed the admiral away. De Ruger shrugged him off and smoothed his great coat.

Five Riverine emerged from a bulkhead hatch no more than a dozen paces from de Ruger. Although they did not know him to be the fleet commander, they recognised the rich gold braiding across the admiral's chest and the inlay on his burgonet helm. A square of silk embroidered with a cartographer's depiction of the Persepian seas, was plastered wetly across his back. 'That's the bastard,' growled a shirtless Riverine, pointing at de Ruger with the thick chopping end of a machete. 'That must be him.' Rebel Guardsmen clattered out from the same hatchway, eager to claim the liver of an Imperial high-ranker.

De Ruger putted his chest as he heard the rebels sloshing through the water towards him. An officer's pride prevented him from retreating in the face of heretics. He stood his ground and flourished a glittering arc in the air with his sabre, a formal salute of the Persepian sword duel.

'Let's have this then,' challenged de Ruger. He stood straight-backed, sword parallel to the ground in a classic swordsman's stance.

But the Riverine running point simply dropped to his knee and fired his autogun into the admiral's chest. De Ruger fell sideways, smoke wafting from the punctures in his ceremonial plate. The burgonet tipped over his face and the sword clattered from his hand. His mouth was open, frozen in an expression of dignified shock. As if he could not believe that he, Admiral de Ruger, supreme commander of the Persepian Nautical Fleet, had just been slain by a Riverine wearing a corporal's chevrons. Blood soaked his powder-blue dress coat and clouded the water around him. Looking up, de Ruger clawed weakly at the Riverine as they fell upon him, tearing at his dress medals and hacking him with machetes.

EXPLOSIONS TREMBLED THE decking. Steel groaned with pressurised creaking. More of the rebels were breaching the hull. Avanti almost lost his footing as the Nautical listed again, sliding candles and papers off his stateroom desk.

'Cardinal, what is happening?' demanded Amadeus Savaat. For once, the cardinal's esteemed guests shared Savaat's outrage.

'The Persepian armsmen have everything under control. They are exemplary soldiers, I assure you. I would not have your investments protected by anything less,' Avanti said, holding onto the edge of his desk.

A trade baron – Groseph Uhring – began to cry. Uhring was the firstborn son of a grain and textiles magnate from the inner Mesalon sub, heir to an illustrious line of merchant aristocrats who owned five per cent of all shipping along from the Bastion Stars to Medina. He sobbed into his tricorn and began to shake. 'Forget the investments!' he wailed. 'Just let us live. Take us to safety and my father will donate untold amounts into the Imperial coffers.' As if to punctuate his plea, there came another distant rumble in the ship. Faint, muffled screams of men echoed in its wake.

Avanti silenced him with a turn of the wrist. 'There is no need to panic. We will proceed to the saviour deck. Valkyries will take us to the mainland, although I doubt the necessity of such precautions.'

'Necessity, cardinal? You promised us this war was as good as over. From what I can see, it is anything but over!' Savaat raged, stamping the plush carpet with his badge-lance.

'We are going to die! I smell leaking gas!' wailed Uhring, throwing his hands up into the air. He was right. Even Avanti could scent the heavy odour of propane. Somewhere, the pipes which provided heating of the staterooms had burst. There was a murmur of worry amongst Uhring's fellow trade barons. Some began to take pinches of snuff from locket pendants in an attempt to mask the stink.

'Gentlemen, please,' shouted Palatine Fure. She was like a siren of calm amongst the babble of panic. 'Follow me. My sisters and I will accompany you all off this Nautical until the situation can be placated.' She signalled to her retinue of Sororitas who began to move out of Avanti's stateroom in a herring-bone formation.

'We are going to die. I can smell it! Can anyone else smell it?' Uhring cried. No one answered but even the hardy mercenary-explorers of the Phalia Trade Company made signs of the aquila.

The cardinal could feel his subsectoral investment slipping through his fingers. Who would be willing to bring trade to a war-torn planet? He could not let such a thing happen. It had taken him the better part of six years to provoke the natives into rebellion alone. The Ecclesiarchy would not look on him fondly if he failed to bring this world to heel.

'Kill that man,' Avanti ordered, pointing to the hysterical baron. Before the oligarchs could fully process what had happened, Palatine Fure creased Uhring's face with a blow from her flanged mace, collapsing him instantly.

'He needed to be quiet,' Avanti muttered. 'I'm under quite significant stress right now and I need to think. My apologies if you thought that was crude, but Palatine Fure cannot risk combusting the leaked gas with firearms. Now please be quiet so I can think.'

The assembly fell very quiet. Even Amadeus Savaat stared uneasily at Groseph Uhring's body, leaking fluid from a split down his face.

'We must proceed to the saviour decks. May I remind you gentlemen, if you have any firearms on your person do not use them while the threat of leaking gas lingers. My devoted bodyguard here will keep us quite safe.'

To prove his point, the Adepta Sororitas lining the stateroom corridor slung their bolters in front of their chests and drew personal arms. Maces, morning stars and chain flails were unhooked from plate girdles. They snapped the gargoyle visors down over their helmets as Palatine Fure took her position at the head of the fighting column. 'My Celestian bodyguard,' announced the cardinal proudly. 'Gentlemen, despite this interlude of excitement, we will be dining on shell-fish in my palace tonight. The Emperor protects.'

BAEDER FLIPPED OPEN the deckhead hatch and emerged in the ship's upper structure. Here the Argo-Nautical more resembled the interior of a ducal manor than the structure of a warship. The staterooms were divided into three separate decks with swirling ceramic stair-cases connecting the mid-tier mezzanine.

Baeder, Mortlock, some forty Riverine and the Carni-balès found themselves in the ground lobby of the state ward. Thickly-padded carpet of Berberian tapestry covered the expansive floor upon which bobbed a family of divans. The regimental flags of various boat squadrons, battle fleets and armadas were draped like heavy curtains on the wall in proud colours of sky blue, white and golden thread. High overhead, a crystal chandelier flick-ered as the ship's main power stations shorted. The air was hot and appeared to haze. Several gas pipes that provided the state ward with warmed water and heated flooring had burst. The air was pungent with a sulphurous stink.

'I'm getting a high read-out of combustible gas in the atmosphere,' Gabre announced.

'Yes, brother,' confirmed Atachron. 'As high as thirty-five per cent in some parts. Set firearms to safe,' he commanded.

As the rebel Guardsmen toggled their weapons from ready, the double doors at the far end of the lobby crashed aside. A female in pearl white power armour entered the chamber. Her visor was open. Palatine Morgan Fure. Baeder recognised the cold witch from their deployment parade. She led a column of some thirty Adepta Sororitas flanking a procession of extravagantly dressed off-world dignitaries.

There was a shocked, split second of stillness as Fure saw the rebel raiders. The sisters encircled the flock of dignitaries like low, growling hounds. The Riverine began to bay for blood, clashing machetes against their bladed rifles. Baeder snorted through his nostrils, barely able to contain the angry shudder in his hands. Avanti was amongst them. The man who had decimated the 31st Riverine Founding. He could see the cardinal's purple robes. He wanted to remember every line and every crease on the ancient planes of his face. They locked stares and Baeder saw no fear in the old man's eyes. Just a righteous glare of hatred. That compelled him more than any fear. He hated Avanti more than anything. More than the orkoids of the swamp. More, even, than the Carnibalès. Cardinal Avanti personified the Imperium and the entire, rotting hierarchy that had spurned his soldiers.

In the haze of gas, the battle-sisters formed a solid wedge of warriors in front of the Imperial dignitaries. Without the threat of projectile weapons, fighters squared, shoulder to shoulder. Like jousting knights, both sides lowered their weapons and charged. Baeder could see his enemies in intimate detail. He could count the brass buttons on their mantles and smell the frankincense of their bodies. Most Guard regiments were not accustomed to combat at such a range but the Riverine howled for it. The forces met in the centre with a grinding crunch of bodies.

Palatine Fure stood at the front of her formation, face to face with Atachron, who towered over her like a rising black tide. Brandishing a holy war sceptre in her left and a plasteel combat shield in her right, she darted at Atachron. The Chaos Marine swept from left to right

with his axe, cleaving through the gas curtain in a trail
of liquid ripples.

Gabre threw himself into the power-armoured wall
of battle-sisters. He slashed with a double-edged
chainsword, the brute strength of his swing cracking
Sororitas armour.

Baeder fought his way to Gabre's side. He brought his
fen-hammer down in a downward arc directly onto a
battle-sister's helmet. She raised her mace in a horizontal block but the weight of the fen-hammer simply
crashed through. Neck buckling at an awkward angle,
her head tilted almost ninety degrees and she fell backwards, throwing her hands into the air. He swung the
hammer up again like a woodsman and sent it crashing
back down. His swings were long and almost comical
in their method, despite throwing up plumes of blood
and armour fragments with every downward arc.

Despite Baeder and Gabre holding the centre of the
line, the rebels were retreating under the crush of mace
and flail. The Sororitas's pearl ceramite deflected all but
the most fortunate of blows from their opponent's
rusting machetes and bayonets. At such range, the
sisters' advantage of armour was undeniably telling.
Moving as one solid block, the sisters pushed through
the rebel mass. Baeder saw Mortlock bouncing the end
of his fen-hammer from foe to foe, bellowing in his
attempt to rally the men.

There came a sudden, sharp bellow, like the spearing
of a bull oxen. Atachron stumbled backwards. Palatine
Fure's power sceptre was sizzling beads of blood off its
crackling disruptor field. Atachron's battle axe and his
arm lay some metres away, a black, segmented limb
lying in a pool of darkening fluid. Fure took two steps
forwards and brought her mace in a backhand across

Atachron's antlered helmet. With a final, sonorous cry, the ancient warrior spilled onto the ground like an avalanche.

'For the Emperor! And the glory of the cardinal!' shouted Palatine Fure. Her battle-sisters warbled curious whistles that bridged into the first high-pitched notes of a hymn. As they sang, their fury was renewed and they pincered the beleaguered Riverine.

'For the fallen!' Baeder bellowed, throwing himself deep into the enemy lines.

MAUTISTA'S HEARTBEAT WAS more a convulsion than a pulse. It soared up to three hundred beats a minute, drumming agony and the hard buzz of adrenaline into his system before slacking down to a weak tremor or two every few seconds. The daemon in his curdled blood was whispering sweet promises in his mind.

Mautista would find death soon.

Four score rebels rampaged through the deckhead with him. They slaughtered any unarmed crew ratings they encountered. Some tried to flee past them onto the deck, while others just curled up and surrendered. None were spared. The Persepian resistance they met was sporadic and cursory. It seemed most Nauticals were more concerned with evacuating the sinking warship than defending it against attack. The few Nautical armsmen they encountered put up a few stray shots before scurrying away.

'Mautista! There!' Canao pointed eagerly. There was a corkscrew staircase leading out of the deckhead into the upper structures. The aperture was open and they could hear the intense clash of metal and cries of pain and anger, even above the creaks and booms of oceanic warfare.

'I can find rest up there,' Mautista said, smiling crookedly. He clawed up the corkscrew and into the hatchway, limping into the plush ground floor of the state ward. Structural damage to the ship had loosened valves and cables. The air was swimmy with a haze of combustibles, but through it Mautista could see a pitched and desperate struggle. Instruments of cutting and clubbing rose and fell. An armoured female lay on the carpet, bleeding from a stab wound to the rubberised underarm of her shoulder plates. An off-world Riverine was slumped on a divan as though asleep, his lower body twisted around unnaturally. Dozens of Riverine bodies lay on the carpet, their arms locked stiff as if trying to ward away the final blow. Several white-armoured bodies were interspersed with the Guardsmen. Mautista followed the carnage with his eyes until he saw the behemoth of dark armour in the centre of the room. It was Atachron.

Mautista's ruptured vision immediately tunnelled. His heart rate escalated to five pulsations a second. He felt a hot, swelling bulge in his stomach. He nursed that hot rage into a fury. For a moment all he could see was the broken shell of Atachron. He had been one of the Two Pairs of visionaries who had given Solo-Bastón the means to fight. Were it not for them, Mautista would have never reached enlightenment. He owed them everything.

The remaining rebels emerged out of the floor hatch. Less than eighteen mixed Canibalès and renegade Guardsmen. They would suffice. With a sharp yell, Mautista the Disciple charged into the melee.

LIKE CRUSADERS IN celestial armour the battle-sisters laid about with maces and chain flails. The order favoured such weapons because they drew inspiration from fossilised woodcuts of thirty-nine-thousand-year-old knights from a period known as the 'First Crusade'. They were like knights driving back the feral hill hordes. The colonel's men were the faceless animals to be felled for their legend.

Baeder fell back into a ring with the eight remaining men in his unit as Fure's Celestians hemmed them in. Baeder ducked a lashing chain flail and swung his fenhammer low. It caught the battle-sister in her shins and swept her legs out from underneath her. She came crashing back down, her legs shattered. Prayer – fervent and pained – escaped from her helmet vents.

Another mace cut the air and this time Baeder had no room to evade. It hit him square in the ribs, the flanged mace-head bouncing off his flak vest. Baeder heard bones break and scrape against splintered ends. He fell. He heard harsh incantations. Baeder expected death. The sisters were intoning his death prayer. But the killing blow did not come.

Instead, the sister turned away, her attention drawn as more rebels had fought their way into the state ward. He saw Mautista, the skeletal Disciple, decapitate a battle-sister with a scything machete. A second wave hit the scrum – Soder, Barlach, Boetcher and a mob of Carnibalès. They hit the Celestian flank and threatened to spill over to where Avanti and his assembly hid in the rear. Once again, Baeder realised, the powers above had chosen to keep him alive.

He rose to his feet. Broken ribs grated. Every breath brought a stab of pain in his right side. Clawing his way up, he led off the remnants of his group. Mortlock moved to his side, slamming a battle-sister into the ground with a downward blow. 'Where to, boss?'

'Find Avanti. I need to see him die.'

The cardinal hid behind a fighting square of his bodyguard as they fought their way beneath the mezzanine towards the foredeck. They had almost broken free until Mautista's party engaged them. Now the cardinal was hollering about the ship sinking. He was probably right, the Argo-Nautical rocked dangerously. But Baeder's focus became one of such singular aggression he did not hear any words.

Gabre bowled into the Celestian flank. He tore at them, picking up the armoured form of a battle-sister and shaking her like a deranged simian. The Celestians rushed to meet him, creating a gap in the formation.

Baeder staggered towards the breach, fen-hammer loose in his hand. Mercenaries rushed to plug the gap with a forest of flagged lances. Each bore a handlebar moustache and neatly-waxed hair. These were no fighters. To Baeder they were typical of the Imperium's ruling elite. Baeder smashed the ceremonial weapons aside with contempt, splitting the polished wood staves and trampling their pennants. Avanti was close now. Baeder looked into his eyes. There he saw not fear, but a flicker of uncertainty. It elicited a thrill of delight in Baeder. He was slavering now, but he didn't care.

'He's mine!' howled Baeder. 'Mine!' He hurled himself against the aristocratic lancers, breaking apart two of them. The burning in his ribs was forgotten. He snorted, blowing strings of blood from his nose. A lance plunged into his thigh. Something collided with the side of his head. Baeder felt none of it, he could see only Avanti and his cold blue eyes, clear and vivid amongst a periphery of grey shapes. He was reckless. He would die here.

'No!' screamed Mautista.

A hand seized Baeder by the back of his jacket and pulled him away from the front-line. Baeder lashed out instinctively, punching Mautista in the face and exploding his nose in a spray of blood. 'What? What?' growled Baeder through his teeth.

'There!' said Mautista, pointing to the mezzanine stairs. Platoons of Persepian Nautical infantry were clattering down the steps, bayonets couched at the hip. Nautical officers blasted their bugles in the cardinal's rescue. A company-sized element at the very least. Several of the vanguard threw themselves into the churning fight, spearing Riverine from behind with their bayonets. He saw Sergeant Colborn sink as a Persepian blade transfixed his spine. A Nautical officer's sabre parted the head of Trooper Bantem from his neck. A Carnibalès screamed as he clutched a stomach wound.

The realisation of sudden defeat sobered him. Mautista pulled Baeder back from the melee as the man continued to protest. 'I have to kill him. To rest the souls of my men, I have to kill him.'

'Let me do it. Gabre needs you to go with him. The ship is sinking.'

Baeder shook his head. 'Damnit Mautista, no. I will not. This is what I came to finish. This is everything I have left.'

'No, this is not why. The Four know there are greater designs for you yet. The gods have promised.'

'This is my fight,' Baeder shouted into the Disciple's face, lashing him with spittle.

'Fyodor, leave! The gods have marked you as their own now. As for me, the gods have chosen to end my mortal life. I am dying already.'

As if to prove his point, Mautista wrenched open the buttons of his leather jacket with his remaining arm and bared his chest. Beneath a cage of distended ribs, his heart was a visible black stain beneath paper skin. With each slow, irregular beat, the black stain pulsated like a convulsing ink blot. 'I have been infused with the blood of daemons. My life purpose is to serve the Dos Pares. Yours is a greater purpose. Go Fyodor, do not anger the gods.'

Baeder could not look away from Mautista's heart. Arterial spider webs of black were spreading out across his skeletal chest. Whatever daemonic entity had been imparted into Mautista's body was claiming the flesh vessel as its own. Baeder was not sure how he knew this, but he was sure he was correct.

A mace slashed towards his head. A black armoured shape took the hit against its ceramite hide and eviscerated the mace-wielder with his chainsword.

Gabre.

'Fyodor. Come with me,' he said, holding out his great gauntlet.

Bader looked around at the crashing battle. More of his men were dying. The last of the 31st bleeding out, dashing themselves against the wall of pearl amour. The entire Persepian company had reached the floor level now. They were surrounded and overwhelmed.

'Riverine!' Baeder ordered. 'Fall back on my mark.'

MAUTISTA SAW THE last of his warband fall. He knew he would fall too, soon, but not quite yet. He knew his purpose and he would play it out to the end.

The ship boomed again. Perhaps an ammunition store had cooked off, or perhaps the boiler room had erupted. The she-warriors in pearl, their polished ceramite dented and stained, maintained a tight circle around Cardinal Avanti, leaving the flock of beribboned oligarchs scurrying in their wake.

Mautista cut diagonally with his machete and sheared a Persepian apart from shoulder to waist. He leapt clear of a toppled divan and sprinted towards Avanti. The last three survivors – Canao, Estima and Azuilgur – followed him, hacking left and right as they ran.

Estima was transfixed by a Persepian bayonet. Stopping to parry a Nautical officer's sabre, Canao was dragged down and lost. Only Azuilgur and Mautista reached Palatine Fure.

The palatine's power sceptre knocked Azuilgur sideways, five metres across the room. His torso ruptured, beads of blood seemingly hanging in the air before pattering to the carpet. Mautista knew, despite the unnatural augmentation in his bloodstream, he could not match the martial skill of the Palatine. He reached for a stub pistol at his hip, a small six-shot revolver. Fure swung her sceptre, gouging away a portion of Mautista's lower torso. As the holy weapon met daemon blood, there was an audible hiss as if the wound itself was crying out in pain. Steam ejected forcefully from the open wound, boiling and bubbling with effervescence. The shock alone would have been enough to kill a normal man, yet Mautista was numb. His legs buckled and he toppled backwards, his stub pistol still clutched loosely in his fingers.

He saw Avanti, now at the front of the procession. The cardinal's eyes were closed, his hands clasped in prayer. He seemed impervious to the carnage around him.

Fure loomed over him to deliver the killing blow, but Mautista was faster. He jerked the finger of his trigger, willing his muscles to contract one last time. The percussion cap struck the round and the stub gun barked.

Mautista saw the muzzle glow before the bullet had left the barrel. A discharge of hot, high-pressure gas flickered. It sparked the volatile gas and ignited. The flame expanded outward, a horizontal sheet of flame that erupted instantaneously from wall to wall.

There was no sound. Mautista felt nothing. He saw, before his death, the room grow white and Avanti open his eyes. Mautista saw fear there. In the fraction of a second before his death, Avanti's eyes quavered. His soul was damned, and he knew it. The cardinal opened his mouth to scream but blooming fire sucked the oxygen from his lungs.

EPILOGUE

THE IMPERIUM'S INLAND campaign pressed on for a further ten months, well into the dry season. Robbed of its initial momentum, the land forces were drawn into a lengthy guerrilla war with the natives of Solo-Bastón. Outmatched by Caliguan heavy armour, the indigenous fighters expanded their tunnel systems and continued to fight, drawing numbers from the sudden influx of refugees dislodged by fighting.

Although the death of Cardinal Avanti did not have any strategic impact on military planning, its impact on the overall campaign was considerable. He had been the embodiment of the holy campaign on Solo-Bastón and the architect for the creation of a post-war industry. Without him, the campaign lost political influence and financial investment fell away. Prospective shipping and holding firms declined to enter into any chartered agreements on the unstable planet. The Weston-East

Phalia Company reneged on their contracts and ceased negotiations to explore the mainland interior. House Uhring, furious at the loss of their heir, lobbied for a protracted trade sanction against Solo-Bastón. The Ecclesiarchy severed their ties with Solo-Bastón and were quick to clean their hands of Avanti's mess.

Without the support of powerful vested interests, the Imperial Guard were left to conduct a war with limited resources. Major General Montalvo succeeded as operations commander upon the deaths of Avanti and Admiral de Ruger. Despite the initial successes of an inland assault, he inherited a stagnant campaign. His men were unused to fighting an insurgent war in such inhospitable terrain. Demoralised and without cohesive leadership, Caliguan crews hid in their tanks and Chimeras away from the heat and disease. Dysentery afflicted one in two men while tropical agues became a conditional norm. Significant quantities of medical supplies were requested, but none were forthcoming and their pleas were ignored. No Imperial officials in the region wanted to involve themselves in the cardinal's disaster.

Despite Imperial superiority in firepower and numbers, the Carnibalès fought an obstinate war on their home soil. With no end in sight, the Imperial Guard lost the will to fight. They languished in camps, unwilling to advance and unable to retreat. However, the poorly equipped Carnibalès were unable to press the advantage and the fighting stalemated into intermittent skirmishes and constant ambush.

The war on Solo-Bastón ended exactly eighteen months after initial deployment. In its aftermath almost a third of the planet's population had perished from conflict, disease or malnutrition. The Imperium declared it a victory. Streamers and processions lined the streets as far as the Bastion Stars. A soapstone statue of Major General Montalvo was erected in Union City. With its arms raised towards the sky in victory, the forty-metre sculpture was clearly visible from the Solo-Bastón coast.

However, only the inner administrative officials knew the truth of their triumph. They had lost Solo-Bastón. The war was an Imperial catastrophe that could ruin Ecclesiarchal legitimacy within the subsector. Restriction of information was imperative.

Many years later, military theorists wrote of a guerrilla network concealed within the rural populace led by daemon-blooded heretics known as Disciples. These Disciples disseminated knowledge of guerrilla warfare far in advance of anything the rebels would otherwise have known. Yet more importantly, the success of the insurgency relied on the support of dissident villages who supplied raw produce, food, labour and concealment for the Archenemy host.

Imperial historians legitimised the massacre of thousands by citing the local support for heresy. No mention was made of the wholesale genocide of loyalist groups. A complete history of the Solo-Bastón Uprising was commissioned by Cardinal Heitor de Silva which omitted the violations committed against the indigenous groups of Bastón. Instead the campaign was repainted as a struggle between Caliguan Guardsmen and Persepian vessels against the barbaric hordes of Chaos cultists. No mention was made of involvement from the 31st Riverine Amphibious.

In actuality, it would be the arrival of Traitor Marines that broke the stalemate on the eighteenth month. Blood Gorgon, in company strength, deployed via a fortress fleet that broke the Imperial picket at Midway Reach. They deployed by Thunderhawk and Raptor into Bastón interior, pin-pointing strikes against command and communication centres. Quick and brutal, the Blood Gorgons routed the Guardsmen back out into the sea, drowning them in their thousands. The colossal monument of Major General Montalvo was demolished by the Archenemy, less than three weeks after its completion.

KHORSABAD WAS BOTH title and forename. It was derived from the Bastónese word '*Khorsa*' meaning corsair or renegade and the honorific '*Habad*' meaning 'the King'.

Maw or '*Mau*' was his true name. It was a name that Gabre of the Blood Gorgons gave him. A derivative of another name, Mautista, whose very fate was intertwined with that of Khorsabad Maw as much as Maw's own organic birth mother's. The threads of fate crisscross and interlock. Although Mautista's thread had ended, it converged and continued along the thread of Khorsabad Maw. His actions in life had bound them. Without following the destiny of Mautista, there could be no Maw.

Fyodor Baeder was a past name. With the passage of time, it was a name that would be forgotten. There existed a young Fyodor, much younger, who had sailed paper yachts in the marsh parks of Ouisivia with his father. Another Fyodor not quite yet a man who had greased his hair, worn leather crêpe-soles and taken a dark-haired girl to the slump dances. The last Fyodor has been the colonel who led his men into interiors of a distant, war-torn jungle. All of those Fyodors would in time be forgotten too.

His title Khorsabad and his true name Maw were chiselled into the newly-forged plates of his armour: miniature, heretic script that adorned every pane of his shoulder, torso and thighs like the cauldron crab shell of Kalisador fame. The ragged remains of his military uniform fluttered like ghostly vestiges, the death shroud of man entombed in a crypt of new armour.

The Blood Gorgons gave him his armour and much more. They gifted him with a mask of iron, so he would not suffer memories of the past each time he faced a mirror. This they welded to his face, forever, as a pledge to his new life. Bands of steel looping like serpents, their tails began sharply at his chin and their heads met atop his crown. They gifted him with a falchion, sculpted from the rending claw of a tyranid specimen, and many accoutrements of war from the Eye of Terror. But most of all, they promised him immortality so he could pursue his vendetta against the Imperium.

Khorsabad Maw lowered himself unsteadily, touching his forehead to the soil. 'My benevolent creator.'

'There is no need for that,' replied Gammadin, Ascendant Champion of the Blood Gorgons. When he spoke, the rich voice that oozed out of his amplifiers reverberated among the ancient gum-saps. Flocks of tiny, dark birds were startled from epiphytic perches. Unseen amongst the broadleafs and tangled roots a panthera roared, as if recognising the power behind that voice.

The Traitor Marine stood before Khorsabad, as large in physical presence as the totemic pillars that surrounded them. Gammadin stepped forward, caped in the severed wings of a giant bat. Stooping slightly, the Ascendant Champion guided Khorsabad up by the elbow. 'We are allies, equals. An enemy of my enemy is to be treasured,' Gammadin said gently.

Khorsabad nodded. 'Fighting is all I know. It's all I've ever done. If you will give me the arms and the purpose, we will fight for you.'

'There will be plenty of opportunity to fight,' Gammadin said. 'The Imperium is vast and the Eastern Fringes uncharted. Harass them. Plunder and worry their shipping lanes, cut them where they are weakest. Fight and flee and fight some more. Can you do that?'

Although Khorsabad's iron mask could express no emotion, his shoulders lifted visibly. 'It will be the only thing we do.'

'You have my patronage in this pursuit. Arms and ships I can give you, but your men will need you to lead them.'

'I can do that.'

Gammadin drew his scimitar, an immensely old weapon. The length of its two-metre blade was pitted and notched, beaten and scarred. He brandished the weapon horizontally towards Khorsabad Maw. In reply, Maw struck the back-edge of the blade with his own lacquered falchion. He did this thrice, gouging teeth marks into Gammadin's thickly rimmed blade.

'That is all?' Khorsabad asked. 'No blood oath? No pledge?'

Gammadin shook his head, the recurved horns on his crown rattling against his armour. 'We are not the barbarians the Imperium thinks we are. I don't need your blood when I already have your word as a commander of men.'

ABOUT THE AUTHOR

Henry Zou lives in Sydney, Australia. He joined the Army to hone his skills in case of a zombie outbreak and has been there ever since. Despite this, he would much rather be working in a bookstore, or basking in the quiet comforts of some other book-related occupation. One day he hopes to retire and live in a remote lighthouse with his lady and her many cats, completely zombie-free.

THE BASTION WARS SERIES

WARHAMMER 40,000

EMPEROR'S MERCY

"Crunchy, vivid and memorable...
next time I need a galaxy burned,
I'm sending for Mr Zou."

WARHAMMER 40,000

A BASTION WARS NOVEL

FLESH AND IRON

HENRY ZOU

HE

UK ISBN 978-1-84416-734-0 US ISBN 978-1-84416-735-7

UK ISBN 978-1-84416-814-9 US ISBN 978-1-84416-815-6